I0716600

OCEANUS

OCEANUS

By Scott Overton

No Walls Publishing

SUDBURY, ONTARIO, CANADA

Copyright © 2024 by **S.G. Overton**

All rights reserved. No part of this publication may be reproduced, distributed or transmitted in any form or by any means, without prior written permission.

Scott Overton/No Walls Publishing
Sudbury, Ontario, Canada
www.scottoverton.ca

Publisher's Note: This is a work of fiction. Names, characters, places, and incidents are a product of the author's imagination. Locales and public names are sometimes used for atmospheric purposes. Any resemblance to actual people, living or dead, or to businesses, companies, events, institutions, or locales is completely coincidental.

Book Layout © 2017 BookDesignTemplates.com

Cover art by Juan Padrón.

Oceanus/ Scott Overton. -- 1st ed.
ISBN 978-1-7782844-6-5

To Robin,
whose wise and gentle guidance provides
the final boost my words need to take flight.

*Limitless and immortal, the waters are
the beginning and end of all things on earth.*

—HEINRICH ZIMMER

*What would an ocean be without a monster lurking in
the dark? It would be like sleep without dreams.*

—WERNER HERZOG

1

January 10, 2042

"How long can the plane fly with both pilots dead?"

"We don't *know* they're dead."

"You're assuming they are. How long?"

Phillip Watanabe leaned against the desk and pushed back his suit jacket to slide his hands into his pants pockets. "It was bound from Guam to Tokyo with Osaka as an alternate. Say, four more hours, give or take, depending on wind conditions."

Alex Rhys wasn't fooled by Phillip's casual stance. "So, it'll ditch in the Sea of Japan. Probably won't reach Russia."

"I didn't ask. You and I are going to make sure it *doesn't* crash."

Breath hissed through Alex's teeth. "Still no communication? Nobody?"

"Nothing from pilots or crew. Air Marshall's not answering. We've even been trying passengers' phones. It's a dead zone for cell signals, but Homeland's database shows nine passengers with satellite phones—nothing from them, either."

Dead zone. Alex's shoulders twitched. "Well, the first thing we need to … *Shit!*" He stood on the brake pedal. His classic '25 Charger screeched to a stop a couple of feet from the rear bumper of a white panel-van. The elderly woman pedestrian at the far corner of the intersection turned wide eyes toward him and waved the van hurriedly through the right turn in front of her. Alex waited until the van was well clear before continuing straight through the green light. He could feel the glare of the woman as he passed and swore again, then wiped his palms on his pant legs.

"What just happened?" Phillip's voice held a concern Alex had never heard in it before.

"Nothing. I freakin' hate handling calls like this while I'm driving!" He should have left the video off, at the very least.

"Suck it up. Listen, you're about a half hour from here by chopper. Find a nice empty mall parking lot—we'll come to you."

Alex stopped at a red light and took his bottom lip in his teeth. On his left, a young couple was coming out of an Asian grocery store pushing a stroller. How many families just like that were on the doomed 787?

"Fine, but you can't wait for me. What's the biggest stratellite outfit in Japan?"

"Stratellites? Hang on … that'd be Nippon Stratellites, based out of Narita airport."

"They'll have maintenance flyers. Tell them to get their best crew in the air and on an intercept course, south, fully stocked with repair gear including plasma cutters."

"Jesus! You're not thinking they can get aboard a jetliner in mid-flight?"

"When you have a better plan, give me a call. I'll be in the northwest corner of the Stonestown Galleria parking lot. Get me first, and apologize to the authorities, after."

Phillip's people would catch hell from San Francisco and Oakland air traffic control, the SFPD, the mall owners, and who knew how many others. That wasn't Alex's concern. As he pulled into a parking space, he commanded his console viewscreen to end the call and bring up specs on the Boeing Dreamliner. The screen blurred until he blinked away wetness as he pictured an aircraft interior filled with three hundred and forty-two souls—people with lives, people with families. In his imagination they were slumped over in unconsciousness, or even, in one flash he quickly pushed away, blackened and burned. It was one of the many nightmare scenarios that plagued his sleep since he'd accepted government work.

His last job for Phillip had ended only a week ago, barely enough time to take Andrea out to dinner. No way he'd make it to their theatre date tonight. He told the car to send a regret message and shook his head at how many times he'd had to send regrets in the past year. No wonder his love life was shit.

He'd been on a high after that last assignment, though. His biggest success yet: eight high-value diplomatic hostages rescued from the Kurdish Hezbollah in Gaziantep. A perfect extraction plan had been spoiled by bad luck. But that was why they needed Alex—his gift for creative troubleshooting when the dice came up snake-eyes. He'd improvised with the help of a passing city bus, an approaching thunderstorm, two pilfered umbrellas to flash a coded message to a rooftop observer, and a couple of well-paid hookers who'd playacted a thoroughly distracting fight in the open street. The story had been worth a lot of free drinks once the team was back home.

But one special-ops soldier hadn't made it back.

Alex had gone to her funeral, standing on the very fringe of the cemetery gathering, but still too close to tear-stained faces with helpless expressions of grief. Thick raindrops sputtering on a dying fire. The cheerful flower arrangements on the casket depressed him: superstition painted to look like hope.

After that, he'd pretty much decided to get out of the business. His idea of "consulting" didn't include decisions of life or death. He'd nearly cancelled Phillip's call without answering—part of him wished he had. But another part thought of all those helpless airplane passengers returning home to Japan from a sunny vacation in Guam.

He had to help them. But he would get out of the business soon. His "retirement package" was almost ready.

# # #

As Alex jogged out from under the spinning helicopter rotors, Phillip met him on the rooftop. The Homeland Security agent's hair didn't budge. His suit seemed to repel the dirt blowing through the air. And maybe it did—there were nano-engineered fabrics designed for that. In contrast, Alex's usual wardrobe would have embarrassed a department store dummy, though his recent government work had compelled him to upgrade a little.

He was as certain as he could be that Phillip didn't really work for Homeland, and equally certain that the other man knew of his suspicions. But both played their parts and never spoke about such things. The bottom line was that Phillip did work for the American government: he had enormous clout when it came to accessing resources, and he accomplished very special tasks. Sometimes he hired Alex. So did a dozen other government agencies and five multinationals so far. Except Phillip's missions were the toughest and dirtiest, and there was almost always a cost in blood.

Alex hoped this one would be an exception.

The door from the rooftop had an old-fashioned key lock, nothing high-tech. Only temporary quarters for Phillip's team. A couple of floors down, there was a suite of offices with windows blacked out and one wall a bluish screen with a half-dozen holographic displays floating in front of it. There were only six staffers on hand, but Alex had worked with four of them before and was awed by their skills. He was quickly introduced to the new members, both women in their late twenties so attractive that he promptly forgot their names. He would have forgotten his own, too, but Phillip supplied it first. Alex ran his fingers through his short blond hair and felt grit stuck to his scalp by sweat. He gave up any attempts to impress.

"The ocean views—are those from a chase plane?" he asked.

"From the maintenance flyer you wanted," Phillip replied. "They're at maximum airspeed, still a half-hour from the target." He crossed his arms. "The company had to ask for volunteers."

"Of course. Flyers don't have the range for a round trip of that distance. These guys either succeed in hitching a ride on the 787 or they go down in the Pacific." The stratellite service vehicle was a stubby wedge of flying wing with twin jet-engines at the rear and a main flight-crew hatch between the exhaust nozzles. There was another hatch on the underside, but that was for when the flyer was doing its intended job: ferrying two-man crews up to stratellites for maintenance work. Even solar-powered gas bags required repairs every once in a while, most often to electronic gear that relayed communication signals of every kind over a big chunk of geography. Alex knew that, basking in the stratosphere like gargantuan whales, Japan had at least one stratellite for each of the nation's islands. Crewless, except during maintenance, their provision for in-flight visitors consisted of a special landing platform with a proprietary female hatch coupling to match the male counterpart on the underside of the flyers. No one relished the idea of walking over the top of a zeppelin in hurricane winds twelve miles above the ground. Once mated, crews could transfer directly from the flyer to the interior of the stratellite without oxygen masks. Since the flyers had vertical take-off and landing capability borrowed from jump-jets, and the platforms were always aimed into the prevailing wind, linkups were reasonably straightforward.

Landing on a jetliner at cruising speed would be a whole different story.

Phillip had returned his hands to his pockets, but Alex noticed them twitch every so often, as if they needed to be touching a control screen, pressing a button, or weaving a complex dance through a holo projection. Doing something. The man was a gifted organizer, but a restless supervisor.

"If you're planning to have the strat team land on the plane's roof and cut into her, it won't work," Phillip said.

"No. The ceiling's all electrical cables and vents." Alex gave a sweep of his hand and brought up a detailed cutaway of the Dreamliner. "This one is twenty years old, you said? But with upgraded engines?"

"Built in 2022."

"Most of the 787's flight functions are controlled electronically instead of hydraulically. Not a good idea to go cutting wires. Anyway, the carbon fiber composite materials of the fuselage and the insulation behind it are a bitch to cut through, even with plasma torches. They'll have to go in here." He tapped the air.

"The top of the cockpit? Isn't that all control systems, too?"

Alex spread his fingers to expand a small section of the picture. "Escape hatches. One on each side, above the pilots. In the event of a survivable crash or a fire on the runway, the flightcrew is meant to climb out and rappel to the ground on retractable cables."

The rectangles looked tiny. Phillip whistled through his teeth. "I hope these guys don't live on pizza and beer."

"The hatches will be big enough. Just. The problem is opening them. They've got safeguards to keep them from being opened in flight, of course, but the bigger obstacle is air pressure."

"All airliner doors open inward, so the pressure differential between inside and outside at 30,000 feet keeps them locked shut." The comment was from one of the new women—the redhead—leaning over a desktop console with her head cocked toward Alex. He became conscious of a cool touch at his armpit: sweat patches on his shirt as he painted the air with his fingers. Naturally.

"So, what's the answer?" Phillip asked.

"The strat crews carry a new epoxy system in their kits. The catalyst, used on its own, is violently corrosive on synthetic sealing compounds like the ones around the escape hatches. But they'll have to cut the locking mechanism with a plasma cutter."

"In a five-hundred mile-per-hour wind?"

"But you'll still have to push against the air pressure to open the hatch." The redhead again. "My name is Jill," she reminded him.

"Right. Two choices on that. One: quick and dirty—an explosive. They've got flares and mini oxygen packs that should combine for a big-enough bang. The downside ..."

"A metal hatch bouncing around the pilots' heads, followed by explosive decompression in the cockpit. Maybe the whole plane, if the flight crew left the door open."

"Only first-class. Since 2024 this model has come equipped with instantly inflating pressure seals between the passenger sections. And the pilots are probably already dead."

"Sure." Phillip frowned. "But if a metal hatch slices into a control panel, that bird isn't coming down any way but hard. What's option number two?"

"The rear hatch on the strat flyer includes an extendable entranceway, basically a tent-like hood for the rare case that the coupling on the stratellite has been damaged. In our scenario, they extend the entranceway over an escape hatch and seal it to the fuselage with the quick-acting epoxy. Then they can equalize the pressure inside the hood with the plane's interior pressure while they cut, and the hatch should just fall open. But they'll have to set the flyer down on the nose of the jet—right over the windshield. They obviously can't match speeds aimed the other way, and they could never extend the hood into the force of the airflow."

"The downside?"

A nervous smile tried to rearrange Alex's taut face but gave up. "For one thing, 'quick-acting' is relative. I'd guess that the cut-and-blast method will take ten minutes or so. Option 2? More like half-an-hour to forty-five minutes. Air temperature, the age of the hatch seals, the skill of the rescuers ... a bunch of other variables could all make it take longer."

"By then the plane will be into Japanese airspace, closing in on the coast."

"Yeah. Not good. 'Cause there's one more thing."

"Which is?"

"Autopilots aren't programmed to compensate for the weight of a truck suddenly planted on the nose cone. As soon as that flyer touches down, the Boeing is going to start to descend. Maybe in a hurry."

# # #

Alex chewed at his lip as he watched the scene from the nose camera of the small flyer and a second video feed from the helmet camera of its co-pilot, who was suited up and ready to move as soon as the craft touched down on the Boeing. Even second-hand, it was hellish to watch the giant jet grow to fill the view as the smaller plane sidled into alignment over the top of the Boeing's fuselage. Forward progress was painfully slow. Alex gripped a chair-back to stop fidgeting. Everybody else in the room, except Phillip Watanabe, was sitting. It helped them portray a calm they couldn't be feeling.

There was a collective gasp as a wind gust dipped the flyer's nose into a nauseating crunch. The view bounced. They heard an exclamation from the flyer's Japanese crew that Phillip didn't choose to translate. The two-man flyer crew understood English, but Phillip repeated Alex's directives in Japanese for insurance. Finally, the ocean reappeared beyond the cockpit roof, there was a second crunch as the small craft's tail touched down, and then a sickening lurch forward as the pilot brought his vehicle down onto the steep slope of the 787's nose. It looked as if the flyer was certain to slide off and plunge to the ocean below.

Alex pressed the microphone button on his headset. "Fire the clamps!"

Explosive-charged needle-pronged clamps stabbed like scorpions' tails, intended to anchor the flyer to a stratellite surface in case of dangerous turbulence. But they were meant to penetrate thick rubbery fabric, not a hard composite shell. It was anybody's guess whether they would hold onto the jetliner.

There came a rapid stream of sounds. Phillip said, "They're getting some grip. For now."

Alex felt his eyes widen as the view tipped forward slowly, approaching the vertical. He opened his mouth to cry out, but a rushing sound told him that the pilot had already transferred engine thrust to jump jets that flared outward. The man would have to be a genius to balance that thrust with the tenuous grip of the clamps; but without the extra lift, the nose of the Boeing would soon point toward the sea. There was a groan that could have been the clamps protesting. The horizon edged ever-so-slowly downward.

"The 787 is still a little nose-heavy," Jill called out as the view stabilized. "It's descending."

"How bad?"

She waited to get a reading. "Couple of hundred feet a minute."

"That gives them enough time," Phillip said.

"It would." Alex looked at him. "Except the flyer will run out of fuel in … thirty-eight minutes. By that time, somebody'd better be in the captain's chair ready to take over from the autopilot, or that descent is going to become a dive."

The view from the helmet camera moved chaotically as the flyer's co-pilot double-checked his suit fastenings and the gear he'd attached to it. He was only a couple of yards from the rear hatch and raised a hand to point at a set of controls.

"Decision time," Phillip said. "Does he extend the fabric hood or go in with a bang?"

Alex's lunch was threatening to leave its resting place. This choice could determine the rescue mission's success or failure.

"Bring up the recording of the fly-over again," he told Jill, wiping a hand over his face. The air to his right filled with footage shot by the flyer as it did a slow pass along the starboard side of the jetliner, then the port side, its cameras zooming in on the Boeing's passenger windows. There was no sign of movement. It appeared that everyone was sleeping. About a third of the window seats known to be occupied showed no human presence at all. Other instruments surveyed the integrity of the hull, as they were designed to do when on stratellite duty. There was no sign of damage anywhere. No leaking gases or smoke.

"There still could have been a fire. Something smoldering. Poisonous." Phillip used a virtual keyboard to search for details on the plane's interior materials.

"A fire should have triggered automatic alarms. Same with smoke. The pilots should have had time to make a call. But there's been no explosive decompression. At least, not yet." Alex glared at the ceiling and rolled his head on his neck. "Could it be something electromagnetic? Radiation? Even a patch of concentrated air pollution."

"At 30,000 feet? There's no sign of anything different from what every other commercial jet has to face."

"Then I'm going to assume whatever it was has come and gone, and exposure duration is no longer a factor. Extend the hood. There's just enough time."

"Because you don't want to risk the first-class passengers?"

"I don't want to sacrifice anybody," Alex said, his voice raspy. Phillip gave a curt nod and repeated the order in Japanese.

Then they waited.

With no outside view except the flyer's nose cameras the only thing to see was the slow extension of the flexible tunnel, its bottom edge vibrating, followed by the copilot hurriedly spreading a sealant along the contact edge. For fifteen minutes they watched glue dry—they couldn't afford to wait longer—and the invisible build-up of air pressure within the hood rendered it more and more rigid. In the meantime, in another display, a small red airplane icon crawled across a map of the ocean toward a rugged coastline. The rescue crewman didn't wait for full pressure before spreading another compound around the seals of the escape hatch as Alex directed, and finally used a hand-held plasma torch to cut away the remaining metal. There was a noise like a cheer as the hatch dropped suddenly inward.

The crewman wriggled through the small opening, even before the surfaces could cool, his suit briefly catching on a sharp edge. His camera soon showed the cockpit, strangely undisturbed.

There was no smoke. The two pilots were in their chairs, hands hanging loosely, heads lolling to one side. A female flight attendant sprawled face down on the floor. Alex hoped the hatch hadn't struck her, but it wasn't nearby and there was no blood. He watched the flyer pilot remove a glove and reach out to touch the neck of the jetliner's captain. There was an exclamation in Japanese, and the captain's head was tilted toward the camera. The eyes were wide and staring and foam speckled the corners of the mouth.

More Japanese.

"He can't find a pulse, but the skin is still warm," Phillip translated. "He thinks the man hasn't been dead for long."

The hand in the camera view moved to the neck of the co-pilot, then the woman on the floor. The lack of any further contact told the story.

"Less than ten minutes of fuel in the flyer," Alex warned. "Follow the program."

The rescuers had been thoroughly briefed during their approach flight. The first priority was to get the aircraft under control. A check on the passengers had to wait.

There was no place to put the unfortunate captain except the floor. The flyer co-pilot climbed into the command chair and began to familiarize himself with the controls. Finally, he made a comment and disengaged the autopilot. There was a slight drop, but he quickly activated the elevators in the tail to raise the nose of the craft again and boosted the throttle to compensate for the extra drag. With the exchange of a few words, his compatriot in the flyer slowly cut back the thrust from his jump jets until he could shut them down completely.

The small craft had now given up its independence, wedding its future to the larger beast beneath it. The 787 would be a bitch to land with another aircraft perched like a bird of prey on its face; but for the present it was stable, and no longer descending.

Alex exhaled a long breath and finally allowed himself to sit. His knees betrayed him and dropped him the last few inches into his chair.

"Now crossing the coast of Japan twenty-five miles north of Tokyo," a male voice in the control room said. "All air traffic has been cleared from our corridor. As expected, there's no possibility of an approach to Narita now. We'll vector to Sapporo."

Once set, the autopilot could maintain the necessary pitch of the aircraft, but the first rescuer stayed with the controls anyway while his partner climbed down through the escape hatch and, after a pause, opened the door to the passenger compartment. His helmet camera flickered to life.

As the team from Phillip's base of operations watched, it was like one of those horror movies that simulated hand-held video: a familiar setting turned grotesque by unsettling details. An abandoned food cart blocked one of the aisles, a flight attendant crumpled beside it with her limbs in unnatural positions. Passengers rearward and toward the windows from her had various snacks and drinks spilled across their laps, some even with food hanging from open mouths. No one moved. Most heads had fallen forward or to the side. Most eyes were closed, but many were open. Staring.

About half of the windows had their shades open, but not in any pattern. Shafts of the brighter sunshine spot-lit protruding tongues, eyeglasses dangling from ears, a candy bar caught in a V-neck tank top.

The shock of the would-be-rescuer showed in his hesitant movements and sudden changes of direction. Unlike his compatriot, it took him a long time to work up the nerve to touch anyone. When he finally did, he gave a cry of surprise.

"Some of them are alive," Phillip said. "Maybe most of them. But they look to be comatose. Could it have been something in the food or drink?"

"It doesn't look like the flight crew had finished serving everyone. Besides, there's always someone who doesn't want a drink or a snack."

Alex saw Phillip's face stiffen, eyes grow wide. He spat some rapid-fire Japanese that made the flyer crewman stop to take a closer look at a pretty woman on the aisle. The man checked her pulse, listened for breath, and carefully lifted an eyelid, then offered a husky string of syllables. Phillip closed his own eyes.

"What is it?" Alex asked.

"A cousin." The voice was a near whisper. "A favorite cousin."

"My God. Why didn't you tell me you knew someone on this flight?"

The other shrugged. "I couldn't take a risk that you would do anything different. Anything ... not for the greater good."

"But for Christ's ..."

Alex stopped at a sound coming from the camera feed. High-pitched. Undulating.

The sound of a baby crying.

The crewman had heard it too: a baby lying at the feet of its mother, partially hidden by the seat in front. The baby's rescuer found a bottle of formula that had rolled a few steps down the aisle. It gave the infant girl at least some temporary relief.

With the child cradled in his arms, he continued his tour of the passenger cabin. What was missing was just as telling as the visible details. There was no smoke. No oxygen masks dangling from the ceiling. No one had vomited. No blood. No clue as to what had taken place. The man found a portable crib for the baby and took her to the flight cabin. For the landing that was only minutes away, two pilots would not be too many.

The passengers might be close to death, but there was nothing obvious that could be done for them by one man. Their best hope was to get the plane on the ground as quickly as possible near good medical facilities. Teams were already standing by at Sapporo's New Chitose Airport. Diverting all but essential traffic from Japan's third busiest air hub would be giving ulcers to a lot of air traffic controllers.

Alex and his companions squirmed in sympathy as they watched the pilots try to control the giant plane with their windshield completely blocked. There had been some discussion about releasing the maintenance flyer's grip on the jetliner and allowing it to drop into the Sea of Japan—it was capable of remote-controlled flight— but the risk was too high that the wind would catch it and smash it back into the Boeing, causing fatal damage.

A blind landing was bad, but the alternative was worse.

Phillip brought up views from the airport control tower. On the left was a jittery close-up of the approaching Boeing, a streamlined beauty with a grotesque growth on its nose. The right-hand view showed the runway flanked by a dozen emergency vehicles, lights strobing chaotically. The image of the Boeing grew sharper as it neared, then smaller as the camera zoomed out and elements of landscape came into view. Alex thought it looked too low—it would undershoot the runway.

The nose of the jet lifted just a little. A ribbon of pavement appeared.

Unbidden pictures flashed into his mind: fireballs of lurid orange and churning black, burning skeletons of metal, pinwheeling wreckage—all the images of plane crashes he'd ever seen.

Then suddenly it was over. The plane was safely on the ground, nose on the runway, the front landing gear collapsing from the extra strain but the aircraft otherwise undamaged. A fleet of ambulances raced across the tarmac. Phillip's team cheered.

Alex could only sit there, stunned.

A ball of cotton had closed around him, muffling sounds, muting sensations, attenuating his connection to reality. His muttered responses to Phillip's exhortations were barely lucid. He permitted himself to be led to a nearby room with a shower, food, a bed. He stood, sat, walked, listened, nodded, ate, slept. Maybe twice—he wasn't sure. It was as if he had stepped out of the stream of time, awaiting a moment of revelation.

Two questions burned in his mind. The first was, of course, *what had caused hundreds of people to lose consciousness?* But the answer to that was not forthcoming, even though investigators rushed to the scene. Passengers still alive were completely unresponsive. Priority autopsy results of the flight crew showed brain damage—minute but widespread hemorrhages—with no apparent cause. There were no traces of poisons in the air, water, or food. No evidence of decompression, of radiation, excess heat or cold, loss of oxygen ... Nothing out of the ordinary.

The second question: how many souls had been saved? After a few very early reports, Phillip had waited for the conclusion to play out—nearly forty-eight hours—before coming to sit in front of Alex.

To tell him that the passengers had died.

"*All* of them?"

"The baby survived. It seems to be OK."

"Your cousin?"

Silence.

Alex stood shakily. Phillip offered praise and platitudes, but was distracted by an aide with an urgent message. When he turned around again, Alex was gone.

Days later, the special government resources that Phillip Watanabe called upon could only conclude that Alex Rhys had simply disappeared.

2

March 2, 2042

Elle Travis thought about running away. Just getting on the subway, riding to the end of the line, and going wherever her feet took her.

Anywhere but the Foster Psychiatric Clinic and her appointment in ... fourteen-and-a-half minutes.

It was only a block away now—she could see its gleaming glass. Such a building needed to be made of glass to allow everyone to see inside, the way shrinks thought your skull was transparent. They thought they could read her emotions, catalog her motivations, chart all her hurts and fears and guilt into a computer spreadsheet that would fill any blanks with a simple command. Tell them what to do with her, where to put her—what drugs to feed her.

She hadn't meant to give in to bitterness. Actually, the doctors amused her a little. They acted like they could read her mind, when the reverse was closer to the truth.

Unfortunately, her amusement never defeated her fear.

There was a coffee shop beside her. A shot of caffeine would be a bad idea right then, so she ordered a glass of milk to wash down a double-chocolate donut with chocolate-cream filling and brown sprinkles on top. A smear of the filling nearly the same color as her skin landed on the back of her hand and she licked it off. Too late, she remembered her resolution not to have any liquids, because the interrogation by the panel of doctors would make her need to pee. Again, she looked longingly toward the subway entrance down the block.

Why couldn't she just think of the doctors as foreign dignitaries—as if she'd been assigned to translate their strange words for the General Assembly? They spoke a language all their own, didn't they? She could handle that—it wouldn't intimidate her at all. After more than a year in the UN translator corps, it was second nature to take phrases of even the most outrageous bombast and convert them into equally over-inflated expressions of a wholly different language without batting an eye.

Overheard snatches of other languages automatically triggered a running commentary in her head.

Two tables away sat a mother and daughter reinforcing familial fetters in clipped Armenian. The mother declared that the girl was determined to spoil every potential relationship with a respectable man by ignoring sensible matchmaking in favor of childish dreams. What could the young know about love?

But then love was unlikely to come to a girl with such short hair, anyway. And penciled eyebrows, mannish clothes. Her future husband would pass by, unnoticed, while she was tapping feverishly on a telephone.

Elle didn't need to know the language to know that conversation. She could have written the script. Hers would have been more subtle, but no less debilitating for that.

She pictured her mother, Alysha Travis, tyrannically herding two-and-three-year-olds in the specially modified lower level of the family home in Toronto. A daycare operator once her own children, Elle and

Tanner, had left home, Alysha wasn't finished molding lives. An ability like hers must not be wasted.

That wasn't an assumption on Elle's part—she had read that conviction in her mother's thoughts. A lifetime together had made that possible, indeed, inevitable. Not from hundreds of miles away, though. Her telepathic 'gift' didn't work over that great a distance. That was part of the reason she'd come to New York. She'd tried taking short road trips into the countryside to get away from people and their constantly murmuring sea of thoughts, but the mental silence was too stark—her mind tried to fill in the emptiness with imagined voices, and she'd feared for her sanity. Better to seek obscurity among ten million strangers.

Her co-workers' thoughts would never be as transparent as her mother's; but now that she'd been in the city and at the same job for more than a year, many of them did leak through. Some of their mental musings were clear enough to be recognizable; but more often, the ever-present background chatter she endured was like the white noise of street traffic that grew more defined and harder to ignore once she arrived at her office. She hadn't allowed herself to grow close enough to any of her workmates to really access their psyches. She didn't want to eavesdrop. Personal secrets could be disturbing, but the inane mental babble of the average person was profoundly embarrassing. Elle blushed easily, and knowing her blush could be a giveaway only made it worse.

She'd never met the Armenian girl at the other table, but she didn't need to read her mind. At any moment, the daughter would forcibly resist throwing her hot drink in her mother's face (probably) and march out alone. Elle had never done that, and regretted it.

She swallowed the last of her milk, but it didn't wash the bitterness from her throat. A look out the window sent a shiver through her. The Foster Clinic building blocked the sun, demanding to be faced. And she would face it. Running was pointless. Her troubles would only follow. Especially since her episode on the airplane. Her boss had learned about that from the media—other potential bosses would too.

Elle stood and walked to the counter. As if spurred by Elle's nearby movement, the Armenian daughter shot to her feet and stormed out of the shop, leaving her mother to pay the bill. The girl had already paid a price of her own.

Elle watched her go, not seeing weakness, but strength.

The time that passed in the clinic waiting room was a force of destruction, carefully calculated to be so—destruction of the last vestiges of a patient's resistance. The institutional sign above the door should have read: *Abandon all hope, ye who enter here.* The thought made Elle snicker, and she had to wrap her arms tightly around herself to quell a fit of laughter. Her judges in the next room might not hear it, but they would hear of it. She was certain that such people didn't consider laughter to be a good thing.

Finally, she was led into a room that was plain to the point of bleakness. A single chair had been placed in the middle to face four figures in nearly matching suits who sat behind a raised table. Although hairstyle and expression provided no clue, Elle was gradually able to distinguish that two of the figures were men and two, women, including her own psychiatrist, Dr. Simcoe, on the far left. But there was no sense that Simcoe was there to support her. In fact, there was a noticeable extra distance between the doctor and her three colleagues. That was a message in itself.

Decisions would be made by the other three. Simcoe was only there to be a witness.

The panel didn't even acknowledge Elle's presence immediately. She swallowed and looked around.

Sunshine was carefully kept from the room by heavy curtains dark enough to transform yellow light into a deep amber, like the last gasp of sunset. Official certificates hung on the walls, but the text was too small to read.

"Ms. Travis." It was remarkable how the tone of the two words expressed that Elle was already wasting their time by not offering her full attention.

Elle said nothing. It irritated her that she had to raise her face to look at them. Doctors on a level higher than the patient. Not subtle.

"I am Doctor Hammond," said the woman. "This is Doctor Price and Doctor Baen," indicating the men on her right and her left. "You already know Doctor Simcoe." Simcoe was the only one who nodded. Price looked pleased with himself. Baen looked at Elle's legs. She shouldn't have worn a skirt. It was going to be a distraction, having to hold her knees tightly together.

Hammond continued. "You've been asked to meet with us because there is some indication that regular appointments with a single therapist might not be enough to provide an effective treatment for your condition. Do you understand that?"

"You're going to decide if I should be in an institution. I've never hurt anyone. I never would."

Hammond's face puckered and she turned that expression to Dr. Simcoe, who swallowed visibly.

"This is *not* about locking you away," Hammond explained in a voice that unashamedly contradicted her words. "We're here to help you. Are you suggesting that you don't need help? Especially after your ... incident on the aircraft?" The words were a stab and a twist. Baen and Price looked toward their colleague as if to compliment her on her form.

Baen cleared his throat. "Ms. Travis, the recent incident isn't, in fact, unusual for you, is it? You've had numerous episodes even as far back as grade school."

"I never blacked out."

"But you would drop to your knees screaming in frustration, with your hands over your ears." He was consulting a data screen on the desk in front of him. "It was enough to convince your parents to take you to a therapist even at that age. The sessions stopped your … tantrums, for want of a better word; but it would seem that wasn't a permanent cure."

No cure at all, Elle thought, but they had made her smarten up. If complaining about the babble of voices meant she'd be forced to spend time answering embarrassing questions from some creepy doctor with bad breath, the obvious solution was to hide her pain. She became very good at that. Good enough that she was still able to hide the suffering, even once she'd begun to understand what the voices were saying and where they were coming from. Though she'd occasionally slipped up in other ways.

"Your records say that your parents took you back to therapy when you were thirteen because you were spying on members of your family. Exhibiting signs of paranoia. A feeling of persecution?" Baen spoke as if he knew every single fact about her life and was hoping for her to contradict him so he could trot out each grisly detail. Elle was not about to give him that pleasure.

It wasn't spying if you couldn't help it. It wasn't paranoia if you knew the people you loved the most were thinking about having you committed.

There had been only one thing she could think to do. Squeaky clean Elle Travis had bought an ounce of marijuana and then made sure it was easy for her mother to find among her school things. The shitstorm that followed had been epic, but not as bad as an endless parade of shrinks. Her parents had been so relieved to be able to blame all of her strange behavior on drugs, that it had diffused the immediate crisis—but also had filled Elle with a cynicism that had sunk deep into her soul.

She should have been able to trust them with the truth. Wasn't that what family was for—to accept her as she was?

From the time she was fourteen, she had lived behind a mask, her family life no more than a stage play. She'd learned words and the actions that would keep her audience content, that's all. She'd learned the script.

It was only much later, when she discovered that living as an adult on her own didn't make her troubles go away, that the pain began to get the upper hand again. Desperate, and fully aware that her best friends were part of the problem, she had only one place to turn for help, though it felt more like reaching for a coiled snake than for a lifeline.

Therapy.

And for the third time in her life, it was a terrible mistake.

It had brought her here.

"Surely you must know that Dr. Simcoe only has your best interests in mind by bringing you to our attention." Price spoke for the first time, a voice too slippery smooth for her ears to fully grasp it. Elle felt her eyes open wide. He couldn't have been reading her thoughts....

No. If he had that ability, he would have genuine empathy for her, instead of just a shrink's simulation of it. He'd simply been assigned the role of 'good cop' within the trio. Caring. Sympathetic. Oh, so trustworthy.

"Yes, I'm sure that revealing our confidential conversations was a very difficult sacrifice for Dr. Simcoe," Elle said, then mentally bit her tongue. A glance at Simcoe revealed shock and fear. But not the fear that her mind might be an open book to Elle—it wasn't; they hadn't known each other long enough. The doctor had never believed that part of Elle's story anyway.

No, it was the three panel members who made Simcoe afraid. Clearly, they had influence in the psychiatric community that she had reason to dread. Elle shouldn't have taunted her, shouldn't have alienated the only possible ally she had in the room.

"I'd like to hear more about your collapse aboard the passenger jet," Dr. Hammond said, leaning forward. "Was it a recurrence of your childhood affliction?"

"I fainted."

"And writhed on the floor in the aisle. A little more than just a fainting spell. You have no history of epilepsy. And you are reported to have muttered *words*." She looked down at her own data screen as if reading an indictment. "Blue fog. Deep water. Deep Earth. Space. Some other things about many eyes, but blind eyes. Only one face. Only one voice. Were these descriptions of something you were seeing?"

"I told you. I fainted. I was unconscious."

"That's not what you told Dr. Simcoe."

"I was feverish. Probably something I ate."

"Or something you were being told. By voices in your head? Not an uncommon occurrence, Ms. Travis. Those of us on this panel have encountered many people with just such experiences. And have been able to help them."

Help them to find padded accommodations, no doubt. To find the right cocktail of drugs to keep them numbed and compliant.

Each individual word hissed through Elle's clenched teeth. "*I...don't...need...your...help.*"

"I agree."

The new voice came from the back of the room, causing every head to snap to attention. Elle spun in her chair.

Two men in dark suits stood in the entrance door, their faces expressionless. But their casual posture said they were enjoying the reaction they'd caused. The one on the left spoke again.

"This panel is hereby released of its obligation to review the case of Elle Travis, and Ms. Travis is free to go." He turned his face to her with his last words.

"Who the hell are you?" Hammond's lips had paled.

The man gave no answer except to step forward and show her a leather wallet that he flipped open. Elle caught a glint of something she assumed was a badge. His partner remained at the door.

Guarding it?

All four doctors stared at the wallet as if it held a tarantula about to get loose. Hammond was livid.

"This is absurd!" she snapped. "You don't imagine …!"

"Save your breath, Doctor," the man said without emotion, then turned to Elle. "Ms. Travis?" He extended his arm toward the door.

She leaped to her feet and hurried out, not caring that she looked like a scared rabbit. The man at the door let her pass; but after a few steps down the hall, she realized that both men were behind her.

She should have known it couldn't be that easy. She slumped against the wall.

"OK, what's this about? Are you policemen?"

"Something like that." A non-answer he was used to giving.

"Am I under arrest?"

"Absolutely not. You're free to go, just as I said. And you're under no obligation to come with us, but we very much hope that you will. Our boss would like to speak with you. It's important. Lives are at stake."

She gave a nervous laugh. This was all straight from a spy movie.

"You must have some pretty impressive credentials to think I'm going to climb into a car with you."

They did.

# # #

Alex could have wrung out his clothes, but the central Florida air would only have soaked them again within minutes. In retrospect, it was a ludicrous place to work in such weather. Even the divers who cleaned the tanks at SeaWorld probably spent more time dry than he did.

For now, he was on lunch break, chewing half-heartedly on a soggy tuna sandwich, willing its strong flavor to overcome the pervasive detergent tang in his nostrils. Eddy was a decent boss who didn't expect too much for what little he paid, but he'd be watching the clock, nonetheless. Seventeen minutes to go. Enough time for Alex to walk a couple of blocks to work the kinks out of his legs and grab some beer at the Express Mart for later, except it seemed like too much effort. Everything did, on a day like this.

A persistent buzzing noise managed to break through his reverie: a fly trapped between the screen and the glass of a window a few feet from him. It could see freedom. Smell it. But couldn't reach it. For a moment Alex considered putting the insect out of its misery, but since it had somehow gotten into the narrow space, it would eventually get itself out.

If it came anywhere near his sandwich, though, he'd hammer it. He hated flies, and anything else that carried germs.

A shadow fell over him.

"Who knew there were still manual car washes?"

The voice was unmistakable, but Alex shielded his eyes and looked up anyway.

"Why in hell would you pick a place like this?" Phillip Watanabe continued.

Alex didn't know if the question referred to the whole town or just Eddy's Sparkle and Shine, but he answered, "'Cause he pays cash. So you couldn't track my cards. My phone's never on, either. And I didn't tell anyone where I was going, not even my family."

Phillip leaned against the frame of the entrance. "Not even Andrea."

"*Especially* not Andrea. I burned that relationship so badly she was probably ready to hire a hit man. So, how *did* you find me?"

"A week ago, one of our analysts was using a broad sweep of facial recognition software. He accidentally spotted you in some month-old surveillance camera footage from San Francisco International when you took off your ball cap to get through security. On a hunch, I asked the Japanese if they had any video from the funerals of the airliner victims. How many did you go to?"

Alex's only answer was a shrug.

"We confirmed you at eighteen—as the only *gaijin* in the crowd, you stood out—a pretty busy few days for you. And I'm guessing that all of that condolence money you handed out pretty much drained your bank account. Then we were able to find your return flight to Louisiana but lost the trail until we got a hit on a surveillance camera in Lakeland. Were they showing a movie you couldn't see here?" The government agent smiled, but it wasn't malicious.

Alex didn't return the smile. Part of him had known it was only a matter of time before they tracked him down, but he'd thought it would take longer than five weeks.

"I have to ask why you ran. My bosses insist, although I think I have a pretty good idea."

Alex looked everywhere except at Phillip, but his unwelcome visitor refused to vanish.

"I swore to myself that I'd never make a life-and-death decision like that again. Maybe … maybe if I hadn't insisted on taking the time to use the hood and equalize the pressure, the plane could have landed in Tokyo. Less exposure to … whatever it was. Earlier treatment. Lives might have been saved." His voice had become husky. He cleared his throat and looked down.

"The evidence doesn't bear that out," Phillip said softly. "The majority opinion is that the cause was a phenomenon of short duration. It came and went long before our people arrived on the scene. Nothing you could have done would have changed the outcome."

Alex badly needed to believe the words, but the other man was a clandestine operative. Lies were just one tool of many in his kit. He'd say whatever would produce the result he wanted.

Running a hand across his mouth, Alex kicked at the dirt. His voice was drier than it was.

"What do you want with me?"

A muscle twitched in Phillip's face, but his dark eyes were blank.

"It's happened again."

3

March 2, 2042

The flight to New York was a little surreal. Phillip refused to give Alex more detail about the second 'event', and the small-talk the two men made was theatre of the absurd. After ten minutes, Alex kept his face firmly turned to the window and Phillip buried his nose in his entertainment app. The molded plastic and synthetic fabric surroundings felt like a stage set, immobile, while a projected world passed behind the small quadrangle of glass.

The cab ride from the airport offered more of the same awkward silence. It was only as Alex sat with his companion at a cramped café table waiting for coffee that his interest was revived. A young black woman came through the door flanked by two men in dark suits that reminded him of Phillip's. Her glowing brown skin, pretty features, and good figure provided a welcome distraction. He was astonished when the men led her to his table.

"Sir? This is Ms. Travis," one of the men said, then they casually withdrew to the far end of the room. Left standing by the table, the woman looked as if the café was the last place she expected to be. Phillip got to his feet, so Alex stood too. The woman hesitated, and slowly took the remaining free seat as the two men sat back down.

A waitress approached their table. "Would you like another chocolate donut, Sugar?"

Ms. Travis blushed and shook her head. It seemed that the waitress recognized her from other visits. "No thanks." But as the server began to turn away, she said, "Wait. You know, sure. Why not? And coffee, please. Regular."

The voice was a little childlike, but charming. Alex wished he'd ordered a chocolate donut for himself.

"I'm sure you're wondering who we are and why we've asked to speak to you." Phillip Watanabe was at his most congenial. He introduced himself with his Homeland Security title—or one of them—but only gave Alex's name, leaving her to infer that Alex worked for them too. The agent's soft-spoken manner made Alex realize how noisy the café was, with loud conversations all around them, a construction crew in the street shattering concrete and loosening dental fillings, the complaint of worn brakes on a delivery truck and the deficient muffler of a passing motorcycle. He couldn't imagine having to live with such noise day in and day out. It was a challenge to keep focused on the woman's words, especially since they were spoken with apparent reluctance.

"I'm mostly wondering how you got me out of that inquisition, and why. What could I possibly do for the government that would save lives? I'm just a UN translator."

"Elle—if you don't mind us calling you that—this has less to do with your job and more to do with a recent experience you had. Aboard a jetliner."

Her face fell. "I should have guessed." She leaned back in her chair, and when her donut and coffee arrived, she didn't touch them.

"I apologize if it's a painful subject."

She shrugged. "Seems to be all anyone wants to talk about at the moment. Elle Travis, airline freak and tabloid curiosity."

"Maybe you'll understand better if I tell you that you're not the only person this has happened to. You're just the only one who survived."

Her eyes opened wide at that, her gaze shifting back and forth between the two men. Alex tried not to show that he was as surprised as she. Phillip went on to describe the flight from Guam and the fate of its passengers, saying little about the rescue attempt.

"But why do you think it was the same thing? From what you say, nobody knows what happened on that first plane. I just had a fainting spell. Just me. Nobody else on my flight. And nobody's said I had *brain damage*." There was fear in her voice and on her face.

"I'm sure you don't," Phillip said, a little too quickly. "But your ... spell happened about fifty miles directly north of where we believe the other passengers were injured. Plus, we have the cockpit voice recorder from the stricken plane. The last words of the pilots were ... unusual." He looked down at his data tab. "The pilots sounded as if they were in a trance and talked about 'blue fog', the 'deep ocean' and 'deeper Earth'. Many eyes, but only one voice. A single face, which they seemed to associate with space—that word came up quite a few times. A powerful feeling of need, of questioning. And the many eyes were blind for some reason." He was stopped by the expression on Elle's face. She looked as if she were about to be sick.

"This is the first I've heard about any of that," Alex said. "But what has it got to do with her?"

When Elle didn't answer, Phillip did. "Ms. Travis said most of the same things in the same words during her attack, or whatever it was. Describing something that no one else could see." He looked directly at her. "Is that what it was like?"

The young woman hesitated, as if answering that question had been cause for regret in the past. Then she came to a decision.

"Yes, but I can't remember what I saw anymore, not clearly. There were ... impressions. Visions, I suppose, but dreamlike—not in any order. A sense of something vast and powerful. Curious. Searching. And images; but nothing I could make sense out of, even when I woke up and it was still fresh in my mind." She looked at them. "I'm not crazy."

"We don't think so either," Phillip said with a smile. "We think you experienced something important. But if it was the same phenomenon that hurt the other people, anything you can tell us might help prevent more loss of life. You're the only witness we can ask about this, Ms. Travis. It's very important."

"But that's all I can tell you. I don't remember anything else. I can't even remember anything about the flight before the spell hit me, but I don't imagine that I was doing anything unusual. I don't drink much alcohol. I don't do drugs." She looked down at her hands, which were shredding the napkin beside the untouched donut. "There's something else you're not saying, though."

"What's that?"

"If you think this was the same ... whatever it was that killed that whole plane full of people, why didn't it affect anyone else on my flight? Why only me?"

Phillip exchanged a look with Alex, who was wondering the same thing.

"We think it's because of your ... unique ability," the Homeland agent said softly. Elle drew back, mouth open.

"Simcoe told you that, too? God, that woman!"

"It wasn't Dr. Simcoe. At least, not directly. Reports about cases like yours are gathered automatically by certain agencies of the government. Unlike most people, these agencies take such things very seriously as a matter of national interest. They've known about you for a long time, Elle. Most of your life."

The woman sat stone still, absorbing the shock. Alex didn't know what her 'special ability' was, though he could guess. She must have thought it a closely guarded secret. He searched his mind for words of comfort, but that wasn't his strong suit. The noise of the pneumatic drill outside was even louder than before, as if it were about to crack open a stubborn vault.

Suddenly Elle snatched up her coffee cup and Alex raised an arm in self-defense, but she didn't throw it at them. She took a large swallow of liquid and attacked her donut ferociously.

It was Phillip's turn to look stunned. Then he broke into a loud laugh that turned the faces of the few customers and staff and drew looks of astonishment from the other two agents. Not surprisingly. Alex had never heard Phillip laugh before—the man rarely even smiled. He was pulling out all the stops.

Elle was taken aback by the laugh, too, her face frozen with a glob of chocolate cream at the corner of her mouth. Alex's hand twitched with an urge to wipe it off, but she caught his look and a pink tongue darted out to do the job. Her eyes focused back on the Homeland agent and narrowed.

"So, what exactly do you think could kill those people and be attracted to someone like me?"

For the first time, Phillip looked around to ensure that the rest of the customers had returned their attention to their own business. Two were just leaving, and the waitress had gone into the kitchen.

"We think it was an emission of very powerful energy—we have no idea what kind, but strong enough to fatally injure hundreds of people—and disable three satellites in low Earth orbit. So far." He looked at Alex, who hadn't heard any of this either. "Fortunately, your flight didn't pass directly through the energy field, Elle, only close enough that someone with your special sensitivity was affected. I know that seems like a stretch, but the similarities are too great to ignore."

"So, you think this was some kind of mental energy?" She swept her bangs away from her eyes.

Phillip gave a shrug. "What is mental energy? Scientists can measure brainwave activity, but they can't tell us the wavelength of a thought, or detect a transmission of what some would call telepathy. The only thing we can detect about such things is their effect on matter, or the mental processes of other human beings." He took a sip of his coffee. "We've diverted all flights along that route to pass at least a hundred miles from the location where we believe the aircraft was struck. Whatever satellites were capable of orbital changes have been moved, too."

"That must have required a pretty creative story," Alex said with a curl of his lip.

"A 'geological phenomenon believed to cause anomalous readings in aircraft navigation equipment.' For the satellites, we persuaded NASA to spread word of a possible debris cloud—they weren't happy, but they did it. It was total bullshit—we'd used every radar system available to comb that area of space in case something new showed up that could be the source of the energy field. There was nothing up there that wasn't already known and certified harmless. But the debris story was convincing because some satellites have been disabled, but a lot of others passing over the same area of the Earth had been left alone. We have no idea why."

Elle said, "I've heard of earthquakes and volcanic eruptions supposedly causing psychic phenomena—hallucinations and such."

"No seismic disturbances were detected anywhere in the area; though it is a hot spot within the Ring of Fire, with seeping hydrothermal vents on the ocean floor."

"A powerful energy source in mid-ocean. Not a human telepath, obviously. Maybe a top-secret weapon created by a mad scientist?" Alex smiled to show he wasn't serious.

"I've spent most of the past month coordinating intelligence teams to eliminate that very possibility. There was a thought that it might have been some new kind of electromagnetic pulse. A nuclear detonation is impossible to miss these days, but there are other ways to generate an EMP. We found absolutely no trace of a weapons development program anything like this by any country or rogue organization. No James Bond villains, either."

"You don't think the source is anything of this Earth," Elle made it a statement, as if daring the man to deny it.

He didn't.

Alex whistled. But his incredulous smile quickly faded as he saw the expressions of his companions: the woman's complacent, almost smug; the man's carefully blank. Alex's gaze escaped out the window.

The sun was still shining, glinting off a passing cab's windshield, a man's designer sunglasses, the frame of a baby stroller. His eyes darted to a teal T-shirt over white pants, a red spandex outfit on a bicycle, the crisp blue of a cop's uniform. A child's blond head bobbed past with a tongue gleefully lapping at a vanilla ice cream cone.

These were things 'of this Earth'. They belonged. Unknown killer energies did not.

When he returned his attention to the room, Elle was staring at nothing, putting the last small pieces of donut into her mouth mechanically like someone in a trance. For a moment, Alex feared she was having another spell; but her eyes cleared, and she turned her head to Phillip Watanabe.

"Even if what you say is true, you already know everything I can tell you, everything I remember. So why tell me all this? What do you want from me?"

Phillip met her eyes and held them.

"We know approximately where the effects of this phenomenon are taking place. We don't know what the source is. Or where it is.

"We want you to help us find it."

4

March 4, 2042

Weapons training. Learning how to field-strip and clean an old Beretta ARX100, swap barrels on a Bushmaster ACR-Series X while on the run, reload an FN Five-Seven pistol in the rain.

Mud. Brambles. Sand in every body orifice. Ears ringing despite protection gear. Livid bruises on upper thigh, right shoulder, other places not revealed to the trainers. Blood blisters in the thumb-web skin of both hands, pinched between metal components.

Exhilaration, yes—burnt propellant is like inhaled caffeine, intoxicating and aphrodisiacal. The aftermath of that adrenaline high, though—shakes and nausea. Not cool. Dehydration. Sugar craving. Forced camaraderie and forced enmity. Copious amounts of alcohol both as social lubricant and therapy.

It was a setting in which Alex's intelligence and education counted for nothing. He would never excel at it—didn't want to. Was afraid to, because a skill mastered was a skill that would surely be put to use. Even though, technically, he was only a consultant for private security contractors, proficiency with combat weapons was a guarantee that he would be put on the ground in hot zones rather than advise and coordinate from the safety of a bunker miles away.

So, he'd learned to complete the training, neither washing out nor impressing anyone. Deliberately under-performing pricked his ego like a thorn, but there were worse hurts that he meant to avoid.

He hadn't been able to. There was a bullet in Afghanistan that had just missed nicking his liver. A wedge of shrapnel in Sri Lanka that caused him to protect the ribs on his left side a little now. A near miss of a sniper's round in Turkey that he still heard in his dreams. His fellow contractors treated such things as badges of honor, but Alex hadn't dared laugh at them. Not out loud.

Cynicism, scorn, shame, all circulated through his bloodstream. Each new combat both tempting and taxing, slowly depleting his stores of courage. All while his youthful ideals seeped away.

He'd stopped working for security contractors. Turned down offers from the DEA and overtures from the Treasury Department. He'd lowered his fees to make himself available to FEMA—there had to be ways to do some good without killing people—but their tangled bureaucracy was too much to take. He could swallow a bit of pride, but his devotion to efficiency was a lump that no amount of expensive whiskey could wash down.

Sitting alone in a nondescript hotel room, beginning to feel nostalgic about an ignominious six-month career as a used-car salesman years earlier, he'd opened his door to find Phillip Watanabe standing there. Phillip hadn't needed another hired gun; he'd needed someone who *knew* things—biophysics, chemistry, engineering, aerodynamics—and could put them together to solve unique problems. With a mind that refused to specialize,

Alex's grades at university had never been top-of-the-class. He came to realize that he was a polymath, interested in too many things, and pretty good at most of them. And that was just the sort of thinking Phillip was looking for.

Over the ensuing months Phillip had lived up to most of his promises. Alex had never again been sent bodily into combat, but the death count he'd witnessed was still far too high, and his hands got dirty at a distance. The human body of flesh and blood is destined to return to dust and ash. But was the human intellect no more than a means to hurry that end? Did vast mental gifts always have to be turned to conflict, carnage, and conquest? The Alex Rhys freshly graduated from MIT would never have accepted that. But ten years of toil at the periphery of government had tarnished his bright idealism like silverware forgotten in a chest.

He'd never been a social person. He'd become content with his own company, though never enamored of it. He could work efficiently as part of a team; he could live comfortably as a recluse. Phillip commented on that only once. Alex had offered no answer, but he'd given it thought afterward. It had led him by a web search to "An Essay on Man" by 17th Century poet Alexander Pope.

> Virtuous and vicious ev'ry man must be,
> Few in th' extreme, but all in the degree;
> The rogue and fool by fits is fair and wise;
> And ev'n the best, by fits, what they despise.

It was a truth Alex Rhys had seen reaffirmed time and time again: good men and women driven by unworthy motivations into unconscionable deeds. The best and brightest, doomed to fall into shadow. He had come to recognize it as the core truth of the human condition. So promising. So flawed.

His own family was a good example: a father who was ostensibly one of the country's respected leaders; yet his list of sins was a long one, as Alex had come to learn bit by bit through various government contacts. He now knew more than enough of his father's dirty secrets to ruin the man, but refrained for the sake of his mother—though she was anything but a paragon of virtue herself, as her longtime affair with the current vice-president attested. Alex didn't know if it was motivated by romance, lust, or political gain, and didn't want to know. Even the love between mother and son had limits.

There must be something better than humankind, of that he was certain. But he hadn't found his answer in religion, or in science either—not yet—though he still held out hope.

The crack of a flag in the wind brought him back to the present. Salt-sea mist in his nostrils. The hiss of a metal wedge charging through waves.

What was he doing here?

Foreign lands, secret buildings, isolated hangers—those were all solid. Known or knowable. Earth beneath his feet. A smooth transit from place to place.

But now he stood on a bobbing mountain of steel that had no business staying afloat. Empty sky above. Yawning ocean beneath. Miles of mystery upon which this metal behemoth was a chip of flotsam at the whims of storm and sea.

It felt like a mistake. A big one.

"I thought you'd be getting some food." Phillip Watanabe's voice startled him as the man stepped up to the railing.

"Not hungry."

"Not seasick, I hope. This is calm for the Pacific."

"The waves don't bother me. Though there's a hell of a lot of water under them. Under us. And how do we know that we're not just as vulnerable to that ... mind-killing energy field aboard a ship as we would be in a jetliner?"

"I'm certain that we are just as vulnerable," Phillip said with a half-smile. "But the effect seems to be confined to a very precise zone. Maybe think of it as a column of air and space, reaching to the surface of the ocean and probably below."

"And the other end?"

"Who knows? The Moon?"

"You said there haven't been any more casualties—human or satellite."

"That's because we've moved all the aircraft and as many satellites as we could. With the cooperation of the International Air Transport Association, we've instituted a no-fly zone for everyone but the aircraft involved in the investigation, based on our belief that the effect is restricted to a limited area—surface area, if not altitude. There could be another reason, though. We can't be sure." Watanabe folded a hand over a fist and leaned his chin on it, elbows on the railing.

"You can't measure it any more precisely than that?"

"With what? Normally we'd use a satellite to scan the electromagnetic spectrum or send a survey aircraft overhead."

"Yeah. Not ideal in the present circumstance. But ...." Alex shook his head and took a hard look at his companion. "Elle Travis floundering around the sky in a helicopter, hoping to blunder into the location of the source without being killed ... it's kind of like dowsing for a well in a minefield. How did you convince her to do it? The same as back in the café? Tell her she didn't have to come—she could just go back to the shrink tribunal?"

"I didn't say that as a threat."

"Of course you did! So, what was it this time?"

Phillip shrugged. "Ms. Travis didn't need convincing, believe it or not. You can ask her. I think she's a little afraid of flying but she seems ... almost eager for this. Maybe she thinks what we're doing could bring her some closure."

"Or death. Or life as a mental vegetable."

"Maybe she has more faith than you do in our ability to cope with whatever we find."

"So, what do *you* think it is? You keep dodging that question in briefings."

The agent took a long time before answering.

"It's some form of energy that we can't identify without instruments that can survive its tremendous power. My bosses think the Chinese could be responsible—they suspect the Chinese of everything to do with abuse of technology. I don't agree." A veil seemed to fall over his eyes.

"You don't think ...? Yes, you do. Are you serious? You think the source is somewhere other than Earth?"

"That's a possibility. But the effects are very localized—the source is probably located on or very near our planet." He turned to face Alex, his mouth tight. "I'm more concerned that the source is *from* somewhere other than Earth."

They said no more as the whine of a helicopter starting up on the helipad took their attention. By unspoken agreement, they walked toward it.

Alex had flown in Sikorsky Black Hawk, Pave Hawk, and Pave Low helicopters, an old Huey once too. He'd sat in an Apache on the ground. But he'd never seen the helicopter that was sitting on the pad spinning up its two sets of rotors—not in person, at least. He had to shout to be heard above its growing whine.

"Is that a ...?"

"Sikorsky Raider ET. Enhanced Turbine."

"I didn't think they ever made it into full production."

"A half-dozen special orders were filled, for organizations that needed something with more than the usual speed."

That made sense. Infiltration missions were hairy in the exfil phase, once the shit had hit the fan and the bad guys' defense forces had been alerted. Speed could make all the difference between escape and capture. The original Raider was able to make 220 knots cruising speed, 80 more than the Black Hawk. How much more would an enhanced-turbine engine provide? The impact-resistance of the composite material airframe would be a factor, too. Wandering birds could play hell with low-flying aircraft.

"You plan on having to run from something?" Alex asked.

Phillip wore a strange expression. "Maybe in our case, the ET in the aircraft's name will stand for something else."

Alex had no response to that.

There was a lot about the slate-grey helicopter to catch his eye: sleek lines, two rotors, one above the other, spinning in opposite directions, and especially the weird pusher rotor at the rear that provided extra velocity. But equally intriguing to Alex was the on-again, off-again helipad attached to the stern deck of the Research Vessel *Orion*. That part of the ship had originally been dedicated to a huge crane to load and launch submersible craft. *Orion* had been adapted so that the expanded crane structure extended beyond its stern and now supported a flat platform just big enough for the thirty-five-foot-long helicopter. He'd overheard someone say "nanotechnology" but didn't know how that figured into the formation of the wide pad over the framework of crane girders. As he followed Phillip onto the platform's edge, he saw that it was black with a hint of gloss, but otherwise completely featureless. The texture underfoot reminded him of ceramic tile, but wasn't slippery despite sea spray.

Two pilots were visible in the helicopter cockpit. An open side door showed that no one else was aboard. Phillip turned back toward the ship's superstructure, so Alex did the same. A bulky soldier in a flight suit escorted a diminutive figure vainly trying to regain control of her hair in the windstorm from the rotor blades. Someone with more experience would have put on her flight helmet before approaching the aircraft; but from Elle Travis's staring eyes, Alex guessed that she'd never flown in a military chopper before.

She gave Alex and Phillip pleading looks before she climbed into the throbbing machine. Phillip leaned toward Alex.

"Well? Aren't you going to go along to hold her hand? I have to stay here to coordinate some equipment transfers with the mainland."

To Alex's surprise, he found an air-support crewman beside him holding out a flight suit in his size. It left him no time to think of an excuse not to go, and the appeal was typical Phillip. Suddenly his bladder didn't feel as empty as he would have liked.

"How long?"

"Couple of hours, max. Less if she can pin down a location."

Less still, if she suddenly collapsed and died. Or the flight crew did.

Alex put on the suit.

# # #

As he climbed into the passenger compartment of the Raider, he was surprised by its interior layout. It was padded with light grey soundproofing material, and the black seats were upholstered and comfortable, not like the benches or slings he'd often had to endure. Clearly, it was used more often for ferrying valuable personnel in a hurry than it was for pulling troops out of a firefight. He caught a quick flash of gratitude from Elle and buckled himself in. The flight crewman was checking her safety harness. He didn't check Alex's. The helicopter was already lifting off and Alex's mind kicked in to what he'd come to think of as survey mode. It was a longtime habit that had saved his life more than once.

His hand felt under his seat for a life jacket. Seagoing aircraft usually carried inflatable life rafts, too. There, on the wall near the floor. There'd be another one on the side he couldn't see, as a backup, though this bird could only carry six passengers and two crew. A fire extinguisher hung within easy reach, but only if he unbuckled his harness, which was part of the reason extinguishers were rarely helpful. A copter spiraling out of the sky pinned you to your seat like an insect on a corkboard. Dry chemical spray might be a good deterrent if the mind-killing beam made anyone go berserk. The bottle was a little too short to use as a good club. His helmet might work, except that would leave his own skull unprotected.

He didn't see much that would be useful in a survival scenario. Inside and out, the Raider's shell was too tough to break off pieces for shelter or to make improvised knives. None of the interior materials would burn well. The polymer windows might make a little solar oven to cook fish. There would be a toolkit in the cockpit, under a seat perhaps. This particular craft carried no armaments—usually good news in the event of a crash. His eyes scanned the compartment for anything that could be pried loose and used as a crowbar, digging tool, paddle, or spear. Nothing looked promising.

Under his flight suit he wore the fatigues he favored on a mission, with a dozen or more pockets. A few of them always held his Swiss Army knife, satellite smartphone, beef jerky, and a flat flask of water. Old-style compass. Plastic zip ties. 20-pound fishing line with a steel hook. Ultra-foldable sunglasses with a magnifying lens that slipped over one eye and could start fires. Stainless steel mirror.

His wrist implant was a chronometer and compass combined, but he trusted his analog compass more. His neural augment contained detailed topographical maps of the entire globe as accessible as if they were in his flesh memory, so he could never really be lost.

No weapons. But he noticed that the crewman behind Elle wore a sidearm. Was he assigned to Elle and Alex as a bodyguard? Did someone not trust the flight crew?

No. The gun was in case the two civilians aboard suddenly went crazy, their brains fried by an unknown energy. Why anyone thought soldiers would be less affected, he couldn't guess. Maybe they wore tin foil hats under their helmets.

Alex put his hand to his own helmet and felt for the radio controls built into it. He flicked a switch and listened for a moment. Within a few seconds he heard one of the pilots describing the Raider's altitude and airspeed. There should be a separate channel for the passengers. He found a sliding switch and tried that. There was a faint background hiss, but no voices. He cleared his throat.

"Testing all stations, this is Alex Rhys requesting a communications check."

"Sergeant Upton confirming communications check, sir." The air crewman.

"No need to call me sir, sergeant. I'm a civilian. Ms. Travis, can you hear me?"

Her face was already turned toward him, and she nodded.

"Good. You just have to talk, and I'll hear you—these radios are voice-activated in this mode. Are you doing OK?"

She nodded again, then remembered. "Fine. I'm fine." Her voice was higher than usual.

"I was kind of a last-minute addition to the crew," Alex said, giving her what he hoped was a reassuring smile, "but we're basically just going to cruise around in a very wide circle, right?"

"And if I sense any feeling like what happened on the plane, we take note of our location and how long it lasts, if possible." Meaning if she didn't pass out.

"So, if you get a positive result at more than two places, we might be able to triangulate a location of the source. And if there's nothing, we shrink the circle?"

She hesitated. It sounded like a swallow. "Yes. Until I sense something, or we get within fifty miles of the point where the first airplane was … affected."

That point was little more than a guess based on the time of the last known communication from the jetliner. The time window was a big one. If the Raider unwittingly blundered into the danger zone, would there be any warning? Probably not.

"I don't know how Phillip convinced you to do this. You're a very brave woman."

She barked a laugh. "Bravery's got nothing to do with it." But she didn't explain further. A minute later she said, "If we get close to whatever it is, you could be in just as much danger as me. Why did you come?"

Why had he? To 'hold her hand', as Phillip had said? To prove he had the guts? Or was the Homeland agent's crack about ET enough to spark Alex's obsession with superior intelligences in the universe?

"That's a good question," he said. "Um, should I be quiet so you can concentrate on sensing this thing?"

She sighed. "If this thing is out here, I don't think I'll be able to miss it."

That brought conversation to a halt. Alex looked out over endless ocean. Sea and sky mirrored each other and blended into one. There were no clouds in sight and nothing to be seen on the dimpled surface of the South Pacific. Soon, they'd probably glimpse a twin bump on the horizon: a sliver of land with a smudge of cloud above it.

RV Orion was sailing a little more than a hundred miles northwest of Guam. The helicopter had set out almost due east. They'd be flying near a chain of islands that formed a beaded arc from Guam northward toward Japan, including Saipan and the other Northern Mariana

Islands. But they were well north of Saipan. He thought they would pass closest to Guguan, or possibly Alamagan. Their circle enclosed an area of ocean called the Mariana Basin, a rugged plain with a lot of seismic activity, bordered by the Mariana Trench. Although the infamous Challenger Deep—the section of the trench that comprised the deepest point of Earth's oceans—was hundreds of miles south of them, he still felt a little queasy at the thought of it. Almost seven miles of implacable water, straight down. A long way to fall.

"Why are we flying so high?" Elle asked. "I thought we'd be lower, so we could spot things on the surface."

Alex waited to see if Sergeant Upton would answer, but the man remained mute.

"This trip isn't about finding anything by sight," he said. "It's really hard to pick out objects from the waves. Everything blurs together and lulls your attention. Even if we were looking, we're trying to stay at least fifty miles away from the thing, so we'd have to be pretty high to see that much ocean."

All true, but none of it was the reason for their altitude.

If something were to disable the flight crew or the avionics, any extra height would provide a slim margin of time to switch the controls over to remote flight (if the pilots died first) or make an autorotation descent to soften the impact if they had to ditch in the sea.

Though some satellites had been disabled, the avionics of the Boeing Dreamliner had survived the attack. Alex tried to take comfort in that. In the event of incapacitated pilots, the Raider could be controlled remotely from *Orion* to bring it back home. But dead avionics would mean a big splash and only seconds to escape a sinking cage.

There was no need for Elle Travis to know any of that.

# # #

The flight turned out to be completely uneventful anyway. Elle felt nothing out of the ordinary at any time. As the Raider returned to a landing on *Orion*, Alex was already undoing his flight suit, urged on by the pressure in his bladder. But he turned toward Elle to help her out and the expression on her face shocked him.

It looked more like disappointment than relief.

█**5**█

The slow bow-to-stern rise and fall of the deck made Elle walk with her legs farther apart than usual. She hoped she didn't look like a cowgirl after a hard ride.

The long ocean swells were comforting, really. Like being rocked by a gentle mother. She hoped the calm would last. She didn't want to experience *this* mother in a bad temper.

If she'd been in the city on a night like this, she probably would've been listening to loud Korean pop music to cover up the ceaseless traffic noise. Her wrist bangle held a weeks' worth of tunes and there was no fear of disturbing anyone else since the signal streamed to decorative studs implanted just behind her ears, and generated sound through bone induction. But here and now, the soft murmur of the ocean was more appealing.

It really was true, what they said about stars seen at sea. The sky was a sparkling canopy stretched tightly to the horizon in every direction. A few shipboard lights interfered with the view, but the stern deck was nearly abandoned for the night.

Not quite. Someone stood near the railing where she'd been headed. She slowed until she could make out more detail. A man in fatigues, but something about the clothes was familiar. The slight bulges. Pockets. Lots of them.

Alex Rhys.

She thought about turning around. He was a congressman's son, she'd learned. That kind of upbringing, along with his good looks, pretty much guaranteed a spoiled snob used to having everything his own way. About as far from Elle's own childhood as you could get. They certainly couldn't have anything in common, so why even bother trying to make small talk? She could find another piece of railing to lean on. Besides, he might think that an evening rendezvous at a ship's rail under the stars was a situation that spoke of romance, something she definitely didn't want. Her life was complicated enough.

On the other hand, Alex had barely talked to her during the helicopter flight when she would have welcomed idle chatter. Maybe he wasn't a risk. And they would be working together.

She scuffled her feet on the deck so as not to startle him, but he mustn't have heard it over the waves. He jumped when she said hello.

"Ms. Travis. Nice to see you on deck. I guess that means you're as comfortable on ships as you are on helicopters."

Was he making fun of her? It didn't look like it. Maybe she really had fooled him.

"I've never been on the ocean before, on a ship. Just an air mattress." She hadn't meant to be funny, but she liked his smile. "Do you … travel on ships very much?"

"Hardly ever. I … um, I don't know what kind of security clearance you have, so let's just say that I work as a consultant for government agencies on special projects. I've been on a few that were run from naval vessels, but mostly I log a lot of flight time."

"Air miles?"

"Funny, the people I fly with don't offer those. I'll have to talk to them about that."

"You're a consultant. Does that mean you don't go into combat? You don't kill people in person?"

God, what had made her say *that*? He suddenly looked like a kicked puppy, though he made an effort to get his face under control.

"I've never killed anyone in person, no." His gaze fell to the deck, and he cleared his throat. "But I have been responsible for deaths. Sometimes of our own people."

He turned toward the ocean and Elle did the same. She brushed bangs out of her eyes. Shit, she wasn't usually a bitch. She was a *nice* girl—a girl everybody brought their troubles to, confident she'd know the right words to say. Was she just lashing out at whoever was closest? Yet she couldn't bring herself to apologize. This man had sat in a room somewhere, nice and safe, and ordered other people to kill and to die. She knew that went on all the time, but it was revolting. Bad enough that men and women still shed so much of each other's blood, but the ones who sat in safety and ordered them to do it ... they were the worst. Warmongers and cowards.

So much for worrying about a romantic entanglement with this guy. That wasn't going to happen.

On the other hand, if they were going to have to work together, she shouldn't piss him off too much.

She looked toward the horizon to the east, brighter than elsewhere. That must be the rising Moon.

"I'll bet the Moon is beautiful over the ocean," she said. "But by the time it's overhead I'll be in dreamland."

"It won't pass directly overhead." His voice regained its strength. "It would have a few weeks ago, but now it'll pass a bit farther north. You probably know that the Moon seems to shift across the sky with the seasons, like the sun and … *Oh my God!*"

"What is it?"

He grabbed her shoulder. "Let's find Phillip. I think I just hit on some answers."

#   #   #

They found the Homeland Security agent in the officers' wardroom with a tall glass of sweet tea in front of him, although the trio of ship's officers at a nearby table all had beers in their hands. Phillip's shirt and slacks looked crisp, as if he changed them several times a day. There was only a small wet patch on his shirt in line with his chin, where condensation from his glass had dripped.

When Alex said they needed to talk, Phillip stood and led them back out onto the deck.

"I could've explained without spilling any state secrets," Alex said.

"It's not about secrecy," Phillip replied. "It's a tradition not to talk business in the wardroom. Bad form. The captain made a friendly concession in allowing me to have a drink there even though I'm not an officer. I don't want to abuse their hospitality."

That didn't fit Elle's image of a government operative who could order up a navy ship at need.

"What have you got?"

"Maybe an explanation for why some satellites have been trashed and others not. Was there any change in the numbers over time, before you altered orbits?"

"Not much. I seem to remember there were quite a few losses in the two days after the jetliner incident, and then the kills tapered off. But we figured it was because the satellites in the most dangerous zone had already been hit. We sent out the alert after five days. With all the satellites being owned by different organizations, nobody noticed a trend until then. That's when we alerted the airlines, too. Luckily, no other planes had been affected; but then Ms. Travis had her ... spell, and we expanded the no-fly zone."

"I think there might be a reason. Has anybody tried to look behind the Moon?"

Phillip's head snapped around. "Who told you that? I just heard about it myself."

"Nobody told me anything. Are you saying somebody has?"

"A Chinese probe has been re-tasked. It was on a trajectory for orbital insertion anyway, preparing to land, but they're giving it a higher orbit to get a broader field of view. We should get results before morning. Now tell me how you knew this?"

"The Chinese cooperating with us? That speaks volumes." Alex gave a slow shake of his head. "I'm only guessing, but when the jetliner crisis happened, the Moon would have been directly overhead. Elle's plane was well north of the original jet's flight path; but by then, the Moon's apparent track through the sky had also shifted northward."

"You think someone on the Moon is firing at a target on Earth?"

"That's a possibility, but I think it's more likely that something at a fixed location near here is transmitting something toward the Moon. The first jet had the bad luck of getting between the transmitter and the target. The Moon was farther to the north when Elle's jet passed, but luckily she was still beyond the path of the most concentrated energy." He gave her a look of sympathy. "Not quite far enough."

"You know the position of the Moon each day from memory?" she asked.

He gave her a puzzled look, then tapped the back of his head. "Tesla neural augment. Moon phases and motions are one of the basic apps from the factory, but it connects to *Orion*'s network, too. My point is, if the source of the transmission only sends when the Moon is nearly overhead, that could explain why a lot of flights and satellites weren't affected. I think if you check, you'll find that the dead ones passed through a line connecting the Moon with this patch of ocean, and only within a small range of longitude."

Elle thought the idea was pretty random, but Phillip's face held respect.

"I've also been trying to figure out why satellites would be disabled but avionics on the Boeing weren't. Most satellites' electronics are hardened against radiation."

"And ...?"

"Three possibilities come to mind, but they all come down to intensity. The first is focus. Picture holding a magnifying glass over a patch of grass on a sunny day. An ant can crawl over either side of the lens and be unharmed. Meanwhile you've set the grass on fire."

"What else?"

"Whatever this energy is, maybe the transmission is a tight beam that diffuses rapidly with distance, but with an intense core. So, a satellite passing directly through the beam has its circuitry fried but an aircraft fifty miles away from it doesn't."

"Except human brain circuitry is more fragile and is affected."

"Or more sensitive to the frequencies involved. Enough to produce tragic results aboard that Boeing; but farther away, only somebody as sensitive as Ms. Travis is affected."

"You mentioned a third possibility."

Alex hesitated. "That whatever is producing this energy knows exactly what it's doing, has full control of it, and wanted to take out those satellites."

"And hundreds of human beings?"

Alex shrugged, clearly uncomfortable. "When we find it, I'll make sure that's the first question I ask."

"I'll get on that idea about the satellite orbits. Anything else you want to say?"

"Yeah. Let's make sure *Orion* is well south of the original jet's flight path six hours from now."

As if with one mind, they turned to look at the bright Moon poised just above the horizon. To Elle, its face seemed uncharacteristically cold.

6

March 5, 2042

Elle awoke from a nightmare and gasped for breath like a drowning victim.

Buried beneath a mile of water so dark it seemed to suck the light from her very soul, she'd felt pressure, brutal pressure, but not from the water. Rather, from questions, unknowns, uncertainties. She didn't know what she was, why she was, why she was there, why she was apart from … from what? So many other living things. Bright things, quick things, hot things, noisy, busy. Alive. She could not reach them. They were near, and yet much too far.

There was a large *something* that called to her, pulled at her. She called out to it for answers, but answers never came.

But the need remained. A very great need.

She realized that she was clenching her eyes shut to keep the water out, yet her lungs were filling with air. She forced her eyes open, longing for light.

And there was light. Blue light, but not light through water. Blue curtains covered the porthole above her bunk. She reached toward the porthole, desperate to know she wasn't trapped at the bottom of the sea.

Her t-shirt was soaked with sweat; but as a shudder passed through her, she pulled the covers over her for warmth—or a shield. It did no good. There was no way she was going back to sleep. She was too afraid of what sleep held.

No going back. That was true of her waking hours, too, she realized. She'd already begun thinking of her job at the UN in the past tense, as if it was a part of her life that was over. Why? Was that a premonition of her death?

It didn't feel like that. Maybe that frame of mind was just an inevitable reaction to an attempt to interact with something utterly alien. But from that interaction, she knew for certain that her whole world would be changed, and she would reluctantly become a part of history. Such a thing couldn't be kept secret, no matter what the conspiracy theorists thought; and it would eventually become known that Elle Travis was not a normal human being.

In a very real sense, she was giving up the life she'd led.

Unless she quit the mission right now.

And if she did?

More people would die.

She slipped on jeans and a tangerine sweater and padded out onto the deck, her footsteps ringing lightly on the metal surface. The muggy night was alight with a waxing gibbous Moon, just less than full, high off the starboard bow, that illuminated the ship, but not the rolling waves. She had expected to find it there, had seen it even with her eyes closed. If it hadn't directly robbed her of sleep, it was implicated in the theft. An accomplice, remote and untouchable.

She heard a light cough from behind her.

"Ms. Travis? Elle?"

Alex Rhys stepped to her side. He wore baggy shorts and a t-shirt, but was hugging himself.

"It's sticky in my cabin but a bit cool out here. What about you? Couldn't sleep?"

She only nodded. He returned it.

His stark eyes in the moonlight showed there was more to say. Should she allow him his privacy?

"You had a nightmare," she stated. "About combat. People dying. Because of what I said yesterday?"

He was slow to answer. "You really do have it, don't you? That 'special ability' Phillip talked about."

Elle hadn't read his mind. That took weeks, if not months, of close proximity. The accuracy of her guess had more to do with her own regret about having said something so hurtful. But he didn't need to know that, this long-distance killer. Maybe his computer brain-implant preserved every one of his transgressions in vivid detail, instead of the merciful impermanence that human memory provides. Only rich people could afford such augments. Served them right.

He gave an awkward shrug and turned his face into the moonlight. It was a good face, and the silvery light turned his windswept blond hair into an aura.

"What you said might have triggered the nightmare tonight, but not all the other nights." His mouth gave a twitch as if he was trying to make a joke of it, but his smile was like a candle that went out with the first puff of air. "You figured out my bad dream, the least you can do is tell me about yours."

No, the least she could do was to keep her mouth shut. Did she want to share something like that with this man, especially in moonlight with both of them feeling vulnerable?

Stupid. Of course, she had to. There was no way it was a simple nightmare.

She told him. He gave a soft whistle and looked up at the Moon.

"Wow. And we're almost a hundred nautical miles from my best estimate of the source's location. Maybe I'm way off, or maybe it's even more powerful than we thought. Are you sensing anything now?"

She'd been trying not to.

"Yes," she said finally, "there's the same sense of urgent need. Questioning. Frustration, I guess. But I can't tell what direction it's coming from, if that's what you're thinking." She wrapped her arms around herself. "Are you going to tell Mr. Watanabe?"

"We have to." He touched her shoulder lightly. "But not right now. He'd have us up in a helicopter within twenty minutes, and something tells me you're not up to that. Better to make a plan and give you a chance to get some rest. Then we'll go for another ride tomorrow night when the Moon's high."

"But I told you I can't sense the direction."

"So, we fly a path like a sine curve: move in close until you feel something, then edge away until you lose contact, move in again, and so on. A continuous pattern of approach and retreat. If the energy field is circular, we'll eventually get some idea of where the center of the circle should be."

"Terrific."

"I thought you were disappointed when we didn't find anything last time. That's what it looked like."

There was no way she was going to answer that. She shrugged and turned back to the Moon, but in the corner of her eye she saw him give a prodigious yawn. "You should go back to bed. You might sleep now that you've cooled off."

She felt him watching her and tried her best not to be rattled by the cold face in the sky. But her body betrayed her with a tremble.

"Nah, I'm not tired," he lied. "People work all shifts on this boat. We can probably get some breakfast already in the mess. Come on."

She let him lead her back inside. Maybe the guy wasn't a *total* asshole.

# # #

While they waited for a decent hour to wake up Phillip Watanabe, they saw him already awake and walking toward them on the deck. He wasn't alone.

"Oh my God," Elle squealed. "Here boy, come here!" She squatted and Phillip released the leash he held. A big yellow dog came bounding toward her and knocked her on her ass. She squealed again as it licked her face, adroitly dodging her arms.

"Ranger. Ranger! Sit!" Phillip called, and eventually the dog complied, though its back end did a dance up and down on the deck while its feathery tail swept back and forth.

"Golden retriever and lab mix. Two years old," the agent said, deliberately misinterpreting Alex's questioning look. "I rescued him from a shelter in San Francisco last year. Stupid thing to do. I travel too much, and Ranger isn't always on his best behavior when I'm gone. It's a constant hunt for dog sitters."

"A dog. And a rescue dog too. Phillip Watanabe, I'm speechless."

"Smartass. You think I don't have any home life?"

Alex's face left no doubt that it was exactly what he thought. How long had they known each other, Elle wondered? Or had they ever really known each other?

She stood up and scratched behind Ranger's ears. He was a well-built mutt with the short, smooth fur of a lab everywhere except his ears and tail, which were shaggy. Light-colored all over, his chest and stomach fur were nearly white. She was surprised to see black blotches on his pink tongue.

"Genetic," Phillip explained. "Who knows how far back?"

"I can't believe this guy could ever be any trouble," Elle cooed, petting the dog's face and neck.

"He's on probation aboard *Orion*. Fortunately, he doesn't seem to like the taste of the furniture here as much as he does at home." Phillip raised his eyes. "Were you looking for me? What have you got?"

Elle gave Alex a look and he explained about her dream at the height of the Moon. Phillip didn't ask why they hadn't awakened him. Instead, he said, "OK, I'll set up a flight for tonight. The Chinese probe was behind the Moon during that time, which would have protected it but maybe also kept it from finding anything. It'll have a chance to scan the daylight side today."

"A light-dispersing cloak isn't out of the question. We've got the technology ourselves."

'True. But the probe's designed to find mineral resources, so it's equipped with radar and magnetic sensing instruments. While they aren't intended for searching open space, the designers think they'd pick up anything as large as, say, some sort of mother ship in lunar orbit."

Elle's eyebrows shot up as memories of old movies came to mind. Giant hovering spaceships. Whole cities destroyed. Was that really what she was involved with?

"What about the Moon's surface?" she asked.

"We've got telescopes and radar dishes like you wouldn't believe scouring every inch. Have had for a few weeks. Anything larger than a Frisbee would've been spotted."

Ranger was nudging his leg with determination. He gave the dog's face a rub.

"A smart intruder would be buried beneath the dust," Alex mused. "Good thermal insulation. Wouldn't block radar, but they might have something else that could. If only we knew what the transmissions were saying."

Elle felt their eyes on her. She paid more attention to the dog.

"I've told you what I see, and what I feel. Ranger probably understands more of what we're saying and thinking than I do of … this thing. Dogs have a history with us. If you really think it's aliens I'm sensing, then there's no guarantee we'll ever understand them. That's what *alien* means."

The men acknowledged that. Phillip said, "I think you're right about having a history. Which is why I'm going to have to ask you to spend some more time with us, Ms. Travis. Time to develop a connection, if you can. I have a feeling we're not going to get anywhere broadcasting mathematical formulae by radio. We'd do as well flashing semaphore."

She was too embarrassed to ask what he was talking about. "How much time?"

"You'd know that better than I would."

Again, Elle wondered how much Phillip Watanabe knew about her 'gift', and where the information had come from. At least he treated the subject with some sensitivity. Although his 'request' for her extended presence didn't make it sound as if she actually had a choice.

A pair of gulls squawked overhead and flapped on a rising breeze toward the ascending sun. Maybe they had a destination, maybe not, but that didn't seem to matter. To them, the whole ocean was available, the whole sky.

"What more can we do in the meantime?" Alex asked. He squatted and scratched the underside of Ranger's chin, dodging a grateful lick. The dog looked happy; the man, awkward.

"We're bringing a stratellite into the area to try to learn more about the signal. It'll be on point within the next hour. The thing is, we don't know how this energy beam disables satellites, or why. As you pointed out, the avionics of the first jetliner didn't show signs of damage at all—even the autopilot worked perfectly well. It occurred to me that a spacecraft hiding in orbit might want to make sure there was nothing nearby that could give the game away, while an aircraft wouldn't be a threat. The human injuries might have been collateral damage."

"You're gambling that it will leave a stratellite alone. Maybe it will. Until the strat starts using active radar or laser ranging."

Phillip nodded. "Which is why that will be a last resort. Fortunately, the electronics that fly the blimps are pretty simple and are already heavily shielded against upper-atmosphere radiation exposure. The detectors we've put on board the strat are in casings developed for monitoring nuclear tests. Nested faraday cages—stuff like that."

"How can they detect something like a radio signal if they're shielded against electromagnetic radiation?" Elle's question was a signal of her own. Their bodies shifted to include her in the conversation.

"I don't understand most of it." Phillip smiled. "I know that one of the detectors emits beams of laser light and then measures how the photons are affected by surrounding electro-magnetism. Hopefully not enough laser power to look like a weapon." He looked at Alex. "You want to add anything? You've got the internet at your beck and call." He tapped his head.

"Come on, Phillip. Your agency paid for my implant. I find it very hard to believe they didn't give you one. Actually, I've been finding the Wi-Fi a bit unreliable over the past forty-eight hours. Even the clock in my implant is glitchy. How's yours?"

"We could probably make you a replacement in the ship's printing room. But I doubt if Dr. Bannerjee would be keen on doing the installation surgery."

"I'm going to assume that because you're not surprised, you're noticing the same things. So, I think you should have the crew keep a close eye on *Orion's* more sophisticated systems. Glitching in the ship's navigation system could pose a risk, and that's just one of many problems that could crop up. If it gets much worse, we won't know how far to trust any of our instruments."

"I agree. But there might be a remedy for that." Phillip didn't elaborate, but straightened and took a firm grip on Ranger's leash. "We'll schedule the helicopter flight for four-thirty tomorrow morning when the Moon is nearing its zenith; but meet me on the stern deck twenty minutes before that. I want to test something."

He and the dog resumed their route around the deck.

Elle didn't want to be alone, but didn't want it to be obvious, so she turned toward the nearest doorway with slow steps. She could imagine Alex's gaze on her back—or maybe her ass—but he didn't say anything to stop her.

Damn.

7

March 6, 2042

Orion was never completely still. There were always duties of one kind or another for its crew to perform. Even so, Alex felt lonely waiting on the aft deck. It was the emptiness of the ocean and the sky, he supposed, although that was certainly an illusion—both were full of life. But he couldn't communicate with any of that life. He might recognize the creatures, but he couldn't know their thoughts. Wasn't that what 'alien' meant in tangible terms? If you couldn't talk to it, it was alien; it was *other*.

The full Moon was climbing high, outshining the stars and making many too pale to see; but Alex never forgot that beyond that bright globe lay an endless velvet void, like vast sheets of blackness held together with bright pins. A quilt stitched together by a wizened Creator? Humankind had detected thousands of planets around those points of light, but no unequivocal signs of life—not yet—and no hints of intelligence.

Or was that no longer true?

Was Elle Travis sensing a consciousness that had been born amid that vastness? There was no way to know. It wasn't inconceivable that the source of the lethal emissions was some previously undiscovered species native to the Earth. The lightless expanse of the deep ocean was still a realm of mysteries.

When Alex thought about the future, he saw two ways that it could go. The first was with humanity left to its own devices. That scenario was filled with flooded cities, ravenous deserts, corporations run amok, and a tree of life barely recognizable because of genetic modification and technological enhancement. The other path involved intervention by an advanced alien species. He'd always believed that a race capable of crossing space would have solved the problems that threatened the human race. Necessarily benevolent, because they'd learned how not to exterminate themselves. Wise, because they'd tested the laws of the universe by trial and error and were still alive to share what they'd learned.

That contact is what he fervently hoped had now happened. If so, it had taken three hundred and forty-two human lives—regrettable, but not a sign of hostility. Humans were fragile creatures, their consciousness more so. Even an advanced race would make mistakes when dealing with a new planet and a new species. *How many life forms have we exterminated over the eons?* he thought. *And we know better.*

"Wondering what's up there and if it's watching us right now?"

Phillip walked along the deck with Elle beside him in her flight suit. He passed another suit to Alex. A short distance behind them came three uniformed helicopter crew already wearing helmets. They took their places in the insect-like craft to start pre-flight procedures. The maintenance team had done its checks during daylight hours.

"One of us might know whether we're being watched or not." Alex looked at Elle. She shook her head.

"You expect way too much. I'm sensing something, but it's the same stuff as before: feelings more than information. I don't even know if the source is anywhere near the ocean. The water was just how my dreaming mind interpreted things." She looked at the full Moon and Alex thought she shivered.

"That level of detail could change if we get close to the source. The intensity, too, so if you feel it getting strong, don't wait. Let your pilots know and they'll back away." Phillip rested his hand lightly on her shoulder for a moment. "I'd planned to come along for this ride, but I was ordered not to."

"Too hard to replace in a hurry," Alex said, then regretted it, but it had clearly already occurred to Elle. He looked back at the federal agent. "What was it you wanted to show us?"

"Not just you. I want to know if it works. Are you noticing any glitching with your Tesla implant right now?"

"Yeah. There's something like a stutter a few times a minute, almost as if part of the system is resetting itself."

"And you're sensing the ... entity ... continuously, Ms. Travis?" She nodded. He spoke to his wrist. "Hit the switch, please, Ensign."

Within a few seconds Elle gave a light gasp.

"It's gone!"

Alex ran some complex mathematical calculations. There was no hesitation. He raised an eyebrow.

"It's an energy shield against radio interference and EMP attack," Phillip said. "*Orion* may be a research vessel but it's still a Navy ship." He gave a tight smile. "It's good to know that it works, even if we can't be sure how effective it will be at close range or how much power it can withstand." He gave the order to turn off the shield.

Alex felt relieved. He was sure that a superior mind would be pacifistic, but it was still comforting to know there was some possibility of a defense, just in case.

It was a long, eerie flight. He'd taken a lot of helicopter rides in the dark; but most of those had been en route to hot zones. There was danger here, too, but he couldn't feel it. The only evidence was in the person of Elle Travis, so he watched her the whole time instead of looking out at the night sky. It was an education.

The flight went as he'd described to her. As the aircraft flew in the direction estimated for the source of the energy field, he could see strain build in her face. She'd call out "Close enough" and they would veer away, erasing the deep lines on her forehead. Another approach, another retreat. Then repeat, and repeat again. They'd only travelled a quarter of the intended circle when Alex instructed the pilots to make fewer approaches and cover the area more quickly. Swoop in and swoop out.

He noticed a tremor in Elle's hand.

He tried to imagine what it felt like to have another mind infringing on your own thoughts, no matter how vague and formless the presence was. He couldn't. And he felt nothing unusual himself.

Elle held her breath for half a minute at a time on the approach runs now. He asked if she had any sense that the 'entity' had become aware of her or the helicopter. An energetic shake of her head showed him the whites of her eyes. Perhaps the thought hadn't occurred to her.

On the next approach he loosened his harness and brought his face close to hers. There were tears.

He told the pilots to head home.

Switching off his intercom he touched his helmet to hers and said loudly, "You're a goddamn strong woman, Elle Travis."

He thought he heard a sob and she reached out to hold his helmet there for a long time.

#   #   #

Phillip was waiting when they landed. He hurried over, ready to begin his debrief, until he saw the shake of Alex's head and his protective nearness to Elle. Instead, they went to the mess for some breakfast. She only nibbled at a danish and held her coffee cup two-handed, though the semblance of a breakfast ritual seemed to calm her. She swept her hair back from her face much more often that it required.

"Don't tell me you left Ranger cooped up in your quarters on a nice morning like this," Alex said.

Phillip nodded. "Yeah, he could really use some fresh air but I'm just too busy this morning."

"I could take him," Elle said quickly. "I'd be glad to."

They went to Phillip's room and the dog's exuberance made her laugh as he led her back out to the deck. Alex was relieved to hear the laugh. The two men walked up to the number three deck where the government agent had a makeshift office in an unused cabin, which spoke volumes about his status on the ship.

At first glance, the decor was little more than an office desk and chair with an extra armchair in a corner. But neither desk nor chairs were Navy issue, so they'd been provided by Phillip's employers. That meant secret compartments, biosensors in the fabric, probably hidden electronics and data storage.

A thin rectangle lying on the desk looked like an ordinary tablet, but Alex knew that it was packed with extras, like DNA authentication, military grade GPS, satellite phone with the latest encryption algorithms and, he was almost certain, a self-destruct device. He also knew that the sports jacket hung on the back of the door had fine wire mesh woven into the fabric—both a receiving antenna and, if need be, a powerful source of radio interference. He wouldn't be surprised if the Homeland Security logo on the man's coffee mug concealed a camera lens and audio pickup.

Nothing in the room was what it seemed except, perhaps, for the maps of the south Pacific that covered the walls, with the local islands grouped together at one end. The rest were hydrographic survey maps of the ocean floor, including the area of the Mariana Basin they assumed held whatever was sending or receiving the signal.

Ground Zero.

"Is she really in bad shape?" Phillip asked as they sat.

"Let's say I'm glad Ranger could be pressed into service as a therapy dog. The flight was very hard on her—actually painful, from the expression on her face—yet she never complained. I hope we don't have to put her through that again."

"We shouldn't. I was getting real-time location data from the chopper as you went. I think it's enough that we can reliably place the center of the energy field right about...," as he tapped a spot at the full reach of his arm, "here."

"Not far from where we figured," Alex said.

"Less than eighty nautical miles off."

"I presume you had the radar going?"

"All clear the whole time. Nothing on the surface, nothing above it. Seems like strong evidence that either the transmitter or the receiver is actually *in* the ocean."

"Are you thinking it could be a submarine?" The arm of the chair was probably checking his fingerprints. He drummed his fingers to screw with it.

"I don't know what to think. But my superiors consider it a strong enough possibility that they've sent one of our own submarines this way. And over the next couple of days, we'll have more company—two survey ships with powerful side-scan sonar. We've even been given an official name—Top Secret, of course—*Operation Oceanus*." He rolled his eyes a little to acknowledge the unoriginality of the designation.

"A transmission that strong from something on the bottom of the ocean? Come on."

Phillip shrugged, looking a little uncomfortable. "How can we rule it out? We don't know what kind of energy is involved. Maybe whatever's in the ocean is only a receiver, but that's only slightly more credible." He leaned back in his chair and steepled his fingers. "Anyway, some news I just heard might change things."

Alex turned his attention from the map with a feeling of foreboding.

"A ship went down in a typhoon just two days before the first airliner incident," Phillip continued with furrowed brows. "Very close to Ground Zero. It was loaded with a cargo of toxic waste from Okinawa. Apparently, every kind of toxin from arsenic to dioxin, radioactive material to nerve gas has passed through the US military bases there. The good news is that somebody finally decided to clean it up. The bad news is that one of the ships involved just took thousands of tons of that poison to the bottom of the Pacific with her."

"Jesus. That timing is too much of a coincidence." Alex ran his hand over his chin. "But why would anyone—or anything—want to sink a ship full of toxins?"

The agent shook his head. "You're looking at it backward. I don't think this entity sank the ship. A major typhoon could easily account for that, and it was blowing pretty hard when she sank."

Alex was still puzzled. Then he got it.

"Holy shit. You think the ship's cargo leaked all over the bottom of the ocean. You think it *woke something up.*"

8

March 18, 2042

Elle felt like the most conspicuous of outsiders aboard *Orion*. But it wasn't long before she began to attract companions. She couldn't really call such people friends, because the relationships were so one-sided. A woman would casually strike up a conversation in line at the mess, or somewhere on deck. Then one of the woman's friends, and another soon after. More. Eventually, a man would do the same, and then others. They'd make small talk. Joke about the weather (which hardly ever changed), ask what she thought about shipboard life (she could usually tell whether they wanted to hear a compliment or a complaint), answer a few questions about the Navy. Then, inevitably, they would start to talk about themselves and their problems.

Did she give off a 'shrink' vibe? Did she look like one of those TV self-help counsellors?

It had always been that way, though, as long as she could remember. All through school. At work. Each time, she'd offer sympathy, commiseration, encouragement, or even occasional advice if something obvious struck her—nothing profound or especially enlightening. Yet the others always thought she'd said just the right thing, and expressed their sincere thanks. And told their friends.

It could be a little annoying, but then she almost never had to pay for a coffee or a limeade. And anyway, it wasn't like there was much else for her to do at sea. After her first few days aboard *Orion*, the mysterious signal had diminished and finally stopped, even when the Moon was visible. Alex and Phillip guessed that it might be because of the Moon being lower in the sky, but they weren't assuming that whatever produced the signal had gone away. Elle still wasn't off the hook.

She hadn't been subjected to any more helicopter flights, though. Instead, two small Navy ships had shown up a week-and-a-half ago. She'd thought they might be frigates but was told that they were called Littoral Combat Ships—no one explained the difference. Their job was to search the sea bottom with side-scan sonar, towing the sonar units behind them while they sailed in a grid pattern.

On the first day, both ships, *USS Kennebunkport* and *USS Tallahassee*, had set out to patrol the area near Ground Zero at the same time, but their crews had quickly suffered an epidemic of headaches. Both ships had been fitted with the same EM-protective screens as *Orion* before leaving port and had utilized them when the headaches struck; but the shields were never meant for use over long periods of time. Phillip and the ships' captains had quickly decided that the LCS's would have to take turns searching, spending less than forty minutes at a time in the 'hot zone.' That had turned a task expected to take two or three days into a weeks-long ordeal. And so far, they'd turned up nothing.

At least the government was paying her for all this lost work-time, though she didn't know exactly how much. Phillip had assured her it would be a pleasant surprise.

As Elle stood at the ship's rail and watched *Tallahassee* out near the horizon, she thought about the vast depths below them all. Somewhere down there was the entity, or alien spacecraft, or whatever, that had drawn them all to this uninhabited patch of ocean. But silently, somewhere in the middle spaces, cruised an American nuclear submarine like a giant grey ghost. She didn't know the sub's name—no one talked openly about it—but she caught the occasional gossip. The sub ranged over a wide area, but never too far away: a guard dog waiting to pounce should anything threaten the sonar ships or *Orion*.

One *unknown* source of danger, but also a *known* one: a nuclear-missile sub. Elle wasn't sure which scared her more.

She felt terribly small poised between the vastness of sea and sky.

"Hey, little lady. Looks like you could use some company."

She jumped and turned her head.

It was a sailor—a big Black man with ostentatious muscles that bulged from his uniform shirt, and a couple of companions just behind him, one white, the other Hispanic. The one who'd spoken towered over her, and she knew they hadn't met. He didn't look like anyone she'd seen on *Orion*.

One of *Kennebunkport*'s crew then—her captain had flown to *Orion* for yet another conference.

"No thanks," she said, and turned back to the ocean.

"Now don't be like that. I heard that *Orion* had a good-lookin' guest aboard, an' I know how nights at sea can get lonely."

"I'm sorry. I can't help you with that." She turned to walk away, only to find the other two men standing there. Blocking her while trying not to look too obvious about it.

She'd been lucky until now. *Orion*'s Captain Jensen had probably warned his crewmen away from her. Clearly the other crews had missed that memo.

"Look, I'm not interested, OK. What, *Kennebunkport* has no females aboard?"

"None as pretty as you."

"You mean none who respond to your idea of charm anymore."

"Hey now ..." He touched her arm and she jerked away.

"Don't touch me!" Then she heard someone calling.

"Ms. Travis. *Ms. Travis.*"

It was Alex Rhys, approaching quickly but making it look casual, his hands in his pockets.

"Ms. Travis, there are some details of tomorrow's operations plans we need to discuss," he said as he came up beside her, barely giving a glance at the big sailor. He jerked his head and began to walk away, expecting her to follow. When she moved, the sailor threw up an arm.

"Get your own sugar, man. This sweet one and I was just getting to know each other."

Alex returned to her side. "Looked to me like the lady's got a mind to move on." He stood straight, looking up into the other man's face. Alex was six feet tall, with the athletic build of a runner or swimmer, but the sailor made him look small. Brown arms the size of Alex's calves slowly crossed over the massive chest.

"Wait. You the congressman's son, ain't you? Rich boy. Think all the babes should belong to you, huh? But maybe that ain't so out here in the ocean. No congressmen 'round here." The man gave an exaggerated look over the empty ocean, then stepped forward until his forearms were almost touching Alex's chest. "What, you think I don't get out your way Daddy gonna see to it I don't get promoted? Maybe thrown in the brig?"

"No, I think your IQ will take care of that."

"Listen asshole …" the sailor growled, bumping Alex.

"*Seriously?*" Elle stepped up to them. "You're expecting me to be the prize in a pissing contest? You gonna show everybody who has the biggest dick?"

Alex looked stunned but the sailor smiled and said, "Ain't no contest there, sugar. I'll show you. Just tell me where and when."

"Oh God help us all."

"*Jackson!* Cooper! Desmarais! With me."

The captain of the *Kennebunkport* approached and swept past on his way to the helicopter pad, giving the slightest of frowns at the group. The two other sailors were quick to fall into step behind him. The Black man grunted and shoved his way past Alex. He sauntered after his captain without looking back.

Alex and Elle said nothing until the helicopter had lifted off and swung away toward the ship waiting beyond the far side of *Orion*.

He gave her a quick glance and a nod, his face expressionless, and began to walk away.

"Wait, Alex. I shouldn't have said that. At least, I didn't mean …." She sighed and started again. "Thank you. You have good timing."

After a moment he turned and slowly walked back. "Just luck. I think." He frowned. "Something gave me the idea to come this way. You didn't …?"

It took her a moment to get it. "What? Call for you with my mind?" She snorted. "It doesn't work that way. I hardly have any control over what I pick up. I can't send—I'm not a radio."

"OK. Sorry. It's all new to me."

"Yeah, well, don't worry. It won't affect you. I can't even get coherent thoughts from somebody unless we're close, like I've known them a long time."

"Good to know." He scratched the back of his neck, looking a little embarrassed. "Feel like walking? Maybe this way? I want to have a closer look at that helicopter landing pad." He set out slowly toward the stern and she followed.

"If that's how your ... gift works, I guess that says something about the power of whatever we're facing, if it could get into your head from a hundred miles away."

"Power? That thing killed the people in the jet you tried to save. I'm sure they weren't all telepaths." She looked at him. "Did somebody say a baby survived? How could that be?"

"Yeah. No one really knows why. It might be because the baby's brain was still so undeveloped. Not so many neural pathways to scramble. Or ...."

"What?"

He gave a shrug. "Or maybe whatever it is figures adults are fair game, but babies should be protected." His mouth twitched, as if to smile, but she didn't think he was really joking.

They came to the landing pad, protruding like an enormous black fan beyond *Orion*'s stern. The helicopter would be gone for a little while longer, and there were no ropes or gates to keep people off, so Alex stepped onto it. Elle reluctantly followed. The pad was a grating with holes that sighed faintly with the sea breeze. She felt very aware that she stood midway between deep sky and endless space on one side, and a cold, unfeeling abyss on the other. Like the balance on a scale: a narrow border between upper and lower worlds. How fragile human existence seemed at that moment, so thinly spread over the surface of the globe like the peel of an apple.

Alex was looking at her. "Does this make you uncomfortable?"

She shook her head. "Just as long as nobody makes me go in that helicopter again."

"Right, you're not fond of flying. What was it that got you up in that jetliner? Must've been a good reason."

"I was at a wedding. In Korea. I worked in Seoul for a year teaching English as an additional language. For the first month I stayed with a family—the Seungs." She hesitated. "I actually … was engaged to the son, Jihun, later. For a while. I broke it off. He was way too set in their patriarchal ways for me—he didn't show that, at first."

"But you got to know him too well. Your gift."

She frowned. Why did he feel he could make assumptions like that? Even if he was right. "Anyway, I stayed good friends with his sister, Jia, and she asked me to come back for her wedding."

"Have any of them come to visit you and your family?"

"Oh, God no! I never told my family about Jihun. My mother would have thought they'd brainwashed me—she could never believe I have a mind of my own."

That killed the conversation for a while. Alex squatted and ran his hand over the black surface of the pad. It had a strange finish, not reflective, even in the tropical sun.

"I don't know what this stuff is," he said, "but when they don't need the pad it just disappears. Packed out of sight somewhere, but I can't see how it's done." He stood up.

"You can't figure it out with that … implant thing in your head?" she asked.

He smiled, and with a glance up at the sound of the returning helicopter, they walked back onto the ship's deck.

"My implant isn't smart on its own. It's like any other computer, except the interface is very fast because I can control it with a specific set of thoughts." His smile was rueful this time. "You know, I guess it's the closest I can come to being telepathic myself. Ready access to the internet is pretty good on its own, but I had hoped that one day, when more people have them, we might use the augments to communicate with each other, without talking. Kind of like telepathy."

"Huh. Yeah, that sounds so … friendly. The real thing is no picnic, I can tell you."

"But from what you're saying, your gift doesn't provide communication. More like eavesdropping when you don't even want to do it."

"It's exactly like that. And I can't help it. And if people only knew …. The absolute worst thing that could ever happen to me would be for everyone to know I was a true telepath. I'd be like a leper. Worse."

"But wouldn't it be cool if you could really talk two-way, mind to mind? You could get to know people—maybe a lover—better than anyone ever has before."

"You say that like it's a good thing." She looked out over the ocean.

He was quiet for a while, then asked, "So when you're at work … do you eventually get to know your co-workers too well?"

She sighed. "Yeah, some of them, after a few months. Sometimes I think I'd be better off in a job that kept me moving around from place to place, working with different people all the time. Your job must be like that."

"It is. I take contracts from companies and a few branches of government. If I get hired a second or third time, I might work with some of the same people, but most of the contracts only last a few weeks."

"All over the world? Lots of exotic places?"

"I don't know. Is Afghanistan exotic? Ethiopia? Palestine? I've been in South American countries a few times, helping to find kidnapped executives. Investigated some bank frauds involving places like Grand Cayman and Niue—but that's probably as close as I've come to 'exotic'." He laughed.

"I thought you mostly went to combat zones."

His smile vanished. After a time, he said, "Those are the jobs that pay the most. And then I end up regretting every single penny."

"Why do you do them?"

"Believe it or not, I think some of them—most of them—are actually necessary. Horrible, often, but ultimately important. I like to think I'm doing some good."

"With war, and fighting? Maybe that's what men like to tell themselves."

His whole body stiffened, and she sucked a breath. Why had she said *that*? She had no right to judge him.

"I'm sorry," she stammered.

"It's all right," he said too quickly. "So ... I guess shipboard life must be getting pretty tedious for you by now."

"Well, the good side is, it's curing me of my addiction to stupid reality TV!" she forced a laugh.

He gave a half-hearted nod. They'd reached a door near the mess hall. Would he invite her for a coffee or something?

"See you later," he said, and went inside, quickly disappearing along the passageway.

He'd come to help her out of an uncomfortable situation, done his best to make casual conversation, and once again she'd driven a wedge between them with her stupid mouth. And then looked like an idiot, talking about TV!

For someone who could read minds, she still sometimes blew it big time when interacting with people. How could she hope to succeed if the phenomenon they were investigating involved a wholly *alien* mind?

9

March 22, 2042

The helicopter dropped out of the storm clouds, and for a moment, Gary Cross considered telling the pilot to abort the landing and return to Guam. But the chopper wouldn't have enough fuel for that.

The bobbing grey thimble below had to be *Orion*, and the postage stamp floating beside it would be the cargo barge that carried the experimental underwater habitat. Given the choice, he'd rather land on the barge—it had enough space to allow for mistakes—but he knew the helicopter was headed for the tail of the research vessel, to a platform barely wide enough to hold the aircraft. He couldn't yet distinguish the landing pad from the rest of the ship, but he could see that the dark grey ocean was streaked with tall wave-tops broken by the wind: ragged stretched Zs like a cartoon depiction of an off-channel TV screen.

Gary wasn't afraid of flying in bad weather—he'd done enough of it. As a Navy Master Diver, the ocean was his workplace. But he'd seen men sink in aircraft that had missed a ship's deck, and it was the stuff of nightmares. Sometimes all the dive training and experience in the world wasn't enough.

He knew the smart thing would be to look away from the rising seascape and focus on something inside the helicopter cabin until it was over. Instead, he forced himself to watch out his window and hummed the theme to *Mission Impossible* all the way to touchdown—which wasn't successful until the third attempt. On the first try, the chopper nearly clipped *Orion*'s radome, like a volleyball on a stand.

The turbines began to wind down as ship's crew rushed to secure the helicopter to the pad, and Gary leaned between the pilots to promise them a round of beers any time they were thirsty. They didn't admit to fear, but he knew they'd felt it. Navy pilots weren't stupid.

A sailor anonymous in yellow rain gear met him on deck and hustled him along the starboard side of the ship to an entranceway that led to a lounge. Its plain chairs and couches in durable fabrics of grey and blue were totally familiar to Gary, but nobody was sitting in them now. Apparently the two men and two women standing in the room were waiting just for him. They moved forward to greet him, while his guide vanished without ever showing a face.

He'd seen pictures of these four among his briefing documents.

Phillip Watanabe looked like the Homeland Security agent he was, trim and well-dressed. Gary had spoken with him briefly by video link the day before.

"Petty Officer Cross is here to take charge of undersea operations," Watanabe announced to his companions. "He's a Navy Master Diver with experience in all aspects of underwater work." Then he introduced the others with him.

Alex Rhys would have been pure Ivy League if he dressed better and his hair hadn't been styled by the wind. There was cool assessment in his eyes, though no challenge. That was good—Gary didn't like macho competitions.

Elle Travis's eyes barely met his and her handshake was a mere touch. Too good-looking, too shy, she triggered his natural protectiveness immediately, and that was a concern. He had low tolerance of civilians on quasi-military operations at the best of times. This woman didn't belong here.

The final member of the group made a stark contrast to Elle. Phillip Watanabe introduced her as Lee-Anna Cavallo, an engineer, who'd only arrived on *Orion* a half hour before Gary. He remembered the barge he'd seen during his helicopter's approach—the one he was told carried an experimental deep-sea habitat. He asked if she was part of its support contingent.

"The undersea habitat on that barge is Ms. Cavallo's creation," Phillip explained.

"The product of a team effort," she corrected. "Very much so." She turned, stepped toward a couch along the nearest wall, and sat in a fluid motion. She was quickly joined by Elle, as if the move was part of an understanding among their sex to help avoid awkward male rivalries for the nearest seat. Alex took a chair near Elle, and Gary and Phillip pulled two more into place.

Where Elle Travis was rich brown skin and deep black hair, Lee-Anna Cavallo was a strawberry blonde with the pale complexion of an English girl. Or Irish Italian, as it turned out. In her late twenties or early thirties, her firm handshake and direct gaze showed a confidence that wasn't surprising in a woman with an engineer's intellect. In fact, her face was very familiar, but Gary couldn't place it. Her bright red sweater and simple black slacks looked expensive and ensured that she stood out from her drab surroundings.

"You flew the habitat to Guam and then towed it here by barge?" Alex asked. "That sounds like fun."

"Boredom is a good thing on a trip like that. I'm not sure why the exciting weather chose to come along just as we reached *Orion*."

"This is where the excitement happens."

Gary caught the look Phillip gave Alex, as if he was surprised by the younger man's behavior. It was obvious that Rhys was flirting. Or maybe that was unusual. Maybe Alex Rhys was a nerdy type who didn't have much to do with women, though that didn't seem likely given his good looks.

"Someone said the habitat was related to *Orion's* landing pad," Alex said. "What does that mean?"

"They're both based on the same nanotechnology," Lee-Anna answered. "One of our developments at Stanford. Nano-modules—we call them 'nims'— that fit themselves together in a thousand possible combinations. Each one is basically a triangle, but their edges have protrusions and gaps that link seamlessly and with exceptional adhesion. The real breakthrough was being able to make each module individually smart enough to recognize patterns and adapt to make a place for itself in them."

"So, you tell the batch of modules what shape you want, and they arrange themselves to make it," Gary said.

"That's right."

"*Zaks*." Alex smiled. "A kids' construction toy. I loved them. But I'm not so happy to think of my helicopter landing on them."

The engineer's smile didn't disguise the frown in her eyes. "When strength is called for, the nims arrange themselves in lattices the shape of diamond crystals, Mr. Rhys. Pressure just makes them stronger."

"A valuable quality in an underwater habitat," Gary noted.

"Exactly."

"I still think it's premature," Alex said. "Two weeks of searching with side-scan sonar didn't find anything conclusive at all on the sea floor. Even a nuclear submarine failed to provoke a reaction."

Gary turned to Phillip, who looked annoyed.

"In hindsight the submarine probably caused whatever it is to stay hidden," the agent argued. "Which makes it all the more necessary for us to establish a less threatening presence. But the habitat is still Plan B. First, we'll scout the bottom with the *Darwin*." Phillip turned his attention to Elle. It took her a long moment to notice.

"What? You're not saying I have to go down in a submersible!" Her eyes were impossibly large, and her fingers curled to grip her knees.

Phillip's voice was gentle. "You'll have help, Elle. I've had some special gear brought to *Orion*. Subliminal teaching equipment. Sleep teaching. You'll learn everything you need to know about coping with an underwater environment, subconsciously. Methods to overcome anxiety, too. We won't send you underwater until you've become completely comfortable with the idea."

"Hope you're not expecting that to happen this century!" she said. No one laughed.

"It will work. Believe me. Alex has used it with great results."

If he was expecting the man in question to back him up, he was disappointed. Alex only looked uncomfortable. Gary'd been told that Rhys was a civilian. Maybe before his assignments in conflict zones he'd needed a sleep-teaching regimen involving weapons or combat tactics. Clearly, it wasn't a fond memory.

"I'm curious about why you turned your nano-engineering skills to an undersea habitat, Ms. Cavallo," Gary asked.

"Call me Lee-Anna. I've always loved the water. A competitive swimmer when I was younger. Then I discovered scuba diving. I did a lot of training as a recreational diver, but a few years ago I linked up with a guy named Ray Proctor in San Francisco. He teaches the pros who work on movie documentaries and TV shows. He's amazing, and inspiring."

"Oh my God. Chase Vizell." Alex's eyes and mouth were wide. Lee-Anna snapped her head toward him. He cleared his throat and looked sheepish. "*The Guardian* online pictures: you and Chase Vizell ... on the sets of some of his movies, right? And those others ...."

"Boudoir photos, Mr. Rhys, yes. Have you never seen a woman in lingerie?"

His blush was epic.

"Chase claimed his phone was hacked, the prick. But I know his publicity guy arranged it because his last couple of movies were underperformers. And so was Chase Vizell, actually." Her smile was meant to be smug, but Gary sensed hurt beneath it.

"And you left him for ...."

"I left him for *me*," she replied coolly. Then she shrugged. "Brett Sumner came later."

"Ice Hands Sumner?" Gary asked. "That's why you looked familiar. They blamed you for distracting him ..."

"I refuse to take the blame for losing a Super Bowl," she interrupted, with a tone that said it was time for a change of topic.

The group fell silent. Phillip coughed.

"Ms. Cavallo will take the lead on any activities involving the habitat itself, but as I indicated earlier, Mr. Cross will be in overall command onsite. I'll stay aboard *Orion* as liaison to the higher-ups."

"Command is the official term, but I prefer to be part of a team," Gary said. "The quarterback, not the GM. The first person to call me Sir gets thirty pushups." He saw Elle Travis react and instantly felt contrite. "I'm only kidding, Ms. Travis. This is a research mission, not combat."

"Let's hope it doesn't come to that," Phillip said softly.

Elle got up and moved to the porthole. Gary followed and saw that she was looking up at the troubled sky. The storm clouds had begun to break up; and through one of the breaks, Gary caught a glimpse of the moon toward the north.

She spoke in a breathy voice. "Let's hope whatever's out there stays asleep."

10

Gary seemed to have made an immediate impression on Elle and he didn't welcome that. Badly out of place on board *Orion,* she acted like a woman who needed a confidante. From what Phillip Watanabe had told him, Elle was crucial to the mission, and they needed her to be focused.

The mission team was headed through the ship toward Phillip's office, but Elle lagged behind. Gary slowed his own pace to match, and for a few moments they were alone in a passageway. He put his hand on the next door but didn't open it.

"I need to talk to you for a second, Elle," he said, dropping his voice. She looked startled but gave a quick nod. "They've put me in charge of this mission, and if we do end up going to Plan B and use the habitat, the team is going to get even larger. I won't be able to keep my eyes on everything and everyone all the time. I'll need some help. I'm hoping you'll give me that help."

"You ... you want me to spy for you?"

"Not at all. But I have a feeling you'll notice things—sense things—that I might not." Her sudden frown surprised him. "And people will probably say things around you that they won't around me. I wouldn't ask you to spy, Elle; it's just helping me gauge the morale of the team and spot any issues before they become a problem."

She was still frowning. Maybe a little flattery was called for.

"You strike me as a naturally honest person, and if I'm going to build a team of people who can work well together, I'll need someone I can count on to give it to me straight. Do you think you could do that for me?"

There was a little extra color in her face as she nodded and brushed her bangs from her eyes. "I'll try. Don't expect too much right away, but I'll do my best."

He wasn't sure what she meant by that, but it was as close to a yes as he thought he'd get for now. He gave her an appreciative smile and put a hand on her shoulder to guide her through the door. He felt the muscle relax under his fingers.

Phillip's office had become a miniature command center. The others were already gathered around a map on the far wall that had a red circle around its midpoint and a handwritten X in the middle of that. Beside the circle, paper graphs were stuck to the map's plastic coating with tape. Sonar graphs. Phillip circled a finger around one section that showed choppy lines in the middle of a flat stretch between large peaks.

"I suppose it would be more impressive on a video screen, but I work better with things I can touch." Phillip tapped the paper. "The sea bottom here is not particularly distinctive—these ridges are hundreds of feet high, but that's typical of the Mariana Basin; and the flat area corresponds to this amphitheater-like space I've circled on the map. It's enclosed by high ridges to the north and south especially. What's worth noting is the profusion of black smokers along the sea floor."

He looked toward Elle and perhaps decided to elaborate for her benefit.

"Deep-sea geothermal vents. They release superheated water from beneath the crust of the Earth—most of it is seawater that's leaked down; the rest is water extruded from magma much deeper underground. They're like the geysers at Yellowstone Park. This whole string of islands with Guam at the southern end is known as the Mariana Arc, and it's an area of the ocean that's volcanically active." He shifted his gaze to the others. "We don't know what link there would be between black smokers and this transmission we're investigating, but the locations are a strong match."

"It's a natural source of energy," Alex pointed out. "Geothermal electricity generation has increased in lots of countries in the last twenty years. And if we can do it, so can they."

"Whoever 'they' are. My bosses' think-tank offered the same guess, but we don't actually know. Sonar can only tell so much. We're going to have to take a look for ourselves."

Lee-Anna laughed. "Maybe whatever we're looking for is just a big fan of seafood. Black smokers are often covered with shrimp and tube worms and all kinds of delectables. Add a little tartar sauce ...."

"No thanks," Gary said. "Smoker emissions are full of heavy metals you don't want to be eating. And then there's that cargo ship from Okinawa that went down. I assume we're going to be testing the water for radioactivity?"

Phillip nodded. "The ship's manifest has been hard to come by. The owners claim there was no radioactive material onboard, but I don't believe them. Anyway, it's only prudent to make sure."

The rest of the briefing lasted a half-hour. Gary had heard most of the information already, so he paid more attention to his companions. He'd learned long ago that his nose could tell him as much as his eyes and ears. Alex Rhys's windblown hair style owed something to a common brand of hair gel, and apparently he'd brought too few changes of clothing for this trip. The innocuous smell of Navy soap was tinged with salty sweat.

Elle's body odor was liquid anxiety, more acrid and less earthy than the product of physical labor. There were undertones of Secret deodorant, L'Oréal shampoo, and a fruity scent that might be fresh lip gloss.

He was surprised that Lee-Anna wore no perfume either. The predominant fragrance that surrounded her was unquestionably sunscreen—Gary thought the brand was the same one preferred by his fiancée, Naomi Sinclair, a California girl transplanted to New York City because that was where most retail fashion buying took place. Naomi only bought the best in cosmetics as well as fashion, so obviously Lee-Anna Cavallo had expensive tastes. It wasn't surprising that someone with such a fair complexion would be conscientious about applying sunscreen.

If Phillip Watanabe gave off any scent at all, it was an impression of efficiency that came from crisply pressed clothes and well-polished shoes. That didn't make the man a dandy, or metrosexual, or whatever the current term was. Gary found that people who paid attention to little details like that paid attention to big ones too. That was reassuring. Especially because Gary himself was already feeling well out of his depth on this mission.

An unknown source of deadly energy that might be extraterrestrial. Possibly hiding under twelve thousand feet of ocean. He felt as much at home in water as any human could, but no human being was ever meant to venture to the ocean floor. He'd never gone that deep before, and he was a little ashamed to feel a twinge in his gut at the thought of it.

The submersible trip would wait until Elle had been given a good dose of indoctrination conditioning to be able to stand the confined environment. "Dose" was an accurate word, too, since the learning was enhanced with injections of enzymes and other substances to induce RNA synthesis. He wondered how Elle would feel about that. In the meantime, it gave Gary a chance to start work on his team dynamics.

After they left Phillip's office, he subtly led Alex Rhys to the ship's rail. The rain had let up, but the sky still brooded, and the waves ran grey and high—an inhospitable display from both above and below, and Gary couldn't help but wonder where the greater threat lay. *Orion*'s captain, Darryl Jensen, had her pointed almost directly into the wind with her screws turning just enough to keep station. Her bow mostly bobbed up and down but every now and again the motion would become more circular and then, briefly, the ship would wag like a dog's tail. Tall waves shed their tops to the wind throwing spray into the men's faces, but Gary liked the taste of sea salt on his lips, and Alex appeared to enjoy the bracing breeze. A few bright shafts of light broke through the overcast.

"I wanted a minute alone with you, Alex," Gary said. The other man looked surprised and a little wary. Gary put on a man-to-man smile. "I hope you don't take this command thing the wrong way. I have a feeling you've had some bad experiences with the chain of command in the military. Fair enough—it's not perfect. But I really meant it when I said I want us to be a team. When a decision has to be made, I'll take responsibility; but I prefer to do things by consensus whenever possible. We're gathering people who have a range of expertise way beyond mine, including your own skills. I'd be an idiot to ignore that. So, I'll want to hear honest opinions from everyone at all times, and I hope we can come up with the best courses of action together."

"Sounds good," Alex replied, though it was mostly a reflex response.

"One other thing." Gary leaned just slightly closer and lowered his voice, keeping his face turned toward the sea. "I'm going to need a special ally on the team. Someone who can help me gauge how things are working and how people are feeling. Someone I can count on without having to second-guess them. You strike me as the person best qualified for that. Are you willing to help me out?"

"Even if it means keeping things from Watanabe?"

"Yes."

"I'd like that."

"Good."

11

March 23, 2042

Elle had a memory of crossing a snow-covered lake at night on the back of a snowmobile, arms wrapped fiercely around her cousin, who was driving. A single headlight struggled to push back the darkness ahead, and its all-too-small pool of light filled with crystalline projectiles might have been all that remained of the world. The ride seemed endless; even its constant bumps and judders were no proof that the small machine was actually getting anywhere. For all that Elle could tell, they were caught in a void, unable to proceed or retreat in a kind of turbulent purgatory.

The trip in the submersible was like that: anxiety-filled boredom that made it hard to concentrate on the details of the ocean floor as *Darwin* passed over it. Even more so because there was much less to see than in the headlight of the snowmobile. The sea bottom was an undulating plain of smooth sediment of unknown thickness. Maybe it was best measured not by inches, but by ages: dust, detritus, and dead diatoms representing centuries, or even millennia of a world in slow motion. No sunlight fell on this plain, only debris.

Then again, Elle wasn't there to use her eyes. There were others with her for that—Gary Cross, and the pilot, Bob Evans. Without touching, the three were still packed closely enough that she could feel their radiated warmth on her stomach and thighs in contrast with the cold of the ocean at her back. Every rise of her chest drew in their used breath and stale sweat after almost two hours in a pimped-out tin can.

It was all that her eyes could *not* see that bothered her. They might be travelling a lonely path across an alien planet for all her senses told her to the contrary. The inky blackness surrounding them might be filled with towering mountains. Or monsters. Except as she watched the sonar readout over Evans' shoulder, it proclaimed that they were crossing a nearly flat expanse of muck with nothing remarkable for a significant distance to either side. The mountain ridges were ahead and behind. They had come down one slope and were slowly transiting toward another.

At first, Gary had kept up conversation, mainly with the pilot, asking details about the craft and then about their region of seafloor. Evans seemed to enjoy Elle's shudder when he mentioned the Challenger Deep, many miles away to the south, but part of the same ocean basin. Then talk flagged, and *Darwin's* interior had been mostly silent for the past half-hour or so. Elle was pathetically grateful for the sleep-conditioning that kept her from clawing the walls to get out.

Evans' voice startled her.

"Smokers ahead," he said.

Jagged lines were already visible on the sonar display but not yet in the view window. Evans brought the nose of the submersible up quickly enough that Elle felt the change in angle. Her fear of a collision lasted only a moment and then was suppressed by a sleep-conditioned mental reassurance that *Darwin* was strong and agile and Evans a pilot of exceptional experience.

Expecting to see rugged chimneys jutting from the sea floor, she was disappointed when stirred-up sediment obscured the view, followed by billows of something that looked black in *Darwin*'s lights. Occasionally, the water cleared enough that she could see the clouds roil up from below, mostly grey and black but with a faint suggestion of other colors. Only the sonar showed the chimneys themselves, ragged spikes in a child's line drawing.

As quickly as the vents had come, they were gone, followed by another narrow zone of stirred-up water. Elle could see its turbulence like heat haze over a desert highway, but *Darwin* reacted gently, rising with the heated water. She couldn't feel any extra warmth from the hull, though.

Instead, she began to feel pressure.

Water pressure? No, there was no way to feel that. *Darwin* was a rigid shell protecting her from harm.

It wasn't a physical pressure, she realized, but a mental one. A powerful weight on her mind, surrounding, enclosing.

Squeezing.

It wrung thoughts from her head and replaced them with a thick mixture of displeasure and distaste: a mental mud of dark thoughts with one focus.

Humans were not welcome.

The sensation grew. Elle's mouth fell open to relieve the pressure within. Her body jerked, and the motion alerted Gary.

"Elle. What is it?"

She struggled to shake her head, jaw hanging open like a fish out of water, and frantically jerked her thumb toward the ceiling.

"Evans! Take her up, as quickly as you dare."

Gary struggled to turn himself so he could take her arms, but the contact was little help. Elle's breath rasped, her vocal cords frozen, her eyes forced wide.

The fearsome strain didn't ease until they'd recrossed the north ridge and risen a thousand feet. She was left shaken and with an urge to retch, desperate for the safety of the world above, for oxygen-rich air, for cleansing sunlight.

But the ordeal wasn't over.

Divers were in the water as soon as *Darwin* broke surface, and the crane quickly began to lift the craft from the grasping waves.

Then, without warning, it lurched to a halt.

Gary keyed the comm mic to ask the crane crew what was wrong. There was no answer. He repeated the call, then asked for any station to answer him. None did.

Darwin hung suspended like a piñata above the hungry sea.

12

March 23, 2042

The cup of hot coffee slipped from Alex's grip and spiraled down in slow motion. Brown liquid swirled over the lip, mid-fall, then geysered upward as the mug hit the hard floor. It shattered into eight pieces—he could count them, track them on their trajectories through the air, tumbling, spinning. The mess hall closed in around him like a tunnel and the jagged ceramic missiles were the shifting objects of a kaleidoscope. He floated in space, fascinated.

Then his body vanished in a deep blue fog.

He wasn't alone—there were others in the fog—but there was nothing about them that he could define. No shape, sound, or smell. That was disappointing because he was powerfully curious. There were impressions of heat and motion, but to what purpose? These others didn't belong in his consciousness. They didn't belong to each other, either. They were scattered particles struggling against unseen currents with no coordination or mutual intent.

They were a disturbance, an intrusion. Insignificant, but difficult to ignore—neither helpful nor hurtful but ... distracting. Like sparks in dark space that provided no context. Not part of a great brightness that pulled at him from above.

Yet these others were dwellers of the in-between, as he was. He existed at the joining of a hard fluid that rarely moved and a dense fluid that ebbed and flowed. These others infested the plane between the dense fluid and a yet much-thinner one. That placed them closer to the great brightness, floating in a fluid of energies, not matter. But it did not pull at them.

If they were not part of the answers he sought, perhaps they were in the way. Or perhaps they were nothing at all, not worth the energy to consider.

Perhaps.

The fog faded to a lighter blue, but dark residue clung like watercolor paint bleeding from lines and curves. Shades of color filled spaces. The blue receded still more until it was a gauze over vaguely familiar shapes.

Objects.

Tables. Chairs. Walls.

The mess hall of *Orion* seen from its floor.

Alex raised his head to shake it, then vowed not to repeat the motion. He must have passed out. It was lucky he hadn't hit his head on the hard pedestal of the nearby table. Carefully, he rolled onto his side and pushed into a sitting position— but the room began to spin. Focusing his eyes on a chair, he concentrated on breathing. After another minute or so, he felt confident enough to get to his feet, but tightly gripped the edge of the table for support.

As he let out a sigh of relief, the air filled with a blaring alert from the speaker above his left shoulder.

"Medical team to crane control. Support team to crane control. All other department heads report to the captain." It

was repeated. Three men and one woman stumbled out of the room.

God, the *Darwin*! It was due to be recovered.

Alex lurched toward the exit, colliding with the doorframe on the way.

13

March 23, 2042

"*Orion* will circle at a distance of twenty miles from the center of the phenomenon for now," Phillip said. "Until we decide what to do, at least. The ship's EM shield came up automatically once the defense system judged the helmsman to be unresponsive. It's now set to respond more quickly if there's a recurrence, but we can't run it non-stop. It's intended for combat only." He looked more unsure than Elle had ever seen him, shaken by the experience like everyone else aboard the ship.

"This wasn't energy on the scale of what killed the airline passengers," Alex said. "Otherwise, we'd be dead too. I think this time was just a probe. Whatever it is knows we're here and was checking us out. Better pray it doesn't turn the full blast on us. Twenty miles won't protect us from that."

"Maybe it won't, Alex, but it might convince the thing that we aren't a threat. And since none of us can remember more than vague impressions of what happened during our blackouts, that's probably all we can hope for, for now." He looked at Gary Cross. "And you were OK … on the *Darwin*?"

Gary shook his head. "It hit us when it hit you, but maybe not as hard. When our heads cleared, we were still just dangling there like a fish on a line."

Elle remembered the building panic as Bob Evans failed to raise anyone on the ship. She'd thought everyone on board must be dead or brain-damaged like the passengers of the jetliner weeks ago. Her sleep conditioning protected her from fears about the ocean depths, but not the prospect of wandering through a ship of zombies.

"Could be whatever it is had already checked us over," Gary offered. "Elle had a spell of her own down at the bottom."

Phillip gave her a look. "And you can remember it?" She nodded. "OK, tell me all about it in a minute. In the meantime, I'd say we've found what we were looking for. The first question is how can we contact it while keeping everyone safe? I'm kicking myself that I didn't turn on the EM shield before sending *Darwin* down. We should have anticipated some kind of reaction."

"The good news is we're not dead." Lee-Anna gave a wry smile.

"I agree. I'm pretty sure that if it wanted us dead, we would be." Alex crossed his arms. "It was probably just trying to learn about us. I wish we knew whether it only investigated the crew or if it has infiltrated our electronics too."

"I've never been probed by an alien before."

Elle shook her head. How could Lee-Anna joke about something like that? Maybe it was just bravado.

"I had Captain Jensen check the computers," Phillip answered. "The core of the main system is a limited AI. It didn't report any sign of an intruder, and our lost twenty-minutes don't appear in the recording equipment. The ship's systems just did what they were supposed to do while we were in la-la land."

"Maybe the ship's brain doesn't remember the intrusion any better than ours do."

None of them had an answer to that.

"So, what's next?" Gary finally asked. "Elle reacted just after *Darwin* passed over the line of black smokers. If I had to bet, I'd say that whatever—or whoever—we're looking for is probably located very close to those vents. Maybe we walked across its front lawn, and it got annoyed. Do we send the submersible back down for another pass? See what reaction we get?"

"No!" Elle surprised herself with the vehemence of her reaction. "Why would you poke a sleeping lion?" She turned to Phillip. "If that's what you've got in mind you can find yourselves another stick to poke with. I'll catch the next helicopter to the States." She sat up. "Where is the helicopter, anyway?"

"It was sent to pick up some people in Guam while *Darwin* was being deployed," Phillip said. "The crane can't operate with the landing pad in place, but once *Darwin* is stowed away, we'll have the chopper back. No, Gary, I do not want to send the submersible down again. In fact, we're going to try Lee-Anna's habitat, though not on the bottom—not yet. We'll suspend it partway down and hope whatever's down there will take that as a friendly overture and not a threat."

Lee-Anna and Gary nodded.

Alex said, "Maybe a peace offering is called for."

"What do you have in mind?" Phillip asked, his eyebrows rising.

"Food. The bottom of the ocean is a pretty desolate place—not a lot of variety on the menu. Maybe we can catch some tuna or a dolphin and drop it down."

"A dolphin? No way!" Lee-Anna snapped her head around, only to see Alex's grinning face, but she didn't seem impressed with his sense of humor.

"Tuna or some other large fish … that's not entirely crazy," Phillip said. "It's just possible that it is a single creature of some kind down there. I'll ask the captain to put some sailors on fishing duty. And as I mentioned, the helicopter will be bringing us more company tonight. The two final members of our team. I recruited them when the evidence began to point to an alien intelligence. They're both fascinating men with amazing credentials. In the meantime, enjoy the return of the sunshine."

As the team was leaving, Phillip beckoned to Elle.

"Now, what do you remember about your spell this time? Did it happen right when you passed the smokers?"

"Just after. It was a kind of mental pressure—terrible. I couldn't stand it, so I motioned to Gary to get us back up."

"Was there anything more to it than pressure?"

She nodded and bit at her lip. "It's not just a force. It's an intelligence—I'm sure of it—and it doesn't want us here. Really wants us gone. I felt a … revulsion, as if we were something disgusting."

His normally guarded face showed surprise.

"I don't think we deserve that. In any case, leaving it alone isn't an option just yet. If you remember anything else, let me know. And thanks again, Elle. I think you've finally confirmed something we were only able to guess at. I know this has been hard on you, but you're doing a terrific job. Outstanding."

He patted her shoulder, and she turned toward the door.

As she came out on deck, Phillip's praise, although patronizing, seemed sincere; and the return of the sunshine made her feel better than she had in a while.

But … what had they been talking about just before that? She couldn't remember.

Her mind had drawn a blank.

14

March 23, 2042

Gary had been told that Bheru Sura was a xenobiologist, specializing in extreme life forms, and Matheus Ventura was a theologian trained in psychology—he supposedly liked the title of *sociotheologist*. Gary knew both men were stars in their fields, true experts and highly respected. So, he'd correctly pictured men in their late fifties or early sixties. But that was about the only part of his mental picture that he got right.

As Bheru stepped from the Raider helicopter his clothes flapped extravagantly in the downdraft as if too big for him. Yet Gary felt the hard thump of the man's weight on the pad. His steps were too regular, adjusting perfectly to the sway of the deck. Then the man reached out his hand for Gary to shake.

There was no glove on the hand. There was no skin on the hand either. It gleamed a polished black, reflecting the light of the setting sun, and its touch was like the grip of an assault weapon. Machined steel, or something even stronger and more supple. But not flesh and blood, oh no.

Bheru Sura had prosthetic arms and legs.

The man laughed at Gary's reaction.

"You weren't told?" he said. "A little joke of Mr. Watanabe's perhaps. I'm sorry to spring it on you like that." His voice was a deep, smoky rasp, a cultured British accent with traces of something more. Hindu, judging by his name and appearance. The man would have been impressive even without the hardware, a couple of inches taller than Gary's 5'11" with a full head of thick, white hair reaching to his collar, but with two streaks of black extending back from the peak of his forehead in a natural V. It was a striking effect and tipped the scale to make the scientist handsome in spite of a complexion badly scarred by youthful acne.

"Well, if you weren't told about me, then Matheus might be a surprise, too."

Gary followed Sura's gaze back to the helicopter as another man gingerly stepped down onto the platform. He was dressed in what looked like pantaloons, and a loose shirt with blousy sleeves that might have been stolen from a pirate movie except a picture of a horse was printed on the front. Curiosity piqued, Gary watched Matheus Ventura closely, but there was no repetition of Bheru's nearly robotic precision. The second man's steps were a little hesitant, and he lurched awkwardly as the ship rolled over a particularly high swell. Shaved bald with a short grey beard beneath a round face and a pair of bright eyes, he looked exactly like Gary's idea of a theologian and academic.

His handshake was firm, but with the warmth of human flesh.

"It's a pleasure to come aboard *Orion* Mr. Cross. Especially since helicopter rides leave me terribly bored. Too little to see." Matheus moved along the line to Phillip Watanabe and then *Orion*'s captain Darryl Jensen. Gary still couldn't decipher what Bheru had meant about the man being a second surprise, although he noticed that

Matheus didn't quite meet the eyes of the person he was speaking to. Many people found direct eye contact uncomfortable.

It was as the group walked along the deck and entered into the superstructure that the truth dawned on Gary. The giveaway was Matheus' ability to navigate corners and dodge obstacles without turning his head from Captain Jensen's face.

"How long have you been blind, Dr. Ventura, if you don't mind my asking?"

Ventura stopped.

"Fifteen years, but I've used this for the past five." He pulled down the neckline of his shirt to show an extremely fine mesh that could have been knit silver from its brightness, yet looked airy and light.

"Not mithril, I assume."

Matheus' laugh was loud and genuine.

"Bravo. I love Tolkien's stories. But I doubt my garment could turn aside a goblin's spear. Or a cave troll's, if you only remember the movie."

"Are you saying this mesh is ... your eyes?"

"Precisely. A web of sensors. And very much more capable than human eyes in many ways. But I still miss the real thing. Those who've said, 'The eyes are the windows of the soul' neglected to mention that you also need real ones of your own to see through those windows. But I can't complain. It keeps me from stepping in the things my horses leave behind." He gave an impish smile.

"Yes, I noticed your shirt. A special horse, I suppose?"

"My favorite of my stallions, Quixote, named after the famous fictional don for his single-mindedness. An exceptional Brazilian breed known as a Mangalarga Marchador. My family has bred them for six generations."

"I don't mean to offend, but will someone with such a sensory system be comfortable in an underwater habitat? You said you get bored in the confines of a helicopter."

The older man smiled without malice. "That is true. But my garment can link to WiFi cameras and other electronics, which is how I use computers. How much will you be able to see through the walls of the habitat, Mr. Cross?"

As the group dispersed to get ready for dinner, Gary wondered whether Phillip Watanabe had deliberately kept him in the dark about Bheru and Matheus' special circumstances as some kind of test or challenge. Was he afraid Gary would object and go over his head to reject the new recruits? Or was it a simple case of a man so used to keeping secrets that he only revealed what was absolutely necessary?

The worst time of Gary's life had been caused by excessive secrecy: a failed mission in the Philippines, when he'd believed there was an excellent chance of rescuing an American delegation taken hostage by pirates. But his superiors had kept important details from him. Like the suspicion that had fallen on a local operative, and the reasons behind an order to abort the extrication at the last moment.

One of the hostages was the wife of a friend.

Gary had disobeyed the abort order.

The intel from the operative was bad—the pirates paid him more—and the mission went all to hell. The hostages were killed, and Gary's team barely made it back.

He'd deserved a court-martial; but since he'd been authorized to retrieve the delegates "at all costs" and could document that he'd been told to rely on the local spook, top brass judged that he'd been given conflicting orders. He didn't go to jail, but he was given the equivalent of grunt duty for two years.

He'd vowed never again to go against orders, but he'd also developed a bitter distaste for those who hoarded secrets like miser's gold.

If Phillip Watanabe was one of those, they were going to have a problem.

# # #

The quarters Gary'd been given were numbingly familiar, the way a traveling salesman must feel about hotel rooms. Still, there was something reassuring about the efficiently spartan trappings of a naval vessel. His various homes on land had never been any more decorative, a non-choice that his fiancée Naomi often laughed about. By Gary's standards, her own apartment in New York was cluttered; although everything in it had been carefully chosen to reflect a perfect blend of trendiness and good taste. Her wardrobe was the same, while Gary was always thankful that Navy life rarely required him to expend thought on what he wore.

It wasn't surprising that they'd irritated each other when they first met. She was dating his dive team's explosives expert Hector Roge, and she had tried to break up Gary and Hector's friendship. Since Gary had saved Hector's life more than once, that wasn't going to happen. By the time Hec lost interest in Naomi (Gary suspected he was afraid of her father, the admiral) Gary had become intrigued by the navy-brat-turned-fashion-girl in spite of himself. Expecting little from their first date, they'd both fallen hard, and Gary had proposed two years later to the day.

He was more than happy to leave the wedding arrangements to her. He knew her plans for the ceremony would be tasteful and carefully considered like all her other choices.

Naomi would not be impressed by his current mission; but having an admiral for a father, she accepted the fact that Gary would sometimes be in danger and could rarely tell her about it. To her credit, she never pressured him or her father to find a safer job for her future husband. Gary planned to ask for a less nomadic assignment on the east coast after they were married in six months, but it had to be his decision, not hers.

As he looked through the file on Bheru Sura, he wondered what Sura's wife Armita thought about her professor husband gallivanting around the south Pacific with the US Navy. The couple had no children; so, other than a few nieces and nephews who had come to study at McMaster University, where Sura worked, Armita would be alone if anything happened to him. However, she was an experienced math teacher and had clearly survived some rough times with her husband, which spoke of her strength and intelligence. Gary would do his best to ensure that she didn't become a widow.

There was a note in the file that said a onetime Glasgow University schoolmate of Sura's named Fergus Simpkin had been considered for this mission, but rejected—which seemed strange since Simpkin worked for NASA. Perhaps it was because Simpkin had five children, or maybe it was because of the man's observed habit of subtly badmouthing his former friend at conferences and other gatherings. The tight confines of an underwater habitat were no place for a backstabber.

The information Gary was looking for was near the end of the document.

Sura had lost his limbs, and very nearly his life, to necrotizing fasciitis—the flesh-eating disease. What would that do to a man's psyche? He'd been given prosthetic limbs right away, but only recently had been offered much more advanced prototypes in return for unspecified services to the US government, an odd arrangement for the government to make with a Canadian citizen, Gary thought.

That would make a man beholden to offer his expertise for certain, but how much more? Had Sura also been asked to spy for Phillip Watanabe? Something like that would have been removed from the file before the agent reluctantly gave a copy to Gary.

Matheus Ventura, on the other hand, had a reputation for ignoring authority—not a good candidate to be an informer. A boyhood friend of the Brazilian foreign minister, Paulo Estevez, Ventura had used Estevez's influence to persuade the American government to recruit Ventura as a consultant, and he'd been well-positioned to be chosen for the current task.

His file said that he'd contracted CMV retinitis fifteen years ago while studying the faith practices of a remote Amazonian tribe, and hadn't been able to reach civilization in time to save his eyesight. But five years ago, he'd used his academic contacts to acquire his cutting-edge sensor mesh, linked to a brain-computer interface embedded in his skull. He often used his enhanced senses to do parlor tricks to impress women, but it also enabled him to be a perceptive judge of people's motivations and honesty, a perfect complement to his psychology and sociology training.

Such a man could be very useful in helping to manage team dynamics. If he hadn't already been pressed into clandestine service by Phillip, he might be worth a private chat.

A yeoman knocked at Gary's door to announce that dinner was ready. Gary muttered a surprised thanks. A personal reminder about a meal seemed to say that the crew considered him part of Phillip's team rather than one of their own. That was disappointing.

As he shut down the computer, he realized that he'd been trying to think like some kind of secret operative himself. Another unwelcome development. One of the things he liked best about dive work was that it was straightforward, without politics or deception.

It appeared that his command assignments had reached a new level, but he wasn't sure that he could consider it progress.

15

March 23, 2042

Orion's crew had already eaten, allowing Phillip's team privacy in the mess hall. The meal was an excellent lasagna, garlic bread, Caesar salad, and fresh fruit; but Gary didn't taste much of it, mulling over the strangeness of his new assignment and the assortment of civilians ostensibly under his command.

Once dinner was over, the conversation turned from the froth of light banter to a deeper current of debate, but only after Phillip had gained their attention to officially welcome everyone and thank them for participating in "Operation Oceanus."

Matheus Ventura laughed. When no one else joined in, he looked embarrassed and covered his mouth with his hand as if to hide the stain of his outburst. "Sorry. I thought you were making a joke. But military men really do use names like that?"

"I'm not military, Doctor," Phillip said with a tight smile, "but, yes, government organizations really do use names like that. This one, by the way, is quite secret."

"Of course. My lips are sealed." The sociotheologist made a key-turning motion at his mouth, the twinkle never leaving his eyes. Gary looked at Phillip, but the man's features had set like concrete.

"I'm interested in hearing your ideas about how we should try to communicate with this entity we've found, Dr. Ventura," Alex said, as he wiped sauce from his chin with a napkin but missed a spot. Elle impulsively removed it with a finger, then realized what she'd done and put a hand to your own mouth in embarrassment. From what Gary'd read, she and Alex hadn't known each other before this crisis, which made the casual intimacy of the gesture surprising. But Alex only looked distracted for a moment before continuing.

"Yes, Elle has been able to confirm that it is, in fact, an entity. Unfortunately, she's also convinced that it is not pleased to have us here."

"I think the question isn't so much *how* we should do it but *whether* we should do it at all," Matheus answered with conviction. The rustle of limbs and utensils around them fell silent. Gary sat up straight and pushed his plate away.

"Are you serious?" he asked.

"Perfectly serious. We have apparently encountered a presence of some kind that transmits harmful energies we've come to believe may be a form of communication. What are our assumptions?"

"That it's alien."

"If you mean extraterrestrial, that's possible, though not certain. What else?"

"That it's intelligent, and more advanced than we are," Alex said.

"Interesting. I wonder why you would make either of those assumptions. Would you, Dr. Sura?"

"Call me Bheru, please. Communication proves little. We know that plants appear to communicate through chemicals in water, air, and fungal mycelia. Bees signal information to each other using dance-like movements. Ants use pheromones. There are many, many other examples, and yet most of us don't make assumptions about plants or bees having intelligence. This presence is certainly powerful in a specific way; and, if Elle is correct, it can express its displeasure, apparently. But the same can be said about a rhinoceros."

Alex frowned. "What do you think, Elle? You sensed animosity, but did you sense that it was intelligent?"

"I can't say that for sure. It doesn't talk. There are pictures, but I don't know if those come from it or from me."

"Have any of the images been of things you've never seen before?"

"No, Dr. Ventura. I don't think so."

"So, the signal might not be putting anything in your head at all, but only prompting your own brain to react by recalling certain images." Matheus positioned his discarded dining utensils in a neat pattern on his plate. Of all the diners, his place at the table was the tidiest, with no spills or fallen scraps, napkin meticulously refolded.

Then a wide grin spread across his face.

"Something amusing, Doctor?"

"The name of this ... operation: *Oceanus*. A Titan, the first of the Greek sea gods, deity of the great world river before Poseidon. At least he was renowned as a pacifist. But I wonder if a son and herald of Poseidon would fit better. His name was *Triton*, known for blowing a horn made of a conch shell with awesome power to calm the waves or make giants quake."

"You figure that our mysterious energy blasts are the call of an ancient god?" Alex asked.

"I think perhaps we should beware of letting our imaginations run away with us."

"Gentlemen and ladies, I'm afraid it could put all of us at risk if we underestimate this being," Phillip said.

"The simplest answer is often the best, Mr. Watanabe," Matheus replied. "It is also dangerous to take action beyond what is indicated by established facts. But let's say, for the sake of argument, that this being is not only intelligent, but, indeed, more advanced than we are, as Mr. Rhys suggests. Why should we make contact with it, and what might be reasons not to?"

"Think of how much we could learn from a being with that kind of power," Lee-Anna offered. "Maybe some super-advanced technology."

"Technology that would render your nano materials comparable to the invention of the horseshoe, Ms. Cavallo? No offence. But now imagine such a result, globally. Every innovator in the world suddenly losing their motivation because aliens already know a better way. Every consumer suddenly dissatisfied with not only their own possessions, but everything in a store window or online catalog anywhere, suspending all their purchasing while they wait for something superior. Research grinding to a halt, while the whole human race comes to understand that it could be generations before we catch up to our new neighbors and are able to make a meaningful contribution to galactic progress."

"Precedents in history are not encouraging," Bheru added. "Less-advanced civilizations have encountered more advanced ones many times. It has never turned out well for the primitives." He drained his water glass, looked around the table for a pitcher, and found it at his elbow.

"People were killed or enslaved by colonial powers, it's true," said Gary. "But many also saw their standard of living and life expectancy increase dramatically."

"While they inherited an unhealthy and stressful modern lifestyle. *And* saw their cultures absorbed and erased! Were they happier? More fulfilled? That is doubtful. In almost every case they became second-class citizens in the broader society."

"Not forever. Descendants of slaves are now regularly elected to the highest offices in the country."

"Native Americans are still waiting," Matheus said with a tight-lipped smile. "Not that Latinos, or even the Black citizens you mention have much to crow about in the United States, either."

Lee-Anna leaned over the table. "But what about medical technology? Aliens might have a cure for cancer. Heart disease. Even aging. They might be able to offer virtual immortality."

"Without new challenges and meaningful pursuits, what would we humans do with hundreds of extra years?" Matheus asked. "Create art? As wonderful as it is, I'm sure that most of the human race would not be content with that. We would be placing ourselves in eternal purgatory, no longer able to pursue our own destiny because our destiny would have been superseded. An entire race rendered obsolete."

Most of the faces around the table were as empty as the dinner plates. A steward came in to clear the serving dishes and immediately asked if something had been wrong with the food. Phillip sent him back to the galley with muttered reassurances. Alex coughed and raised his water glass to his lips. Gary looked around at what had been a product of effort and pride from the galley staff, and reflected that only trash remained.

Phillip cleared his throat. "If that's the way you feel about it, Dr. Ventura, I have to wonder why you accepted my invitation to join our team. Do you truly feel we shouldn't try to contact this being?"

"Of course, we should contact it!" Matheus boomed. "I simply believe that before one takes an action, one should have a good understanding of the reasons for doing so. And the possible repercussions."

"Then ... what are your reasons? You've done a good job of puncturing ours."

"Knowledge, of course. Not technology or medicine, but answers to the great questions of the universe. How was the cosmos created, and why? How many intelligent races have arisen from galactic dust? Is there such a thing as universal morality? Is there a God?" A smile of delight played over Matheus' lips, while Bheru Sura sheepishly wiped a hand over his own face, and everyone else sat with sour expressions and crossed arms.

Gary sincerely hoped for an affirmative answer to that last question, because if he was expected to mold this group into a functional team, he was going to need powerful help to do it.

16

March 24, 2042

"I have to sleep between two snoring seniors, and you get to bunk with the ladies? How about we flip a coin?"

Elle stopped at the bottom of the ladder on Deck Two of the habitat, perversely curious about the direction of the conversation above her. Alex and Gary were on Deck Three, the crew's quarters. The top half of the habitat was still above water for now, and the whole thing rose and fell slightly with the ocean swells; but it wasn't like being below decks on *Orion*. The habitat's much smaller size resulted in a lot more secondary motion: slight wobbles like a dinghy at anchor. Not enough to throw her around, but she found herself clinging to railings anyway.

"We're testing out a prototype submersible habitat in the Pacific Ocean and you're concerned about bunk assignments?" Gary gave a laugh, but it was thin.

"Sleep is important in stressful situations." She could hear a genuine smile in Alex's voice. In the week that she'd known him, she'd seen him use humor to cover his own insecurities. But sometimes it was no more than it seemed. As for his complaint about sleeping arrangements, he was no skirt chaser. He'd made no passes at her—had only ever been attentive to her well-being. In fact, she'd had to reassess her preconceptions about Mr. Rhys.

"Well, I don't know about the rest of you men, but I know that I'm trustworthy around women. So the bunk assignments didn't require a lot of thought. By the way, Dr. Ventura isn't even sixty yet."

"Is someone using my name in vain?" Elle heard two sets of feet on the ladder rungs, one of them much slower. Matheus and Bheru had been checking out the electronics and communications station on the top deck. Now they were descending. She had trouble telling the difference between the heavy tread of Bheru's mechanical legs and the clunky shoes Matheus had brought aboard because he said they adjusted to the strain his aging feet had to bear through the day.

"Gentlemen. I was just showing Alex the bunk assignments. Dr. Sura, are you having difficulty with the ladders?"

Bheru's bass rumble seemed to penetrate the whole structure.

"It's a fairly specialized motion. My old prosthetics were slower and more rigid. I've only had these new ones for three weeks. But I'm very grateful to Mr. Watanabe and his people. I definitely got the better of the trade: cutting edge cybernetic limbs in return for my dubious expertise in this matter." His smile was in his voice.

"You have me sleeping on the men's side of the habitat, Mr. Cross? I'm disappointed."

"Please, Dr. Ventura. We need to focus on more important things. We're due to submerge within the hour, so if you see anything of urgent concern, now's the time to tell me. What did you think of Deck Four?"

"I'll be interested to see the robotic arm in action, and it was a wise decision to have analog readouts at the sensor station rather than handling everything through the computer. Electrical instabilities and computer glitches are still facts of life, especially during shakedown ventures." There was a rustling sound as someone sat on a bunk. Elle gripped the ladder, deciding that it was safe to join them, when Matheus continued, "Is Ms. Travis really a communications expert? She didn't strike me that way."

"Elle is a UN translator on leave to help us with our mission. Fluent in five languages and with a knowledge of a half-dozen more, it's not the equipment that's her expertise, it's the nature of communication. So far, the entity hasn't chosen to talk to us using conventional means, but that could change at any time, and we feel that Elle has a better chance than most to make sense of what it might say. Coincidentally, she was a victim of one of the entity's early transmissions, and she's been able to sense those transmissions much more readily than the rest of us. All good reasons to include her."

"Of course, of course. However, it doesn't take a psychologist to see that the young lady is fragile. I hope you will bear that in mind."

She didn't like the sound of that.

"Elle Travis has more inner toughness than a lot of soldiers I know," Alex said. "Believe me, she'll surprise you."

"Don't worry, Doctor," Gary said. "I'll look after her."

Really. Maybe while he was *looking after* her, she'd tell him about her Masters degree in linguistics and her undergrad studies in non-verbal communication. Although that might not be enough to impress Matheus and Bheru—they probably had three or four degrees each. She'd once planned to go back to school for her PhD, but the UN job-posting had caught her interest because languages had always been fun for her. Then, too, her one-time dream of becoming a field researcher in exotic locales had come up against the reality that she wasn't a good traveler.

But Alex thought she had "inner toughness." Huh.

There were more noises of bodies shifting, so she quickly climbed down the ladder to Deck One where Lee-Anna was double-checking equipment in the laboratory bubble.

The sloping curve of the walls took some getting used to. The habitat—already conversation-shortened to "the hab"—was egg-shaped for strength under pressure—but the lowest of the four decks was even more strange with its two round protrusions. One was the airlock for exiting the hab, and the other was a small laboratory facility with work benches on either side and a round table near the outer wall. Equipment clung to walls or ceiling or, in the case of the cutting laser, merited a four-foot-tall stand of its own. And technical gear wasn't always what it seemed to be. For example, the boxy thing that looked like a microwave oven was a soil and water analyzer. The gas analyzer was cylindrical and shiny like polished stainless steel. She'd wondered why the habitat required a safe, but learned that it was actually a high-temperature oven.

Lee-Anna was checking over a box of glass test-tubes and a carton of flasks beside it.

"Nothing broken so far," she said, looking up. "I was expecting a little breakage after the rough seas we had coming here, but it'll be nice and calm once we submerge." She put the boxes away and leaned back on the cupboard. "What do you think of the place?"

"It's amazing. The design makes great use of space, and the equipment is obviously state-of-the-art. How could I not be impressed? But the thing I still find hardest to believe is that the hull is all one piece."

"All but the flat base, which is one big chunk of ballast made to be instantly detachable. The clamps for the flotation balloons, and the manipulator arm with its track around the hab's middle are attachments, too. The rest is nano-material, most of it locked into the rigid egg shape, but more malleable on this deck."

"What do you mean?"

Lee-Anna waved toward the airlock. It looked as solid as the rest of the structure, extending from the far side of the deck and flanked by the special diving suits that hung full-length in two rows of three on the wall.

"When we want to go outside, the nano-modules, which we call *nims,* spread out from those thicker strips around the entrance and link together to seal off the airlock as if it were a separate craft of its own. It can be, in fact, since it can sever itself from the habitat and act as an escape pod able to float to the surface. Under normal use, valves let water in, and the outer wall splits open once the lock is flooded. But we'll only use the full airlock for large items or groups of people because it takes a lot of air to pump it dry again. You'll notice those three smaller indentations in the outer wall just big enough for one person. They're mini-airlocks that operate the same way as the big one, but require a lot less air to cycle.

"Other than the valves, there are no moving parts to break, or seals to leak. Although I suppose you could consider the material itself to be all moving parts." She smiled and nodded at the lab walls. "The lab can separate too. Neither of the pods has a motor to take it anywhere, but in an underwater emergency, the most important direction is up." She began going through the other cupboards removing and then replacing containers of unknown substances.

"Do we really need two escape pods? The airlock looks like it could hold all of us."

"True. The lab was designed that way for protection of a different kind. If an experiment goes wrong, it might be necessary to eject it and send it as far from the hab as possible."

"Are you talking about an explosion? Or some biological danger?"

Lee-Anna only replied with a shrug.

Elle felt a sudden chill.

She deliberately pictured herself trapped in the separated airlock, falling to the bottom instead of rising. The thought was a test of her sleep conditioning to see if it might be wearing off: mentally probing it the way a tongue probed a new filling. After all, she was waiting inside a giant hollow egg about to plummet into the depths of the sea. But her concern grew no worse. Without the conditioning, she'd be a basket case.

"Have you tried out this habitat yourself? Underwater?" She asked Lee-Anna.

"Of course. Although it was only for a day ... in San Francisco Bay. But everything worked perfectly. Don't worry. It'll be great."

"Wow. Wouldn't you normally test it out a bit more before something like this?"

Lee-Anna had her back turned, but Elle could see her neck muscles stiffen.

"We tested a scale model the size of a minivan down to five thousand feet with all kinds of sensors hooked up to it. It passed with flying colors. No leaks, no overstressed areas, no brittleness. No problem. OK?"

"Sure. Fine. I'm ... going upstairs to the communications room. I need to get to know the equipment better."

Lee-Anna only nodded and returned to her busy work. Elle fled up the ladder. The men were all on the second deck now as Gary showed off the features of the galley, and she stopped for a moment to listen.

"Not just a microwave, either," he was saying. "We also have a ceramic stovetop. The oven is not very big. That's mainly because of needing to vent the heat. You don't want smoke in an environment like this, either."

"Damn, no bacon," Alex said, then looked at Bheru. "Oh, sorry, I didn't mean …"

Bheru laughed. "No offence taken, Alex. I choose not to eat pork, but I am not scandalized when others do. During my time at Glasgow University my friends were mad about sausages. I even tried them once or twice, but I can live without them. I have a feeling, however, that some of my own favorite recipes would be judged too aromatic for these confined quarters."

"I expect most of our supplies have come from *Orion's* stores," Gary said. "So, I doubt if they'll include anything very spicy or exotic. But we should probably talk about a schedule for cooking duties."

"I know how to cook Kraft Dinner," Elle volunteered. The offer was met by blank faces. "Americans call it 'macaroni and cheese'. You know, the stuff in a box? It's better with cut-up bits of hot dog cooked in it."

"And ketchup, I suppose?"

She shrugged at Alex. "My brother likes it that way. I don't."

"But then you Canadians eat french-fries with cheese curds and gravy on them."

"Mmmm. Poutine. Don't knock it until you've tried it." The others still looked unimpressed.

She gave a sigh and climbed the ladder past Deck Three into the more cramped upper chamber that held the communications and electronics station. The small space also included a manual-control center for the robotic manipulator arm and a third workstation with analog gauges showing outside and inside pressure, temperature, and a host of other readings. Each station also had a touchscreen display connected to the habitat's main computer. There were identical displays on both sides of the central access shaft in the crew's quarters, two workstations on opposite sides of the lounge and galley deck, and two more in the lab bubble and outside the airlock on Deck One. The computer stations were apparently capable of producing holographic displays and controls, but Elle wasn't sure how she felt about technology that didn't involve touch.

She hadn't used the computer yet, but she'd been told that its *Help* files would provide everything she needed to know about the communications gear. A good thing, because she felt horribly unfamiliar with it. Gary claimed it wasn't very different from what she'd used before, but she was skeptical.

As she took a seat at her duty station, the habitat gave a downward lurch.

"Just venting some air preparatory to submerging." Lee-Anna's voice came from the workstation speaker, and also more faintly from the access tube that ran up the center of the habitat. "Once we start down, I'll begin inflating the flotation bags to slow our descent and we'll level off at about two hundred feet. We'll spend a day there before going any deeper. You probably won't feel anything, but we'll be heading down in one minute."

Elle did feel it when it came, like the drop of a slow elevator. More noticeable was the sudden absence of a repetitive sibilant noise she hadn't even realized she was hearing. It must have been waves against the top half of the hull. The silence was a bit unnerving. Everyone had stopped talking to experience the moment, but she wished they'd start again.

She was startled by a sound like a cat scrambling across the roof over her head.

God, it couldn't be a Navy diver, could it? Snagged on the submersible, being dragged down ....

"Lee-Anna!" Elle bellowed down the access shaft. "There couldn't be anyone on the upper hull could there?"

From thirty feet below Lee-Anna called up, "No, certainly not. The divers got well clear—I'm watching the view from the upper cameras right now. See for yourself."

Elle touched the display screen. As it powered up it showed the camera feed, perhaps slaved to Lee-Anna's control by default. The picture cycled through three side views of 120 degrees each, then straight up and straight down. There was no sign of any divers nearby, though Elle could just make out the underside of *Orion* against the surface. Four billowing streamers extended upward—the flotation bags, still mostly empty of air. In anticipation of her next thought, the cameras swiveled to show sections of the outside of the hab hull. She saw the brackets where the flotation bags were attached, and other camera mountings, but nothing else.

The skittering noise came again. This time it seemed to stop right beside her. She hurriedly looked around her desk, but there was nothing unusual to see.

"Did you hear that noise?" she called. Gary had just come up the ladder and gave her a look of concern, but the sound repeated on the far side of the room.

"Oh, that's nothing," Lee-Anna replied from the workstation. "That's just the hull contracting—the nims adjusting themselves. Nothing to worry about."

There was a low muttering from the decks below until Matheus's voice rang out.

"You've only tested it *how deep*?"

"It'll be all right, OK? God damn it!"

Elle looked at Gary and saw him frown.

"This isn't going to be easy, is it?" she said.

"No, I don't think it is."

17

March 24, 2042

The first thing Alex had noticed when they boarded the habitat was its new-car smell.

The nanomaterials of the hull probably didn't have any odor. But the interior was completely covered by a tough synthetic coating with the texture of fabric. The smell likely came from that and furnishings that looked like leather but surely weren't. Probably some dirt-repelling microfiber with good flexibility, but minimal stretch and low moisture-absorption. Humidity could be an issue with so many bodies perspiring and exhaling in an airtight environment. Add a slight hint of lubricants and sealants to the metallic tang of electrical components, and the olfactory aura could have come from a Detroit showroom.

The wall coatings were the same color everywhere, a shade Lee-Anna called 'white opal'. It was a warm, creamy tone with the barest shimmer of iridescence, especially in peripheral vision. The bright colors of the furniture and other fixtures made a striking contrast:

poppy-red in the lounge deck (though the galley was mostly light grey), robin's-egg blue on the communications deck, and leaf-green in the lab, except for clean white counters and tabletops. According to the hab's creator, the color scheme was meant to produce a feeling of spaciousness and energy amid one of the most oppressive environments on the planet: the deep ocean.

Habitat uniforms were matte-silver with accent panels of metallic blue; and when he saw their filmy material, Alex had to suppress a laugh. He'd worn something similar, called a dive skin, under scuba wetsuits, and they truly were little more than a skin—they didn't hide anything. These suits were worse. Two-piece, though they looked like one. He thought about his luggage and realized with chagrin that he'd only brought two pairs of briefs. The rest of his underwear were boxers, and they'd look ridiculous under these foil-thin garments. He certainly wasn't going to wear the uniform without underwear—he wasn't an exhibitionist.

Almost as annoying, they had no pockets to put his hands in.

Why silver? Was it because the color complimented fair skin and strawberry-blonde hair to perfection and made Lee-Anna Cavallo look like a space goddess?

"They're an experimental material," she explained. "Meant to allow the skin to breathe better than previous clothing material, allowing sweat to evaporate freely while still keeping some heat in. Plus, they're embedded with nanoparticles that prohibit bacterial growth. No need for frequent washings. Or that's the theory. I've never worn one longer than a day."

Great, Alex thought. Locked up in a tin can with strangers for days, trusting to an untested fabric to prevent his body odor from making him a social pariah. Preserving his modesty seemed like a hopeless cause.

Would he be able to wash his briefs in one of the sinks?

There was a logo on the right breast of the suits: a circle with a hand pointing up from the left toward a hand pointing down from the right, the fingertips only a small space apart. The image was naggingly familiar, but he couldn't place it; and before he could ask Lee-Anna, she'd gone off to supervise the storage of some gear.

The computer-brain interface embedded in the back of his skull was linked to the habitat computer and from there to *Orion*'s satellite internet, but it wasn't capable of taking images directly from his eyes. Instead, he went to the nearest computer station, resigned to the thought that he'd have to run a net search to track down the 'reaching hands' logo. To his surprise, it was the computer display's default wallpaper. Was it a Stanford symbol? Clearly painted, not a photograph—he could make out age lines in the right hand, and the color tones spoke of something very old.

"It's Michelangelo," he said to Lee-Anna as she climbed up the ladder from the bottom deck where the largest storage lockers were located.

"What is? Oh, you mean the logo. Of course. The most famous detail from his Sistine Chapel fresco: 'The Creation of Adam.' Adam reaching up to God."

"I think it's God reaching down to Adam, giving him the gift of life."

"Not the way I see it."

"You don't strike me as the religious type."

"There's a religious type? Do tell. Wait, let's call Matheus and Bheru over to ask them."

"OK, but to use a Judeo-Christian symbol as your logo on a scientific expedition ...."

"I don't see it as exclusively religious. I don't even know if I believe in God. Certainly not as some bearded patriarch. To me, Michelangelo was trying to show humankind reaching out to something greater than itself. That's why it's a perfect logo for scientific research. Even more so for this mission."

Alex shrugged but didn't reply. He was still convinced that the painting depicted a more powerful entity giving a gift to inadequate humanity. Knowledge? Wisdom? Life itself, perhaps, or at least life at a higher level of existence. That's what he'd hoped for all his life, and even more so as he'd witnessed the depths that humans could sink to.

While he waited for the washing facilities to become available just before 'lights out' that night, he downloaded a portion of the Michelangelo painting and set it as the screen saver on his personal tablet. But he included the heads and torsos of the figures in his version.

It was more than just a reaching or a yearning. It was a gift from head to head. Maybe even heart to heart.

# # #

"Did *Orion* ever drop any food offerings like I suggested?"

Alex cut vegetables while Gary poured canned tomatoes and tomato paste into a pan to make spaghetti sauce. The crew had been divided into three pairs to rotate dinner duties. Breakfast and lunch were do-it-yourself.

"Sure. They caught some tuna and some mahi-mahi, I think. Dropped it in weighted mesh containers open at the top, with the fish secured by dissolvable cord. There wasn't any reaction that anyone could measure. Were you expecting a thank-you card?"

"I was just hoping to persuade this thing not to eat us."

"Or we may just have given it the idea to connect us with food," Bheru said from the computer workstation to their left. "Some people are foolish enough to feed wild bears and then be surprised when the animal comes after them. I've been checking into this section of ocean. If we believe that the entity we're searching for resides on the sea bottom, it's too deep here to host many species of fish. It may not have developed a taste for tuna."

"So, what would something live on down there?"

"Species of all sizes die in the upper ocean all the time, and their carcasses eventually fall to the bottom. But by then they've been thoroughly picked over and rotted enough to fall apart into small pieces. It's like a snowfall most of the time at the seafloor, except the snow provides nutrients."

"Like manna you mean?" Matheus gave a broad smile as he descended the ladder from Deck Three, where he'd probably been trying to nap, and went to the workstation on the right.

"I make no assumptions about the religious proclivities of sea creatures. To them, it would be no more a miracle than a field of grass to a cow. But the material falling from above is sparse—not enough for large species, I shouldn't think."

"Giant squid?" Gary asked.

"They probably hunt at shallower depths. Although there are species of flatfish, eels, and stingrays that live near the bottom. Don't forget, there is another source of nourishment: the biomass supported by geothermal heat and expelled gases, like from the black smokers below us. They sustain many types of microorganisms which in turn feed tubeworms, shrimp ... lots of creatures that never see sunlight. Certain species of bacteria can convert volcanic emissions into food energy—chemosynthesis instead of the photosynthesis that surface plants use. Both processes require water, carbon dioxide, and a source of energy. In place of sunlight, it is the chemical energy of compounds like hydrogen sulfide that do the job down there, except that the waste product of chemosynthesis is sulfur instead of oxygen."

"Remind me not to make a shrimp cocktail."

"No, the sulfides of copper and zinc that give the vents the name 'black smokers' would probably ensure that it was your last meal, and not a very tasty one at that."

Alex had finished cutting up salad ingredients and was embarrassed to find that chopping onions for the sauce was making his eyes tear up. He dabbed at the moisture with a sleeve, but the fabric wasn't absorbent.

A skittering sound ran across the wall beside him and made him jump.

"I expected creaking or banging sounds from the pressure changes," he said, trying to cover his discomfort. "That's what they always show in submarine movies."

"Submarines have seams with rivets and expansion joints. This material is a billion joints you'd need a microscope to see." Gary filled another pot with water for the pasta.

"After all this ... adjusting, should we go outside and check the hull? I'm kind of eager to try out those new dive suits."

Gary dropped his voice. "Don't be in such a hurry. They've only had a little more testing than the habitat itself." He grinned and spoke louder. "Anyway, what would you expect to find? A tiny black crack in a solid black wall? Maybe if you had a portable x-ray machine. If these nim things fail, it'll be because of a programming or circuit flaw in the manufacturing, which means they'll all go at once, or in a long strip, like a zipper breaking."

"You're not filling me with confidence."

"The nanomaterial will be fine. Besides, we'd have to use scuba gear at this depth. Lee-Anna's suits are like space suits; they're meant for walking, not so good for swimming around. And we're a long way from anything solid to stand on."

"But the hab's always kept at surface air pressure, right?" Alex asked. "So, if we use scuba gear, we'd actually have to bring ourselves up to the surrounding water pressure before we go outside and then decompress before we come back in. Like diving down from the surface and back up."

"Yes. The airlock on Deck One has the capability to do that. At this depth. But I don't plan to test it if we don't need to."

"Maybe we should have used ambient pressure in the habitat."

"No thanks," Gary said. He nodded toward the sauce pot and Alex tossed the chopped onions into it. "Then we'd be into breathing special gas mixes—probably helium—trying to understand each other when we all sound like we've been huffing from circus balloons. There can be wicked side effects, too. Very long decompression afterward. Not my idea of a good time. And that's only at our current depth—about seven atmospheres. Deeper than this—no way. There's just nothing we could safely breathe at those pressures."

"What about liquid breathing? Down at the bottom, I mean," Alex asked.

"Oxygenated perfluorocarbons? They keep trying to make that work, but nobody's succeeded yet. The problem is the viscosity of the liquid—once we're out of the womb, our lungs and diaphragm aren't meant to handle something that dense. And the flow of fluid would have to be intense to supply enough oxygen and remove enough CO_2. Our lungs just can't move that much liquid on their own."

"I've never been scuba diving," Matheus said. "I suppose I never will now. My sensor mesh can't see through neoprene."

"The nano-suits are equipped with multiple cameras," Gary said. "If we end up using them, you'll be able to plug into them the way you connect with that computer."

"I look forward to that."

"What about you, Dr. Sura? Have you ever used scuba?"

"Indeed, I have, when I still had my own limbs. I just had to see firsthand the biodiversity of coral reefs. Absolutely inspiring and humbling."

"Some of God's most wondrous handiwork, I'm told," Matheus said.

"Or a miracle of synergistic evolution. Each organism adapted to fill its own special niche. I wonder if that's what we'll find here?"

"Wait. You think something that emits enough energy to reach the Moon could have *evolved* here?" Alex asked.

Bheru smiled. "I have seen far too many ingeniously adapted forms of life to rule anything out. It wasn't so long ago that most people didn't believe living things produced auras. Who is to say that a biological entity couldn't evolve the means to accumulate and store an enormous quantity of energy and release it in one short, powerful burst?"

"Not so short," Gary said. "Even that transmission Alex calls a 'probe' held the *Orion* crew entranced for nearly twenty minutes."

"Elle has sensed emissions for hours when the Moon is overhead," Alex added, "although we have no way to know if they were full transmissions."

"Yet if we don't know what kind of energy we're dealing with, we cannot know how difficult it is to generate. Perhaps we're on the verge of a new discovery in physics as well as biology." Bheru's smile was a bright beacon, his teeth amazingly white for someone his age. Alex had a feeling he was pulling their legs, but didn't want to be the one to ask.

"Mr. Rhys is clearly skeptical, Bheru." Matheus slouched and swung his chair back and forth.

"Well, it's just that ... that's ridiculous. When scientists first bounced a laser off the Moon it took ..." He consulted the augment in his head. "Fifty kilojoules in half-microsecond bursts. A hundred kilowatts. To think that a living creature could produce that amount of energy is silly."

"I'm not often called *silly* anymore," Bheru said, his smile losing a little of its own wattage. "When scientists first bounced radar off the moon, they used only *three* kilowatts. Electric eels can dispense a jolt of more than half a kilowatt, which is very impressive for their size. As it happens, some microbes found near hydrothermal vents generate electricity thanks to chemicals in their diet. Why not something larger? We could be dealing with a life form very much bigger than an eel and an as-yet unidentified type of energy. So, you attribute this signal to what, Mr. Rhys? Space aliens? And that is not silly?"

"I think it's a lot more likely that advanced extraterrestrials have finally come to Earth. It's long overdue."

"You speculate entirely without facts. More than half a century of listening to radio frequencies for signs of technology, plus decades of probing the far reaches with space-based telescopes has failed to provide a single piece of evidence that life exists elsewhere in the galaxy, let alone intelligent life."

"If you don't put some seasonings in this sauce soon, there won't be any point," Gary said, reminding them of the task at hand.

Alex added salt and pepper, garlic powder and oregano, measuring only by eyeball, then complained about the lack of red wine, though he'd known not to expect it.

"When you're on a special underwater mission run by the Navy, you learn to do without alcohol. Remember, the US Navy has been dry for over a century."

"Even the most delicious pasta is only half a meal without a good Portuguese wine accompanying it, Mr. Cross."

"Maybe when our job is done, Dr. Ventura, but I suspect we're going to need to stay sharp on this mission. All the time."

With that assessment, the group fell silent. Alex stirred the sauce. He didn't have high expectations for its flavor. No wine, no Worcestershire sauce. Tomatoes all from cans. The spaghetti would be edible, but nothing memorable.

Bheru's comments about the biota around black smokers came back to him. Even if it were possible for an organism to evolve a means to harness and emit such powerful energies, what would be the evolutionary benefit? And how could the ability to telepathically invade the minds of surface dwellers like humans help a deep-sea creature to survive and reproduce?

There were lots of explanations to account for the failure to detect intelligent life around other stars, along with plenty of reasons to think such intelligence existed. Humanity could take a giant leap ahead with knowledge from space travelers. What could be learned from a creature that spent its life in the lightless mud of the abyss?

He tasted the sauce and grimaced before adding a little more salt. Should he put in more garlic too? It might not make Gary very popular with his female bunkmates that night.

Maybe just another pinch or two.

18

March 24, 2042

Gary followed Lee-Anna up the ladder to Deck Four, trying to ignore how she looked in the ultra-thin material of her uniform. He liked to think that he kept himself in good shape, too, but the damn stuff was just so revealing it made him uncomfortable.

Elle wore it well, he observed, as he came into the upper room. But she also wore an expression of dismay. One red light blinked above the communications workstation. He had no idea what it signified.

"We've lost the link with the *Orion*," she said. "It won't lock onto any frequency." Anticipating Lee-Anna's request, she slid out of the chair and allowed the engineer to take her place. "I didn't touch anything other than the usual. I don't know what happened."

The habitat's creator scanned the panel in front of her and pressed a series of soft buttons. Each one produced a new set of numbers on the display, and she leaned in to read them, but made no comment. One switch made the red light stop blinking, but it resumed about ten seconds later. She shook her head and tried again with the same result. Finally, she typed a string of characters and the comm system began to run a diagnostic check. While it worked, she ducked underneath the equipment panel to check physical connections.

"Uh, maybe we should go downstairs to be out of the way," Gary said, already moving.

One deck below, Matheus lounged on his bunk. When he saw them appear, he sat up straight and pulled in his abdomen until Elle had passed down the ladder. He gave Gary a wink and said quietly, "These damn uniforms. At first, I was impressed with the way they accentuated physical assets. Unfortunately, they do too much to reveal a man's excess baggage."

"I know what you mean."

"No, I really don't think you do. In another twenty years, perhaps."

Elle stopped on Deck Two and sat down on one of the two couches against the wall in the crew lounge. There was lots of room for Gary to sit beside her, but he took the upholstered chair facing her, instead. He'd expected to find Bheru and Alex there, but there were sounds of motion below, in the lab.

"Have you had any sensation of the entity since we submerged?" he asked, voicing a question that was never far from his mind. Elle shook her head.

"There's a kind of constant sense of something being aware of us; but, you know, people sometimes get a feeling of being watched when there's nothing around. It could just be my imagination."

"Are you the imaginative type?"

"No more than most, I think; but this isn't exactly a normal situation."

"I have to wonder what you consider a normal situation. I mean, you work at the UN. What's that like?"

"It's great. I like it. I used to really love it when I first started. Being among people from so many different countries was glamorous. And I hoped I'd play a part in momentous decisions that made the world a better place."

"You're using the past tense. It isn't that way now?"

"Actually, most of it is just squabbling among people who have no interest in being convinced of anything they don't already believe. But it can still be interesting. You do get a better understanding of the reasons behind world politics, even when they're not good reasons." Self-consciously, she crossed her legs, perhaps aware of how they were revealed by the clinging fabric. Gary tried not to look at them.

"What about meeting all those VIPs—heads of state, sheiks, princesses? Or Hollywood stars fronting for prominent causes."

"Usually, I just meet UN delegates or ambassadors and their assistants. The ambassadors act like politicians—most of them are the cronies of politicians, and that's how they got their jobs. And the assistants are yes-men. But sometimes you meet guest speakers who're really sincere about what they do and are out to accomplish something important."

"You must have some standout memories."

"Not what you think. But one that does stand out was a time I had to pinch-hit for a sick colleague. My Russian was a bit rusty. A Russian cabinet member hosting a lavish reception announced that his daughter would provide some 'light entertainment.' I used a word that meant 'easy'. Basically, I called her a hooker." Elle laughed at the memory, covering her face with her hand. "What about you? Being a Navy diver, you must be sent on some dramatic missions."

"I could tell you, but then I'd have to kill you."

She laughed as if she hadn't heard the old line before. The reaction made him remember an ex-girlfriend who'd laughed at nearly everything he'd said. That relationship hadn't lasted long.

"You'd be surprised how dull it can get, searching over the hull of a ship for the twentieth time—they all look the same. Looking for contraband if it's a foreign ship; for mines, if it's one of ours."

"God, that must be frightening." She leaned forward, and again he had to avert his eyes, this time from revealed cleavage. He hoped she wasn't flirting.

He shrugged. "If a mine went off it'd be worse to be inside the boat, I think. A slower death. But most of the time there's not a lot of danger involved in my job. It's just routine."

"That's what they all say." Lee-Anna came down the ladder and dropped into the other chair. "I found the problem. It was the signal checking system."

Their blank faces prompted her to continue.

"The comm system uses ultrasonic sound waves because radio doesn't travel through seawater worth a damn. Everything we send—voice or data—is converted to digital form and back using special modems, and the signal itself is high frequency sound. I'm sure you've used wireless comm systems between divers, Gary. Well, those are lower power, but also higher frequency because they don't have to travel far, and higher frequencies provide faster data transfer. The hab is designed for depth, so we have to use a frequency around 100 kHz which makes for very slow data transfer but gets us the distance we need. Following me so far?"

Elle and Gary nodded. Most of this had been covered long ago in his dive training, but he'd never needed to remember it.

"Sound can be bounced around by objects, altered by a thermocline or a change in salinity. There can be doppler shifting ... a lot of stuff can distort the signal. So, to keep it reliable, our comm is constantly linked to *Orion*'s. Every few seconds they do an electronic handshake to make sure what's getting through is consistent and accurate. Because we could be sending sensitive information, a severe change in the signal will cause the system to break the link and trigger an alarm. Somehow, that checking program was shut off and our comm didn't adjust for signal drift—it lost contact with *Orion* and then wouldn't recognize *Orion*'s transmission identifiers to restart the conversation. It just started scanning the spectrum to find a signal it liked."

"How would the checker shut off by itself?" Gary asked.

"It wouldn't." She gave Elle a look.

"Could I somehow have hit the wrong button? Or a couple of buttons? I don't think I did, but ...."

"No, you have to dig down about three menus deep to get to that setting," Lee-Anna said. "But, I ... can't see how it could happen by accident."

There was an awkward silence that Gary knew wouldn't benefit any of them. He slapped his palms lightly on his knees and stood up.

"Well, I'm glad you found the problem. Obviously, Elle will have to keep watch in case it happens again."

This time he was the recipient of Lee-Anna's skeptical expression; but she just nodded and said, "I hope Alex and Bheru haven't been messing up my lab." She spun around to the ladder and dropped out of sight.

Elle touched Gary's arm and mouthed 'Thank you.' Her eyes held his longer than necessary, so he broke the contact by stepping to the side as if making room for her to climb back up to her duty station.

She did, but the view as she negotiated the ladder made him look away and suppress a sigh.

19

March 25, 2042

"Whales!" Elle called out, realizing too late that her voice would carry through the entire habitat, and that Lee-Anna, Alex, and Gary were still in bed after a late night of strategic analysis. Bheru and Matheus were at the workstations in the crew lounge—Bheru doing research in the archives of the Woods Hole Oceanographic Institution while Matheus reviewed some esoteric philosophy. Alex's head was the first to poke up from the dorm deck.

"What kind of whales?" he asked in sleep-raspy voice.

"Not very big. Five meters long, maybe a little more. Four of them just swimming around the hab."

There hadn't been any communications to handle, so she'd been at the second data station trying to learn what each of the analog readouts represented. Outside cameras, part of the display, were left on routinely, cycling from one to the next every half-minute. A shadowy movement had caught her attention; and when she'd taken a second look, the view of a passing whale had filled the screen.

Alex squatted beside her to watch. They could see only two whales most of the time, but changing camera views confirmed that two others were circling farther off and slightly below the hab. The topside camera showed nothing but flotation bags. Elle tapped the screen to go to the next camera in time to see the tail-half of a whale slide past. The large fluke gave a flip just as it passed the lens.

"A beaked whale, probably a Cuvier's," Bheru's voice called up from below. "Very common in these regions."

"Does everyone have to yell around here?" Lee-Anna's voice was a moan. It was followed by heavy footsteps and Bheru climbed onto Deck Four.

"You'll notice the fluke—the tail," he continued in a softer voice, though Elle could still feel it through her elbows on the desk. "The fluke of a Cuvier's doesn't have a split in it like most whales, and it has a pronounced snout somewhat like a dolphin's except shorter. One of the few whale species that isn't yet considered endangered."

The fluid motion of the creatures was entrancing, especially the way they could spiral around each other so gracefully without obvious coordination. One of them looked uniformly grey, but the others varied in color; and each had patterns of light blotches across their bodies. The smallest looked polka-dotted and more energetic than the rest. They continued to do haphazard passes around the egg-shaped habitat but avoided the flotation bags above.

On impulse, Elle closed her eyes and reached with her mind. She could sometimes sense the presence of animals without seeing them. After a few moments, she had a sensation of flying—dipping and rising up, slipping into a downward roll and a long glide. There was a feeling of gentle curiosity, too. With more concentration, she recognized a roughly circular shape floating in her mind; but it bore none of the details of the habitat.

"Could they think we're another kind of whale?" she asked, opening her eyes.

"You mean, is that why they're investigating us? I suppose that's possible. A blue whale would be comparable in size to the habitat. Maybe they think we're hanging head down, in which case we should be singing." Bheru launched into a wordless piece of operatic music that Elle recognized from "Carmen", she thought. The man's singing voice was amazing, even richer and more penetrating than his speech, and he clearly took great pleasure in it.

"Bheru, seriously?" snapped Lee-Anna. The biologist stopped mid-phrase and favored Elle with a sheepish smile. The group watched the outside performance in silence for another ten minutes until the whales decided they'd seen enough and slipped away into the shadowy distance.

"You look puzzled by something, Dr. Sura," Alex said.

"Bheru, please." The man removed his hand from his chin. "Well, as I said, Cuvier's beaked whales are fairly numerous, and like all other whales they have to surface to breathe, but they prefer to hunt at much greater depths, sometimes more than nine thousand feet—deeper than any other mammal we know of. But during the past decade, there have been a number of these whales stranded on beaches. I have to wonder if there is something in the deep that is encouraging them to spend more time at shallower depths."

"Maybe they're just not hungry," Elle said.

"Ah, yes, well that's as good a guess as any."

"But Alex is," she noted. "Come on. I was going to fix scrambled eggs with salsa for myself. I can make enough for the rest of you."

Bheru went first. Alex hesitated at the ladder and said quietly, "That was perceptive of you."

Elle laughed. "Hardly. I grew up with a brother. Guys are always hungry. For food or … other things." She flashed a smirk and went down the ladder.

# # #

It was later, while she was reading on her bunk, that she felt hungry again.

At first it was just a notion that she should have made more of the breakfast eggs for herself, but it quickly grew into powerful discomfort that gnawed at her. Was something wrong? Had her blood sugar suddenly crashed? At the thought of eating a sandwich, her stomach rebelled. So, apparently, it wasn't a real hunger, a normal hunger—that sensation was just the closest parallel her mind seemed able to make.

Because the feeling wasn't her own.

She shuddered. She should have known the strange touch instantly.

The entity.

She'd always sensed that it had a potent need for answers of some kind. This was more visceral, more urgent. And, she couldn't help feeling, more threatening, as if humans might be the object of its hunger, or an impediment to its appeasement.

There came an image of a dark space: a hole, a mouth, and a vague impression of the habitat approaching it. No, being drawn to it. Into a chasm large enough to swallow it whole, and hundreds more along with it.

She nearly cried out. She tried to draw reassurance from the brightness of the habitat's lights, but they began to dim, and objects around her to fade. The craving in her stomach was replaced by a feeling of sinking— except the hab wasn't sinking. Only Elle.

She pushed shakily to her feet and reached for the ladder. There was no one else on Deck Three and she badly needed company, but Deck Four was empty and going downward felt dangerous.

She finally forced herself down the stairs, and for a panicked moment she thought that the deck below was empty too, that the whole habitat had been abandoned and she'd been left alone. But Lee-Anna stood in the galley, looking for something in the cupboards. Elle went to stand beside her, then impulsively threw her arms around the other woman, quivering.

"What's wrong? Are you OK?" Lee-Anna hugged her back and Elle raised her head to blink back tears.

"It was … I guess it was a nightmare, but I sensed the entity. Really strong. It startled me."

"Did you think you were in danger?"

"I … I don't know. It has killed before, maybe by accident. I guess I was afraid of that." Before she came aboard, Phillip had asked her to carefully consider how much she told the rest of the crew for the sake of morale, and because they might react badly if they learned how far her abilities extended.

"Is it gone now?"

The powerful hunger had faded, though a brooding presence remained that she was sure wasn't her imagination.

"Mostly." She pulled away, feeling embarrassed. "You must think I'm a big baby."

"No, of course not. I can remember when it hit us on *Orion*. That feeling of losing control of my mind and body. Not something I want to experience again anytime soon. And you nearly died your first time. Don't apologize. But I think you should tell the others and report it to Phillip."

Elle nodded and gave a quick squeeze of Lee-Anna's hand, then took a deep breath and climbed back up to the communications deck.

# # #

"Are you sure it wasn't the whales you were sensing?"

Phillip's face didn't move—the data transfer rate was too slow for streaming video—but his voice sounded fairly normal.

"I sensed the whales when they were nearby. They were nothing like this. This was a painful need. A *hunger*, Phillip—do you hear what I'm saying?"

"Of course, Elle, and I believe that it must have been hard on you. We all need to remember that this is non-human intelligence we're dealing with. We can't be sure of how to interpret its signals. You've said so yourself. We can't know that the feelings you get from it are in any way comparable to any specific human emotion."

"But what about what Matheus said, about how it could be triggering my own mind to produce equivalent images or sensations? This felt like hunger. Maybe it really does want to eat us!"

"No. No, there are plenty of other sources of food down there. Whatever it uses for food or fuel, it's already been doing so for weeks at the very least. And no matter what its appetites are, it would find the habitat a pretty indigestible meal. Remember that there's still a good chance you're sensing an attempt to communicate by beings from another planet. If they were hungry for humans, there are seven billion of us scurrying unprotected all over the land masses. They wouldn't be interested in a few measly morsels inside a hard shell."

He was trying to make a joke, but Elle couldn't laugh.

"You didn't tell the others that it was hungry, did you?" he asked.

"No."

"Well, I'd suggest you don't. The mission is stressful enough for everyone. I don't want to add to that without evidence that there's an actual threat. OK?"

She nodded and then said, "Yes," out loud when she realized he couldn't see her.

"Good, Elle. You're doing a terrific job. Outstanding."

Phillip ended the call and she slowly got out of the chair, a little tired, and now she really could do with a snack. Real hunger, this time. Something from the galley. She moved toward the access shaft.

Or should she talk to Phillip?

No, she'd just been talking to him about ... something. Anyway, there was nothing urgent to report.

She climbed down, feeling as if a load had been lifted from her mind.

20

The crew had just finished a meal of corned beef hash when the hab computer sounded an alert. Alex gave a look of regret at the chocolate pudding he had to leave on the table.

"It's one of the flotation bag cables," Lee-Anna said to Gary. "One of the clamps on the cable for bag number three isn't delivering full pressure. Magnetic sensors assess whether good contact is being made. The faulty clamp may be prying open."

"That doesn't sound good. What do you recommend?"

"Well, if it goes, we'll be dangling from three cables, putting a lot more strain on them. We won't lose a bag because they're attached to one another, but the hab won't be level, and things will get worse in a hurry if other clamps start to go. I think the safest plan is for us to go outside and check the clamp. If it's weakening, we can rig a short safety cable to relieve the strain and act as a backup."

"Couldn't that be done with the manipulator arm?"

"The arm has a camera at the claw end, so we can take a closer look, but if we want to feel the tension or check the mechanism, the claw's tactile feedback isn't sensitive enough for that."

"Scuba it is, then. Let's do it."

Lee-Anna moved toward the ladder, but Gary stopped her.

"Not you. You're the only one who can interpret the readings of the sensors quickly, and we'll need real-time advice. Alex and I will go."

Alex took a deep breath and regretted eating so much dinner.

He enjoyed scuba diving—it was like being in an alien world—but the gear was a nuisance. A survival suit for a hostile realm. Neoprene wetsuits were annoying to pull on and confining to wear; but in the water, the skin-hugging material offered protection as well as warmth. Without it, water would conduct heat from skin twenty-five times more quickly than air. Over the neoprene went a cumbersome vest, heavy tank, and awkward weight belt, all of it accessorized by snaking hoses with uncomfortable mouthpieces. But since immersion equaled zero gravity, it was always a real relief to finally 'get wet.'

Pumping water out of the airlock wouldn't be an issue at this depth, so they used the whole space. It was a strange feeling for Alex to watch the room fill. He and Gary stood in full gear as the sea surged in through four vent plates in the floor. As soon as the water entered, Alex felt the pressure increase, any remaining air quickly compressed. The weight of all the water above the habitat pressed down on every square inch with a force seven times greater than what a diver would experience at the surface. Gary waved a signal to Lee-Anna, and the inflow of water slowed. The divers needed a more gradual change so they could make the pressure in the air spaces within their bodies—especially the sinus cavities and inner ear—equal the force pressing on them from outside. Otherwise, fragile tissues could be badly damaged. With his nose pinched shut, Alex gently blew air into his ears every few seconds and felt them pop a little. That was necessary any time he descended in the water. When rising, the inner air spaces relieved excess pressure on their own.

Water gushed over his fins and then his knees, soaking through the porous wetsuit. Cool at first touch, a thin layer of liquid between suit and skin warmed quickly from his body heat.

He'd learned scuba in fresh water, but preferred ocean dives because of the ocean's great visibility and beautiful blue water. North America's Great Lakes were almost as good, but most smaller lakes were the color of tea, in shades ranging from milky green to Earl Grey left in the pot for days. He'd dived in flooded river valleys with near-zero visibility thanks to constantly stirred-up silt (an experience not worth repeating), but even the clearest of wilderness lakes rarely offered more than thirty feet of visibility in any direction.

Here, he could see something bright or high-contrast a couple of hundred feet away. When the hab wall finally opened and the divers kicked out into the open sea, *Orion* might have been visible, but he couldn't pick it out from the silvered underside of the ocean surface because of the angled sunlight.

The rasp of his inhaled breath and the blocks-falling-down-a-plastic-tube rattle of the exhaled bubbles were loud. He'd hear better if he held his breath, but that was something you never did during a dive. Rising even a few feet with full lungs could rupture the bronchial tissues like an over-inflated balloon, and maybe even cause a fatal embolism.

He was startled to hear Gary's voice in his ear urging him on. The headgear enclosed his chin and ears to allow for earbuds and a microphone, but it wasn't a rigid helmet. The soft rubber molded to fit closely over his nose made him sound like he had a cold. He gave a quick affirmative reply and kicked faster.

The computer's error message had indicated a problem with the cable of the number three flotation bag but didn't show which end. They checked the upper end first, at the bag. There was no play in the connections.

The two men descended along the cable toward the habitat. Alex remembered to pinch his nose and blow every few feet. Equalizing made the sound of his bubbles drop in pitch.

Gary reached the clamp first and gave it a slight turn to get a better view.

It happened like the strike of a cobra, leaving an afterimage of fizzing bubbles.

Gary was gone!

Alex watched helplessly as the habitat lurched downward and began to bounce. Heart pounding, he raised his head to look for Gary.

There, only ten or fifteen feet above, but clearly in distress. His testing had made the clamp come loose from the habitat in a fierce recoil, the cable wrapping itself around Gary's arm and yanking him upward. The number three bag was still harnessed to the others, keeping it from shooting to the surface and dragging Gary to his death. But he was in obvious pain and unable to free himself.

Horrified, Alex looked toward the other clamps. If the sudden extra stress made them all fail, the habitat would plunge to the bottom twelve thousand feet below. No one knew if the hull could stand such a rapid increase in pressure. Gary would rocket to the surface, his bloodstream filling with a froth of deadly bubbles of absorbed nitrogen expelled too quickly from his tissues.

Alex would be left alone at two hundred feet of depth with only minutes of air left. He might reach the surface, but without stops for decompression he would be courting death anyway.

He reached Gary's side and tugged at the tangled cable. Gary kicked listlessly but without effect. He'd had the presence of mind to bleed some air from his buoyancy vest to keep from rising, and Alex did the same. Between rasping breaths, he tapped the microphone button at his jaw and gave a report to the others. Lee-Anna asked about Gary's condition and Alex could see Gary's free hand move to his face, but there was no sound.

"I think his microphone is broken," Alex said.

When Gary's entangled arm was finally freed it hung at an unnatural angle.

"I think his arm is broken, too."

"Bring him back to the hab. We've got medical equipment."

"Not yet. I don't like the look of those other cables."

"Shit, you're right. I'm getting warnings from two of them. But there's nothing you can do about them. We'll have to surface and hope they hold until then."

"And if they don't, you get a fast ride to the bottom. I think it's best for Gary to hang on to the cable for now." He saw the man nod. Alex's throat was so dry he could barely talk. He worked his mouth to create some saliva and swallowed. "What if you release the base on the bottom of the hab? That's for ballast, isn't it?"

"Sure, and the hab would pop to the surface. We'd be OK, but you two ...."

"Right. Let me think."

He swept his eyes back and forth over the hull, hoping for inspiration. Gary had brought a couple of safety cables out with him but must have dropped them when he was hit. Was there time for Alex to re-enter the hab and get more? Not without switching to a fresh air tank. The strained clamps might not hold that long.

He did a double take as something caught his eye.

There were bumps on the lower section of the hull forty feet beneath him. He reached for the end of the cable that had struck Gary and worked the clamp mechanism with his hand. It didn't appear to be broken. Maybe if it were re-fastened it would hold for a while, but doing so would be a tall order.

"Lee-Anna? There are four large lumps on the hull of the hab below me. Are those air tanks?"

"Two for water, two for air."

"Detachable?"

She hesitated before confirming it.

"Pretty heavy, I bet," he said. "If you ditch them, that might raise this side of the hab enough to let me reattach the cable. With a lot of luck."

Her reply didn't sound optimistic, but she didn't have a better plan. Alex reached out to Gary to help him move into the clear in case the hab lurched upward. He had a mental flash of the mission logo: a hand reaching for another hand.

At his signal, Lee-Anna released the tanks. For a terrible moment, as they tumbled into the abyss, he thought the hab might go with them.

Instead, it rocked in a small arc, began to twist, then rotated back. Alex sped to the dangling end of the cable and pulled it toward the housing where it belonged, but he couldn't latch it on before the hab swung downward again. Cursing, he hoped that the hab's pendulum motion would carry it as high on its return swing. When it did, he frantically snapped the clamp into place, jerked at it with as much force as he could to test its hold, then kicked out of the way while the hab began to drop and the cable took the strain.

It held.

The habitat would settle with that side higher than the other because of the lost weight, but Lee-Anna could probably restore the balance a little by shifting water supplies among interior reservoirs. He gave her the good news about the clamp and kicked toward Gary.

Gary held out his gauges to show his air supply.

"Jesus. Lee-Anna, you'd better see how fast that airlock of yours can cycle because we're sucking on empty tanks here."

"You'll still need to decompress. Use the spare air tanks in the airlock."

He watched the wall of the airlock split open. It seemed terribly far away.

## 21

March 25, 2042

The smell of iodine was all too familiar, but Gary still hated it. It was an odor associated with blood and pain, and the field hospitals that featured into the worst memories of his service as an 'individual augmentee' with the army in trouble zones: comrades with faces ravaged by homemade incendiaries, limbs missing, guts riddled with shards of scrap metal. Field hospitals were places of dying, not healing; and in the Middle East, they were not even safe havens, but targets. He'd never imagined he could be so glad to get back to his Navy job.

He hadn't expected to smell iodine on this mission—the dangers involved were of a whole other level. Go figure.

The ship's surgeon on *Orion* was a young woman named Bannerjee. She'd done a good job on his arm. Fortunately, it was a clean break, but the force of the blow from the cable had nearly pushed the broken bone through his flesh. In battle zones, infection was nearly guaranteed with an injury like that; but it wasn't a concern this time. The cable was made of nano-materials—probably carbon-60 fibers—without the ragged filaments and barbs that formed the surface of steel cables that readily shredded flesh.

He'd been lucky.

Lucky that Alex Rhys had kept his head. Gary had to admit that he'd underestimated the man. There were times when he was glad to be wrong.

Modern arm casts still weren't comfortable, but they were a lot lighter and durable than the old plaster kind. You could also get them wet, which was a bonus because Gary could really use a shower. That was the thing he was most looking forward to, now that the hab had been recalled to the surface.

But that pleasure would have to wait until after he met with his team.

He left sick bay with a warm thank you to the doctor and went down one deck to the conference room and library where Phillip Watanabe had gathered the others. He'd already briefed Phillip while the surgeon was doing her work, but there was more that hadn't been said.

As he entered the room, his companions gathered around to offer sympathetic touches and words of relief. Ironically, they finally seemed like a team; but that didn't change his mind. He would go ahead with his plan, because there was a second reason to do so—a more sinister one.

"Thanks, everybody," he said. "The good news is that my arm should heal without any complications in about six weeks. The bad news is that I also suffered a slight concussion." He noted the sharp look Phillip gave him, but at least the agent didn't say anything. The other five made noises of surprise. "Yeah, so that means it's too risky for me to go back down with you. Concussions are unpredictable, and so is a habitat environment on the ocean floor. The doc won't let me take the risk."

"You mean we're going down to the bottom without you?" Elle asked, eyebrows disappearing behind her bangs.

"You can handle it. We'll maintain constant contact, and I'll still call the shots from up here. Underwater, Lee-Anna will remain in charge of everything to do with habitat operations. For any other decisions in the event I'm not available," he turned his head, "I'm putting Alex in charge."

Lee-Anna looked pissed. Alex actually gasped.

"I don't want to be in command. I'm a consultant. I don't *do* command."

Gary laughed. "Command isn't a dirty word. This is a team, remember? So, you're the backup quarterback because I've been sidelined with an injury. No big deal. You've got the smarts, you're a quick thinker, and you keep cool under pressure."

"Lucky me."

"You'll do fine. And I know everybody will give you their full cooperation." He found himself meeting Lee-Anna's gaze. She looked away. "Besides, we've got to get this done. We know that the entity is fully aware of us, but there shouldn't be any more daily energy transmissions to worry about for a while because the Moon has moved and will remain hidden by the sea-bottom mountain ridge to the south of Ground Zero. We have to take advantage of that time window. The downside is that because of this circumstance, our superiors, in their wisdom, have cancelled the 'no-fly' zone. Prematurely, if you ask me; but I don't want any deaths on my conscience because we didn't get the job done. While the hab is repaired and checked over, we'll take a day tomorrow to re-evaluate plan details and get a little rest. The hab goes back down the day after. All the way down."

He expected questions, but everyone seemed stunned. Either that, or they were all waiting to race to the showers. He dismissed them and hoped there'd be some hot water left for him.

Phillip remained behind.

"A concussion? And Doctor Bannerjee didn't see fit to tell me?"

Gary kept his face impassive and said nothing.

"Fine. I'll let you explain that little deception to your superiors when they ask, as I'm sure they will. Especially since you're abandoning your responsibilities and leaving the decision making to civilians with no command experience."

"I'll still be close enough to keep on top of things."

"And what if we lose communications again, or something more serious happens?"

Gary hesitated, then said, "Let's face the facts. Once the hab gets down to the bottom, it's the entity that will be calling the shots."

22

March 26, 2042

When Gary arrived for breakfast the next morning the other team members were hurrying out of the mess chattering urgently about something.

"What's up?"

"Ranger's missing."

"Phillip's dog? How? Where could he go?"

Elle bit at her lip. "That's the thing. Phillip's frantic. He's afraid Ranger might have fallen overboard. He wanted out of Phillip's cabin in the middle of the night; but when Phillip opened the door, he took off like a shot. The crew's being questioned to find out if anybody saw him."

Gary couldn't picture the Homeland agent frantic about anything, but he was devoted to his dog. The group split up to help the crew with the search. Gary went with Lee-Anna.

When they were alone, he said, "You're not happy with my decision to put Alex in charge."

"You heard him—he doesn't *do* command. We all know that consultants consult because they can't *do*: they only spit out somebody else's ideas and let others do the work."

"Is that what happened yesterday when the cable broke loose?"

"OK. He handled that well, but everybody gets lucky sometimes."

"According to Phillip, Alex Rhys gets lucky more often than anyone his department has ever dealt with. He gets thrown into bad situations and he comes up with good solutions—solutions that work. Now we're dealing with a force, possibly an intelligence, that we can't even identify. I have a feeling the rule book isn't going to do us much good. We'll need onsite improvisation, and the best we can get."

"So far, his only response to this entity resulted in a plane full of dead people."

He took hold of her arm and stopped her.

"That's not fair. Alex's plan worked. The passengers were already too badly damaged to survive."

She pulled her arm free and continued walking.

"He hasn't criticized your habitat. Even when the failure of a component could have cost him his life."

This time she stopped on her own and glared at him, eyes filled with blue-green fire.

"The problem was a torque setting on the clamps. The specifications were correct; the implementation was at fault. It's been fixed now, but I don't know if it was shoddy installation work by your Navy guys, or another deliberate attempt to block this mission."

"Another .... You think the comm system was sabotaged? But it was easy to fix."

"Smashing components would be too obvious. Better to have a failure that might go unnoticed until it's too late. Or make the system look unreliable to force us to scrub the use of the hab altogether."

Gary crossed his arms. Lee-Anna Cavallo was even smarter than he'd expected. She was right—two such incidents were too many, even for a shakedown dive. He'd reached the same conclusion the day before, but hoped that no one else would. He still couldn't think of a motive for anyone to delay the mission, but it wouldn't do to allow paranoia to gain a foothold within the hab crew.

"I think you're taking this personally. And you seem to suspect Elle even though she was the one who called our attention to the problem."

Lee-Anna leaned back against the railing, her hair caught by the breeze. She looked like the cover of a sailing magazine but was oblivious to the fact.

"Elle had both access and training. She plays all innocent and out of her element, but the woman is sharper than she seems. I have a hard time trusting somebody who puts on an act like that."

Gary sighed. "Elle has … issues that you don't need to know about. But her 'act' is a defense mechanism, not anything sinister. And she's tough. Cut her some slack. You might find she'll be the one you can count on the most down there."

Lee-Anna held his eyes for a few more seconds then swept onward toward the bow.

It was Matheus who found Ranger. The sensory mesh Matheus wore could be attuned to acoustic signatures—he tracked the dog's whimpering. But effecting a rescue was a challenge of another kind. Ranger had managed to make his way into the cargo area on the bottom deck where dry stores were kept, presumably while chasing a rat, and had fallen between two large bins about five feet tall. The bins were too large to move without a forklift. As Gary and Lee-Anna arrived, Alex had just slid headfirst over the edge of one bin into the gap while Bheru, spreadeagled on the bin lid, held his legs. Elle and Matheus held Bheru's feet for good measure.

Phillip came upon the tableau and gave a look of surprise. He reached into his pocket and tossed something that rattled over the lid and into the crack.

"It's OK, Ranger. We're coming to get you. Take it easy." He wasn't frantic, but the relief in his voice was obvious.

From the scrabbling sounds it was clear that the dog wasn't sure he wanted to be grabbed, but Alex finally grunted, "Lift me up" and was pulled into the open with the big golden mutt in his arms. Ranger scrambled to his feet and dashed to Phillip as soon as his claws could get purchase on the smooth metal deck. His rescuers slid off the bin and came to check on him.

"He looks all right," Phillip said. "Just scared. Thanks, everyone, for your help." He had trouble getting the words out as Ranger enthusiastically licked his face, causing laughter all around. "Are you OK, Alex?"

"Maybe a bruise or two on my legs." He turned to Bheru. "You don't know the strength in those hands of yours."

"Still getting used to them, sorry."

"We thought Bheru might be able to shift one of the bins," Elle said.

"But it doesn't work that way." The biologist flashed a smile. "One of my rehabilitation therapists once introduced me to a really old television show about a bionic man. Have any of you seen the one I mean? He could lift cars with his prosthetic arm, and I always thought, 'That's ridiculous. The trunk of his body is still human—it couldn't stand the strain.' Little did I know that one day I would face the same constraints."

"I'm grateful to all of you," Phillip said. Lowering his voice, he added, "If anybody wants to celebrate with something more potent in their breakfast coffee, drop by my quarters. I keep a little something hidden away for celebration. Right after I get this guy settled down with a walk along the deck."

As the group dispersed, Gary found himself beside Matheus.

"I didn't know your mesh could detect sounds, too."

"Oh yes, even very faint ones. Heartbeats sometimes. Like when our Ms. Travis looks at you."

Gary snapped his head around to see the man's conspiratorial smile, then replied with a frown.

"Yeah, that's a potential problem. Not just because of the command situation, but I'm also engaged to be married. My fiancée's a very special woman—way out of my league—and there's no way I want to mess things up. Especially since her father is Admiral Norwood Sinclair, Commander in Chief of the US Pacific Fleet, who probably has me watched like a hawk." He laughed awkwardly. "So, temptation of a sexual nature is something I'd prefer to do without."

"Don't complain too much. I only wish women's hearts beat quicker at the sight of me. There was such a time, but I fear it has passed."

The breeze had picked up on deck and waves were crashing against the hull of the ship. Gary paused and looked around to see that they were alone. Matheus might have been doing the same, but his head didn't have to move.

"So, if you can hear heartbeats, you might have a pretty good built-in lie detector."

"True. Sometimes. Along with other observations based on long experience. I know, for instance, that you don't have a concussion."

Gary straightened and gave the man a hard look.

"I'd appreciate it if you would keep that to yourself."

"Certainly. I'm sure you have your reasons. Other than that, I find our team members are mostly truthful, or have not yet had strong enough reasons to lie. My ability does not help much with our friend Phillip, however. He is much too accustomed to concealing the truth."

"Of that, I have no doubt."

23

March 27, 2042

Alex checked the time.

10:45 am.

The habitat had been scheduled to submerge at 10:30.

He leaned against the yellow submersible, the *Darwin*, and looked around its hangar. The hangar walls were undecorated steel, but racks of various kinds of equipment were everywhere: hoses, extendable boat-hooks, padded grappling-hooks, and lots of coils of rope, as well as assorted sizes of metal tanks with labels he couldn't read at that distance. Some would be for breathing gases; others could be for cutting-torches. One shallow alcove appeared to contain a welding unit of some kind.

There was lots of gear, but none of it should be needed with the submersible not being used. No one had reason to come to the hangar.

But Elle found him there five minutes later.

There was no valid excuse for him to be there. He didn't even try.

"Did you find me with your telepathic powers?"

"I really don't know. I just had a feeling you'd be here. You want to talk about it?"

"Not especially." He only meant to glance at her, but her eyes held him. They were beautifully liquid. Sincere. Worried about him. He pushed away from the submersible and slowly began to pace. "It's not that I'm afraid of going back down in the habitat." That was mostly true—it wasn't his main fear.

"I believe you."

"I just ... I don't want to be *responsible*. I've made decisions before—lots of times—life and death decisions that often did cost lives. Sometimes enemies, sometimes our own soldiers. Sometimes ... innocent civilians. I ... went to the funeral of one of the special-ops guys we sent into a firefight and felt as if every mourner there knew it was my fault." He swallowed hard and waited until his throat opened up again. "It's one thing to risk your own life, but another to choose whether someone else lives or dies. I don't want to *do* that again. I swore to myself that I wouldn't."

"I understand that. I don't think I could do it either. But Gary will still ultimately make those kinds of decisions. If we fail, the government will come up with some other approach. It's not all on us. You certainly can't blame yourself for the airliner passengers who were killed, and you can't be to blame if it happens again."

"Do you think I haven't told myself the same thing? But it's a lie. If your job is to protect people from harm and they still get killed, you failed them. It's that simple. I can't do it anymore."

She stepped close. Her eyes were dark wells of feeling. He looked instead at her soft hair and her slender arms. Gentle. Vulnerable.

"Is it the strangers in airplanes that you're worried about? Or the rest of us—your new friends?"

His only response was a shrug.

"OK, I get that. But we have to do the job anyway, with or without you. With you, we stand a better chance of succeeding, and a better chance of not getting hurt. We all might have been killed if you hadn't thought of a way to reattach the flotation bag."

She put her hand on his arm, and he could tell it wasn't easy for her.

"I *am* scared of going back down. I'm scared of the water; and of that thing that keeps getting into my head. It would really help to know I've got the best people looking out for me."

"Gary should be the one going."

"Even if he went, Gary would want you down there beside him. He's an experienced commander, though he doesn't talk about it, and he's a good judge of people. He has full confidence in you, that much I can tell."

Alex thought about that. In his experience, members of the military looked down on people like him as outsiders, not part of the fraternity. Especially him, because as a congressman's son, they saw him as privileged—someone who'd achieved status through connections rather than merit. Was Gary really any different? But then, he had put Alex in charge.

Elle sounded sympathetic, but what did she really think of Alex?

"How about proving something else?" he asked. "During our helicopter searches and your submersible dive, you were upset. Frightened. But I was sure you were also disappointed when you came back, instead of relieved. Was I wrong?"

"No."

"Why?"

She hesitated for a long time, and he was just about to send her away when she said softly, "I wanted that thing to overload the psychic part of my brain. Cauterize it. Burn it out so I could never read minds again. I still want that."

"To just be normal."

She nodded. Her face looked incapable of telling a lie. Her hand was still on his arm, and he found he liked it there. He put his own hand on top.

"Let's go," he said.

The crossed arms and rigid faces of the others said it all. No one else was missing—they must have known Elle could find him.

"He fell asleep in the computer lab," Elle said with a big smile. "Reading some report about tidal forces or something." Apparently, she could lie on someone else's behalf.

"Sorry about that." He didn't trust himself to say anything more. No one else spoke, but as they turned toward the suspended habitat Gary's brief grip on his shoulder was a little warmer than camaraderie alone would require.

# # #

Descent was incredibly slow, taking even longer than the submersible's dive to the same depth. Although Lee-Anna had full confidence in her creation, Phillip and Gary wanted to give the habitat lots of time to adjust on its downward path. For every thirty-three feet of additional depth, the force of water on the hull increased by one atmosphere of pressure, one atmosphere equaling the weight of the Earth's ocean of air as it pressed down on a person standing at sea level: 14.7 pounds per square inch. The site picked for the habitat was nearly 12,500 feet deep, which meant the structure would need to withstand a force of nearly 380 atmospheres, or almost three tons per square inch. Its egg shape was designed to use that force to push the nano-modules more tightly together to provide even greater strength.

But it had never been tested at anything close to that depth.

The crew should have been used to the skittering noises as nims shifted, but it was impossible to forget that they were traveling sixty times deeper than before. Although the hab could have descended on its own, the cable attached to it provided greater control. It was a cable of woven nanofibers, much slimmer but also much stronger than an equivalent cable made of steel. A repetitive *thrum* traveled all the way down the tether from the surface. Habitat crew members gravitated to the lounge deck where conversation helped them forget about the sounds, and the occasional lateral motion as the habitat passed through ocean layers of different density or crossed weak underwater currents.

Alex couldn't help looking over Lee-Anna's shoulder at the readouts.

"Looks like the stress on the cable clamp is staying steady."

"Don't worry, I checked it myself manually. In fact, I took a little swim over the whole habitat this morning. Looked over the replacement tanks for the ones we jettisoned the other day." She dropped her voice and kept her face expressionless. "I even removed Mr. Watanabe's little gift package."

"What do you mean?" Alex matched her lowered volume and checked to make sure the others weren't paying them any attention.

"The explosive he arranged to have planted on the hab. Are you saying you didn't know about it?"

"*What?*"

"On the hull, just behind our central electronics hub on Deck One. If it blew, it would take out our escape systems and distress beacons before flooding the place. I thought we were better off without it."

"You're serious. How did you know what it was? And how do you know Phillip had it put there? God, why would he *do* that?"

Tight lines at her mouth revealed that she wasn't as composed as she pretended.

"It wasn't labelled, but I've seen underwater demolition packs before. A guy I dated a couple of times was into stuff like that and loved to show off. As for who put it there and why, do you think some terrorist could have sneaked up on us in the middle of the Pacific Ocean? Or maybe one of *Orion*'s dive crew has a locker big enough to hide fifty pounds of explosives? Most likely, Phillip Watanabe's superiors want to be able to keep a lid on what happens here if things go sideways."

"By killing all of us?"

Lee-Anna swept her long hair behind an ear. "Geez, Alex. I thought you'd been playing with the big boys for a while. This shouldn't be a surprise to you."

He thought about how long he'd known Phillip. They'd worked together on at least half a dozen missions, but it wasn't as if they were friends. The man was secretive, of course, but had no qualms about prying into the secrets of others. He could be cold. Yet it was hard to believe he'd deliberately plan Alex's death.

On second thought, no it wasn't. The two of them had probably ended many innocent lives. Alex lost sleep over them. But he'd never seen signs that Phillip did.

24

March 27, 2042

Elle had just finished giving Gary a progress report when Matheus came up the ladder into the top deck.

"Do you need me?" she asked.

His face came alight. "My dear, what a wonderful question for a beautiful woman to ask a man of my age. Do I need you? There can be only one response to that."

Her face turned warm. "You know I didn't mean that. Although I'm sure you've swept many women off their feet."

"Again, you are kind and gracious. Yes, I suppose it would be false modesty to deny it. But I know that you don't feel that way yet."

"How do you know? And why did you call me beautiful? Can you see my face in that much detail?"

"Yes, this sensor mesh of mine is quite remarkable. The information it gathers about my surroundings is expressed to me through my other senses. My brain has learned to interpret certain sonic and tactile inputs as a visual image, while sonar measures the distance to objects but feels like varying pressure on my skin. Infrared radiation feels like heat and shows red in my vision. Electromagnetic fields cause a tingling sensation when I'm near them. My hearing is enhanced over a much greater frequency range than humans, which is how I found Mr. Watanabe's dog. And, sadly, I can also tell that your heart does not race because of my nearness, nor your skin flush—except your face, from my comment having embarrassed you, perhaps?"

She blushed again, but the meaning of his words made her sit up straight.

"You can tell all that? Wow, you could be a human ..."

"Lie detector? Yes, Mr. Cross said the same thing a short while ago. So, you see, when you eventually fall in love with me, it will be no use trying to hide it."

This time she laughed, but touched his arm gently to remove any insult. He laughed too.

"I'd better not try to lie then," she said. "I guess it would be best if I don't tell you anything at all."

"Oh, there's no need to go that far. After all, it may surprise you to know that I am an ordained member of the clergy. Not the Catholic priesthood—I am not saintly enough for them—but the Methodist church. It was a natural outcome of my theological studies at one point. So, I'm officially recognized as a source of spiritual guidance, should you wish to ... confess, for instance. About a secret love, or anything else." He smiled wickedly.

The frown in her eyebrows couldn't override her wide smile. "I'm not Methodist, but I happen to know they don't do confession in a little booth with a priest like Catholics do. Besides, what makes you think I have anything to confess?"

"Everyone has things to confess."

"But I thought you were a psychologist. In fact, I was afraid you were brought on board to keep an eye on me."

His expression became more earnest. "I'm more sociologist than psychologist, though I've studied both. My official task is to provide some analysis of this entity's thought processes in the context of its behavior toward others. But if I were also to give regular reports about how our team is getting along, I'm sure Mr. Cross would be glad to have them."

"A clever answer. And after that you expect me to tell you anything?"

"Why not? We can trade—confession for confession."

"Don't you know that if you want a girl to spill secrets you've got to buy her a hot chocolate?"

He did. And she did. But first she closed the hatch to the deck below.

She confessed to him about how her mother had started her own daycare center, professing that it was her duty to humankind after doing such a wonderful job with Elle and her brother Tanner, who'd spent even more of his life in psychiatrist's offices than Elle had.

Matheus confessed to her that he'd come along on the mission due to the sin of Pride, because young upstarts in his field were hogging all the attention, and he needed a prestigious breakthrough to regain the spotlight. But he was beginning to fear that the US government would throw a cloak of secrecy over the whole mission. He still couldn't understand why his seminal research paper about commonality among world religions and the psychological needs they serve had been so vehemently rejected by the Catholic church in Brazil. He'd felt like an exile ever since, and compensated with an unwise consumption of the Brazilian sugarcane liquor *cachaça*, as if his taste buds could transport him back to his youth.

She remembered the way she had decorated her childhood bedroom with photos of her namesake, because she'd wanted to be blonde and beautiful like the actress Elle Travis. And now she hoped that her chance to do something authentically important would cure her of her love of stupid reality-TV.

In return, he told about his restless and reckless wandering as a child that led to a night trapped in a cave full of snakes and poisonous spiders. He'd been spooked by slithering things ever since.

Elle admitted that she'd come close to being married once, briefly, in Korea, where she spent two years teaching English, and had never told her family about the engagement. She'd gone a little wild during that time, willingly seduced by the attentions of men as the exotic Black girl among them, and by the alcohol they gladly provided. The most ludicrous part was that when she'd returned to Canada to save herself from her burgeoning addictions, she found that her parents showed her a new respect because she had finally done something on her own. Though her independence had only lasted until her money ran out and she'd had to move back in with them for a few months before landing a job at the UN.

"You pass the test," Matheus said with a broad smile.

"The test?"

"Not a single lie in any of those stories. Did confession ease your soul?"

"Not especially. I'll probably just kick myself tomorrow for blabbing everything. I'm not used to revealing so much about myself."

"I'm sure that's true. You are much more accustomed to knowing the intimate secrets of others, though perhaps unwillingly."

"I don't know what you mean."

"Hah! The first lie!"

25

March 27, 2042

A sudden sideways shift of the habitat threw Alex off balance. Until then, the ride to the bottom of the ocean had been smooth.

"We're just passing the level of the mountain peaks," Lee-Anna said. "There's a bit of a current streaming off them. I can make adjustments with the water jets just above the hab's base, but I'll wait to see if we drop out of the current first. We should. In the meantime, the flow has pushed us right over the line of black smokers. In a few more minutes, we might be able to see something from the base cameras."

She switched on the camera feed just as a fist of roiling cloud slammed into the habitat and knocked them off their feet—a geyser of heated water spewing from the black smokers below. The base of the giant egg swung out and up, tumbling everyone onto the wall, and then another upward surge pinned them there. The hab began to roll along its axis like a barrel in a circus balancing-act. Small objects slid and bounced. Alex was struck in the face by a shoe. He saw Elle forced into a somersault and slammed against a table. Bheru had a fierce grip on the couch, but Matheus fell into the access shaft and just managed to wrap his arms around a rung of the ladder.

Lee-Anna crawled along the wall, clutching at a shelf and then the computer desk to reach the control panel again. She was just able to slam a palm onto a raised red oval before she was flung across the room. An alarm sounded.

Why? It wasn't as if anyone aboard was unaware of their danger. Then Alex realized that she'd triggered the signal for an emergency retraction of the cable. That should pull the hab upright again and forestall the most serious danger—if the giant hull rolled out of the upsurge and plunged down too quickly, a slack cable could snap as it came under full load again. Or the coupling at the top of the hull might be yanked out like the cork of a bottle.

Alex lay spreadeagled between one of the computer workstations' shelves and the galley cupboards. Over the clatter of pots and dishes inside them, he yelled to Lee-Anna, "Are there water jets that aim downward from the base?"

"Yes, to soften the landing if we were making a free descent."

"Try giving them full thrust—this geyser may not be very wide, and if we can get clear of it ...."

Gritting her teeth, she allowed herself to fly loose again, landing hard, but close enough to Alex that he could grab her outstretched hand. He pulled her to him, and she climbed down his body to the computer screen. With one arm wrapped around his leg, she raised the other hand to tap out commands. An agonizing thirty seconds passed while she waited for *Orion* to take up more of the slack cable, then she tapped the screen a final time.

There was a noticeable push from the direction of Deck One.

The hab began to bounce as it rolled—the upthrust of water from below wasn't even. Matheus' legs shook loose of the access shaft and his feet swung toward Bheru, who ducked his head just in time. Alex tried to imagine what the psychologist was feeling, dangling straight out from the ladder, his eyes not able to see what was going on. Would his sensory mesh be able to sort out such confusion?

Elle was in a bad way too. Her spine had taken a vicious blow from the table edge. Barely conscious, she was thrown again. Her head made a thump as she landed flat on her back across another section of wall. Bheru reached toward her, but she was too far away. Alex tasted his last meal threatening to come back up. He looked down at Lee-Anna, who'd slid farther down with the last jounce and seemed to have a good grip on the computer console.

"Can you hang on there? Elle's in trouble."

"I'm OK. Go!"

He had to judge the hab's roll perfectly. Pushing off, he dropped through the air to the ceiling just above Elle, rolled to soften the impact, and ended up beside her. Before another bounce could pluck him away, he scrambled on top of her and braced his legs between the back of the couch and the underside of the deck above. Nearly doing the splits, his thigh muscles protested immediately. He pushed harder, hands scrabbling blindly to find a grip. Most of the hab's walls featured narrow storage shelves wherever they were unlikely to be struck by heads. His right hand found a shelf edge and gripped hard while the fingers of his left clawed into the couch fabric. He could feel Elle's breath on his neck and the pounding of her heart. She moaned, and her arms shifted but didn't go far.

The hab made another lurch upward and rolled faster. For long seconds Alex took all of Elle's weight and his spread legs shook with the strain. He was grateful for the solid latches on the cupboards and restraining bars on the shelves—without them, the air would have been full of projectiles.

His right foot slid a few inches on the ceiling, and he groaned. Soon he would have to take a chance: let go of his handholds, wrap his arms around Elle, and hope the impact would be on him when they landed. Even better if they could hit something soft.

As suddenly as it had begun, the turbulence stopped; and the hab began to right itself as it dropped. Alex's stomach clenched, but the fall lasted no more than a few seconds. The cable took the weight again, and held, turning the giant hull into a yo-yo that danced in slow motion at the end of its string.

Gravity pried him loose. He clutched Elle tightly, kicked with his right foot, and landed on his back on Bheru's prosthetic legs. The impact forced a grunt from all three. The hard shoes dug into his ribs, but the biologist pulled them free as quickly as he could and swung around to see what he could do to help. Alex lay gasping, pain in every muscle and joint.

"I've got to get up to the communications deck to tell *Orion* to stand by," Lee-Anna panted. "Is Elle okay?"

"We're not sure," Bheru said. "I'll see what I can find out."

Lee-Anna nodded with a look of concern, then hauled herself stiffly up the ladder. Matheus was already at the hab computer asking it for information about impact injuries. Alex couldn't quite make out its reply. Blood still pounded in his ears.

Elle gave a moan and stirred.

"Maybe you should help me lift her off me," he said to Bheru.

"Not yet, I think. She might have a head or spine injury. I don't want to move her any more than we must until I can be confident we won't do more damage."

With a louder moan, Elle tried to raise her head and managed to bring it up onto Alex's shoulder, facing him.

"Oh, fuck! That hurts!" For a few seconds she just concentrated on breathing, but gradually lifted her head again, her hair in Alex's face. As her eyes focused, her mouth opened wide.

"Jesus, Alex! What the hell are you doing?" She tried to climb off him, but Bheru's hands on her shoulders kept her from going anywhere. "What the fuck?"

"Please, Ms. Travis," Bheru said in his most soothing voice. "You've been hurt. As a doctor, I'm asking you to lie still until we can tell how badly."

"I'm not gonna lie on ..."

"Alex was only helping you. You were being thrown around by the motions of the habitat and he used his own body to protect you. Now please just lie still and answer some questions for me."

She didn't move for a few seconds, but then her body arched and shivered; and she stopped pushing with her arms. With her mouth beside Alex's ear, she harshly whispered, "You dare enjoy this and you'll be sorry."

He couldn't hold back a laugh, despite the stab of pain it caused in his back and head. She gave a growl.

Bheru asked her dozens of questions about what she was feeling and asked her to carefully move each part of her body. Everything seemed to be working; and other than a bad headache, she felt no sharp pains or tingling. Alex couldn't say the same—his left arm had fallen asleep and his neck and back were on fire—but he lay patiently, waiting for Bheru to be done.

Matheus joined them by the couch.

"Are her eyes equal and reactive?"

"Yes," Bheru said, "and her pulse is returning to normal. I'll check her blood pressure—I think there's a cuff in the medical kit."

"I'll get it."

"It's too bad your sensor mesh can't do a CT scan or an MRI."

"No, but if there was bleeding on her brain or spine, I think it would show in infrared and I don't see anything like that. A section of her back is extra warm but that's likely just a bad bruise. Do you feel any sharp pains in your back or neck, Ms. Travis?"

"Not sharp. My whole body aches like hell, though. I'm not looking forward to going anywhere."

"It's probably best if you don't then, for a little while. You might go into shock so the less strain and pain, the better. Are you all right, Mr. Rhys?"

"I'm fine," he lied. "I don't think anything's broken. Elle can ... stay still for a little longer."

"You did enjoy this, didn't you?" she breathed.

"Only once the hab stopped throwing us around the room. Just relax, and go when you need to."

To his surprise she did relax, so he moved his arms a fraction to hold her more securely. After a time, he feared she might be falling asleep. He told Bheru.

"Her breathing sounds natural, but you're right, we should keep her awake for a few hours, just in case." The man gently roused her, lifted her up while doing his best to keep her neck stable, and began to walk her around the room. Alex sat up but went no further while he did a mental inventory of his own battered body.

26

March 27, 2042

Twenty minutes later Lee-Anna came down the ladder looking puzzled.

She'd briefed Gary and Phillip. Though they agreed that a large geyser must have erupted from the geothermal vents, they couldn't agree on what to do about it.

"Phillip ordered us to surface, and I heard him start to give the order to the winch crew, but then the signal cut out. A minute later Gary came back on to tell us to stand by. I don't know what to think. If Elle has suffered a concussion ...."

"She did bump her head and her spine," Bheru said, giving Elle's shoulder a squeeze as they stopped walking, "but I think it was the combination that stunned her. I don't think she actually lost consciousness, and she's not showing any signs of cognitive impairment now. Of course, that doesn't necessarily rule out concussion; but her vital signs are all normal: she's fully aware and alert, and there are no signs of shock, either. How do you feel, Ms. Travis?"

"I feel that if you're going to be my doctor, you have to start calling me Elle. Other than that, I suspect you all did a dance on my back while I was out; but I'll forgive you if you make me a nice cup of hot chocolate."

"Done." Bheru went to the galley cupboards while Elle moved to the couch, and, after a little hesitation, sat beside Alex.

"I'm going to recommend to Phillip and Gary that we bring the hab back up to have Elle checked out by *Orion's* medical staff," Alex said, looking straight ahead.

"What? No, I'm fine."

"We don't know that, and a habitat under two miles of ocean is no place for someone who could have a spine or head injury."

"No way! We've already had a serious delay; and the longer we take, the more chance that innocent people could be hurt or killed."

"I'm with Elle," said Lee-Anna. "If this is some kind of chauvinistic thing because she's a woman, Alex ...."

He gave her a hard look. "Don't ignore facts just because you want more time to test out your toy."

"You son of a bitch! You just want to get your rabbity ass back to safety on the ship!"

"Please, everyone. There's no need to make accusations. We're all colleagues here." Matheus had raised his hands as well as his voice, but wasn't facing anyone in particular. "Alex, you've been put in charge, and no one is questioning your authority; but at least tell us your primary concern."

"Elle's life could be in danger."

"Unless I'm badly mistaken, all our lives are in danger. We agreed to take that risk for the sake of others. Do you have reason to believe that her potential injuries now outweigh those considerations? Or do you think she has become a liability to the mission?"

"No," Alex said. "I don't know. But ...."

"But *nothing*—I'm staying!" Elle snapped. "If it had happened to you, there's no way you would bail out. And I won't either. Besides, you can't do the mission without me."

Alex started to say that it would only be a delay while she got checked over, but that wasn't true, and he knew it. If there was a possibility she'd suffered a concussion, they'd keep her on *Orion*. That was what had kept Gary behind, wasn't it? And Elle wasn't wrong. Her loss to the mission would be a major handicap. Might not only make it riskier for the others, but possibly even make continuing pointless.

The prevailing opinion was clearly against him, so he just folded his arms over his chest and stared at the floor. Gary would still have the final say.

Bheru resumed his rummaging in the cupboard for the hot-chocolate fixings. "There doesn't appear to be much damage in here. A testament to your design as well as your packing skills, Lee-Anna."

"Yeah, there wasn't much room for anything to move around."

Two containers, one of jam, the other of olives, had split open. Lee-Anna found small replacement tubs for the contents. The dishes they used for meals were all plastic, and intact; so she went to check on the lab equipment, as if glad of an excuse to leave the room.

Alex cleared his throat. "You must have had a hard time through all that, Dr. Ventura."

"After what we've been through, I think we're done with formalities. Matheus, please. Yes, my sensors have marvelous capabilities, but I had difficulty keeping oriented during all the motion. I was fortunate to land on the ladder and be able to hang on."

"It wasn't something we planned for."

"No, and the timing was quite a coincidence, don't you think?"

Bheru looked up from stirring Elle's chocolate. "You think the geyser wasn't an accident? That's a bit of a stretch, isn't it?"

"Is it? We really have no idea what's down there—how big it is; how powerful it is. How friendly, or how malevolent. It doesn't want us here, does it Elle?"

She shivered. "No. It doesn't."

"It—or *they*, if you believe it is an alien craft or outpost—have caused death and injury, plus a great deal of fear. Nothing positive or welcoming. We descend to the sea floor despite all that, and suddenly there is a force violently pushing us away, back toward the surface."

"A natural force."

"Natural in form, Bheru, but in cause? How can we know that?"

There was a thoughtful silence. Alex would have loved to refute Matheus' implication, but he couldn't; though he was still convinced that alien beings would not deliberately be destructive. Where would a man of religion like Matheus stand on that subject?

"I have to admit Dr. ... uh, Matheus, that I've wondered about your joining this mission when your main interest seems to be in theology?"

"You don't think theology has room for aliens from other worlds, Alex? You'd be surprised. At least, in my theology. I am, perhaps, not considered orthodox by the Catholics who raised me. My God is not necessarily some supernatural being separate from the world we know. Although I believe the universe was created according to design, I don't rule out that it could have been created by beings who were once much like we are, but perhaps in a different universe, or in an earlier manifestation of this one."

"You subscribe to an anthropic cosmological point of view?" Bheru handed a mug to Elle who sipped on it gratefully. Alex accepted his offer of a drink, Matheus declined, and Bheru fixed one for himself. Intellectual discussion was an obvious reaction to their brush with danger, but it was a healthy one.

"It's undeniable that the forces of the universe, its physical laws, as well as the position and other qualities of the Earth, Sun, Moon, and stars are all exactly as they must be to produce and sustain life. Any variation at all, and there would be no life as we know it, nor any other forms we can imagine. The odds of that happening by accident are nearly beyond calculation; and since I don't feel any need to deny the existence of God, I will save myself the effort." The man's smile was as charming as ever. It was clear that he enjoyed such debates.

"There have been a number of such calculations; and the odds are, as you say, astronomical in the truest sense of the word. Though not impossible. But rather than argue the existence of God, I simply wonder, along with Alex, what brought you here when you seem convinced that the being we face is hostile."

"That was not established when I agreed to come. The deaths could have been an accident. Now?" He stroked his short beard. "I don't assume that we face outright hostility in the sense of meaning us harm. But perhaps we are going against some larger plan, and some force is trying to keep us from interfering. To be honest, I believe that what we've encountered may be superior beings; and any lifeform at that level must be closer to a supreme being. I have a powerful urge to communicate with something more advanced than we are, and with a greater knowledge of the cosmos."

"That's assuming they want to communicate with us," Alex said. "They might be malevolent, or just indifferent, or even paternalistic and determined to make sure there's no interference in our development, even from them. Or they could be just a little beyond us in their technology, didn't plan to be discovered and want to get away without any more contact."

"Well said. Except you don't believe it." Matheus' blind eyes twinkled.

Alex laughed. "No, you're right. I'm like you. I'm hoping it's representatives from an advanced species, and they'll help us pull the human race out of the mess we're in. Give us their knowledge, and especially their wisdom, so we don't blow ourselves up or poison the planet so badly that it kills us."

Matheus softly intoned, *"This is the way the world ends. Not with a bang but a whimper."* To Alex's look of surprise, he replied, "I think T.S. Elliot knew that the Great War was not the end of humankind's destructiveness."

"Yeah. No bang required," Alex answered with a rueful shake of his head.

"You don't have a very high opinion of human beings," Elle declared. Alex didn't feel a need to answer.

"Both of you are extreme optimists with regard to *alien* beings, however." Bheru looked from Alex to Matheus. "I have studied thousands of species, products of millions of years of evolution. Life has adapted to every environmental niche on this planet, with a mind-boggling variety of specialized abilities that, in context, make one species superior to another, but only within a narrow range of criteria. No one species, including our own, is superior to any other in every way. Our drive is just to survive and reproduce. If that happens, we are successful." His lips pulled into a small smile and his eyes narrowed. "Of course, beyond survival, there is the question of intelligence. But, you know, Alex, there's no body of evidence that equates intelligence with benevolence. There are many species that we would consider to have some level of intelligence. I can even name instances in which members of one species seem to have used that intelligence to be generous in some form to individuals of another. *But* I can think of no creatures that are altruistic to an entire species not their own."

"Humans care about animals," Elle interrupted.

"On the whole, our occasional beneficence toward them is far outweighed by our exploitation and outright callousness. But my point is that we have no reason to expect an advanced alien race to want to help us reach their level of development. Indeed, they would have many reasons not to, from the competition for livable space and resources, to the possibility of our being a threat to their safety. We're very warlike creatures, after all."

"Maybe they went through similar self-destructive phases and feel it's their duty to help other intelligent races survive them."

"Duty is a very human concept," Bheru said wryly.

Alex cocked an ear, trying to locate the source of a dry rattle, then realized it was prosthetic fingers drumming on prosthetic legs, a sound he would come to associate with irritation on the part of his learned companion.

"Well, I don't think we're doing our duty just hanging here in the water," Lee-Anna said as she returned from the deck below. "Any of that hot chocolate left?"

"How'd the lab equipment survive the shocks?" Alex felt the need to stand and stretch. He walked to her side.

"In good shape. Fortunately, we didn't have any experiments or tests underway yet." She looked at Matheus. "Your aliens are going to have to try harder than that to put us out of commission."

"At least you agree not only that the eruption of a geyser just at the moment of our arrival is an unlikely coincidence, but also that it argues for the existence of powerful technology rather than it being a natural event."

"No, I don't. I don't see how you figure aliens could trigger something like that. Black smokers are formed when seawater seeps through cracks in the ocean floor, or sometimes water from deeper magma rises up. Water meets very hot rocks, and pressure from that expansion forces it through any opening it can find."

"Much the same way a geyser works."

"Sure, but they follow a cycle of their own—there's no controlling it."

"Mineral deposits in the water build up over time and build pipe-like formations. Some holes become smaller and even close over. It's not hard to imagine pressure building up in such a spot and being released suddenly through some action, natural or artificial."

"They knocked the top off a smoker cone?"

"Or several at once. Or something increased the amount of water in the pressure chamber. Any number of things could have been responsible, and done on purpose."

Lee-Anna crossed her arms. Alex quickly put a hand under her mug before her chocolate could spill. She paid no attention, her glare focused on Matheus.

"I suppose that means you agree with Phillip that we should call this off and return to the surface?"

"Not at all."

They looked at him in surprise, and he laughed.

"If there is a higher intelligence responsible and they feel compelled to discourage our efforts to find them, what better way to prove our worth than to refuse to be discouraged? Personally, I never like taking *No* for an answer. And I like being patronized least of all. If Phillip orders us to the surface, I may just steal a suit and stay behind."

His smirk said he wasn't serious, but his crossed arms and deeply knit eyebrows said otherwise.

Bheru leaned back against the counter with a scowl on his face. "If your commitment to this mission depends on plans to publish a landmark research paper, don't get your hopes up. Phillip as much as told me that the American government is going to keep a tight lid on this story. Which is outrageous! To invite people such as you and me to witness the event of a lifetime and then to forbid us to tell our peers ....”

“I have come to the same unfortunate conclusion,” Matheus commiserated.

A chime sounded from the communications deck above.

“Guess we might find out about our orders right now.” Lee-Anna climbed toward Deck Four. Alex followed her.

It was Gary on the comm. He told them that the habitat would resume its descent when they were ready, but with a landing site a little farther from the smokers than originally planned.

“Did you go over Phillip’s head?” Lee-Anna asked.

“Let’s just say my people overruled his people for now because it’s a Navy ship. That might not last, though; so you folks shouldn’t waste time once you get settled.” The signal cut for a few moments, then Gary said, “Phillip is here now, and he’d like to speak to Alex. Alone, please.”

Lee-Anna wasn’t happy, but she went back down to the galley. Alex closed the bulkhead behind her, then returned to the comm station.

“There’s something you should know,” Phillip said. “There’s an explosive device attached to the habitat. In the event this alien, or whatever it is, were to infiltrate the hab or get control of it, we can’t let it get to the surface.”

“No, there isn’t.”

“What do you mean?”

“Lee-Anna found it and ditched it just before we submerged.”

“Shit. Never underestimate that woman. Well, then you’re just going to have to rig something. Figure out a fail-safe so if your team loses the hab, it stays on the bottom of the ocean forever. I’m sorry, that sounds cold. But if the survival of the whole human race is at stake ....”

"I know. OK, I'll think of something." He ended the call, cursing under his breath.

Had the operative always intended to tell Alex about the explosive? Or had he somehow discovered that it was no longer attached? The geyser might have knocked it off, but Phillip would assume human intervention and figure Lee-Anna would have told Alex about it. In that case, he'd put on a good act.

It was a bitch, not knowing who to trust.

The worst part was, Phillip was right. There had to be some way to ensure that whatever they encountered couldn't launch a deadly global infection via their crew, co-opt their nanotechnology for weaponry, or find some other unforeseeable means to turn the habitat and its inhabitants into a threat against humankind.

But whatever he devised would also be a death sentence for this crew, with Alex as executioner.

## 27

March 27, 2042

The geyser changed things.

Gary ordered the crew to probe the ocean floor with sonar before landing.

Bheru strongly objected that powerful sonar pulses could damage the hearing of nearby whales. Beaked whales like the ones that had visited the habitat only days earlier often dived to those depths. He was overruled.

"The geyser seems like strong evidence that a powerful technology is involved," Gary said over the comm. "If it is a spaceship buried under the silt, I'd rather you know about it before you land on it."

Lee-Anna sent the agreed three sonar pulses. The returns showed nothing more than flat expanses of silt with the occasional outcropping of rock and the jagged line of smoker vents they already knew about, although a change in the elevation of the vent ridge along its northern half caught their interest. A very large chunk of rock had disappeared, either the cause or the result of the geyser.

"This is rather like poking a sleeping giant, isn't it?" asked Matheus.

"And what was the geyser? A sneeze?" Lee-Anna gave a half-smile. "We're going to poke it harder once we get down there. One of the first orders of business will be to go outside and place some sounders in the silt—see if we can't penetrate a lot deeper into the ground."

"Seismic charges?"

"No, these are big cartridges that use a compressed-air mechanism to make a hell of a thump, but there's no explosion."

Matheus muttered, "Let's hope whoever's under there gives us a chance to explain the difference before they shoot back."

"It's not sleeping," Elle said softly. "The giant." She could feel the presence at the edge of her mind, a pervasive puzzlement that required effort to distinguish from her own thoughts, it had been there for so long. She had felt an increase in its strength just before and after the geyser eruption, but it had eased since then, as if the mysterious entity's full interest could only be held for so long.

"Pull up your top."

"Excuse me?"

She turned to see Alex with a tube of medicinal cream in one hand and a blob of the contents in the other.

"The back of your shirt. I want to make sure your abrasions don't get infected. I've seen it happen before, especially in a humid environment like this one."

She obliged and felt him rub the cream into the scratches on her lower back. Beneath the scratches was a large bruise, and she winced a few times, but the coolness of the medicine was soothing. The touch of his hands wasn't bad either, really. Surprisingly gentle, for a guy.

"Sonar is negative," Lee-Anna said into the comm. "Do we have a go to descend to the bottom?"

"I'll give the word to the winch crew," Gary said. "As agreed, you'll use the hab's water jets to keep well clear of the smoker zone, right?"

"The non-smoking section it is."

Within a minute they heard a hum from above and felt the habitat drop slowly. Elle had a sudden twinge of nervousness, thinking about the possibility of two miles of cable plummeting onto their heads in the event of a break, but she'd been told that the cable was made of super-strong braided nanofibers and weighed only a tiny fraction of what steel cable would.

Everyone had their eyes on display screens fed by three cameras: one of them in the hab's base, the other two on either side of the hull but aimed slightly downward. Powerful lights had been switched on to illuminate the scene for a radius of about a hundred yards. They were intruders in a zone of eternal darkness. In the harsh white glow, the grey-brown plain of the sea bottom finally came into view.

Elle wondered why Lee-Anna didn't use the jets to cushion their landing, but as the base of the habitat touched down the silt boiled up past the highest cameras. If even such a minor impact could stir up silt that badly, the water jets would have produced a cloud hundreds of feet high. And the wispy particles didn't settle quickly, either, like sand or other mineral sediment would have. This was like the densest of blizzards, with snowflakes in no hurry to end their flight.

Lee-Anna quickly signaled the winch crew, but the hull continued to sink for several seconds. Its base would be buried deep in the muck.

"How are we supposed to walk in that?" asked Bheru. "It must be like quicksand."

"Perhaps not even that dense," Matheus said. "We would sink up to our waists with each step."

"Not what I was expecting." Lee-Anna looked at Alex, her face a combination of chagrin and … could it be embarrassment?

"The suits have some buoyancy control, don't they?" he asked.

"There's an air bladder in the back of the headpiece—its volume is controllable. Just the right amount of air keeps you head-up without robbing your feet of traction."

"But a little more would make you lighter, or maybe neutrally buoyant. So, we can keep ourselves from sinking into the muck."

"Sure, but good luck getting anywhere."

"Is there any way you could rig the suits with additional air bladders, maybe at the back of the thighs?"

She looked thoughtful. "Should be. The suit nims are programmed to be form-fitting for streamlining, but I can set them to be a little bulkier at the rear of the thigh. Might take a bit of experimentation to get the right amount. You want us to be able to get neutrally buoyant in a horizontal attitude, right?"

"Exactly. We still have the scuba gear aboard, so we'd just have to adapt the fins to fit over the boots to let us swim. The main issue I see is that the headgear isn't made to allow the head to tip back—it might be impossible to look ahead to see where we're going."

"Not a problem. They don't use transparent visors to see anyway—it's a viewscreen in front of the eyes linked to cameras that offer wraparound vision through simple mental commands. Which is why there's no difficulty for Matheus using the suits—he can link his mesh directly to the cameras."

The engineer went to work on the adaptations while Alex communicated with *Orion*. The cable was given a little more slack, but the habitat didn't sink any farther. Alex used lateral jets at the top of the hab to try to rock it, without effect. Silt covered the attached base and a yard or so of the bottom of the egg, providing enough support to keep the hab vertical. *Orion* slowly reeled in some cable to test if the hull would easily pull free again, and there was little resistance, although a protracted stay would no doubt allow the silt to compact to a greater density.

After the hab was lowered again and its stability checked a second time, Gary ordered the release of the cable. Elle imagined it snaking upward into the inky vastness, their last solid link to the world of air and sunlight. Their own world had shrunk to the confines of a small ball—a meager bubble of light and air keeping out the oppressive night; a tiny oasis of life in a barren universe. She looked at Matheus who had a sheen of sweat on his forehead but gave her a reassuring smile.

Alex and Lee-Anna were now the most experienced divers on board, but Gary didn't want them both outside at the same time, at least not at first. Lee-Anna knew how to plant the depth sounding canisters. She took Bheru with her.

Elle's heart raced in sympathy as she watched the airlock flood and then begin to crack open. Lee-Anna directed the aperture to form slightly higher than normal because of the depth of the silt. The divers moved awkwardly around the lock for a couple of minutes before venturing outside.

"The joints are very stiff." Lee-Anna's voice came crisply through the speakers. "I'll need to make some adjustments, but I have to do them from inside the hab. I think we can manage for now."

They both had buoyancy challenges, too. Bheru tested the silt and did sink in up to his waist, but Lee-Anna pulled him out easily. After that, they tried to achieve a horizontal position; but it required a kick or two every twenty seconds to keep them level, and that tended to lift them from the bottom and stir up the silt.

Resigned to fixing the problem later, Lee-Anna and Bheru re-entered the lock to pull out one of the canisters, three feet long by half that in width. They manhandled it to a clear space a hundred feet from the hab and pushed it endwise as far into the silt as it would go. Their attempts to pack silt around it were a failure. In the glare of the lights, it looked like trying to make a snowman out of moths.

As they returned for the second canister, Lee-Anna asked, "Bheru, how's your air? Is your temperature good? How does the suit feel?"

"I'm fine. The readout says the suit is now replacing the air faster than I'm using it."

"Yes, it breaks down seawater to make it. Are you warm enough?"

"I'm sweating a little, but that's probably excitement. This is wonderful. I feel like an astronaut on the Moon, except there aren't any stars. The suit is a bit rigid, but not chafing badly. I feel terribly awkward, though—please tell me no one's taking pictures."

"Every moment is being captured for posterity and distribution on the internet," Alex said. "Didn't you sign the release form?"

"I would never live it down," Bheru grumbled. "Like when one of my cousins posted a video of me doing the robot dance."

"I have got to look for that one," Elle said with a laugh, glad of a break in the tension. Maybe Bheru had some psychological skills too.

They wrestled the second canister into place on the opposite side of the hab from the first, then returned to the airlock. Although the sound discharge would be very focused, there was no reason to subject the divers to any risk. Once Bheru and Lee-Anna had been freed from their suits, the crew congregated on Deck Two and Lee-Anna prepared to trigger the sounders.

They fired simultaneously, the muffled *crump* loud enough to be felt in human lungs like bass notes at a rock concert. There was a residual ringing immediately afterward, and a rustling sound like sand thrown onto a tin roof that lasted for a few seconds.

Lee-Anna tapped the air of her holographic display to fine-tune the way the returning frequencies of sound were shown.

"Looks like they worked perf..."

Elle cried out in pain, her head gripped in a vise that dug needles into her brain. Needles of ice, lances of fire. Reverberations made her teeth chatter, and her limbs began to shake as if she were in the throes of a seizure. She forced her eyes open and saw the others slowly collapsing to their knees, mouths opening and closing like fish.

Lee-Anna put a hand to her throat and coughed, "Fight back. Eject a seismic charge out the lock."

"No!" Alex croaked. "Can't escalate. Could retaliate more."

Agony played along Elle's nerves like St. Elmo's fire. They were all going to die like the passengers on the jetliner! She longed to escape into unconsciousness, except she might never awaken.

"Whale sounds," she gasped. "Play whale music. Matheus." She slid onto her back and vibrated on the hard decking, tasting blood from where she'd bitten her tongue.

Matheus crawled to the workstation where he'd been browsing that subject less than an hour earlier. Elle heard erratic taps and then, finally, the droning and swooping notes of whale song. He increased the volume until the habitat resonated with it.

Her eyes were closed. She couldn't feel the rest of her body. All was darkness streaked with blue fire that came and went, bringing waves of pain. She was no longer Elle Travis. She was injury. She was anger. She was curiosity like a blade that peeled back skin, and flesh, and bone, and carved warning messages into the soul.

Consciousness receded down a long tunnel. She welcomed oblivion, but it would not come. Not quite.

At long last, the suffering eased. Her body fell limp, and she could sense liquid evaporating on her cheek and chin, but she couldn't move her hands to wipe it away.

There was a feeling of arms sliding beneath her and then she was lifted and carried awkwardly to be set down on something softer—where she willingly succumbed to sleep.

28

March 27, 2042

"She's awake."

Alex's voice. The touch of a hand on her own, but now gone.

Elle struggled to open her eyes. It felt as if her eyelashes were stuck together. Finally, her eyelids fluttered open but quickly squeezed shut to block out the light, though she recognized that she was in her own cot and the lighting had been dimmed.

She swallowed, her tongue thick and dry.

"Do I have drool on my face?" she rasped.

There was relieved laughter. An arm under her shoulders. The lifetime-of-cologne smell of Matheus.

"Have a drink of water," he said as he lifted her upper body.

"Any excuse to put your arm around me."

"And I thought I was being subtle."

She felt a straw against her lips and sucked on it while carefully opening her eyes. Some water spilled down her chin and Lee-Anna dabbed it with a cloth.

"You don't all have to look after me. Haven't you got better things to do? An enemy to … piss off?"

"Hopefully not an enemy, not yet." Alex sat on the bed as the others drifted away down the ladder to the lounge where she could hear them talking in low tones. About her? Or had something new happened?

"How is everybody else? How long was I … asleep?"

"Only about an hour. Everybody's shaken up but OK. You were the hardest hit—much more sensitive, as we'd expect." He lowered his voice. "Do you think there's some way you could, you know, build a mental shield to protect yourself? Like in the movies?"

"If I could do that, I would have done it a long time ago. I don't want to sense thoughts. Especially not from that … whatever it is." She took another drink of water. "Why did you tell Lee-Anna not to fight back?"

"Fight back with noise louder than the sound that pissed them off in the first place? That's all it would have amounted to—the sounder charges don't have enough force to do real damage. Except maybe to us. And who knows what would have happened to you then? We were better to back off and hope the aliens, or whatever, would realize we weren't attacking them. That wouldn't have been a fight we could win."

She felt her nose running, and wiped it with her hand, embarrassed. Alex handed her a tissue.

"Maybe we couldn't, here in the habitat; but I'll bet Phillip has friends who could arrange for a major shitkicking."

"I don't blame you for feeling that way. You've suffered a lot. Part of me agrees with you. But part of me doesn't."

Matheus poked his head above the deck floor. "I brought you a cup of tea." At her grateful nod, he carried the mug to her, and she pushed herself into a sitting position. It was apple and cinnamon, very soothing.

"I was in fucking agony. How does that thing even know how to do that?"

"It's like I said before," Matheus offered, standing at the foot of her cot. "It seems as if this being, or beings can send signals that our brains interpret as sensations we are accustomed to have. They may not even feel pain in the way we do, but perhaps they somehow express a *concept* of suffering, or weakness, or vulnerability and our own brain produces responses our bodies would experience in a similar context."

Elle pictured a grotesque witch-doctor playing with voodoo dolls.

"Let's also recognize that an alien intelligence might not have a true understanding of the responses they create," Matheus finished.

"Don't make excuses for it. That bastard knew it was hurting me. And it's not the first time. I've had enough! I want to hurt it back." She choked back a sob and tried to hide her face. Matheus patted her knee in a fatherly way.

"Well, to do that we're going to have to learn a lot more about them," Alex said. "So, Bheru, Matheus and I are going for a walk over to the black smokers first thing in the morning. I hope you're able to get to sleep."

"Shouldn't we wait to make sure the thing doesn't attack again? Before you go so far from the hab?"

"Phillip is adamant about our coming back up—I don't know how Gary is holding him off. So, there isn't any time to waste if we want to find out what's down here."

"We could refuse to hook up the cable." Matheus probably wasn't serious, but it was hard to tell.

"They can send remote-controlled drones to do that. Phillip insisted on sending one down anyway. He says it's to give the habitat a thorough inspection in case the geyser caused damage. Unless that's just an excuse."

"In the meantime," Matheus said to her, "you should know that while you were out, we used the hab's medical scanner to check you over, and you still appear to be in good health. There's no sign of lingering damage—except perhaps emotionally, of course."

"I'm beginning to feel like a punching bag. Not to mention a practice dummy for a bunch of amateur doctors. I'm not crazy about either, frankly." She lay back again and pulled her light coverlet over herself.

The sociotheologist patted her knee again.

"Your sense of humor is a very encouraging sign."

29

A tiny oasis of light, of air, of warmth, the habitat rested on the abyssal plain, now inhabited by the only representatives of their species, in a world as alien as any distant planet, and no more hospitable.

The residue of eons surrounded them: degraded molecules of life forms that once had moved, fed, reproduced and died millions of years before humankind's most remote ancestors had crawled from muck into light. A depository of history before history was ever conceived—a final resting place for atoms used, then discarded.

This world had never known sun or stars, the dance of leaves in wind, or the music of birdsong. Its very emptiness, its utter absence of illumination seemed the antithesis of life; yet there was life. Life that belonged, even in this place.

And now, too, there was life that did *not* belong.

Alex's memory dredged up scenes out of cheesy old movies in which an outraged Mother Nature finally began to fight back against human oppressors.

Maybe the whole ocean was allied against them.

He shook off that morbid thought and turned away from the outside camera view. Food might make him feel better.

The crew had formed a habit of eating dinner together, but breakfast and lunch were informal—most often prepared snacks taken back to wherever the individual had been working, or to some relatively quiet space. Forced to spend so much time close to near-strangers, crew members craved solitude, but had to be satisfied with only an approximation of it. Otherwise, small matters became large irritants, as Alex was now finding out.

It was astonishing to Alex that Elle, with the build of a dancer, had footsteps that were almost as heavy as Bheru with his prosthetic legs, although Bheru seemed to be becoming more agile. But the man had a habit of humming and singing to himself that got on Alex's nerves—bits of Broadway show tunes, snatches of opera, a sudden chorus from a 1980's pop hit—except he almost never knew any of the words. His singing voice was pleasant; but, like the tones of his speech, impossible to escape.

With Lee-Anna, it was her efficiency and superiority that were hard to take. She was never wrong, and never pretended otherwise. Matheus, by contrast, was almost *too* conciliatory, with his damned cheerfulness and enthusiasm wearing thin after a time.

Alex wasn't impressed by the habitat's minimal facilities for hygiene, either. High humidity ensured that smells were pervasive. Their uniforms were supposed to dispose of shed skin and dirt to inhibit bacterial growth and keep bodies odor-free, but they must have been tested under ideal conditions. Despite regular washing with small microfiber cloths, he smelled sweaty. He was almost sure that Elle and Lee-Anna kept their distance because of it, especially at mealtimes. Who could blame them?

Although everyone's diet was nearly identical, Bheru's body odor had a slightly spicy tinge. Matheus had obviously brought aboard some expensive cologne; but, mercifully, understood that a very little went a long way. The women, too, gave off perspiration and other odors that were distinctive to each, but subtle—no perfume or scented shampoo. So, it was possible to tell with a single inhaled breath who was on each deck before confirming it by sight.

Alex wasn't offended by the smell of the men—he'd spent a lot of time in the company of soldiers. He was more disturbed by the scents of the women because they were making him horny. The air must be full of pheromones, and there was nothing he could do about it. It didn't help that Lee-Anna was the epitome of a west-coast knockout, and Elle was just as gorgeous but in a less ostentatious way—fresh-faced and supple, with an irresistible vulnerability that triggered his masculinity to an irritating degree.

At the moment, he was grateful to find the air filled only with the smells of breakfast, especially the appetizing combination of fresh coffee and toaster waffles that Elle was just finishing. Alex had taken his time coming to eat and was surprised to find everyone still on the galley deck.

Unsurprisingly, they were speculating about the unknown entity. The consensus that its energy transmissions were aimed toward the Moon meant that the crew should have a reprieve while that direct line was blocked by the surrounding ocean ridges. But there were still too many unanswered questions to permit total confidence, even about that.

"We keep calling the emissions an energy beam, but we have no idea what kind of energy it could be," Alex said as he surveyed the cupboard for breakfast choices.

Lee-Anna nodded. "I'm stumped by that, too. Communication is always a major headache for underwater vessels and habitats because electromagnetic frequencies don't travel well through water. Radio is almost useless. We usually rely on sonar, but it can be badly hampered by topography or different water densities."

Alex agreed. "Even gamma rays quickly attenuate in water, which is why plans for interplanetary spaceships often include water to shield astronauts' living quarters. I can't imagine what kind of power could punch a coherent beam through twelve thousand feet of ocean."

"A laser?" Matheus asked.

Alex shook his head and consulted his neural augment to provide specifics. Linked to the hab's wi-fi, it still connected with *Orion*, but the communication was very slow. "LIDAR depth-finders use a pulsed laser and they reach a little more than two hundred feet down with enough power to reflect from a shallow sea-bottom to the surface. So, say, five hundred feet of distance altogether, and the beam loses almost all of its energy along the way. A whole lot of the light is just scattered by the water." He waved a hand. "Pumping up laser power would likely just turn the water around the beam to steam instead of extending range. If the beam was coming *from* the Moon, it ought to boil the ocean where it hits. The same objections apply to radio frequencies or microwaves."

"Sound can travel a huge distance through water, though, right?" Elle said. "I've heard that whale sounds can travel hundreds of miles."

"Possibly thousands." Lee-Anna nodded. "That's infrasound—very low frequencies. Plus, it's usually through special channels of water in the ocean between thermoclines that bounce the sound waves back and forth over a relatively narrow range, so they're concentrated instead of being dispersed. Different story making a noise that reaches from the bottom up to the surface, though certainly possible. The bigger hitch comes after that."

Alex picked up the thread. "Yeah, the hitch is that air doesn't propagate sound nearly as well as water. To reach an aircraft flying at thirty thousand feet would take a lot of power. By the time you get up to a satellite orbit, there's almost no air at all to conduct sound; and from there to the Moon in a near-perfect vacuum, there would be no sound whatsoever." He put a couple of waffles in the toaster.

Bheru smiled. "We've assumed that the entity was trying to signal the Moon, yes; but we have no evidence that any signal actually reached that far. Perhaps the entity doesn't know the conditions that surround the Moon, and that it's doomed to failure."

"It would still have to be one hell of a potent sound wave to reach passing aircraft," Alex said, reaching for a plate and some syrup. The toaster caught his attention as it popped. It had no cord. Created in a 3D printer with circuitry built right into its structure, it drew its energy wirelessly from a source in the galley counter. Nikola Tesla would have been delighted with it, Alex mused.

"I witnessed a protest in Sao Paulo once." Matheus sat up. "Authorities used something I think they called an LRAD to transmit a warning to the protestors to disperse. The protest was quite a distance from the transmission tower."

"Right." Alex chewed and swallowed. "Long Range Acoustic Device. But I don't think those can reach more than a couple of miles. And with this entity, we'd be talking about a sound wave that would have to pass through that much ocean and then through the air into the upper atmosphere."

"I'm no expert on quantum physics, but what about the possibility of quantum entanglement?" They all looked at Bheru. "I mean, if this entity is so incredibly old, isn't there a chance that our ships, aircraft, satellites, our own bodies … even the Moon itself could contain particles that were once part of the ocean floor? I'm sure I read somewhere that large asteroid strikes in the past could account for that. And if such particles had once been quantum-entangled with particles over which the entity now has influence …?"

"It could control the distant particles and disrupt electrical circuits in our computers and brains? Wow, conspiracy theorists would love that one."

Lee-Anna gave Alex a disapproving glare then said to Bheru, "It might not be impossible, but that kind of control over sub-atomic particles implies a level of technology I'd rather not think about."

They lapsed into silence. Alex tried to chew more quietly.

Matheus cleared his throat, a sheepish look on his face.

"I was searching the internet for this kind of thing the other day—Phillip doesn't seem to have any of our incoming traffic blocked. Anyway, I came across something called scalar waves…." He hesitated and looked around. "Why are your faces turning red?"

"Speaking of conspiracy theories," Alex muttered, but turned away at another disapproving look from Lee-Anna.

"'Scalar' has a precise meaning in physics," she said, "but the idea of scalar waves … well, let's just say that's still considered pseudoscience at best. The theory gained some attention because a few reputable scientists like Nikola Tesla believed in it, though all his experiments produced was excess heat. The idea of non-electromagnetic energy that could travel through substances like water without being impeded at all was very appealing. But since then, the concept has attracted all kinds of flaky ideas about long-distance communication and even how to extract free energy from nothing."

"Theories about energy leaking from other dimensions," Alex added. "The zero-point field—also linked to some far-fetched ideas about psychic abilities." He gave a quick glance at Elle. "But no one's ever been able to produce consistent experimental results and most of the drivel just makes no sense."

"Didn't Einstein himself try to disprove quantum entanglement?" Matheus asked. "But he couldn't. It's demonstrably real." He gave a rueful shake of his head. "The older I get the more uncomfortable I am with the word impossible."

After an awkward moment Bheru chuckled and said, "There is one way to learn the answer." He folded his hands together. "We ask the entity, itself."

30

March 28, 2042

"Don't you think the adjustments could wait until another time?"

"Don't be a baby. You're not going to spring a leak. I'm only adjusting the adherence of the nims around your joints to make them less stiff. Give you more fluid motion."

"Fluid is what I'm worried about."

A thin layer of linked nano-machines was all that stood between Alex's fragile body and icy salt water at tons of pressure per square inch while Lee-Anna tinkered with those microscopic linkages wirelessly. It was true that the suits were still unwieldy—he, Bheru, and Matheus had been in the airlock for five minutes trying to get used to the suits' limitations on movement—but if the adherence of the nano-modules to one another was reduced too much and even the tiniest hole created, the invading water would slice through Alex's flesh like a laser.

He looked at the bottom of his viewscreen and was disgusted to see his heart rate so high.

As if reading his mind, Lee-Anna said, "As the nims shift, the gaps created are less than a quarter of a nanometer. Water molecules can't fit through."

As with the habitat itself, the suits were so strong that the interior could stay at the same air pressure as the surface of the sea while the nanomaterials kept the enormous weight of the ocean at bay. That meant that, unlike when they'd used scuba gear to deal with the loose flotation bag, the deep-sea suits would never require divers to pressurize or decompress. Alex could use one to rise all the way to the surface if he had to, at any speed, with no fear of getting 'the bends' or any other decompression injury. The suit was a miraculous achievement.

Getting 'suited up' was strange, though, begun by stepping into a hollow in a pile of dull black material, like the hole of a fat inner-tube. Triggered by proximity, the nano-stuff began to climb quickly up his body with the more rigid headpiece sliding up his back until it was ready to tuck over his head. There was no manual intervention required—the suit put itself on the wearer: a dry black tar that crawled over clothing and skin as if alive. It reminded Alex of scenes from old superhero movies of Batman and Iron Man.

Unfortunately, it felt like an army of ants using his body as a parade ground.

Once the suit had fully enveloped its user, it shrank inward to fit like a hard second skin. Alex experimented by rapping his knuckles against his chest. The material had become like armor, with only a thin space on the inside to allow the circulation of air for heating and moisture control. The viewscreen was outstanding: most of the time it aimed the suit cameras by tracking the wearer's eye movements, up, down, or to either side. But if he kept his eyes at their limit in one direction, the camera would keep turning in that direction until a reverse eye movement changed it. The various cameras handed off to each other seamlessly, so it was possible to view a nonstop 360-degree rotation. Other features like zoom, macro, infrared and ultraviolet views were available with a simple thought command. Communications were voice-activated.

He had to hand it to Lee-Anna: She built good toys.

If she'd just quit *tinkering*.

In the meantime, he asked Bheru and Matheus to give him some room and gave a little kick to move himself into a horizontal position. Small bulges in the back of his thighs added flotation—increased just a little from Behru and Lee-Anna's earlier outing—and the air volume at the back of his headpiece was controllable by thought. His legs floated nicely, though his head was higher. Decreasing the head buoyancy brought him parallel to the floor. The usual scuba system—a weight belt to counteract the buoyancy of a wetsuit and an inflatable buoyancy vest to counteract the weight belt—seemed hopelessly clunky in comparison. They were necessary with regular equipment because the increased pressure with greater depth squeezed wet suits and the human body itself into a smaller space. Less displacement of water meant less buoyancy, so air was added to the vest to compensate. Since Lee-Anna's suits didn't compress, their buoyancy, once set, did not change unless at the command of the user.

When he was done, Alex pushed to the side and let the other divers take turns finding their own balance.

Lee-Anna spoke again. "Try your arms now Alex. Shoulders? Now, elbows. And now your wrists. Better? Do you want me to make them any softer?"

The improvement was considerable— any more flexibility wouldn't increase the benefit, and he said so. Lee-Anna adjusted the other suits to the same settings, which took only seconds, then left the airlock.

With the adjustments done, Alex forced himself to relax as the airlock flooded, and then led the way through the gap in the airlock wall.

A casual swim in the ocean, twelve thousand feet deep.

As he relinquished the hull's protection for the open sea, the enormity of their hubris struck home with full force. Even inside the habitat, any rational mind could never forget the danger that surrounded them; but there, it was at arm's length. The hab's interior was clean and relatively comfortable—for brief interludes they could even be lulled into a feeling of security. But out here ....

Death given a realm of its own: fatal to the human organism by every conceivable measure. Devoid of light, heat, air—hope.

From outside, the habitat looked like a plaything: a child's toy in a place it had no right to be, just waiting to be crushed beneath a giant foot. No refuge at all.

Alex's mind teetered between opposite viewpoints, like one of those optical illusions that could be variously seen as faces or candlesticks. Inside the airlock, he'd felt his physical body wearing a manufactured covering within an artificial construct. Then his perception flipped, and he became a disembodied consciousness in a dark space, witnessing a virtual world through technological senses: a world that moved across his vision while he floated motionless in a lightless limbo.

It was the utter isolation of the suit that was so disorienting. His skin could feel the material that enclosed it, but he had no other sensory input from the outside world that was not delivered via electronics. He had to concentrate hard to regain his sense of reality, of self—to re-inhabit his body. To remember that *this* action had *this* result; and it was not the universe that was moving, it was him.

With the return of full awareness, a shudder passed through every molecule of his being. Deep within his hindbrain, the entire panoply of his most primitive instincts was sounding an alarm: His system flooded with stress chemicals refined over millions of years of evolution, all proclaiming that *he did not belong here.*

There was no need to imagine monsters in the dark. The stygian blackness was a monster on its own.

The habitat lights illuminated the water for a hundred feet or so. Beyond that, their suits' headgear took over. He saw Matheus and Bheru each crowned by six bright LED lamps. Each diver travelled within his own globe of illumination, the movement of limbs casting only faint shadows. The brightness of the lamps was also thought-controllable—too much light bouncing back from the specks of long-dead organic matter floating in the water was distracting. It reminded Alex of driving in a snowstorm, when high-beam headlights were more hindrance than help.

"How is your suit interfacing with your brain augment, Matheus?" Lee-Anna asked.

"I miss the extra senses of my mesh, but the link with the suit's instruments is working perfectly well, as far as I can tell." The sociologist's voice sounded strained. He must be enduring some of the same alienation as Alex. And because of his sensory impairment, maybe worse.

Along with the view from the cameras, the headgear display offered a chronometer, depth gauge, compass, temperature gauge (both inside and outside readings), and a display of the remaining supplies of air and battery power. Air shouldn't be a concern—as long as there was power, the suit fractured seawater to replenish oxygen, and exhaled carbon-dioxide was captured. For long periods of activity outside the hab, there was a small reservoir of drinking water with a straw leading to the wearer's mouth. Alex tried it out—tension had already made his mouth dry. The water was flat, but welcome.

Lee-Anna had pre-programmed the suits with the compass heading for the black smokers and the return to the habitat. A red arrow in the bottom-left corner of his screen pointed up when he was heading straight for the target or to the left or right if he needed to make a correction. Without that, the absence of landmarks in the featureless seafloor ooze would have sent him off course within minutes. He knew that most people gave a stronger kick with one leg than the other, which would send them in circles, if swimming blind.

The vents cast no glow at that distance. He nervously looked behind him every minute or so to make sure he could still see the lights of the habitat, lonely sentries in the unforgiving night.

They were about halfway to the vents when Alex's headlamps caught an unusual shape on the seafloor at the edge of his vision to the right.

"Hold up a second," he said. "There's something over here." Bheru and Matheus stopped while he kicked slowly toward a pair of shadows that looked too regular to be natural. He paused to see if there was any movement, then continued. Within another ten feet, he caught a hint of a light color. Before long, he could make out the shape of a crate.

"It's the bait we dropped. Two of the crates, about fifteen feet apart. The crates are intact but the fish inside are gone. Not even a trace that I can see. Something did quite a cleanup job."

"There are small fish at this depth that could do that," Bheru said. "Other creatures too, like shrimp."

"Shrimp I can handle. I'm just glad there aren't giant bite marks."

"Large sucker marks would be more likely, from giant squid. But the smaller species got here first. That probably means there is a substantial colony around the black smokers."

Alex rejoined them. He wished Bheru hadn't mentioned giant squid. They could move very quickly, he knew, and there would be no way to see something like that coming. Should he ask Lee-Anna to send out a sonar ping? No, that would be hard to justify. But he kicked a little faster toward the vents, reasoning that a large creature wouldn't be comfortable there.

"Will we feel heat in these suits?" Matheus asked.

"If it gets extreme enough, you'll feel it," Lee-Anna replied, "but by then you'd be at risk of melting the camera lenses; so keep a close watch on temperature readouts."

"Temperatures at the vents can reach four hundred degrees Celsius—four times the boiling point of water," Bheru confirmed, "although, of course, water cannot boil because of the pressure. The heat also dissipates very quickly. Water just outside the flow is near the normal temperature of the sea. I don't think we'll blunder into a discharge, though; because unless there are cracks that are very new, residual deposits will have built up chimneys around the vents and we should see those easily."

"Why easily? I thought the chimneys were the color of the seafloor and the smoke was black," Alex said, automatically looking at Bheru. He turned his view forward again.

A giant finger of orange and white blocked his way. He gave a yelp.

Bheru laughed. "Just so. See there? The mineral deposits are yellowish from sulfur, and tinted by other mineral salts of iron, magnesium and so forth. The white patches are alive. Most likely bacteria. Perhaps shrimp. Let's have a look."

"It must be twenty-five feet tall. Look beyond it—like a miniature mountain range."

"Swim, don't climb. Some structures can be very fragile. If you were to break through a crust or snap off a chimney, you'd be directly in the flow."

"Boiled in the shell like a lobster," Matheus muttered.

"A thing best avoided."

The next thirty-five minutes were stitched-together fragments of dreams and nightmares. Spires from a vividly imagined fairy world, creatures of pristine white, billowing columns of smoke like the breath of volcanos, and barely visible plumes of water rippling like liquid fire. In place of soaring dragons or flitting nymphs, there were bulbous-nosed eel-like fish and darting, ghostly octopuses.

Bheru made running commentary, often using the blended Greek and Latin classifications: *bathymodiolus, neolepas, bythograea thermydron, lepetodrilus,* and even *vulcanoctopus hydrothermalis.*

To keep them grounded in science instead of myth.

He pointed out that as with other smoker outcrops, the white portions of the first chimney appeared to be bacteria clinging to the roughened surface like sea foam on a drowning sandcastle.

"These, and other bacteria known as *archaea,* form the basis of smoker ecologies. *Archaea* use chemosynthesis to produce energy by oxidizing hydrogen sulfide spewed from the vents, and use that energy to convert carbon dioxide into organic carbon. While some of the bacteria are eaten by shrimp and mollusks, many of the lifeforms, from tubeworms to crabs, are infused with *archaea* in a symbiotic relationship, relying on the carbon from the bacteria instead of using intestines to digest food like their shallow-water counterparts do."

Alex had a feeling that Bheru's monologue was a response to stress, but that was OK—it still was valuable information.

He was drawn to one peak that glowed vividly in his lights, only to find hundreds upon hundreds of colorless crabs, an inch across, scuttling over each other in search of unclaimed morsels of food. On a neighboring ridge, a colony of squat lobsters formed the snow of the upper slopes above a vast forest of shaggy mussels on the lower reaches. The mussels were mostly orange mottled with black, sometimes with dark fringes.

"A seafood feast," Matheus declared.

Bheru snorted. "Full of copper salts, arsenic. Hydrogen sulfide, of course. So, unless you like the smell of rotten eggs, I'd suggest we not bring any samples into the habitat for now."

The crags and valleys had none of the eroded smoothness of most surface mountains and rifts. One long gully of orange spires reminded Alex of Bryce Canyon in Utah with its water-carved and frost-weathered hoodoos pricking at the sky. But unlike the desert rock-columns, these spikes often had vents at their tips, or along a branching arm, or in semi-circles at their bases from which billows of scalding water and dissolved metals surged in a toxic brew that would have thrilled the cauldron-stirring witches of *Macbeth*. He swam well clear of those vents but tried to shine as much light on them as he could for the sake of Elle and Lee-Anna watching monitors in the hab. Once, he accidentally passed his hand above an innocuous funnel and jerked it clear, remembering a childhood dare to hold his palm over a candle flame.

Thirty feet away, Bheru crowed with delight.

"Here they are! I was wondering why we hadn't seen any."

Alex swam closer. The scientist hovered over a wide peak completely obscured by things that looked like props from a cheesy sci-fi flick. Orange tubes, ten feet tall, with red plumes protruding from their ends. Tongues or flowers—Alex couldn't decide which.

"I saw others like these over there," Matheus said, "but they were white."

"Giant tube worms, one of the most common species in these vent communities; but it appears they prefer the warmer waters of the middle zones rather than the outskirts. Yes, they are often white. These owe their color to chemicals in the water. Aren't they amazing?"

Among the tall columns shrimp, crabs, and a few pale fish wended their way. It was as if the tubes formed a whole city in comparison to more isolated outposts of life along the ridge. Yet weren't all these creatures both predators and prey? They didn't seem to realize it. Or perhaps they just didn't dare wander far from the warmth and rich chemical broth of the smoker vents, no matter what the risk.

Alex's attention was drawn to another wormlike creature. This one sprouted fronds all along its body that faded from deep red at their stems to white at their tips.

"Pompeii worms," Bheru explained. "The white along the filaments is the bacteria they rely on for food."

"Have you noticed the shrimp don't have eyes?" Matheus moved a hand through a swarm of the tiny creatures. Unperturbed, they returned to their perches on the nearby rock or flitted across to the next to continue their search for micro-particles of organic matter.

"Well, they never experience light, although some species have patches on their skin that appear to be a sense organ analogous to eyes. You have something in common with them, my friend." They shared a chuckle.

"I had no idea it would be like this," Alex confessed. "It's as active as a coral reef." The profusion of vibrant life had almost made him forget the threatening darkness all around.

"Indeed. Scientists have identified more than four hundred species and find new ones all the time. And it all exists where no life was thought to be able to exist. Nature is unfathomable in its wonder." Bheru dodged around a vent and swam closer to the colony of tubeworms. "Do you know they use hemoglobin? Not exactly like human hemoglobin because ours carries only oxygen, and theirs can carry sulfide as well. But they bleed red if you cut them. Look."

He used the tip of one of his swim fins like a blade and sliced into the plume of a tube. The result was gruesome, like a movie murder victim having his throat slit in a swimming pool. The blood oozed rather than spurting, but it was indeed red.

"What's happening?" Matheus called out. "Something's disturbed them." The sociologist was surrounded by a swarm of shrimp. As Alex watched, vast numbers of them freed themselves from the smoker mount nearby and launched forward. Hundreds, maybe thousands. Matheus swung his arms to swat them away and shake them loose as they began to cling to his suit. Then Alex's view was obscured by blotches of white.

His own arms were covered by shrimp too. Pale crabs climbed his legs. An eel-like fish latched onto his chest while another passed within inches of his face. He switched camera views. All his cameras were becoming blocked by shrimp and smaller creatures like barnacles, and finally a dense white cloud of tiny dots that might be only a few cells in size.

"I'm covered in them," Alex said, trying to sound calm. "My cameras are blinded. What's going on?"

"I don't know," Bheru said, his voice far higher than usual. "I can't imagine why they'd be interested in us."

"I scrape them loose, but more just pile on." Matheus was breathing heavily. He gave an occasional grunt of effort.

"Lee-Anna, is there any chance these things might be able to eat their way through our suits?"

"No way, Alex. It's an acidic environment—some of them may even use that in their digestion—but nothing strong enough to damage those suits. I'd suggest just getting out of there. Move back out to cold water. They won't like that."

"I'm not sure that will stop them," Bheru said. "Smoker vents often don't last more than a dozen years, so the life forms must have a way of surviving until they reach another vent."

"Well, I don't recommend trying to burn them off in hot water. Some species can tolerate those temperatures. You can't."

"Everyone, stay still for a minute," Alex said. "Check your power gauges. Have you got lots of juice? OK, we have our compasses to steer us back to the habitat, so we'll be fine. We just have to swim up thirty or forty feet to make sure we'll clear any chimneys and avoid the hottest smoke clouds. Lee-Anna, can you see our suit lights?"

"Barely. But I can't see the smokers to tell if you're clear of them."

"Does everybody remember which way is up?"

"Boost the flotation of your headgear—it'll lift you up. You can kick, too, if you want. But don't rise for too long. Memorize the percentage of maximum buoyancy that your headset is showing now, then return it to that setting once you think you've risen far enough. That should level you out again so you can swim horizontally."

Alex swallowed and tried to calm his breathing. He'd never been claustrophobic, but he'd also never been encased in a human-shaped coffin at the bottom of the sea, blinded by creatures from a bad drug trip while scalding fountains frothed on all sides.

If the comms suddenly cut out, he would be completely alone. Helpless. A pathetically fragile organism at the mercy of the most hostile environment on the planet.

No, the others would come to find him. Lee-Anna, or someone. He had to get a grip, for God's sake. Everyone was waiting for him to take the lead. He cleared his throat and was appalled at the weakness of the sound.

"OK. Let's do this at the same time so we have a chance of staying together. On my count, make your headgear buoyancy eighty per cent, then follow my instructions. Three—two—one—change." He waited as he felt his head rise into a vertical position. "Now strong kicks: one, two, three, four. Stop kicking and let's just rise. Rise. Five thousand, six thousand, seven thousand, eight thousand, nine thousand, ten. Return your buoyancy to what it was before, including your headgear. The water density should stop our climb. When you're pretty sure you're horizontal again, start swimming until your compass lines up with the hab. Make sure it's the hab heading, 180 degrees from the way we started out. All good?"

There were sounds of confirmation. Maybe they didn't trust themselves to speak. Alex was conscious of a tremor in his own voice. He took a few more deep breaths, then said, "Lee-Anna, you don't see us spreading apart, do you? Nobody's getting farther away?"

"You look good so far. Maybe a bit high, but better to be on the safe side."

"Roger that," Alex said, imitating a military intonation. It gave his spirits a lift.

His head bumped into something.

"Jesus! Who's that?"

"Matheus."

'Oh, good. OK, well let's hang onto each other's arms. Can you see anything yet?" He immediately felt stupid for asking such a thing of a blind man.

"My cameras are still covered."

Just then a flicker caught Alex's eye. He did a quick check on each camera. The one on his left side was letting in some light. He swam on, keeping his attention on that side. Within a minute there was more light, then more again. He saw something fall away.

"I think I'm losing my hitchhikers." He checked the other cameras again. Only one remained completely obscured. The rest were opening up. He looked ahead. A shiver raced up his neck as he saw the lights of the habitat through a small, creature-free hole.

"Mine are coming off," Matheus said with obvious relief.

"Mine too. I'm not sure if the creatures are dying or if they just decided to go back and get warm. And I don't care, as long as they've decided I don't taste good." Bheru gave a nervous chuckle.

"You think that was the reason?" Matheus asked. "You think they were trying to eat us?"

"What other reason would there be?"

"To me it's obvious. You damaged one of them. I think the rest attacked us, either to kill us or to drive us away."

"That's ridiculous. They don't have the brain capacity for something like that. Nor the instinct. Some percentage of them succumb to predators all the time."

Alex felt a chill, even as the last crab dropped away from his headpiece. He let go of Matheus and rolled to look at his limbs, brushing the few remaining shrimp off with a hand.

"There may be another factor at play that could account for that," he said. "But I sure as hell hope Matheus is wrong."

## 31

March 28, 2042

Bheru slammed a prosthetic hand against the ladder. Lee-Anna's eyebrows rose as she stared at it, but there was no dent in either ladder or hand that Elle could see.

"You're imposing your own belief system on a series of events without evidence," he growled.

"It has nothing to do with beliefs." Matheus perched on the back of the upholstered chair, arms crossed. Through eyes that couldn't see, he glared at his fellow academic. "I'm not saying that God made those creatures attack us. It was obvious cause and effect. They'd ignored us entirely up to the point when you sliced into the tubeworm. Then they swarmed us. Blinded us."

"To what purpose? An instant's contact would have told them that they couldn't damage our suits."

"So much for your theory that they suddenly saw us as potential dinner. But maybe all they planned to do was immobilize us. Keep us from escaping until something bigger came along to deal with us."

"Rubbish. I'm telling you that none of these creatures has the mental capacity to conceive of such a notion. They are little more than mouths with a few sensory abilities to point them in the direction of prey. Directed entirely by instinct—to feed and to avoid being food. That's the limit." He shook his head and looked at Alex. "I suppose the two of you think that space aliens told them to attack us."

Alex looked sheepish, but didn't say anything. Matheus thrust out his chin.

"Told. Controlled. Who can know? The frustrating part is that there is an intelligence here that is sending us messages, and we have no means to talk back to it. Until then, we are handcuffed."

"Messages. From shrimp." Bheru rolled his eyes.

Lee-Anna looked uncomfortable about entering the fray, but she raised her hand a little to get their attention.

"The vent animals certainly don't have intelligence on their own," she said, "but simple instincts can't explain what we saw. There were at least four, different, complex species involved—and probably more—plus the micro-organisms. It's not credible that all of them would decide at the same instant that you looked like food. And swarming a threat your size wouldn't be good survival strategy for an individual. Could these things somehow have developed a sense of community, and a mutual desire to protect that community?"

"I'm telling you, their thought processes are much too primitive for that! Why am I even here if you won't accept what I say?"

"Get off your high horse!" Matheus snapped. "You're a member of a team—you have no special status. You ask for evidence, but you won't acknowledge it when it's right in front of you. And you think I'm the one who's blind."

Bheru snorted, climbed the ladder, and threw himself on his bunk. Matheus grabbed his little book of

Portuguese poetry and went up to the communications deck.

Lee-Anna shrugged and spoke softly to Alex. "When did Gary say he'd get us an answer?"

"You know what it's like up there. Two sides who can't agree." He raised his eyes to the deck above and smiled. "I meant on *Orion*. But I don't expect they will have answers. The experts are down here. The best equipment is here. And we're the ones with front row seats. We find the answers, or no one does."

She ran her fingers through her long hair, holding Alex's attention. Elle felt a pang of envy.

"Well, we won't come up with answers unless we have a whole lot more information. I think we have some equipment that will help." She descended the ladder, and Elle could hear her opening compartments on the bottom deck.

Alex went to sit on the couch and waved her over.

"Matheus had a good thought," he said in a near whisper. "We don't know how this entity—or maybe entities—are communicating with us, so we haven't tried to talk back. But maybe we could. Have you ever tried to use your ability to send information instead of just receiving it?"

She was taken aback. "It doesn't work that way."

"Just because it never has doesn't mean that it couldn't. I imagine you've always been uncomfortable about picking up thoughts from others and never wanted them to be aware of it. But maybe it is a two-way channel. You can't know until you try."

I screamed at the thing to get out of my head, she thought but didn't say. Alex would consider that a defensive move, like a mental shield, not an attempt to communicate.

He touched her arm.

"I'm sure the last thing you want is to encourage whoever it is to notice you. I get that. I don't ever want to feel them again and you've suffered much worse. But there's a chance that they don't mean us harm; that we're victims of a misunderstanding. Unless we can somehow set the record straight, we'll never make any progress and things could become outright hostile. Could you try, at least? Maybe ... I don't know, focus on that blue fog and then picture us being friendly or something?" He gave an awkward laugh.

"And should I tell it that we're just harmless busybodies who don't have a warship sitting overhead with tons of explosives aboard and a whole fleet of more powerful ships on call?"

"Definitely don't picture the explosives." He smiled. "Yeah, I know it sucks. But if it's any comfort, it may already know our capabilities from sensing our aircraft and satellites, and by scanning our minds on *Orion*. What it may not know is that some of us just want to be friends." He gave her arm a squeeze then let go. She only nodded. When they'd first met, she'd thought she could never have more in common with this man than she had with the entity they were sparring with. Now, though, she could see heart behind that intellect. He might not have a high opinion of people in general, but he truly cared about them as individuals. She believed that he sincerely cared about her welfare and hated to feel he was putting her at risk.

"Do you hear something?" Lee-Anna's voice startled them from the access shaft, her head just above floor level.

Elle listened. A hollow clang, she thought, but very faint. Then a scraping noise. And finally, the hum of machinery. It sounded like it came through the hull.

She saw a look pass between Alex and Lee-Anna.

"Is there something going on in the airlock?" she asked.

"No, it's nothing internal," Lee-Anna said. "Probably a remote drone. I think Phillip wants to check on us for himself." Her eyes and mouth narrowed into slits.

"Well Phillip should get a better driver," Elle said. "There's no need to bump into us. They could damage something."

That look between them again.

"Yeah," Alex said. "Could be dangerous."

## 32

March 28, 2042

"Are you in love with me yet?"

"Matheus, I think you need to take a little less vitamin E."

He gave a loud laugh and winked at her. "There once was a time you might not have resisted my charms. I was considered quite a ladies' man."

"I have *no* trouble believing that," Elle said.

"A leading citizen, too; but now I'm afraid I'm an outcast in my former community. After my seminal work was not well-received by the Catholic Church in Brazil, members of Brazilian high society shunned me, although I had never been truly welcomed by them—but worse, they shunned my wife Beatriz who was born into their class. She deserves far better. So do my daughter Lia and my son Breno."

"You must love them very much."

He was slow in answering, his smile tempered with regret. "Love is complicated, my dear. My family and I have not been close for some time, I'm afraid. I realize now that I lavished more affection on my prize Mangalarga Marchador stallions than on my own wife and children. But love is like skin—it shapes you, defines you. It may change in small ways, but it is always the place where outer and inner worlds meet to make peace with each other. Sometimes, when love cools in one place, you must find its warmth somewhere else."

"Oh my God, you have a *mistress*! Maybe more than one. Of course, you do, you're a Latin lover."

He laughed. "You give me too much credit, especially at my age. My assistant Milena has been with me for six years and accompanied me to the United States, but was not allowed to come to *Orion*. But rest assured that my wife has *assistants* also; although I may have driven her to that."

"You're a complicated man."

"I certainly hope so."

"Did your children follow you into academic studies?"

"My daughter, yes. Breno is not so studious, though. More gifted with objects than words, he works as a truck mechanic." He smiled. "I'm afraid I was harsh with him when he dropped out of school, and my efforts to undo that damage are not welcomed."

"It's never too late. As long as you're both alive, there's hope you can reconcile."

With a strange look, he said, "Of course, you're right."

They continued preparing the food in silence. When he was done chopping the carrots, he reached for the plastic measuring cups. The clack they made against each other made him smile. He began clacking them in a flamenco rhythm and stomped his feet together. Putting his arm through Elle's he swung her away from the counter and spun her through some dance steps still wielding his improvised castanets. Somehow, he managed to encircle her waist without dropping a beat, completing the dance by dipping her gracefully, down and then up tight against his chest.

She burst out laughing and put her hand over her mouth in case any of the others were trying to nap.

"You don't act like the professorial type," she said. "You're so full of life."

His bright smile dimmed as he stood catching his breath, and he replaced the measuring cups on the counter.

"Sadly, I am actually full of death."

He patted her arm. In a near-whisper, he said, "I have cancer. Cancer of the colon. We have sparred for years, the disease and I, and it has allowed me temporary victories. But I fear it is determined to win in the end, and perhaps before too long, though I was cleared for this mission, short as it is. It was a difficult parting from Milena, and I recorded farewells to my family before we left *Orion*, though I feel fine for now."

Elle didn't know what to say. She'd always felt it was disrespectful to offer platitudes in the face of such misfortune. Then a thought struck her.

"Are you here hoping for a cure?"

He shrugged, holding her gaze. "Perhaps you could say that. Anything is possible. You are very perceptive."

He turned back to the food and began to hum a tune she didn't recognize.

33

March 29, 2042

"We might all be safer if you stay in the hab. You know how to run everything."

"No! I have to get out of here and do something before I go stir crazy."

Lee-Anna had already stepped inside the airlock and into a suit. It started to climb up her legs. Alex sighed and turned to the ladder.

"We can't both go out. I'll get Matheus," he said.

"Bheru is stronger. If you want me to have help with the lights."

He nodded and climbed upward.

"Do you want to come, too?" Lee-Anna asked Elle. "You haven't been outside yet. Don't you want to see what it's like?"

No, Elle thought. "Maybe later." Her conditioning had almost magically kept her claustrophobia at bay in the habitat, but those confining suits would be another story. Especially if they were swarmed by creatures. She shuddered violently, but Lee-Anna didn't see.

"Where are you going to place the cameras?"

"Bheru might have some ideas about that. We should probably get a view of each of the main species. Certainly, the tubeworm patches—they seem to host a lot of activity. The camera stands only extend to fifteen feet, with adjustable tripod legs; but they each have a flotation bag that goes above the lights so we can make sure the feet have a light touch on the surface. They shouldn't break through the crust around the vents." She touched a protrusion near her collarbone that stopped the headgear from completing its motion over her head, and began to tuck her dangling hair into the neck of the suit. Elle stepped forward to help. "It's not ideal to have the cameras mounted on the same stands as the spotlights because of bounce back—reflections straight back into the lens—but we don't have more stands. Whatever's out there might not let us spend much time on their doorstep as it is."

It seemed like Lee-Anna was thinking out loud just for something to say. Her normal days were filled with hands-on research projects and her nights with society soirées alongside her current guy, David Drury, a Silicon Valley executive. Being cooped up in a big can, her restlessness was beginning to show.

"Be careful out there," Elle said. "Don't do anything … impetuous."

"Me? Nah. I'm the epitome of caution and restraint."

The women laughed just as Bheru descended the ladder.

"I won't even ask what that was about," he said. "My wife has a wonderful sense of humor with her friends, only I can't understand any of it."

"What does she think of you being here … your wife?" Elle asked as he stepped into his suit.

"She much prefers my usual boring life as an academic. Not so sure about my gallivanting around at the bottom of the ocean. But she understands what I do, and why. She always says she's 'only a math teacher', but she's one of the most intelligent people I know."

"You'll have lots to tell her when you get back. To Hamilton, right? I'm originally from Toronto."

"I heard that. We're practically neighbors." His full hair reached past his shirt collar. She hesitated, then helped him tuck it in.

"Did you meet in Hamilton?"

He gave a loud laugh.

"No. In my hometown of Durgapur, India. Our parents arranged for us to be married."

"Oooh," Elle said, then mentally kicked herself for sounding judgmental.

"Yes, except I skipped out two weeks before the wedding and left the country for Glasgow." He laughed again. "I was an ass. It was years later that I met her in Canada. I barely recognized her. But she forgave me, we fell in love, and were married after all."

"Wow. So, it all worked out."

"Not entirely. My parents never did forgive me and were killed in a train wreck before the story had its happy ending. My sisters and I have made up, and several nieces and nephews have come to study at McMaster since then." His headgear sealed itself and concluded a rare glimpse into a private man.

"I'll keep an eye on the two of you from up here," Alex called from the galley.

Elle left the airlock and watched it seal itself. It wouldn't do so as long as it detected an unprotected human inside. For the first time since their descent, Lee-Anna and Bheru used the mini-airlock compartments on the inside of the outer wall. Elle couldn't help thinking that it must be like stepping into a stand-up coffin, but the mini locks required much less air to pump them dry again. Since the crew had used up most of their original stores of air and were now manufacturing it from the surrounding seawater, it paid to be frugal. They were able to fit the light stands and lights into a third mini lock.

The suits signaled the lock mechanisms once internal sensors had confirmed a good seal, and flooding began. There was a monitor just outside the lock door, but Elle climbed up one deck and pulled a chair beside Alex to watch from his workstation. As usual, she felt a shiver as water climbed over the heads of her friends, and she could barely watch when the wall split open to expose them to the ebony unknown.

"I'm not sure I'll ever be able to do that," she said.

"You will if you want to. You haven't let anything stop you yet." There was warmth in his smile, maybe even a little pride. Was that condescending? No, she had to stop reading things into what people said. Even when she knew their thoughts were innocent, she often convinced herself she'd misread them.

"I wanted to ask you," Alex continued in a quieter voice. "When we were swarmed by vent creatures, did you sense anything different from the entity? Anger ... or protectiveness? Or hunger?" He tried to smile, but it stalled halfway.

"No, but I was totally focused on what was happening to you. I was terrified. I'm not sure I could have noticed any other feeling. But ..." she hesitated, confused. "I did feel a strong sense of hunger from it once. I'd totally forgotten about that. It was around the time the whales came around."

"Are you sure it wasn't from the whales? You can sense things from animals sometimes, right?"

"I can, but it wasn't from them."

"Why didn't you tell us?"

"I ... I'm not sure. I should have. I thought I did. Now I don't know."

She became aware that their faces were only a foot apart, and her breathing had gotten faster. She must be experiencing the fear over again. She had to get better control over that.

Lee-Anna and Bheru weren't saying very much. That would probably change when they reached the vent zone.

Clumping footsteps rang from the ladder as Matheus came down.

"Did I hear you say something about hunger? Did someone skip breakfast?"

Alex dropped his gaze and his hand tapped on his thigh as he turned back to the computer display.

"A few days ago, Elle sensed hunger from the entity. It was before we descended all the way."

"Oh. That would be disturbing. But we associate feelings of hunger with many other states of mind, not only from a desire for food. Maybe a powerful ambition—a need for success at some endeavor. We can hunger for answers to important questions. Sexual desire is also experienced as a kind of hunger—a very powerful one sometimes." Was that a smile on his face?

"You're not suggesting the aliens want to *breed* with us," she said with a look of disgust.

"I am not. Lurid tabloid headlines and low-budget films notwithstanding, no alien species would be able to breed with us, nor would they have any reason to want to. Sexual attraction has everything to do with compatible chemistry as well as physiology. Pheromones. Body language. An extraterrestrial species would have none of those things in common with us, and no interest in mixing their genes with ours, likely considering us to be inferior to them."

"We mix our genes with pigs and mice," Alex said with a straight face.

"Only to provide tissue for experimental purposes or potential organ transplants. And, please God, never through sexual means."

"Lee-Anna and Bheru have reached the smokers," Elle interrupted.

The view was in extravagant color and just as impressive the second time around. How much more mind-boggling must it be in person? she wondered.

"There's no sign of them being swarmed," Alex said.

"Let's hope they can set up the stands without crushing any of the inhabitants." Matheus' voice had lost its playfulness. He walked to the workstation on the opposite side of the circle and set it to the suit camera feed before sitting down. He increased the volume, and the voices of the divers filled the deck, discussing the best locations for the cameras.

"Maybe now would be a good time to try to reach out to the alien mind," Alex said in a low voice.

"Wouldn't that just call attention to Bheru and Lee-Anna?"

"What better time to project thoughts about us not meaning it any harm than when some of us are tromping around its turf? We want to be sure it knows they're not planting weapons or food harvesters or anything like that."

"OK, I'll try." She held no hope of success, but if it would please him … or at least get him off the subject.

His hand lifted a little, then returned to the arm of the chair and his eyes flicked away.

She climbed up to her bunk, dimmed the lights, and lay down with her arms on her chest. The position always reminded her of corpses at funerals, but it was the most comfortable and least distracting pose for thinking about things. Determined to ignore her fears, and with an involuntary shiver, she closed her eyes and took five, deep, measured breaths.

She began to picture a deep blue fog.

After several minutes, she added other images to the haze. The full moon, of course. It was what she'd seen when she'd first been consumed by the alien presence aboard the airliner, and what she often saw during other contacts. She pictured herself: her face and then her human form. *This is us.*

Was there a difference between images received and those transmitted? She didn't know, but she tried to infuse her mental projection with a sense of power, and an impression of it spreading outward from her like cartoon images of radio towers.

It was important to project peace. Benevolent intent. Harmlessness.

She imagined Lee-Anna and Bheru among the tubeworms and mussels, and was happy for them, but then thought such a representation might be interpreted as self-serving, even food-related.

Instead, she pictured humans sitting in a circle with beatific smiles and did her best to summon feelings of joy and good will. A healing circle. A prayer circle. A circle of cooperation and mutual assistance.

She may have drifted off for a few minutes when she heard Alex call, "They're on the way back."

There was no concern in his voice. A good sign. She climbed down the ladder and leaned over him to see if any detail revealed where the divers were, then stepped quickly back when her breast touched his shoulder.

"I, uh … tried to project peaceful thoughts," she said. "Nothing about explosives. Nothing about food."

He laughed. "Good. Maybe it worked. They got the cameras planted without any trouble. Good choices, too, see? The big tubeworm colony of course. There's the pinnacle covered with crabs that I saw. This depression is mostly mollusks, I think, mussels or some clams. And this one has a bit of everything: lots of shrimp, some white tubes, fish, a lot of squat lobsters."

"Oh my God!"

"What?"

She put a hand to her chest and tried to calm her racing heart.

"When I was trying to reach out … I wanted to say that we're peaceful. I projected the Moon, and … and a group of people in a circle." She reached a shaky finger toward the screen.

In the view from camera number four many of the shrimp had moved to the edges of the picture, but a large number had occupied the abandoned area in the center and grouped themselves together.

In an unmistakable circle.

## 34

March 29, 2042

"I didn't put you in charge so you could countermand my orders."

"I'm sure of that." Gary looked into Phillip Watanabe's eyes from less than two feet away. The man was definitely into his personal space. That was how he intimidated people—he didn't raise his voice: he just made himself impossible to ignore.

Details about the mission were not shared with *Orion*'s crew, yet Gary was convinced that the level of tension had risen over recent days. Some of it might have been restlessness from having so little to do. The ship had maintained station for a long time with almost no productive activity, and rumors flew around a Navy vessel as readily as they did in any community. Somehow *Orion*'s community had become aware of increasing international attention. They might even have sensed the rise in animosity between one of their own and the mysterious man responsible for their current assignment.

"So, what makes you think you know better than I do when it comes to this mission?"

Doing his best to keep just as cool, Gary said, "When you brought me onboard you gave me a thorough briefing on the goals of 'this mission.' Now it seems you've changed the game. I don't think you're pursuing the same mission as I am, Mr. Watanabe. I'm beginning to think you never were."

"Nonsense. We're to identify the source of the energy transmissions, assess the potential threat it poses, and deal with it appropriately."

"Except you no longer seem interested in the first part. Or even the second. If you were, you'd take advantage of the only source of intelligence we have: the crew in the habitat. Something tells me you're eager to skip ahead to the third phase, and your trigger finger is getting itchy."

Phillip scowled and turned away, pacing across the room. He probably wished the encounter was taking place in his office where there was less risk of being overheard. The lounge door was always kept open by tradition. Phillip closed it.

"With a phone call I could have you swabbing decks on some floating antique cruising the Antarctic Ocean," he said.

Gary laughed. "Now look who's talking nonsense. But I guess threats are easier than telling the truth. Why not just tell me what's going on? Why are you looking for any excuse to bring the hab back up and go in shooting?"

"You have no idea what you're talking about."

"Enlighten me."

The response was an undisguised sneer. "I don't think that would be productive."

Gary bristled. "Are you suggesting that I wouldn't understand? That I'm not smart enough to understand?" The words had carried him across the distance until the two men were nearly nose to nose. He was sure he outweighed the agent by forty pounds or more, all of it muscle, but he also knew that strength wasn't everything. Phillip would be trained in weaponless combat. On the other hand, Gary was a champion kickboxer in Navy circles. Right then, he was itching to put it to the test.

"Put your testosterone back in the drawer, Mr. Cross. Picking a fight with me would mean an instant ticket home. I wouldn't even have to ask." He slowly moved his face even closer. "It's not that I think you're stupid. It's that I think you'd be unwilling to see the broader context, so I won't waste the effort to paint it for you." His glare was ice and every move deliberate as he turned back to the door and opened it.

"You've managed to stall things," he continued. "But in thirty-six hours Navy brass will give in and you will order *Orion*'s winch crew to bring the habitat to the surface."

"If I don't?"

"Your superiors know that you remained behind pleading a non-existent concussion. Including your future father-in-law, Admiral Sinclair. I was quietly asked for my assessment of the reason. I haven't given my answer yet."

Gary tried to hide the clenching of his fists. "Look, those people down in that habitat are all geniuses in their field, but they weren't working together. It was a barnyard pecking-party down there. They figured they could snap at each other as long as I was around to give orders and keep everybody from getting too far out of line. So, the answer was to remove me from the equation. Close enough to keep making the key decisions, but far enough to force them to cooperate. And it's worked."

"You've had lots of time to come up with that explanation."

Gary had no quick comeback. The teamwork problem was the truth. But only one of the reasons he'd stayed behind.

His instincts had told him that the communications shutdown and the failure of the flotation bag clamps were too much of a coincidence. Someone aboard *Orion* was trying to derail the mission, and there was no way he could find out who it was from twelve-thousand feet beneath the ocean. Especially since, though he could think of no satisfactory motive, the list of suspects included Phillip Watanabe.

If it came to proving wrongdoing, the man would be an incredibly elusive quarry.

Gary had no training in detective work, but his instinct was to keep the suspect on the defensive.

"I think I do see the big picture," he said. "When you first learned of this energy that can destroy minds at a distance, your people hoped it could somehow be harnessed and used as a weapon. But now you're beginning to think that whatever it is will be too much of a wild card—not controllable. Better to cut your losses and just wipe it out."

Phillip's eyes had grown even colder.

"Thirty-six hours, Mr. Cross."

Gary strode through the door, keeping his face calm by recalling memories of the many ways to kill a man.

## 35

March 29, 2042

Lee-Anna's face glowed as the suit retracted from her head, radiating excitement. She shook her hair, glossy with sweat.

"I'll have to crank up the cooling next time we do something that strenuous," she said. "But it was fantastic. Are you getting the camera feeds. Do they look great?"

Alex assured her they were perfect. Surprising.

"What's that supposed to mean? Oh, there was one piece of bad news—I don't know if you heard us." Her jaw tightened. "Bheru and I took a look at the thing Phillip's drone planted on the hab's hull. I don't think I can remove it. Phillip must have gotten some of the specs of the nims from Stanford—they wouldn't have suspected anything—and figured out how to weld onto them underwater. Or use some kind of super adhesive. Anyway, it's not coming off."

"What *thing*?" Elle asked.

Lee-Anna looked at Alex, who nodded. "Phillip has attached an explosive device to the habitat so they can detonate it from *Orion* if the entity, or aliens, or whatever-it-is takes us over. They won't risk our infected habitat getting to the surface. He planted one before we submerged, but I removed it. This one—no such luck."

"Oh my God!"

"Not truly surprising, though," Bheru said. "We have no way to assess the risk involved with what we are doing. Humanity must be protected."

"While we are killed with no say in the matter." Matheus' habitual smile had been replaced with a look of disgust.

"We might not be in a position to reason," Bheru asserted. "I know that might sound like B-movie paranoia—*Invasion of the Body Snatchers*—but it *is* possible we could become a danger to ourselves and others."

"You're not saying you agree with the idea?" Lee-Anna turned smoldering eyes to the biologist, who stood his ground.

Alex felt a kind of relief to know that the responsibility for a failsafe device had been taken out of his hands. "I can't completely disagree, either. We're in unknown territory here; and yes, the fate of the human race might be in the balance. I wouldn't want to make that call. I couldn't. Better that the decision is not ours to make."

"But we're the only ones who'll really know what's going on! You want your life in the hands of some government spook who's already itching to pull a trigger on someone?"

"There's something you all should see." Alex motioned her upstairs. Lee-Anna angrily followed, the others behind her.

The view from camera number four had changed. A colony of shrimp and other creatures placidly went about their business. None of the other cameras showed anything out of the ordinary. Alex rewound the footage until he found what he wanted, then stepped back to let the rest take a look.

"That's incredible," Bheru breathed. "How would creatures like that have the ability to realize they were in a circle? Why would they want to be? It looks perfectly proportioned."

"A circle is a universal, natural shape," Matheus said, sounding only half-convinced himself. "Like globes. Even the planet itself is one."

"Of course, but this is not natural. Look at the way the others have moved to clear space, to make the circle stand out."

"Or the space is just where the shrimp in the circle moved from," Lee-Anna said. "The circle is probably just coincidence. No, I know what it is. It's a reaction to light from our stands. They produce a circle of illumination; and even if those things don't have eyes, they can probably sense something like that."

Alex huffed.

"So, what do you think it is?" She glared at him. "Aliens sending us messages? Grow up!" She stood and began to move toward the access shaft, then turned back. "If you go telling Phillip Watanabe that's a signal from aliens, it might be exactly the excuse he's looking for to blow this rig." She stomped down the ladder to the airlock and noisily moved things around.

"She could be right," Elle said softly, fear in her face.

Alex carefully considered, then raised his voice.

"I asked Elle to try to contact the entity. On purpose this time. And to try to tell it that we're friendly. She pictured a group of humans sitting peacefully *in a circle*."

Elle looked betrayed, but Matheus and Bheru's eyes were wide. Lee-Anna's voice came from below.

"You asked her to get its attention while Bheru and I were outside the hab and vulnerable? Brilliant! I'm so glad they put you in charge."

Alex only sighed and wiped a hand over his face. The others dispersed, saying nothing, but he felt Elle's disappointed eyes on him. Yes, he'd taken a chance that the crew would put two and two together and realize that she was a full-blown telepath, but they hadn't. They'd already accepted that there was a special connection between Elle and the entity but hadn't extrapolated any further. Still, he'd known how she'd feel about taking the risk.

His own gaze fell to the logo on his chest: Michelangelo's pointing hands reaching toward each other. Hell, maybe he was wrong, and it wasn't about humanity seeking enlightenment from a higher being.

Maybe they were pointing fingers of blame.

## 36

March 29, 2042

There was almost no conversation for the rest of the day. The group took turns using the galley then carried their food away to eat on their own.

Orion called twice for progress updates. While Alex stood next to her, Elle told them about the camera setup, but said nothing about the circle of shrimp. Or the bomb. He thought he heard suspicion in Gary's voice, but the man didn't question their report. It sounded as if he had plenty to occupy him up there.

On a pre-planned cycle, the hab's lights dimmed for a collective sleep period. The day-night cycle of the surface world had no meaning in the deep realm, but it was easier if their circadian clocks weren't messed up too badly.

Alex lay with his hands linked on his chest, thinking about the day's events. The circle. The bomb.

Elle.

He might just be falling for her.

His senses went into overdrive when she was near, his skin drawn to touch hers. And he was nearly sure she had begun to feel something for him, too. Neither was a good idea.

She'd obviously had a crush on Gary; but with Gary left behind, maybe Alex was next in line. Maybe she just appreciated anyone who treated her kindly. She suspected the things he'd done, but probably preferred not to know. No matter what, this would be the last time he'd ever work for Phillip Watanabe and his type. His 'retirement' plan had to work—they had to finally leave him alone. Then, someday, maybe his hands would feel clean again.

Even so, getting involved with Elle wouldn't be doing her a favor. He couldn't offer commitment or stability. She deserved better.

He'd never had trouble attracting sex partners, but meaningful relationships were a different story. Lila Malone had felt like his soulmate, and he'd let her get away. Close friends through high school before they even started dating, they'd hit a roadblock when her Baptist-minister parents were called for missionary work in Africa and Lila went with them. Alex should have found a way to go too, or kept up consistent correspondence, or at least tracked her down after she came home four years later; but he had done none of those things, letting his injured pride make him stupid.

There'd never been anyone since who had understood him like Lila, not even his fiancée Lydia Colton. The daughter of one of his father's business associates, Lydia was considered to be a perfect match for him; and he did fall in love with her—for a while. But after he changed course-paths for the second time in university, she'd accused him of being indecisive and unambitious. That was the beginning of the end, but not the worst of it. When they called off the engagement, Lydia's father couldn't let it go. He foolishly tried to put pressure on Alex's family. Alex's father Curtis pushed back using information Alex had unwittingly supplied him; and when he was done, the Colton business interests were in ruins.

From then on, Alex had avoided serious relationships as determinedly as he'd avoided his father.

He would discourage Elle somehow. For her own good.

He finally fell into a restless sleep but was awakened by movement in the room. Each sleep cubicle was closed off by curtains; but in the dim light that got through, he could just see a form standing over him.

Elle?

No, the scent was very different.

Lee-Anna.

He was only covered by a sheet. Silently she slid in beside him on the left. He shifted to make room.

Putting his mouth to her ear, he whispered, "What are you doing?"

"Seriously?" she whispered back.

Their sleepwear was shorts and a t-shirt, made from the same fabric as their uniforms. With a slight rustle, she slipped hers off and dropped them on the floor. He hesitated, thinking for a moment that he could refuse, and maybe should. There was no possibility of going unheard. Elle had probably noticed when Lee-Anna got up and would certainly guess where she'd gone.

But maybe that was a good thing. For her sake.

He wasn't given more time to think about it. Lee-Anna was rather insistent. She'd probably never been refused sex in her life.

The touch of her skin sent a shiver through him. It had been a long time.

Her lips were full and moist, her breath sweet. Their tongues found each other and gently danced. Then their urgency took over and he lost himself in the press of full breasts, nipples firm against his chest. Taut abdomen thrust against his hardness.

He slid his hand down the smooth skin of her back and cupped perfect curves, then brought it over her hip and between her thighs. She couldn't hold back a sigh. He was sure she wasn't used to restraining herself when making love.

His fingers moved with skill, and when she climaxed, he thought the whole habitat would vibrate, but only the slightest of moans escaped her.

Content to wait, he held her close, enjoying the feeling as her muscles fully relaxed, punctuated by the occasional shiver of pleasure. Then, when her breathing had recovered, she kissed him deeply, brought her mouth to his ear, and whispered, "Again."

He was happy to oblige.

This time she arched so high he thought she'd strain a muscle, the sheet sliding from her and revealing her perfect form in the meagre light.

When the rise and fall of her chest finally returned to normal, he almost thought she'd fallen asleep, but then she rolled on top of him, pressed her lips fiercely against his, and breathed, "Now your turn."

## 37

March 30, 2042

When he awoke in the morning, he was alone in the bunk. Alone on the whole deck. There were sounds from the galley below, and the beckoning smell of coffee. He dressed quickly and descended.

Elle was scraping eggs onto a plate, but she didn't turn or speak. Bheru gave him a weary glance from the couch before returning his attention to his e-tablet. Matheus looked up from the computer workstation, his habitual smile back on his face. The man's hand moved slightly, and Alex realized that he was giving the OK sign.

Well, it was too much to expect the nighttime escapade could have gone unnoticed.

Once Elle had carried her breakfast up to the comm deck, he poured a cup of coffee for himself and climbed down to the lab where Lee-Anna was working on a long rod-like device with holes at intervals along its length. She looked up and her eyes lit with amusement.

"You're trying to think of something meaningful to say. Don't. Last night was fun—don't get hung up on it." She went back to fitting a wire coupling together.

"Everybody heard."

She laughed. "You didn't seriously expect them not to. I wasn't thinking of privacy when we built this place. We forgot two things: an exercise room and a love nest—or maybe just the one space to do double duty."

"Yesterday, I thought you hated me."

Lee-Anna waved a hand. "I was getting twitchy—too much pent-up energy. I needed an outlet for it. A release." She smiled. "Thanks for the therapy."

"Will you need another treatment?"

"Maybe." Her eyelashes were lowered, the smile a tease. "If you're concerned about my guy David, don't be. With both of us travelling for work, we spend so much time apart it isn't realistic to expect celibacy, and we don't."

He shrugged. It wasn't his place to judge.

She leaned toward him and whispered, "I'm sorry if it screws things up between you and Elle, though."

"Elle? But we ..."

Her scornful look stopped him. Instead, he scratched the back of his head and asked, "What are you working on?"

"It's a sniffer—a chemical sensor. I figured while we're watching the vent communities, we might as well get readings on the gases and minerals being released. They might not tell us anything, but you never know. Two of the camera stands are close enough to vent outlets that I should be able to attach a couple of these and extend them into the flow."

"Makes sense." He sat on the other stool. "Do you really think that the shrimp circle was accidental? Just a coincidence?"

She hesitated. "No, I don't. There's an intelligence here that can access our thoughts, and especially Elle's. No point denying that. But I do think it would be unwise to tell Phillip too much. The man has an agenda we know nothing about, and he makes me nervous."

"Fair enough. Do you need any help?"

"Only once I'm ready to plant them. And Bheru or Matheus should come with me, not you. Besides, we can't make out in dive suits. Although with the right programming …."

His face must have showed his surprise because she laughed and said, "I'm kidding. Go find something to do."

He'd reached Deck Two when Elle's voice came from above.

"Phillip wants to talk to Alex. Alone."

Her face was as expressionless as her words when he entered the comm deck. Without looking up or saying anything more, she climbed down the ladder. Alex put on the headset and plugged it in.

"What's with Elle? Did you two have a fight?"

Phillip wore no trace of a smile. Alex cleared his throat.

"No, it's nothing. What's going on?"

"Have you made any progress?"

"We, uh, have reason to believe that the organisms at the vents can be affected by whatever's down here."

"Really? But they don't have developed brains."

"Maybe their nervous systems just react to the energy frequency like ions to an electrode. We don't know, but we've set up cameras to watch the vent communities and Lee-Anna's going to place chemical sensors to monitor the output of gases and such."

"Has Elle picked up anything more?"

Alex looked toward the ladder and spoke even more quietly. "I've asked her to try to communicate but there's … nothing so far. But she would have told you all this. Why did you ask to speak to me?"

"Our intelligence services have kept the Russians and the Chinese in the loop about the energy transmission since the beginning—we weren't able to cover up what happened to the airliner passengers, and we needed the help of the Chinese moon probe. Now they've become aware of the habitat's presence here. They know it's not just routine exploration, so they're both assuming we've found something that might be a potential threat. Political paranoia being what it is, they're not willing to risk our making use of whatever we've found, or having us botch the job and let it get loose."

He rubbed the tip of his nose with a finger. "We're not anticipating any belligerent action yet, and you're too deep for a conventional submarine to reach; but we don't know the full capabilities of their robotic drones. *Orion* will keep watch, but there are thermoclines that interfere with her sonar. I suggest you activate the habitat's own passive sonar. If anything comes snooping, just let us know immediately and we'll take it from there."

"Shit!" Alex swallowed. "It's weird enough down here. You expect me to do this without telling anyone? Lee-Anna will know right away."

"That's up to you. If, as you say, the situation is strained already—nothing will be gained by burdening everyone with things they can't do anything about."

"That seems to be your mantra, Phillip."

The other man frowned. "Let's not forget that we have an important mission to perform. There's no place for personal opinions. Or hasty judgements." He ended the call.

Alex returned to the lab deck, ignoring quizzical looks from the others as he passed down through the Deck Two lounge, annoyed at Phillip's obsession with secrecy. Lee-Anna swiveled to face him, arms crossed. He told her what Phillip had said.

She nodded. "I'll look after it. Does it strike you that this is a little convenient, setting the stage for a quick pull-out if or when Phillip feels like it?"

His answer was a shrug. He sat down at the counter beside her and picked up a wire stripper, squeezed it closed and looked at the diminishing size of the holes. "I don't think he's lying, but there's a good chance the Russians and Chinese want us to know they're keeping an eye on us."

She gave a half smile and shook her head, turning back to a screw she was tightening.

"You guys have odd concepts of foreplay."

38

March 30, 2042

Elle didn't care that Alex and Lee-Anna had spent the night carrying on like alley cats. What they did was their business. But it had disturbed everyone else's sleep.

That was inconsiderate.

And a lack of sleep could seriously affect the crew's ability to carry out the mission. Which made it irresponsible, too.

Now Phillip and Alex were sharing secrets and making plans without the rest of them being consulted. That was ... inefficient.

They expected her to make a crucial breakthrough somehow, while keeping her in the dark. She felt like telling them to screw themselves. She still might, except if there wasn't some progress soon, they'd all be screwed.

And not in the way Alex and Lee-Anna had so enthusiastically demonstrated.

She was cleaning out the coffeemaker when Alex came down the ladder.

"Little boys with their secrets," she muttered. Alex paused and came to lean on the end of the counter.

"If you really want to know what Phillip said, I'll tell you. But it's not going to make you feel any better."

"I'm stuck in a giant metal egg on the bottom of the ocean waiting for some alien to take another shot at wiping my brain. What's going to make me feel better is a ticket home."

"I wish I could arrange it. Honest. For the rest of us, this is our job in some form or another; but you don't belong here, and I'm sorry about that."

"You don't want to be here either."

There was no point denying it. She knew better, and he knew she did.

"Look, I hate to ask you, but could you maybe try to send a message again? Now we have cameras set up, we can see right away if there's an answer."

She finished putting the coffee things in the cupboards and turned to him.

"It's probably the only thing we can try right now—I understand that. But I'm a translator. I don't write the speeches. Why don't you brainiacs get off your asses and tell me what to send that will get us the response we want. Then I'll do my best."

Alex and Bheru looked stunned. Matheus' laugh made the habitat ring.

"She's absolutely right! Absolutely," he said with a huge grin.

"OK," Alex said. "But what do we want to say? We don't know if we're talking to one being, or dozens. Is it some strange Earth mutant or aliens from another planet?"

"The message would be the same," Matheus answered. "We've come in peace to talk to it. We're intelligent beings trying to communicate with another."

"It must already know we're intelligent from our technology."

"No, my friend. If this being is biological, and from Earth, it may not recognize technology at all. It may consider the habitat nothing more extraordinary than the shell of a mussel."

"The most urgent thing we can say is that we're not here to harm it. That's why I pictured people sitting in a friendship circle. Cooperating." Elle said.

"Ah, a very good choice. Now how can we improve on that—make it clearer?"

"Not that I subscribe to your fantasy about space aliens," Bheru said, "but if you do believe we're dealing with an advanced race, mathematics is usually considered to be the most likely area of commonality."

"Do you expect Elle to picture the Fibonacci sequence? The calculation for Pi? What species will have in common is their planets, which are round—yes, I know this one is under the ocean, but it's obviously aware of the Moon. They will have suns—also round. They almost certainly will have a physical form themselves, which is why we included line drawings of naked humans on the Voyager spacecraft."

"You want Elle to picture herself naked?" Bheru showed no sign that he was making a joke. Elle gave a huff and moved to the ladder.

"I'll be helping Lee-Anna until you geniuses agree on something sensible."

"I don't really need any help," they heard Lee-Anna say as Elle moved down the rungs. "I've finished what I was doing. But I don't mind some company. A talk. Maybe we can do a better job than the men. That wouldn't be a first!" They laughed.

Elle reflected that she was being cold to Alex, but was sharing jokes with the woman who had gone to his bed. Well, that Lee-Anna would engage in casual sex was no surprise—she practically telegraphed her availability. Made no apologies for it either. But Elle had hoped for better from Alex. No, not better—that was judgmental—but for something … else.

"Maybe some engineering concepts would be more universal than math equations," Lee-Anna continued. "Like a suspension bridge, or an arch. Or the simplest ones: a lever and a wheel."

"Wheel—also round." Elle said in Matheus' voice, and they laughed again.

"Have you been practicing that accent? I've sometimes thought so."

"Really? I haven't meant to. I have an ear for languages. Whenever I'm with somebody who has a noticeable accent, I have to watch myself, so I don't unconsciously start copying it."

"Does that happen?"

"Oh yeah. All the time."

"What about Bheru?"

"Well, the simple fact is that there is nothing simple about any of that whatsoever."

Lee-Anna gave a snort of surprise and then covered her mouth with her hand.

"The thing is," Elle said in a hushed voice, "Bheru's accent is all over the place. Indian, of course, though both north and south. Oxford English, but obviously learned in India. Then a lot of consonants and a few vowels straight out of Glasgow, and a handful of Canadian pronunciations. I love it. I wish I could always talk that way."

"He might be hurt."

"I wouldn't want that. He's a sweet man."

"A bit of a temper, though." Raised voices were plainly heard from above them. Bheru's made the lab equipment vibrate.

"Both too smart for their own good," Elle said.

"Not Alex?"

Elle tried not to react, but it was too late, she'd already turned her head away.

"Look," Lee-Anna said, "Us getting together last night—it was just sex. As I said to him, it was therapy. I don't have any claim on him nor him on me. We're OK with that, but if you're not ... I'll keep away."

"No, no. Alex and I aren't .... We don't ...." She slumped against the lab table. "Shit! I don't even know what I feel. But I don't have any claim on him either. Do what you want to do."

"Turns out I like his company. And he's a considerate lover. You may want to find that out for yourself." Lee-Anna brushed her hair back over her ears. "Change of topic. About that alien. What if you projected a big egg like the hab, and then pictured a human figure and showed it inside the habitat? That might at least show that we're the thinking beings and the hab is where we live."

"Either that or it'll think we're descended from chickens."

Their laughter finally brought the men down to see what was going on.

39

March 30, 2042

Elle stared at the screen and tried to project the isosceles triangle it displayed. Camera number four showed shrimp in a circle. There was nothing special in the other views.

She pictured a perfect square. The shrimp kept to their circle.

She envisioned the habitat with small humanoid figures inside and outside. She formed an image of two shrimp, then added two more, and added another two. She even tried humming the tune of "Mary Had a Little Lamb" as it played in her headset.

The shrimp formed a circle, and only a circle. Finally, they dispersed and there was only random activity in the colony.

"We lost its attention," Alex said, spinning his chair away from the screen.

"We never had much of it," Bheru said. "It didn't even try to form the other shapes."

"Or maybe it was simply telling us that the circle is so much more important," Matheus offered. "The circle of life, even."

"Did you feel any response from it, Elle? Anything coming back at all?"

She shook her head.

"There's almost always a sense of its presence, especially curiosity, but there was nothing more. Even that's faded right now."

The deck fell silent. Eventually everyone went to their own places to rest, read, or think. Elle stayed in the galley surveying the ingredients in the cupboards and trying to think of recipes that could be made from them. That often helped to clear her mind.

A little while later, Alex came to her. He sat close and his voice was soft.

"If you don't want anything to do with this, it's OK and nobody has to know."

She raised her eyebrows, wondering what he was about to say.

"The only thing I can think to try next is to go out there and communicate in person."

"What do you mean?"

"I mean me taking you out to the vents to see if you can get this thing talking to you face to face, so to speak." He grinned. "Your face to whatever passes for faces on the creatures out there. We know there's a connection. Maybe this intelligence is located under the smokers. Or maybe it just doesn't get the concept of us speaking from inside this big shell." He waited, watching her with his mouth held tight.

Her heart hammered. Go out there in a suit and holler *Come and get me?* Hell no! That was the last thing she wanted to do. Couldn't Alex see that?

Yes, he could. He knew. But he still asked because he thought it was important. More, he thought she could do it. He believed in her, even if she didn't.

"It's your decision," he said. "If you can't … it stays between you and me."

She swallowed hard and fought the urge to vomit.

"I'll go."

"Good. Great." He rose and moved to the access shaft.

"What, you mean right now?"

He laughed. "Waiting is the hardest part. Always better to get it over with."

The feeling of confinement had been bad in the submersible, but at least she'd had Gary and the pilot with her. It reached a whole new level as the dive suit enclosed her.

Just before the headgear slid into place Alex held her shoulders and looked into her eyes.

"I'll be right with you, within reach the whole time. But you could do this without me. You've got strength inside that you haven't even tapped yet. Trust yourself."

She nodded and let the hood go. As it made its seal, she was suddenly sure that there was no air circulating. *There was no air!*

She raised her arms to pull at the headpiece but felt Alex seize them, and there was a thump as his forehead pressed against hers. She could see the head of his suit—she wished she could see his face. He didn't say anything, though—he didn't want the others to hear.

Even though her reason told her that he was only inches away, she felt cut off from the world. The wide viewscreen filled most of her vision—a good simulation of a glass visor—but she knew it was dependent on cameras and wires and circuits, any of which could fail and leave her utterly blind.

Stepping into the mini airlock like a wrapped mummy being entombed, she closed her eyes and took a deep breath. Despite her doubts, air filled her lungs. Again. And again.

Finally, she was able to slow her breathing and open her eyes. The mini lock was already flooded. The worst had passed.

Or so she thought until the wall split apart and revealed the void.

Her body began to shake.

What had happened to her goddamned conditioning?

Alex appeared in front of her and took her hand, but she couldn't move.

He took her other hand too, and then gently began to pull her forward.

Bheru, Matheus, Lee-Anna—they had all gone through this, and worse. But she felt that if her feet lost touch with the habitat, she would float away forever into the endless darkness.

Maybe Alex had suddenly become psychic and read *her* mind, because a cable now hung from his hand, about two meters long, with clips on either end. He attached one end to his suit and the other to hers.

It was said without a word: Wherever she went, he would go too.

She kicked loose and balanced her suit in swimming position.

There was another bad moment as they moved away from the hab, the void all around her. She pictured astronauts on spacewalks—imagining what it would be like if their tether broke and they drifted off into infinite space, beyond rescue, to die alone. This place, too, seemed infinite and implacable. Maybe even more immediately threatening, because of the inconceivable pressure all around her. Death only an eye blink away. Never had she felt so strongly that she didn't belong. No living thing could belong here. It was Hell, the true Hell.

But Alex was with her, her Vergil, leading her through all nine circles of it.

The darkness wasn't total—the lights both of the habitat and their suits pushed a little of the blackness away.

"How's your air? Are you warm enough?"

She swallowed and cleared her throat. "Um, yes. I'm good. It's fine."

"OK. You see that smudge of light over there?" He pointed. "That's from the cameras. That's where we're headed, and it's not far. The habitat lights show up just as well from over there. You can't get lost."

She tried to nod, but the headgear was too stiff for that. "OK," she said, and was appalled at how high her voice sounded. Like a little girl's. Shit! She made her throat relax and said, "Let me know when you think I should start projecting." Much better.

"Let's wait until we're right there, so it's clear where your thoughts are coming from."

There was no sensation of her feet and legs pushing against the water, or any other indication of motion, which made the swim to the lights seemed endless; but once there, the panorama took her breath away. The cameras had been placed within forty feet of each other; and together their lamps lit a space about the size of a suburban lot: a spectacular palette of color, though heavy on whites, oranges, and reds. Much of it was in motion—all manner of strange shapes undulating and crawling over each other. She should have been creeped out—spiders and crabs had always unsettled her—but this was fantastic in every sense of the word.

There were towers and castles and plains and valleys. Banners flew and armies marched. Fish-shaped dirigibles floated among the turrets, while armored scouts conquered steep walls. From fantasy, the scene shifted to reality, and she marveled at the myriad forms life had found to exist in such an inhospitable place. Each creature filled a niche—each had its place.

They did belong.

"Do you feel like making contact?" Alex's voice came through as clearly as if they were next to each other in the hab. He floated close enough for their shoulders to touch. "Maybe start with the friendship circle again, then show our human form with empty hands. It might get the idea."

"OK." Closing her eyes made her feel disoriented again, so she reached out and he took her hand. Forcing herself to relax, she filled her mind with the blue haze and gradually pictured people, this time standing in a circle with their hands linked. She closed in on the basic outline of a woman and showed her form in simple detail.

She didn't know anything was wrong until she felt Alex's arm jerk. Her eyes popped open.

Something had obscured the image of the vent community. She brushed a hand across the face of her suit and felt it bump into *things*. That cleared her view for a moment; but then, blobs of white blocked it again. She held out her hand and saw it covered by crawling things.

God. *Oh God, they were swarming her!* She couldn't hold back a scream.

Alex swept his hands over her suit, trying to knock the creatures away, but the cleared patches didn't last. None of the organisms clung to him. Only her.

Her panting turned to moans, and she began to thrash, trying to get away. Alex gripped her, but she fought him. Everything was dark now—she couldn't see a thing, but she knew forces of death were clawing at her, sucking, biting, seeking any way to reach her body and invade her soul. She couldn't see them. *Couldn't see!*

She wanted to open her mouth to scream again, but was terrified of what would crawl in.

A force gripped her psyche with cold fingers. Pressed and squeezed and probed. She floated in a relentless grey-blue mist—it ran like liquid into the crevices of her cauliflower brain, seeking a way *inside*. Its icy touch was the slither of a poisonous serpent.

In her mind, she raged, *go to hell, go to hell, go to hell!*

From far away, oh so far, she heard Alex's voice saying reassuring words, and then Lee-Anna's: "I've turned her CO2 up to keep her from hyperventilating." And Bheru: "They can't reach you, Elle. They cannot get through. You're safe. We'll keep you safe." And finally, Alex again: "They're gone. Elle, they're gone. They're gone."

She opened her eyes, shaking too badly to focus on anything, but there was light. Lots of light. Coming from Alex's dive suit. Beyond him were the camera lights and the colors ... the colors of the crawling things, and she moaned again, but they were already far away. Alex had pulled her to safety.

He turned her around, and she saw the lights of the habitat, close and getting closer.

Then they were in the airlock, flooded with blessed light, and the suit was collapsing, and she was in Alex's arms shaking, shaking, sobbing helplessly into his neck.

# # #

With a mug of tea warming her hands, she sat at the galley table staring at nothing. The others were all nearby, but they were giving her space. And time. She hadn't spoken. Didn't know if she still could.

She lifted her eyes to find Alex close beside her, worry creasing his face. She examined every line and fold.

"I'm so sorry," he said. "So, so sorry. I should have expected that. I should never have asked ..." His voice cut out as he raised his face toward the ceiling for a moment, eyes glistening. He hesitated before lifting his hand to gently touch her cheek.

"Thank you," she rasped, then coughed and tried again. "Thank you for pulling me away. For getting them off me."

"No. They left on their own. I think … I think maybe you scared them off."

She looked deep into his eyes, and he gave the slightest of nods.

He had felt it. He had felt the scream of her mind.

How …?

She thought back, though reliving the memory was like peeling her skin with a razor. She couldn't help a powerful shudder.

"No," she said. "That wasn't it. They left on their own because the thing lost interest in me." She drew a harsh breath as her body flooded with outrage. "After all it's put me through, it suddenly decides I'm not worth its *attention*? Fuck that!"

Her lips pulled back in a snarl. Hot tea slopped onto her leg, and she didn't flinch.

This was not going to happen again. She was not a toy to be played with and then discarded.

She was going to find that bastard. She was going to find it with her mind, and it was not going to ignore her.

Not anymore.

## 40

March 30, 2042

The sonar's dull susurration lulled Alex into a contemplative mood.

There was no real need to listen to it. Very little of any size moved in the lowest zone of the ocean, and the habitat was in a flat valley with ridges to the north and south. The system's database eliminated extraneous alarms, which included virtually every naturally occurring sound in the ocean. So, if anything artificial were to come within range, an alert would sound, and the crew would have the option of going 'active'—sending a strong *ping* to use returning sound waves to paint a picture.

The main reason they weren't running active already was the obscure game of power politics being played above. It wasn't that they were afraid of revealing the habitat's location—an intruder would presumably be pretty certain of that already—but active pinging would show that they were expecting company, and that was still supposed to be a secret.

So far, their equipment had picked up nothing but a faint murmur from the geothermal vents, and some distant whale-song.

Matheus entered the lounge and sat, with a faint sigh. Alex reflected that they were like soldiers stationed near a battlefront: bored and tense at the same time, with little to do but wait for events beyond their control.

Sometimes talking helped.

"With recent developments, do you still think we're dealing with extraterrestrial aliens, or is it just as likely this is only some Earth creature we never discovered before?" Alex asked.

"The word 'only' doesn't belong in that question. *Only* another powerful intelligence on the planet Earth? I think that would be just as newsworthy as a visit from aliens."

"Important and interesting, certainly, but not as significant. Aliens could teach us so much."

"Do you think we've learned as much as can be learned on this planet? I am certain we have not. The black smokers themselves are a good example. Geothermal vents along volcanically active ridges in the oceans had been predicted, but no one suspected that such vents would support huge communities of living creatures. The discoverers were gobsmacked—such an evocative expression!—and you said yourself that even a knowledge of such things could not prepare you for the reality. The discovery of these life forms challenged our whole way of thinking about how life arose on Earth. I would say it even changed it."

"Why? Because the creatures can tolerate the pressure of the ocean depths and the heat of the vents?"

"No, because our theories about Earth life assumed that all of it depended in some way on energy from the Sun. And here, suddenly, were colonies of life where no trace of that energy ever reached. It is life based on chemosynthesis, not photosynthesis. Energy from within the Earth, not the Sun. So instead of organic molecules being produced by lightning strikes in the so-called primordial soup of chemicals on the surface of ancient Earth, it may be that the bacteria of these vents—the *archaea* especially—are the earliest forms of life and led to everything else."

"As I said, that's interesting but ..."

"Don't you see? If this is an Earth-born being that we've encountered, it could be far more ancient than anything we've ever known. Perhaps anything we could imagine. Very likely far older than a race of space-faring aliens." Matheus' beard twitched—he was enjoying this immensely.

"Are you just pulling my leg, or do you really believe that?"

"We will probably be travelling among the stars within a few hundred years, yet we are babies compared to the oldest life on this planet. We can't know if intelligent life arose that long ago, but what if it did? It may have solved the greatest riddles mankind has ever posed. It may know the *meaning* of life. It may have met God."

Alex leaned back and crossed his arms.

"Now I know you're pulling my leg."

Matheus laughed. "I assure you, I'm not. Humans and our forerunners have been toolmakers for a couple of million years. But this entity could be from a far more ancient race. Here at the bottom of the sea, it could have survived all five major extinctions that took place on the surface. Why not? And you'll say it wouldn't have had the stimulus or perhaps the physical challenges required to learn science and mathematics, or develop wisdom. But even from two miles beneath the ocean, this being is aware of our Moon floating in space. It became aware of us. Maybe it has been aware of us for our entire history and can tell us what the world was like when we were climbing down out of the trees. What *we* were like."

"And God?"

"Those of us who believe in God believe that God is within all of us. How much more of God might be in something nearly as old as the world itself?"

Alex looked into the man's eyes. There was a fervor there, fierce and enduring. A spark of humor, too. But he wasn't lying or joking now.

He beckoned Alex to the workstation. "Here are some of the entries I've been reading to learn about smokers and non-photosynthetic biologies, the beginnings of life on Earth and such things. They're very illuminating. And if you have more questions, Bheru probably has the answers in his head."

The data did back up some of Matheus' inferences, but Alex remained convinced that ultimately it would be alien life they found, not Earth life. Or maybe that was just what he'd hoped for since reading his first science-fiction stories, and yearned for as an adult. Why?

Because life as a human adult of the twenty-first century was disappointing: full of falsehoods, shallow priorities, undesirable tasks and unwanted responsibilities. Status was increasingly important, and status had come to be fed by consumerism. A consumer society had sucked dry the world's reserves of oil, filled its skies with carbon and its seas with acid. In general, there was very little about modern times that Alex could celebrate, and, personally, virtually nothing very worthy in his own life, either.

The coming of visitors from another star would shake things up. Life would never be the same; and, to him, that was something to be desired. Yes, there was a risk that human ambition could die, but he didn't believe it. There was a streak of cussedness in humankind that would never be sidelined—that would desperately strive to accomplish something just because others said it couldn't be done. That was the part of the human animal that would come to the fore if aliens arrived, for better or for worse. The critical factor was that such an advanced race would have learned how to avoid the pitfalls that had hampered humanity's progress. That wisdom coupled with human drive could bring about a true golden age.

Still, Matheus' argument couldn't just be dismissed. When the question arose about why the search for extraterrestrial intelligence had never borne fruit, prevailing opinion said that technological societies detectable by human methods probably didn't stay in that phase for very long. From the time they began to use electromagnetic frequencies for radio and television, it might only be a few hundred years until they surrounded their home star with a Dyson sphere to allow no more energy to escape. Or traveled on long space voyages in some form of deep-freeze hibernation. Or uploaded consciousnesses into giant computer simulations. Or just plain evolved beyond any need for physical bodies.

Was that what he and his companions were dealing with? A disembodied intelligence beyond anything they could comprehend?

It was also true that the crew of an alien spaceship come to Earth might not necessarily be far advanced in technology, knowledge, or wisdom. Perhaps only by a few hundred years, by the standards of human progress.

Maybe they would not have all the answers. So why would they be playing so damned hard to get?

But what if this being belonged to a race so far advanced that it no longer needed to take physical form? It would be seen as a demi-god.

And what would a sociotheologist make of that?

Matheus sat back with a look of surprise when Alex mentioned it.

"You're right. That possibility is just as valid. A demi-god indeed. Or possibly God himself, in the sense of being the creator of this universe."

"How is that possible?"

"Consider an alien life form so advanced, so powerful, so fully evolved by the time its universe finally collapses that it is capable of not only surviving that cataclysm but intelligently creating the next iteration of the universe. Ours."

His eyes glittered with the vision. "Thank you, Alex. Thank you for helping me clarify my thoughts." There was something strange about his expression as he left for the crew quarters.

"But what ...?" Only, Matheus was no longer listening.

Why would God be so coy? Alex wanted to ask. How could God have killed the passengers of the jetliner in such a horrible way, or treated Elle so cruelly?

Centuries of theological argument had not been enough to find answers to such questions. Perhaps they really were unanswerable by a finite mind.

Alex had never bought into that, which was why he'd never practiced any form of religion.

Now, though, he realized that Matheus' words opened up a whole new range of speculation about what they might be facing here in the oceanic abyss, a world apart from the one he knew.

Alex tasted a whole new fear.

## 41

March 31, 2042

When Lee-Anna and Matheus went out to install the chemical sniffers on two of the camera stands closest to vent water flows, adding them to the stands wasn't difficult, but aligning them in just the right position to capture fresh chemicals without overheating was finicky. And then their output had to be added to the camera feed without causing interference.

Alex hadn't been sleeping well, and when he started to yawn while watching the divers, Bheru offered to take over surveillance duties.

It was a chance to grab a quick nap. As Alex stepped off the ladder into the crew quarters, he noticed Elle sitting on her bunk.

She looked as if she were meditating, cross-legged with her arms resting on her knees, except that her face was anything but serene.

"I'm not sleeping," she said. "Or doing yoga either." Her eyes opened.

"I didn't mean to disturb you. What were you doing?"

"Giving that asshole a piece of my mind."

"That ... do you mean the *entity*? Are you serious?"

She gave him a look. She was serious, all right.

"None of you has any idea what that thing has put me through, and then when I go out there to talk to it, it tortures me with my worst fear. And it *knows* that's my worst fear. Then it just ... ignores me? Dumps me like a high-school cheerleader who finally put out for the captain of the football team? I don't think so. I'm sick of being treated like that."

Alex was torn between a laugh and a whistle of surprise. He didn't think either would be well-received.

"Is it a good idea to be projecting anger when Lee-Anna and Matheus are out at the vents?"

"Are they covered with crawling things?"

"No."

"And neither were you last time. This is between that thing and me, and it knows it."

"That might be true for the moment, but it's certainly aware of the rest of us. And we're here to take our share of the load too, if we can. It's not all on you."

"When that thing scares the piss out of you, you're welcome to join me in the fight. Speaking of which ..." She leaned forward and her eyes opened wider. "Did you really feel me scream out there? Not the voice scream, my mental scream?"

He nodded. "Well, I thought I felt something. More likely, I sensed a mental scream because that's what I expected you to do."

"You're just rationalizing."

"How can you be sure?"

She hesitated and looked away. "I just know."

"So ... if you've been sending out all this anger ... has it responded? Did you get a reaction?"

"Yeah."

"*What?* Why didn't you say so?'

"I'm telling you right now."

He moved to sit on the end of her bed. She should be terrified. Need comforting. But she didn't look it.

"What's it been saying? 'Back off sister, this is my neighborhood'?"

She actually smiled. "Maybe that was what it was saying at first. It felt like … well, it felt like it was trying to ignore me again. Turn its back on me. I wasn't having any of that. So, I kind of said, *What's your problem?*"

He laughed, trying to picture a mental conversation between a higher intelligence and a pissed off Elle Travis.

"Are you laughing at me?" She swept her bangs from her eyes.

"It's a funny image. Especially after what we've been going through. But I'm impressed. Go on. What did it do?"

She shifted on the bunk, leaning over her knees. "Well, the rest is hard to be sure about. I think it was trying to tell me it knows who we are, what we are. I sensed images of ships and planes and things. But then … garbage."

"What?"

"Garbage and pollution. Plastics, and oil slicks, and … and drums of chemicals, I think. But also storms and lightning." She gave a look that was almost apologetic. "I think it was trying to say something about pollution and climate change. As if it knows we're to blame."

"Shit. Are you sure you weren't projecting your own feelings and attributing them to the entity?" She glared at him. "That wasn't a criticism, Elle—I'm sure I would. Especially on that topic. It would be only natural. The thing is … we've been trying all this time to make contact and understand what it wants, and suddenly you get a clear-cut message about climate change?"

"It's not clear-cut, OK? I said those were the images I got and, yes, I put them together in a way that made sense to me. If you have another interpretation, let's hear it."

He sighed and held up his hands. The last thing he wanted to do was to fight with her. She was in an impossible position, being asked not only to submit to a horribly invasive process that posed a very real threat to her sanity, but also translate the signals of a totally alien mind. It was a miracle that she didn't go mad, and he feared she was always poised on that razor's edge.

"Did you respond?" he asked softly. She shook her head.

"I started to get all angry back at it, but … if that is what it was saying, then it was right. That *is* who we are."

"Yeah, it is."

After several minutes lost in their own thoughts, Elle asked, "Are you going to tell Phillip and Gary?"

"I have to. But I need to decide how to tell them and how much."

He gave her a sympathetic smile and rested his hand on her shoulder before going to his bunk to lie down. He'd just closed his eyes when he heard her march across the deck to the side of his bunk.

"And by the way …." She bent over and kissed him, hard and hot. Before he could react, she stalked back to her own bed. "There's more than one woman in this rig."

Oh, he was aware of that, he thought, touching his lips with his fingers. He was very aware.

## 42

March 31, 2042

The whole team had gathered around the comm console within moments of hearing Alex's cry of outrage.

"You can't bring us up. We just started making progress!"

Gary gave Phillip an *I-told-you-so* look.

"It's the consensus at headquarters," the agent said into the webcam. "Judging from what you've told us, it appears you could be just as effective topside without the risks of the deep ocean."

Was the man implying that the crew hadn't told him everything, and this was just a ploy to get them to come clean? But he'd already been determined to bring the habitat to the surface and the 36-hour deadline had come.

In spite of the poor resolution of the video signal, Gary saw a look pass between Alex and Elle.

"We disagree," Alex said. "The entity has received images sent by Elle and almost certainly can distinguish between her and the rest of us. We have no way to know if her messages can reach it from the surface; and once aboard *Orion*, she'll be among many more humans whose thoughts will confuse things."

"Our government and its top military leaders are fully informed and in charge here, and Elle's loss of connection is a risk they are willing to take."

"Because you want to be able to take a clean shot at it!"

"Ms. Cavallo, we have no plans to shoot anything at anyone." Which was an outright lie, Gary knew. The plans were in place. It only remained for the brass to give the order. Gary had fought as hard as he could, and the decision wasn't final yet, but they wanted the hab out of the way so there'd be no delay if that order were to be given.

"We have enough food, water, and air to last another week, even without a visit from your supply drones," Lee-Anna continued. "And by the way, were you planning to remove your remote-control bomb from the hab's hull before or after you haul us back to *Orion*?"

Gary's eyebrows shot up. This was the first he'd heard of any explosive device on the hab, though he shouldn't have been surprised. Phillip's face was tightly under control as he ignored the question.

"Are you suggesting you might refuse to come to the surface? I'm not sure your own superiors at Stanford would appreciate your holding their multi-million-dollar facility hostage. Or possibly you've got lots of job offers from other topflight universities."

Lee-Anna's look should have melted the camera.

"Ok, you're good at bullying, Phillip," Elle pushed into the view, "but I'm not letting you use that crap with me anymore. Threaten to send me back to the shrinks—I don't give a shit. But you know what I can do? I can tell our little friend down here all about bombs and missiles and torpedoes. All the things you might be considering sending its way. And then we'll see how friendly it decides to be."

Phillip took a step back.

"You wouldn't do that. You and your team would be the first ones to suffer if you make it angry."

"Not if I make it clear where the threat is coming from."

"So, you'd rather endanger everyone on *Orion*—maybe the whole human race?"

"I'm not the one pulling our team out just as we're coming close to learning what this thing is and what makes it tick. Doing something violent without those answers is what will endanger humankind. Tell *that* to your superiors!"

Suddenly the picture was gone. Elle had broken the connection.

"Shit!" Phillip slammed the desk. It was the strongest display of emotion Gary had ever seen from the man.

"The lady thinks she has you by the balls," Gary said. The response was a vicious glare.

"She has no idea what we're facing. What they're facing."

"Neither do I. So why not fill me in; and if you can convince me, maybe I'll try to convince her."

A parade of thoughts passed behind Phillip's eyes. He threw up a hand and paced across the floor of his office, finally turning and perching on the edge of the desk.

"Our intelligence services believe there's a Chinese submarine in the area. Equipped with nuclear-tipped torpedoes."

"Jesus!"

"It's not certain they could fire on an object two miles below them, but they could drop very powerful mines. Or, conceivably, launch a torpedo with a timer and just let it drop to the ocean floor. Pinpoint accuracy wouldn't matter with a nuke."

"Wouldn't an underwater nuclear blast cause a tsunami? Guam isn't that far away. There'd be hell to pay."

"No, the blast itself wouldn't do anything like that. The only risk of that kind would be if it caused a major seismic event—a large earthquake."

"The whole area is seismically active."

"Our analysts feel that risk is very low; and so, I'm sure, do the Chinese. No, the threat is to the entity—the habitat would be collateral damage, and so would *Orion* if we're overhead at the time, so if we're going to winch up the habitat it has to be now."

Gary raised his arms over his head to stretch out his spine, deltoids, and biceps, then rested his interlocked fingers on his head in thought. His eyes roved over the maps on the wall and the sheets of writing and graphs pinned to them in a fashion that looked haphazard, but certainly wasn't. His mind didn't really register the details, though. He was picturing black space scattered with stars.

He dropped into a chair.

"I don't understand. The bigwigs on both sides probably don't believe this energy beam came from something that evolved on Earth, right? So, we're talking about aliens—advanced aliens, who presumably have a whole lot more firepower than we do. Why in hell would the Chinese take a chance on pissing them off?"

Phillip stepped around the desk and sat down.

"Think it through. Earth is blanketed by radar and other detection systems. Some of it is civilian, but a lot is military. Near-Earth orbit is well-covered too—we have catalogs of space debris, some of it only inches across. Then there are the programs searching near-space for potentially threatening asteroids—there's a growing catalog of those. And we're pretty sure the signal was aimed at the Moon; well, the Moon is under surveillance all the time in dozens of different ways, by a dozen different nations—including that Chinese probe that was re-tasked just to make sure there's nobody hiding on the far side. Nothing has been detected. No alien presence has ever been detected."

"Thousands of conspiracy theorists would disagree." The line didn't provoke a smile. "But what if they have some kind of cloaking technology, like on the legendary *Star Trek*?"

"Yet they betray their presence this way?" the agent said. "OK, maybe they had some kind of emergency, except after nearly two months nothing else has arrived. So, if there is an alien spacecraft under the ocean floor, what would be your conclusion about it?"

Gary took the question seriously and didn't answer for a minute or so. Then he raised his head.

"It's been here since before our detection technology got to this level. Or it was small enough to look like something natural when it came down. Disguised as a meteorite, maybe."

"It sends a signal, but gets no response?"

"It was a lone scout ship, or it's been abandoned."

"And that's why the Chinese feel confident in being able to destroy it without fear of reprisal."

"Shit, that's all speculation! We can't be sure of any of it until Elle makes better contact and gets some answers. That's why they *have* to stay down there."

"You're very cavalier with their lives!" Shocked by his own outburst, Phillip raised his hands in apology and leaned across the desk. His usually impassive face was tense with conflicting emotions.

"Even apart from personal considerations, what if the blast doesn't destroy the aliens? It will certainly destroy the habitat, and we'll have lost the only person who's succeeded in communicating with them at all."

It was a cold assessment, but Gary suspected there was more emotion behind it than Phillip Watanabe would ever let on. It was also perfectly valid.

Gary cleared his throat. "What can you do?"

"Haul them up against their will."

"Really? Do you have spare dive suits like Lee-Anna's? Because that cable isn't going to attach itself. Maybe one of your drones can do it, but the hab crew will hear it coming. The cable and the drone. They'll be waiting, and they'll think of lots of ways to interfere."

Phillip sat back and swiped imaginary dirt from his desktop.

"There might be another way," he said. "I need to talk to Elle again. Could you ... please ... get her on the comm? I have a feeling she might not be taking my calls." He gave a self-conscious smile.

Gary didn't know whether to be relieved, or afraid.

## 43

March 31, 2042

Elle stared at the communications console with its touchpad and rim of indicator lights. Like the other computer workstations, this one could be operated using a holographic interface. She'd tried it once, darting her fingers at images of buttons projected in mid-air, but she was more comfortable touching a real surface. Even the touchpad reacted to the proximity of her skin, though, with each 'button' changing shade slightly as her finger hovered over it. She waggled her fingers over the pad for a while like playing an imaginary piano and watched the dance of the lights.

But wasn't there something she was supposed to be doing?

Talking to Phillip. She leaned toward the display and saw that she'd just completed a call with him. That was strange.

Gary had called her—she remembered that—and then passed the call to Phillip, but she wasn't clear about what she and Phillip had said. There was something about the habitat being recalled to the surface, but she didn't want to go. That's why she was mad at Phillip. But then he'd still said she was doing a terrific job. Outstanding.

Alex poked his head above the deck.

"Were you just talking to Phillip again?"

"Yeah, he wanted to change my mind. Get us to agree to surface the hab. I said no."

"Good. I guess we have to give him credit for persistence."

She didn't reply, and Alex went back down. She returned to the touchpad, making the lights move. It was sort of hypnotic, in a way.

# # #

Alarms went off three hours into the next sleep period.

Elle saw Lee-Anna fly to the ladder and drop into the lounge. Alex wasn't far behind. She swung her feet off her bunk, but felt strangely heavy as she stood up.

"It's the base of the hab," Lee-Anna cried out. "It's been detached! We're going up."

That was the strange feeling—the habitat rising. She clutched at the ladder and tried to think how she could help. Bheru went down to the next deck. Matheus began to stand, then sat again, looking at Elle with a shrug.

"Flood the airlock!"

"Already done. But it's not nearly enough. I'm going to have to flood the lab, too. Fuck! Everything will be crushed."

"Wait!" There was the sound of thudding footsteps on the ladder. Elle looked over and saw Alex drop to the bottom deck.

"What are you doing?" Lee-Anna yelled. Alex was already partially covered in black. He was putting on a suit!

"If you flood the lab, we'll have no other way to get outside without blowing the water out. That'll make us rise again. Give me a minute."

"Make that two. He might need help." Bheru hurried down the ladder and snatched a suit from the rack.

Their headgear was just about to slide into place when the laboratory wall closed. Elle remembered Lee-Anna saying that it could be used as an emergency airlock or escape pod, but the pressure of the water would destroy a lot of the equipment. Obviously, there was no choice.

Going a few steps down the ladder she watched over Lee-Anna's shoulder. The airlock seal indicator glowed green. Moments later there was another green rectangle on the display—the lab was sealed and beginning to flood. Jesus, the men had better have their suits sealed. The main airlock wouldn't flood unless they did, but did the lab have those safeguards?

Lee-Anna must have had the same thought. She drew her fingers over the display, and a square in the corner expanded to show a camera view inside the laboratory. As water rose slowly up the walls, sealed containers of all kinds crumpled instantly. Even containers above the water line were imploding—the air in the room had been compressed that much. Elle felt sick watching Alex and Bheru with debris swirling around them, as if at any moment she'd see them crushed too, though it didn't happen. Of course not. Their suits were closed.

The fully flooded room was still so brightly lit that the screen showed a slow-motion video of a cyclone in a junkyard: crumpled cans, flattened plastic tubes, nearly invisible shards of glass, all floating in long arcs that changed as they collided with each other, or the walls. Or humans. The men flinched, although nothing moved with enough force to harm them.

Alex's voice came from the speakers. "Are we still rising?"

Lee-Anna checked a readout. "It's slowed, but it hasn't stopped. Shit, what else can we do to get heavy?"

"What about letting water into the rest of Deck One?" he asked. "There's a bulkhead to keep it from getting to the other decks, right?"

"Sure, there's one at each deck level. But we can't. The air processing plant is down there. It's not pressure proof, and if it fails, we can't make any more air. There's enough in the tanks to empty the airlock and still leave us a few days of breathing. But if we have to blow out more water than that ... we'll never get back off the bottom on our own."

The comm frequency went quiet as each of them faced the prospect of being trapped under two miles of water while their air slowly went bad.

"The drinking water ... is it possible to filter what comes from the tank?" Alex asked. "There must be room in the holding tank by now."

"Yes." Lee-Anna gave a tense smile. "That might be enough. But you'll have to remove the holding tank's filler cap manually from the outside. That won't be easy—there could be air in the chambers. Fortunately, there's a system of valves designed to prevent over-pressurizing the tank so it can be refilled by drones at depth." She tapped some computer commands. "We're rising much slower now, but you'd better get moving. I'll talk you through it."

A black split began to open in the wall of the lab. That set debris swirling again. Some of it tried to escape, and Alex and Bheru did their best to bat it back inside as they moved out. Their movements were clumsy.

"They don't have swim fins on."

"Right. We've been keeping them in the airlock. That's going to make things extra challenging." Lee-Anna sent the command to re-seal the lab.

Elle could barely breathe as she watched the men through the hab's outside cameras. The filler cap was high on the hull and there wasn't much to hang onto. Alex had used a length of rubber tubing from the lab to tie Bheru to him; and he held tightly to the clamps that had once held the flotation bags, while the biologist tried his skills as a repairman. It took all of five minutes to get the cap off, even with his prosthetic hands. The problem was finding a way to wedge his arm into a gap and let it do all the work—his human torso couldn't take the strain. From the look of it, the nanomaterial of the suit did not grip well.

Once the cap was off, he was able to trigger a series of valves that let in a little bit of sea water at a time. Opening the tank fully to outside pressure would have ruptured it instantly. Within ten minutes Lee-Anna announced that the tank was full, and the habitat had begun to descend. It was very gradual—a good thing because none of them could think of a way to control it. Blowing water from the airlock would risk tipping the hab badly, and if it landed on the silty bottom at an angle, it would stay that way.

"You'd better come back inside," Lee-Anna said.

"Not yet," Alex replied. "Are the water jets still working? Can you maneuver a little?"

"Some. What do you have in mind?"

"If we can land within a few yards of the base maybe we can tie the hab down to it. Otherwise emptying the airlock to let us in will make you rise again."

"Damn, I should have thought of this! There's a cable and winch system. It was added to allow the habitat to float above the bottom. The cable's only a hundred feet, though. By the time you climb down there I'll have it unlocked." Her fingers wove patterns in the air.

Alex and Bheru made their way to the bottom of the habitat and unshipped the cable connector from the middle of the shallow well where the stem of the base normally fit. It required a strong pull; and when it suddenly came free, Bheru lurched backward, the clamp was knocked from his hands against the edge of the well, and he nearly went spinning off into the blackness. The rubber tubing safety-cord stretched to its limit as Alex clung to a clamp housing on the hab. Bheru kicked back to where he could grab the cable fitting again and locked his prosthetic legs onto its ridged curve. Elle couldn't forget that the two men were on the underside of the giant hull plunging downward toward the sea bottom in impenetrable darkness.

"How far are we from the bottom?" Alex asked, rising anxiety in his voice. He straddled the lip of the well and sawed the rubber safety hose across that edge until it parted.

"Less than two hundred yards. About one hundred ninety now. I suggest you get out from under."

"Pump a bit of water out of the airlock. Maybe half of what you took into the drinking water tank. We're dropping too fast. And pay out all of the cable." There was a soft hum that must have been the winch release. It was followed by a bubbling sound as air pushed into the airlock forcing water out through the valves.

Elle bit her lip as Alex went into an upside-down crouch and launched himself toward the bottom, trailing the cable behind him, its end wrapped around his left arm while he pulled himself through the water with his right. Behru, with legs still locked on the cable fitting, guided the cable as it emerged.

In less than a minute Alex's crown of lights was all that was visible. The cable reached its limit. He dangled, helpless, between an anvil and a falling hammer.

"Look over there." Matheus had come up behind the women and pointed to the left of the display. There was a noticeable glow. "That must be the lights of the cameras at the vents, so at least we're clear of them. We haven't come down on the north or south ridges either, so we might be in luck."

Lee-Anna fired the water jets. "I don't think we drifted enough to be on the far side of the vents, so I'm going to assume we went almost straight up and down. I hope somebody has been stroking their lucky rabbit's foot ...."

"I see the base!" Alex called. "And ..." They heard a grunt as he plunged into the muck. Bheru, secure on the hab, quickly pulled on the cable to free him. Alex's suit cameras showed nothing but dirty grey clouds, but he chose a direction, trusting to memory. They lost sight of him for a moment in the roiling silt, then his lights appeared again. He must have somehow managed to extrude a fitting from his suit to hold the cable and now put all his strength into a breaststroke.

Seconds ticked past. Elle couldn't shake the thought that the habitat was going to come down on Alex. How could he swim clear without fins? But he must have gained some distance. The trailing cable had a curve now that caught the light and looked like a glowing eel had suddenly attacked out of the darkness.

"I'm there! I'm at the pad. Just a second." There were panting breaths. "OK, start the winch, but take it slow."

They immediately felt the lateral tug as the spooling cable pulled the bottom of the hab down and sideways. Lee-Anna carefully watched a display that revealed distance between hab and base. With a lot of luck, the pull of the retracting cable would position them over the base before they hit the seafloor.

"Blow just a few more pounds of water, Lee-Anna! No, too late!"

Alex suddenly appeared in the bottom camera view furiously pulling the cable toward the side. He jerked as he saw the hab only yards away. There was no time to swim clear. As he released the cable, a black form shot through the water and knocked him tumbling into the silt, where both vanished in a cloud.

There was a grating crunch as the hab struck the base, sending a jolt through their knees. Lee-Anna flailed the air with her fingertips but cursed in frustration.

"Did they make it? Alex! Bheru! Did you get clear? The clamps for the base aren't holding!"

"Hang on." Alex's voice was a groan. Some metallic sounds came through the hull, harsh breaths through the comm.

"OK, try the clamps again. The cable was in the way."

The display showed new patches of green. Lee-Anna gave a whoop. Elle clambered down the ladder and called to her to start opening the airlock.

"There's no rush now," Alex panted. "Let the silt settle a bit."

Thunder rumbled through the hull. A violent shudder passed up Elle's legs, nearly making her knees collapse. It lasted for a count of eight, then gradually faded.

"Was that an explosion?" she yelled.

It took agonizing seconds for Lee-Anna to answer.

"No! I don't see any signs of system failure or damage on the panel. I think ... I think it must have been a seaquake."

"Oh my God."

The outside camera showed a fountain of mud. Tumbling human forms flashed across the view before they were obscured by grey. She called the news to Lee-Anna who said they'd have to wait. There was a risk of an imperfect seal if she opened the wall and allowed too much silt to come in. Elle stared at the monitor, willing the stubborn cloud to subside. Her uniform pulsed with the pounding of her heart.

A black shape loomed in front of the camera, startling her.

"It's OK. We're both OK." Alex's voice. "When the silt settles, we'll come in."

Twenty minutes later, they were safely inside, and Lee-Anna began to purge water from the round space. Alex asked if they could pump water from the flooded lab too. Visibly angry, Lee-Anna explained that there was no provision for draining the lab at depth—it was only meant for emergency escapes, and now even that was lost to them.

As soon as the pressure equalized, Elle rushed into the airlock to see if they needed help. Their hair was plastered to their heads, and they looked bone-weary. Still, Alex managed a smile.

"Bheru jumped from the hab and knocked me out of the way. You should have seen it."

"I always wanted to be a superhero." The professor gave a deep belly laugh.

"You *are* a hero." Elle hugged him. Turning to Alex, she said, "And you, you macho shit, you almost got yourself killed."

He was too stunned to answer right away. He finished sliding the suit off his legs and picked it up before meeting her glare.

"If the hab had come down in the silt, do you think we could have just bounced it over to the base?" he asked. "Maybe Bheru could've picked it up like Atlas and walked it over?"

"Lee-Anna could have made the hab buoyant and tried again."

"Not for a while, she couldn't," Lee-Anna said, coming halfway down the ladder. "Not until we've had time to make a lot more air. A day should be enough to refill the tanks. Meanwhile, did you feel that quake?

"The silt just turned to liquid and sent us flying. What was it?"

"Come have a look."

Lights illuminated the sea floor on either side of the habitat, but what the cameras showed was hard to process. It looked as if the hab was now sitting in the middle of a one-lane road that disappeared into the darkness both ways. A closer look revealed that the roadbed was slightly lower than the rest of the sea bottom, and its center was darker than its edges.

"A depression caused by seismic activity?" Matheus asked.

"A crack, or a partial crevice," Bheru said. "There's a slight slope toward the middle."

"And we're sitting right on top of it." Lee-Anna sat back, crossing her arms. "What are the odds of that?"

"Maybe we should release the clamps after all, and float at the limit of the cable," Alex said.

"If that crack opens, the base will still pull us down. Look at this." She tapped a small red icon that was flashing. "Possible damage to the cable clamp, probably when we came down on top of it. It might not release. If I try it now and it does come undone, there's no way to reattach it without separating the hab from the base."

Elle's stomach clenched in anger. "Maybe we have to surface after all, and Phillip gets his way. The bastard remotely triggered the base to separate."

The others looked at her wide-eyed, but the same thought must have occurred to Lee-Anna.

"That shouldn't be possible. I'm going to check that now. Regardless, we won't be surfacing on our own at all if that cable clamp is buggered. We can't get buoyant with the base attached—at least, not with the lab flooded."

There was a somber silence. Elle's throat tightened. She had to suck each breath, alarmed at the sound it made.

A hand rested on her arm. Matheus. His voice was gentle but not patronizing.

"There's nothing to worry about. *Orion* would raise us, or in the unlikely event that they couldn't, the dive suits are perfectly capable of taking us all the way to the surface on their own."

"No question," Lee-Anna said. "They're kept fully charged, make their own air. No decompression problems. It'd be a slow trip, but each suit has more than enough drinking water. Even so, I'm damned if I'm going to leave my habitat behind. Let's see how the base got separated."

The whole crew watched as Lee-Anna went through a systems check. She insisted that a remote hack from the surface wasn't possible. Although the hab was designed to allow remote control, she had disabled any remote capability after discovering the first explosive device on the hull.

The systems check confirmed her assessment. There had been no remote access, no system failure. The base had been released in response to a manual command that came from *inside* the hab.

Lee-Anna looked at each of them with uncertainty and her hands hesitated over the holographic interface. Alex gave a small nod. She triggered a playback of the top deck's internal cameras.

Four minutes later, Elle scrambled to the head on Deck Three and threw up violently.

44

April 1, 2042

The crew sat in the lounge in a rough circle, Elle in the middle of the couch with Matheus and Alex on either side, and Bheru and Lee-Anna in the chairs. She couldn't look at any of them. Her mind was still held captive by the images she'd just seen.

"No one thinks you did it knowingly," Alex said, his voice barely rising above the ambient noise of the hab's air-circulation system.

"I *know* you did not," Matheus said, and looked around at the others. "As I've told you before, my sensor mesh would tell me if she were lying. She is not. It is certainly a case of subliminal suggestion, obviously implanted during the sleep conditioning for your claustrophobia, Elle. I've seen it used many times for positive behavior modification—to help people break addictions, for instance. Rarely have I seen anything so sophisticated or so potent; but then, I don't travel in spy circles." His last words had an angry edge, and his face was turned toward Alex, who didn't deny the implication.

Alex couldn't have been involved, could he? No. A quick look at his face showed anger and disgust, but not guilt. Her extra sense confirmed that. With more than three weeks close to him, she was beginning to get a good read of his mental states, if not his actual thoughts.

They'd looked at several playbacks of video footage, all remarkably similar: Elle sitting at her communications console, dreamily tapping at the touchpad just minutes before the communication breakdown on the hab's first descent. Just a half-hour before the flotation bag came loose. Four hours before the habitat shot free of its heavy base.

She remembered none of it. Of course, she didn't. She didn't even know how to give those commands; had no clue how to access those areas of the control system.

She had been a puppet.

Other hands folded over hers, dry but warm. Her eyes drifted reluctantly up to Matheus' face.

"There would have been a trigger phrase," he said. "Something that Phillip said. Not common, but not too unusual. Does anything come to mind?"

Elle opened her mouth to reply but her dry throat made her cough. Lee-Anna jumped up to get her a glass of water. Water bottled and chilled before the recent crisis, she remembered. The rest of their drinking supply was now contaminated with seawater and would have to be distilled to remove the salts. She sipped from the glass with appreciation, coating her throat and licking her lips.

"Maybe," she said. "Yes, I think …. He'd say … he'd say I was doing a terrific job. Outstanding." A tear ran down her cheek. "It was a lie. Always a lie."

Matheus shifted and put an arm around her, drawing her head gently onto his shoulder.

She sniffed and drew her hand under her nose. Alex passed her a tissue.

"I only remember it because it was a weird thing to say after we'd just had a fight over bringing the hab to the surface."

"What an asshole!" Lee-Anna hissed, unable to sit still. She paced to the computer workstation and back again. "I don't even know how he could have learned the commands to control those functions."

"He has *resources*," Alex said with his head down. "And people in his circle have means of persuasion that no one can refuse forever. He probably got to one of your partners, Lee-Anna. Don't blame them too much."

"And you've been his fucking right-hand man all along!"

He flinched as if she'd slapped him.

"I ...." He looked up at Elle. "I didn't want to be. I knew nothing about Elle's hidden conditioning, and I haven't done anything to sabotage the mission. That's the truth."

"It is," declared Matheus. "Or, at least, he believes it to be."

"I believe in both of you," Bheru spoke for the first time. "The question in my mind is, why would Phillip Watanabe want the mission to fail? Why would his superiors want it? He recruits this team, but then does everything he can to tie our hands?"

Elle looked at Alex and noticed the others doing the same. He was aware of the attention and shrugged.

"The man is completely paranoid, but he isn't stupid. And if he wanted to use weapons to destroy the entity— and us—he'd just go ahead and do it without shedding any tears. But you're right, why bring us here in the first place?"

"Is it possible they thought this entity could be recruited as an ally, or even used as a weapon?"

Alex returned Bheru's look. "Absolutely. They analyze everything as a potential weapon. I wonder if that means they really have made contact with aliens before, or even just alien technology?"

"Something has made them decide that this presence—whether aliens or not—cannot be used for their purposes and is better destroyed."

"Maybe that's not the reason he wants us out of the way," Elle said. "What if we've done a better job than they expected and we're getting too close to finding out something they don't want us to learn?"

She looked at Alex, but he gently shook his head.

"It's not like we could reveal secrets to the world. You can bet our internet use is completely monitored and controlled. If we learn something too sensitive, they'll … well, they'll just make us disappear. Make sure the hab never makes it back, and incriminating evidence is destroyed."

Lee-Anna cursed. "That's why the bomb was placed by the air-production plant. So they could make it look like the plant malfunctioned and exploded."

"Any rupture of the hull would cause an implosion from the water pressure, so an external bomb wouldn't automatically be suspected. Then they'd find a way to ensure the computer data wasn't recoverable."

"Do you know what is deliciously ironic about this?" Matheus asked. "The small extra weight of Phillip's bomb probably made the difference. Without it, we would have floated to the surface, despite all our efforts." His mouth twitched at the corners.

"But by programming me he wasn't trying to kill us," Elle protested. "Nothing I did under suggestion would have trapped us down here. It was all calculated to make us return to the surface. Even the flotation bag—only one clamp released. We weren't really in danger. We just had to suspend the mission."

They all looked at Alex again for his take on Elle's comment. He'd operated in clandestine circles and knew the government agent best. He put his elbows on his knees and rested his face on his clenched fists.

Finally, he sat back.

"How about this? Phillip thinks we know things we haven't told him, so he wants us back alive. His bosses have decided the only safe course of action is to have this mystery intelligence destroyed—they were probably all but convinced of that from the beginning, only they want it to look as if they did everything possible to reach a peaceful solution and have *someone else* take the blame for destroying it."

"Jesus," Lee-Anna breathed, turning away. "I'm going to go active with the sonar."

"Yeah. Phillip said there could be Chinese drones sniffing around."

"But you think it's more than that," Elle declared. "A Chinese submarine?"

Alex nodded and cleared his throat. "Does that change how we all feel about going to the surface?"

"No!" Lee-Anna snapped. "I won't give that shit the satisfaction."

"We still have answers to find," Matheus pleaded. "This could be an incredible breakthrough. Momentous. Surely our presence will make the Chinese hesitate before firing, and perhaps even force the United States government to warn them off. But if we leave …."

"The entity will be unprotected," Bheru finished for him.

Elle gave a bitter laugh.

"God, I never thought I'd be trying to protect that son-of-a-bitch from humans."

# # #

Later, she lay quietly on her bed, her mind in chaos.

Did she bear any blame for what had happened? Should she have known?

It was easy to claim the excuse of malicious conditioning, mental programming, but *her mind* was different, wasn't it? Shouldn't it have detected an intrusion like that? Sensed something foreign, the way she sensed the signals from other minds?

She sensed one now.

Alex sat on the edge of her bed.

"I feel like I should apologize for people and plans I want no part of," he said in a voice meant for only her to hear. "But the way you're feeling … it's about more than just being tricked, isn't it?"

She couldn't answer right away. Her eyes suddenly welled with tears.

"You can't imagine what it's like to know that your mind isn't your own. Mine never has been. I couldn't keep other thoughts out. When I was a kid, I always imagined that I'd grow up and grow strong. Learn how to block everything. Instead, things got worse; and like an idiot, I thought there might be professional help for people like me." She wiped her cheek with her palm. "Once you let people think you're crazy, they fall all over themselves to give you drugs and more drugs. Just admit that you're sick, and they'll be helpful as hell. Except the only way they seem to know how to treat you is the same way they treat people with multiple personalities, or voices in their head telling them to do bad things, or people who see angels or demons, or try to hurt people, or hurt themselves. If you refuse to understand that you're not like other people and never will be, then things go bad for you."

She looked up at him and wished the dim light could hide her tears.

"You know, I was suspicious when Phillip rescued me from that mental health assessment panel. But I told myself I shouldn't be ungrateful, so I worked really hard to *be* grateful. Then this … thing kept getting into my head, worse than any of the human thoughts I'd always tried to keep out. I tried to build a defense, but there *is* no defense. The only answer for me was to run—to get as far the hell away from it as I could." She sighed. "Phillip told me I needed to face it. That was how to make everything all right. And he told me I was 'doing a terrific job. Outstanding.'"

"I'm so sorry," Alex said. "He kept that from me completely. I hope you can believe that."

She reached out tentatively to touch his hand and then brushed at his sleeve instead.

"I know how Phillip persuaded me to come on this mission, but how did he convince you?" she asked. "It wasn't for a chance to boss people around. You were willing to hide on *Orion* and let people think you were a coward. So why are you here?"

"You mean apart from the chance to meet little green men in person?" He actually smiled. "Well, because this is the last time. It sounds like a movie cliché, but with the help of a hacker contact I cultivated a while back, I set up a hidden file detailing secrets about clandestine ops I was involved with—stuff that would be very embarrassing to the government if it got out. That's my insurance, to make them let me go. When this thing is over, I'll be free." His eyes shone. "You don't know how much I'm looking forward to that."

"I can imagine."

They sat in silence for a while. It seemed as if he was about to leave but changed his mind.

"I've been trying to think of how to say this without it sounding like some cheesy half-time speech in a locker room. But the thing is, you're stronger than you think you are, Elle. I've seen it. When the entity scared you out of your wits, you didn't fall apart. You got pissed off. You became determined to beat it, and you made the best progress we've had so far. That's what you've got to do about this subliminal conditioning thing. Get mad. Show Phillip Watanabe he doesn't control your mind."

"But he does. He can."

"No. Now you know the trigger phrase, he can't trick you with it. And you know, deeply, not to trust that man ever again. So, you won't."

"I'm not sure it's that simple."

"Maybe not, but you're tough. You've also got a card up your sleeve. You'll probably sense his next move before he even tries it."

"I can't do that except with people I've known for a long time."

"Are you sure? I think you might be wrong. That it might not be true anymore. Try it. Try sensing the thoughts of Bheru or Lee-Anna."

It was a dumb idea. She knew the limits of her 'gift'. Anyway, it was easy to guess that Lee-Anna was trying to find materials outside the flooded lab that could be used to make a water still. And Bheru would be checking his right arm to see if it had been damaged by prying at the docking ring of the hab's base when the cable got pinned. She said so.

"Really? Did you even know that Bheru had used his arm for that?" Seeing the expression on her face, he nodded. "The thing is, your mental ability has been a trial for you all your life, but it really could be a gift. Bheru lost his legs and arms; but without his new ones, I'd probably be dead right now. Matheus lost his eyes, yet he's been able to tell us more about our surroundings than we could ever have learned on our own. It's easy for me to say, I know; but I think you could turn these painful ordeals around to see the ways they've made you strong, then use your gift to make up for all that pain."

"You don't know what you're talking about. Please leave me alone."

Hurt carved lines into his face, but he just bobbed his head and left.

A memory of Bret Sampson came unbidden into her mind. Blond hair and blue eyes—like Alex in that way; but Bret had a football-player physique and business smarts. No amount of effort had enabled her to forget their best times together: their first date at the country fair near Orillia with a Ferris wheel sunset and cotton-candy kisses under a star-strewn sky. Sailing on Lake Ontario and using her beer-cooled lips to ease his sunburnt skin. The camping trip her parents never knew about, when two days of rain meant two days of lovemaking in a sodden tent. A New Year's party in a dress he'd bought for her that made her feel like a queen.

That was near the end. He'd begun to act a little strange after that, a little more distant. She came to suspect that he was cheating on her. It was stupid—he wasn't like that—but the fear wouldn't let her go. So, she made the fatal mistake of sifting through his thoughts.

He'd been planning to propose to her.

Dumbfounded, she'd fumbled an innocent conversation about house prices and let slip what she knew. As his first shock quickly turned to suspicion, he accused her of conspiring with a friend to manipulate him into marriage.

It was all over after that.

Before Bret, her relationships had been ruined because she was too afraid to let anyone even get that close. After Bret, she vowed never to let it happen again.

Yet it had, against her will. When Alex had given her his pep talk, she'd known everything he was going to say.

## 45

April 2, 2042

The crew celebrated Lee-Anna's first gallon of distilled water by making a batch of hot chocolate to go with their Meals Ready to Eat breakfast. They'd avoided MREs until then, but with less cooking-water available, there was going to be a lot less variety in their diet. Dissolved salts weren't the only contaminants now in the drinking water tank. The tank's automatic impurities sensors showed a disturbing assortment of heavy metals and other toxins that had come with it, almost certainly from the cargo ship with a load of toxic waste from Okinawa that had sunk two days before the first airliner incident. The organisms in the smoker zone were probably being poisoned. Lee-Anna could have tested for that if the necessary gear hadn't been crushed, though Matheus reminded them about what had happened when Bheru had sliced into the tubeworm.

"In any case," Bheru said, "there's nothing we can do to stop the toxins."

If the tubeworm's injury really had triggered the swarming by the vent creatures, how would the entity react to a major die-off because of manmade chemicals? But Bheru was right. They were helpless to prevent it.

Alex turned to Elle, who was blowing gently on her drink. "You said the entity showed you man-made pollution and climate change. Was it complaining just for its own sake, because it had been hurt by those things? Or was the complaint more general? Knowing that could reveal a lot about its nature."

Lee-Anna spoke instead. "It's strange. You'd expect a sea creature would be affected by higher ocean acidity caused by all the excess carbon dioxide we humans pump out. So Orion did tests on the local seawater that *Darwin* repeated at various depths, and then I tested some samples down here to compare with the water among the smokers. The average pH of most of this area is a little above 8.05—somewhat *alkaline*, where 7 is neutral, of course, and anything under 7 is acidic. But in this valley, up-current from the smokers, I got pH readings above 8.2. That's what we expect the ocean was like before the Industrial Revolution."

"What are you suggesting?" Bheru asked. "That this entity is somehow able to neutralize dissolved CO_2 in seawater?"

"You know I can't draw any conclusions from such limited data." She paused. "But what if it could reverse acidity? Maybe as a defense mechanism. It could hold the key to reversing one of humankind's most damaging environmental crimes."

"But I have a sense that the toxins from that cargo ship are hurting it," Elle said. "I don't think it knows what to do about them. Now that you mention it, I think that could be what got it stirred up—made it try to communicate with the Moon. No one's reported anything like that energy beam before now, have they?"

Alex shook his head. "Phillip thought the same thing," he said.

# # #

Lee-Anna had rigged the new still with an extra filtration step, making every effort to eliminate all contaminants, and it would have to run nonstop to provide for the crew's water needs. That was a serious drain on their energy stores, already under a heavy draw to keep their air supply replenished. The excess heat from both operations had also raised the temperature inside the hab. That saved energy for heating, but they were reluctant to waste those savings on humidity control. The result was like a tropical island before an afternoon rain. Bheru and Matheus smiled and said it reminded them of their childhood homes, but Alex, Elle, and Lee-Anna changed into short-legged sleepwear.

Alex's stomach was still unsettled since his angry confrontation with Phillip that morning. The agent hadn't even bothered to deny Elle's brainwashing. Instead, he belittled Alex for his naiveté and blamed him for the mission's failures. More significantly, Phillip had sent a robotic submersible to reattach *Orion*'s cable to the habitat so it could be raised to the surface. Alex's explosion of profanity was wasted because Phillip had already broken the connection.

He felt a little bit better after a few sips of hot chocolate and a lot better after a call from Gary.

Three thousand feet from the ocean floor the robot sub had gone dead and all attempts to reestablish contact had failed. It was being hauled back to *Orion* by the cable.

There was a small but enthusiastic cheer when Alex broke the news. Matheus raised his mug in a toast.

"To forms of intelligence capable of putting us cocky humans in our place."

"I'll drink, but I'm not entirely sure we should be celebrating that," Bheru said.

"Why not?"

"Think about it. This entity has the power to kill our electronic devices, not only in the ocean, but all the way to Earth orbit. Nor does it appear to have any compunction about doing so."

"Still, that is a limited ability. We'll eventually discover a countermeasure against it. *Orion*'s anti-EM shield does quite a lot already."

"We won't want to have to shield every aircraft, watercraft, spacecraft, or satellite we launch," Alex said.

"Why would we?"

"This entity is located between two high mountain ridges to the north and south. That's why it stopped beaming energy toward the Moon—when the Moon's orbit carried it farther north, it was hidden by a mountain. If the entity got into the open ocean with clear sight-lines all around, it could send its energy transmission in any direction—cover the whole sky. Depth of water doesn't seem to affect it. So, nothing we float or fly over the south Pacific would be safe from it."

"That is a disturbing thought."

"Let's not forget the other examples of its power," Bheru said. "The eruption from the smokers when we were descending in the habitat, and the quake when we returned after the base was released."

"So now you agree that this *being* is somehow able to command the seismic forces of the Earth."

Bheru countered Matheus' smile with a frown of equal strength.

"I do not believe in coincidences, my friend. I'll admit that the geyser just as we were passing overhead strained my credulity to the limit. And then to experience a seaquake that produces a crack in the Earth's crust directly under our habitat ... that cannot be accidental. Therefore, although we have no experience with a life form that has such power, we must give credit where credit is due."

Alex shuddered and hoped no one saw.

"There's something else worth considering." Lee-Anna left the computer workstation and settled in a chair. "I took some core samples from the smoker mounds and I've finally had a chance to go over the data. Comparing the buildup of material and especially the distribution of sulfur compounds on the surface of the mounds, I'd say these vents are pretty recent. They're a close match to a vent system not far from the Galapagos that's only three months old. Smoker formations often don't last much beyond a decade, but this one's still a baby."

"Is it possible that such a large community of life could have developed in such a short time?" Matheus asked.

"It could." Bheru nodded. "We still don't know if such communities somehow move to a new home when vents shut down, or if only their spawn makes it to another oasis. Even so, I think you're missing a more important point."

"Which is?"

"If this entity is connected to the heat and discharge of the vents, and possibly the life-forms as well, as I'm becoming convinced it is, then we are faced with the prospect that a being only a few months old has the power to cause seaquakes, cast some sort of beam through two miles of water, and destroy electronic devices from here to the Moon."

They were shocked into silence. Matheus' was clearly skeptical but had trouble finding a counterargument. Alex didn't want to believe it either.

"Have you ever had that impression, Elle? That the entity was just a ... fledgling?"

"The thoughts it sends me are pretty basic, I suppose, and there's that curiosity I've mentioned. But ... if it doesn't sound too stupid to say this, its anger and resentment feel very adult. Children get upset when they don't get their own way, but this feels more sophisticated than that, as if it has legitimate grievances against us. Pollution and climate effects, like I mentioned before. Maybe other things too." Then her eyes widened.

"You know, now that you mention it, I'd say the entity feels like an adult but it's treating *me* like a child. I don't know why that is. I don't appreciate it when people don't take me seriously."

"That's not a complaint against us, is it?" Matheus asked.

"No. Well, maybe about Alex staring at my legs while I'm trying to explain something."

He hadn't even realized he was doing it. "Sorry. Although it doesn't mean ...."

"He's welcome to stare at *my* legs," Lee-Anna interrupted. "'Cause he knows that if he ever sells me short on my brains, these legs will kick his ass." She brushed her hair back and smiled.

Alex knew when to keep his mouth shut.

Matheus offered Lee-Anna his brightest smile.

"Until now I have only seen such a combination of beauty, brain, and fire in my own wife," the sociotheologist said with a laugh and a lift of his shoulders. Then his face turned serious. "As to our discussion, I don't believe this 'entity' is an infant. If it is not from 'outer space', I find it much easier to believe that it's a very large but possibly tenuous organism that exists within the crust of the Earth and expresses some of itself outward through openings such as the geothermal vents to interact with the outside world. In all likelihood, it is very ancient, having travelled over centuries or even eons from its original location."

"So, then, it inhabits large portions of the ocean floor?" Behru asked. "That's so radically different from any other form of life we've encountered on our planet that it sounds more like fantasy than scientific extrapolation."

"If I did not have such a high opinion of your intelligence and expertise, my learned colleague—and friend—I might be insulted," Matheus said with a grin. "Since I believe that a species native to the very deepest parts of the oceans could have survived the mass extinction events our planet has endured, it must, almost by definition, be radically different from everything that has evolved since. And, I think, wiser."

"The question of where and when it evolved is secondary as far as I'm concerned," Lee-Anna said. "I want to know its immediate intentions, and its abilities. For example, since it apparently can take out a robot submersible at will, does that mean we're safe from Chinese submarines?"

Bheru stood up to get the last of the hot chocolate from the saucepan. "That doesn't necessarily follow. If I had to guess, I think it's getting more from Elle's thoughts than just images. It may very well sense her resentment of the people on the surface. In fact, you should probably try to control that, my dear. You have just cause to be angry at Phillip Watanabe, but we don't want the entity acting out that anger against the whole crew of *Orion*."

He settled back on the couch, took a sip, and smacked his lips.

"Perhaps the question of intentionality is more my colleague's territory," he continued, "but we have to assume that there are many vessels within the being's range of detection, and it does not attack them all. It may not consider a Chinese submarine to be a threat, at least, not until it fires a weapon. Then again, it may not recognize a weapon until it's too late. Or it may feel secure against such an attack itself, but have no special interest in protecting us."

"So, you don't think it disabled the robot drone to protect Elle?"

"More likely it sensed that Elle wanted the drone gone, and it obliged, though for what reasons, I can't be sure."

"Well, I sure as hell would want a Chinese submarine gone too, if I knew it was there." Elle looked at Lee-Anna.

"Our sonar's been active for five hours with only very faint returns that could be anything. And we have no way to know that a sub isn't hiding just behind one of the mountain ridges."

"So, have we completely given up the idea that this intelligence is aliens from outer space?" Alex asked.

Bheru and Matheus said, "Yes," and "I think so," at the same time. Elle and Lee-Anna let silence signify agreement.

"Shit." Alex leaned on his knees and stared at the floor.

"You were hoping that visitors from space would usher in a new era on Earth?" Bheru asked softly.

"At least shake things up enough to make secret agencies and covert missions a relic of a more paranoid time. I guess that would qualify as a new era. In fact, it would qualify as a miracle."

"Don't stop believing in miracles, Alex," Matheus told him. "My belief grows stronger every day. Maybe this will be one."

"I'm just trying to wrap my head around all this. We've got a zone of black smokers that's only months old, but an organism that could be more ancient than the sea. It probably has no sense of compassion that we'd recognize. It can fry electronics and human brains at great distances, can influence or even control local sea life, and seems able to shift the Earth's crust at will, at least over a small area. Did I miss anything?"

There was no response.

"All of the modern weapons we can bring to bear against it depend on electronics. Submarines, bombers, missiles, even guided depth charges. We could drop poisons or nuclear waste on it, but ships that do that would be sitting ducks long before they could get into position. Hell, we have to *find* it, first."

"I'm alarmed that all of you are so quick to assume this intelligence means us harm," Matheus said. "That we should take a defensive posture, or even an aggressive one, and that it could possibly be meaningful to do so. Surely, the only sensible approach is to learn what it wants and join it to pursue a course of action that will benefit us all."

"That's a very admirable stance, my friend." Bheru leaned back and linked his fingers across his abdomen. "But when negotiating peace, I prefer to do so from a position of strength."

"That's just it," Alex said. "What strength? Do we have any weapon against it?"

After a moment Bheru narrowed his eyes and said, "We may have one." He turned to face Elle.

"Also, our best hope for peace," Matheus insisted.

46

April 2, 2042

Lee-Anna came to Alex's bed during the dim-light hours, but this time she urged him to join her down on the lounge deck. She manually slid the bulkhead into place between the two decks, presumably to block noise. Then they administered a treatment for her restlessness.

Afterward, she was in no hurry to return to her bunk. With a gentle finger she traced the short, sharp scar on the underside of his chin, memento of a knife blade that nearly took his life. Shifting a little, she gave the small crescent shrapnel scar below his left breast a light kiss, then did the same to a rippled patch of tissue on his shoulder that a bullet graze had left behind. She missed the small pucker in his abdomen and its twin on his lower back.

"Don't get the wrong idea about those," he said. "I'm no action hero. Just not so good at getting out of the way."

"If you say so." She kissed his lips and rested her cheek against his. In a voice barely above a whisper she asked,

"Do you think our government will warn the Chinese to leave us alone?"

"Yes. But it'll be a hollow gesture. By now they probably want the Chinese to attack so they can watch what happens. I think this entity has everyone scared—more so with every action it takes. The possibility that it can trigger a seaquake must have them shitting bricks about Los Angeles and Tokyo."

"So should we give in and go to the surface?"

"No. There's a chance the Chinese will hesitate to shoot with us here, afraid of a bad global reaction in case word got out. If the entity is anywhere near as powerful and mobile as we fear it is, we do not want to go to war against it. This crew is the only hope for some kind of negotiated peace."

"You mean Elle is."

"Sure, but I have a hunch that it can sense a lot from the rest of us too. At least it sees our actions. If we show it an example of peaceful coexistence, and treat it with friendship instead of hostility, we may be able to give Elle the proof she needs when she argues for peace."

"What if we could hurt it by blowing up the hab with Phillip's bomb—would you do it?"

He was shocked by the question, but he gave a short nod. "Sure, if it was the only way to stop it from hurting other people."

"Me too." There was no need to elaborate on personal consequences.

They heard someone going into the head on the deck above.

"Speaking of Elle."

"How do you know?"

He shrugged. "I just know. And I'm sure she knows what we're doing, too."

Lee-Anna pushed up onto her elbows and looked into his face.

"Why don't you make a move? With her."

"Now your needs have been met you're trying to get rid of me?"

She jabbed him in the ribs.

"You and I are just friends with benefits, and you know it. But you and Elle ...."

"All I do is irritate her. I've thought we made a kind of connection a couple of times, but then she slapped me down."

"She just wants your full attention. Some kind of demonstration that you're really interested in her, in something serious. I know you are. Everyone does. But it's not something she can ask for."

"Why doesn't she just read my mind?" he said, but then he clamped his mouth shut as if he could stop the words that had already spilled.

"Are you serious?" Lee-Anna's eyebrows arched.

He hesitated. "Forget I said that. She doesn't read people on purpose, and she has to know somebody for a long time before it works at all."

After a moment of thought, her lips pressed into a hard line, and she held his eyes.

"What about knowing them for a short time but in close proximity and under a lot of stress?"

He didn't answer.

"Damn. I've never considered that someone might be able to tell what I'm thinking. Really? Shit, that's creepy. That's worse than the freak who broke into my apartment one time to steal my underwear." She sat up, contemplating the far wall, her thumb between her teeth. "If it were anybody but Elle ... no, it's still wrong. It's just wrong. Shit."

Alex admired her body in the low light, then decided he might as well get dressed; but as he shifted on the couch, she surprised him by rolling on top of him. "At least she'll forgive us for this because she'll know it doesn't mean anything," she said with a smile.

She pressed her lips to his and began to move her body in a practiced rhythm.

Maybe she was right, but Alex tried to make his mind blank anyway, though it wasn't truly necessary since another body part was soon thinking for him.

47

April 3, 2042

Alex awoke to Lee-Anna yelling Matheus' name.

He was in his bunk but had trouble orienting himself. The lights were still dim. Was it the same night? Had another day passed?

No, only a few hours.

"Matheus! Jesus, come back in. It's not safe to be out there on your own."

Lee-Anna's voice held a mixture of concern and anger. Alex dropped down the ladder and went to her side. The display showed the view from Matheus' suit camera: nothing but black water surrounding a cone of light that included a short strip of grey silt and a semicircular glow beyond that. The other half of the screen presented two of the hab cameras aimed toward the smoker ridge. If Matheus was swimming, his shape seen end-on had already disappeared into the halo of light.

"Why is he out there?"

"God only knows," Lee-Anna spat. "A noise woke me up and by the time I got down here he'd already gone out the airlock." She tapped the controls. "Matheus, if whatever you're doing is so damn important, just wait a few minutes and one of us will join you."

She gave Alex a meaningful look. He spoke for the microphone. "I'm on my way."

"No, Alex. Please don't." Matheus' words came from the speaker with a strange calmness. "I am in no need of assistance, and I ... would like to be alone."

Lee-Anna pointed to a readout of the man's vital signs. They didn't represent calm. Heart rate, blood pressure, and respiration were all high enough to indicate some kind of distress.

"Are you in pain?" Alex asked him. "Or under duress—is the entity making you do this?"

Matheus actually laughed. "No, Alex, I'm simply excited."

"Then wait for me and you can show me what's got you excited. I want to see it."

"It's not something that can be shared," he said, and then refused to respond to any more questions. He'd reached the smokers and was floating carefully between them as if searching for a special spot. By then Elle and Bheru were on Deck Two, watching from behind.

"Oh my God," Elle said.

"Did you know he was going to do this?" Alex's words were more accusatory than he intended.

"No, I swear. I didn't." She looked as if she were about to be sick.

"I'll go bring him back," Alex said as he swung onto the ladder. With the lab full of water and sealed off, the remainder of the deck was significantly smaller.

"I'll go with you." Bheru followed him down.

Alex slammed the ladder with his hand. "Shit! He flooded the whole airlock and left the outside wall open.

No, he blocked it with something. It won't close. Lee-Anna!"

"It looks like a container of some kind," she called. "Hang on. I might be able to reach it with the manipulator arm." They heard her race up the ladder to the arm control station on the top deck. Within a minute Alex saw the claw-shaped end come into view from above. The object Matheus had used to keep the wall from sealing was too large for the claw to grasp directly. Lee-Anna swung the arm to the limit of its reach and tried to push the container out into the ocean from behind. It stubbornly rotated instead, but she was finally able to bat it out of the way. As the arm withdrew, Alex stabbed at the controls and the wall began to close up, but it would take a long time to empty the full airlock, if they had enough stored air to do it.

With another curse, he tapped the view screen near the airlock door to show the other camera views. Matheus' suit camera showed nothing, but one of the video units monitoring the vent colony revealed the man standing upright in the center of a ring of spires. He was brightly illuminated, light prisming off a thick coating of creatures that covered him. The humanoid shape surrounded by a fierce aura reminded Alex of special effects shots of people being struck by lightning. His throat spasmed in its effort to keep down a surge of bile.

"Jesus God! Matheus, no!" Lee-Anna's wail of anguish was followed by a scream from Elle.

Alex couldn't see anything different at first. Suddenly there was a single spray of some dark substance from within Matheus' living cloak, and then an eruption of lurid red with a nauseating mix of green, brown, and black. It was as if the man had exploded. The bright water filled with a charged thundercloud that rained blood.

Alex and Bheru both vomited on the deck and stood shaking, their heads hung over their knees.

Dimly, Alex registered the sounds of sobbing and retching from above. He should do something. He should take some kind of meaningful action. But all he could do was stand there rasping breath, his face flowing with tears.

Time passed—an interval of emotional and physical paralysis. Eventually, he found the strength to tap the monitor screen and saw that the airlock had sealed and was being drained. He should go outside, but he couldn't. Not now. Not yet.

Stepping out of his suit and around the mess he'd made on the floor, he wiped an arm across his mouth and climbed the ladder. Elle and Lee-Anna were holding each other, still shuddering. Lee-Anna turned red eyes toward him.

"He opened his suit," she said, nearly gagging on the words. "He found a manual override and opened it. Why would he do that?"

Alex had no words. He collapsed onto the couch.

"He had cancer," Elle said, though they could barely hear her. She coughed, her arms wrapped around her body as if trying to hold herself together. "He had colon cancer, and probably not very long to live. He'd recorded messages to his family."

Alex and Lee-Anna only looked at her in shock.

"But why would he choose *that* way?" Bheru had climbed the ladder until his torso was above the deck but came no further, his face a crumpled mask of anguish.

No one answered. They couldn't look at each other, couldn't focus on anything.

Elle spoke again. "He was sure that the entity is a large nebulous intelligence, but strongly linked to the life at the vents. I think he wanted to commune with it somehow—communicate directly. It's like he said yesterday, but we didn't understand him. He wanted to join with it to bring about a better understanding for the sake of all of us."

"Why give his life?" Lee-Anna whimpered. Alex was dismayed to see such a strong woman incapacitated by her pain. He went to her and cradled her head.

"Maybe I'm wrong," Elle continued, "but I don't think he saw it as committing suicide. I think he meant to transcend death."

"He once said a being as ancient as this entity might be full of ... God. Maybe, one with God?" Alex found himself remembering Matheus' gentle voice and the even gentler way he tried to help others see what was so wonderful to him.

"*Vá com Deus*, my friend," Bheru said, voice cracking. He pulled himself up the rest of the ladder as if he'd aged a hundred years and slumped in a chair, his head in his hands.

Lee-Anna sighed like the passing of an evening breeze. "He didn't say goodbye."

"He did, though," Elle said, wiping her nose with a clenched tissue. "Yesterday. To each one of us. We just weren't listening the right way." She went to the computer and accessed the internal camera feed for their conversation of the day before. It was true. Matheus had gone out of his way to acknowledge Bheru's brilliance and friendship, Lee-Anna's combination of beauty and brains, to insist that Elle was their hope for peace, and to tell Alex to believe in miracles. Each was a heartfelt goodbye, recognizable only in hindsight.

After a long silence, Alex said to no one in particular, "I should go out and retrieve him."

"There's no rush now," Lee-Anna replied, "and it would be better if we manufactured more air first."

He accepted the offered excuse. Instead, he grabbed some rags; and, as a kind of penance, went down to the airlock deck to clean up. He wasn't clear about why he felt a need to atone. Perhaps it was just that he was alive when his friend was not.

Afterward, he slowly made his way up to Deck Four and stood there in front of the communications console. He didn't know how much time had passed when he heard Elle come up behind him. He turned to her.

"I don't know what to tell them topside. How to say it." The weakness of his voice shamed him.

Elle moved close and they held each other for a long time.

"I'll do it," she said, and he let her.

48

April 3, 2042

It was the second time in three days that they'd lost half a night's sleep. Bheru, Lee-Anna, and Alex slowly circulated about the lounge and galley deck making coffee, pouring and drinking it—but it was only a way to fill time. None of them was able to eat. They just traded places in the room, as if doing so constituted something meaningful. When Elle came down the ladder, Alex was glad to get a cup of coffee for her.

"How did they react?" he asked.

"Phillip didn't say anything at all. Not a word. He looked fit to spit nails, though. Gary asked me if there'd been any change in the entity's signals to me."

"You mean, since Matheus' death?"

She nodded.

"And ...?"

"I told him no, not really." She took a swallow of coffee. "But it wasn't the truth."

The others gathered around her.

"I could just be imagining things, but the entity has been in my mind ever since, and I think its messages have changed. There are still the usual ones, plus some unpleasant undertones that I've finally decided represent toxins in the water. But there are also some glimpses of sun rays breaking through a shallow sea—shafts of light filled with darting fish. A sloping beach with surf frothing above. A coral reef seen from a slight distance, with brightly colored sparks of light against shadow. I don't know what any of it means, but it's certainly ... friendlier."

Lee-Anna's face was even paler than usual. "Are you thinking that ... I don't know ... that Matheus' spirit is somehow coming through?"

"No, it's not like that. Not like him. But maybe it's a new attitude from the entity that we humans are worth a little attention. Possibly even a dialogue."

"If Matheus was right, those could be pictures of other places it's been," Alex mused.

"Yes. But I think the tone is as important as the content. For once it doesn't feel as if I'm just a barnacle it's trying to scrape off its back."

Bheru touched her arm. "Maybe our friend has succeeded in giving you the extra edge you needed to really communicate with this being. That could change everything—finally give you a chance to get across our message of peace."

"I'll do my best."

#   #   #

Their sorrow left them with no appetite, but their bodies needed food. Bheru cooked some thick, breaded-chicken patties that they ate on tortillas with lots of chopped peppers and spices. It returned a measure of strength to their limbs and, to an extent, their minds.

Alex noticed that Lee-Anna was keeping her distance from Elle. A few yards would make no difference if Elle decided to sense thoughts, and the engineer would know that rationally. But her reaction was subconscious, and Alex could hardly blame her for it. The thought of a true mind-reader in their midst would be profoundly disturbing to anyone—he couldn't understand why his own reaction had been so minimal, right from the start. Maybe it was because he'd seen how much Elle suffered from her gift, and how reluctant she was to use it.

An hour later, he announced his intention to go to the vent ridge to retrieve Matheus' remains. Bheru and Lee-Anna argued that the body would be difficult for one person to tow over that distance. The cameras showed that the vent life forms had left the suit, but they had no way to know what remained inside. Looking at it, Alex had the unsettling thought that it would rise up and begin to move on its own. In the end, Elle was left alone in the habitat. Someone had to stay, and she couldn't face the idea of touching the lifeless remains of her friend who had once been so vital.

The three divers were silent as they swam to the smoker ridge. It occurred to Alex that Matheus had been swarmed by the sea life even though he hadn't harmed any of the creatures, yet other divers had been there often without provoking such a reaction. Had the sociologist somehow been able to signal his intentions to the entity?

If so, Alex wondered how to send the opposite message and be left alone.

The body hadn't moved far when they reached it. Weak eddies had turned it around a few times, but it was still within the ring of cones where Matheus had breathed his last. Alex steeled his nerve and swam to it.

There was a split in the front of the suit as if it had simply been unzipped from the waist to just below the collarbone. All that remained inside was a bare skeleton, its torso covered by the shiny sensory mesh Matheus had dubbed his 'mithril cloak.' The bones were spindly, compressed into wiry versions of their former shapes by the extraordinary pressure, and there was a noticeable fuzz over them, as if microorganisms were patiently working to make the bones disappear, too. The sight triggered a few moments of nausea for Alex, but it passed.

It was surprisingly awkward to lift the remains while floating at neutral buoyancy, because the water inside the suit had mass, and any lifting motion pulled the lifter downward. Lee-Anna was able to manipulate some pads within Matheus' headgear to give the suit just a little more flotation so they could pull it by the arms between the highest pinnacles and over a couple of lower ones.

It was a relief when they got clear of the mounds; but as they set off for the habitat, clouds of silt suddenly sprayed up from the bottom. A powerful bass note made Alex's suit throb. He selected a camera view of the smokers, zoomed in, and saw that the columns of mineral deposits were shaking. The top quarter of a spire slowly tumbled down its slopes to raise another fountain of dust, then a second peak broke off. It wasn't hydraulic pressure bursting the vent chimneys open from within. He'd seen what that looked like.

The sea floor below him was covered by a nebulous layer of disturbed silt that reminded him of their landing after the crisis with the ballast.

"Another seaquake," he said to the others. Then the implications struck him.

Oh God.

He spun toward the compass heading for home.

The lights of the habitat were gone.

49

April 3, 2042

Alex let himself sink into the silt at the edge of the crevice and simply stared at the gaping chasm in the sea floor, a hideous jack o' lantern mouth that had consumed the habitat—and with it, Elle Travis.

He'd begun frantically calling Elle's name as soon as he realized the hab had vanished, but there'd been no response. Letting go of Matheus' suit, he'd charged through the water even while he'd known that the gesture was futile. Hovering over the edge of the new precipice, even the maximum magnification of his suit's cameras wasn't enough to pick out the lights of the habitat. They should have been visible for hundreds of feet, but were probably obscured by silt clouds from the quake.

Lee-Anna's hand came down hard on his suit shoulder. He realized that he'd been gulping air in great gasps. He fought for calm.

The habitat had fallen but that didn't mean that Elle was dead. It was far too soon to despair. Why was he suddenly overcome with fear?

"Sorry," he stammered. "I don't know what hit me. Elle might still be OK."

"The hab's tough, as long as Elle wasn't tossed around too much," Lee-Anna agreed. "No response from her on the communicator, though."

Alex cleared his throat. "I'm going down to find her, but I want you two to head for the surface. It's too dangerous here. I don't want any more deaths on my watch."

"You're not responsible if we choose to go on our own," she replied.

"Please surface. Get somewhere safe. This is a nightmare, and it'll only get worse if you come with me."

"This isn't about you. It's about Elle. And we're going."

He exhaled raggedly. "Could we talk to *Orion* from here? We need to tell them what's happened."

"I'll boost my signal to the maximum—they should be able to hear that if there isn't a lot of other noise in the water—but we won't hear them." She made the adjustments, then her voice boomed in Alex's head. He wished he could plug his ears, but not half as much as he wished he could blow his nose.

"Gary and Phillip would only say we should surface on our own," Bheru gave a harsh laugh. "We've heard that song before. Why listen to it now?"

"We'll go after her, no question," Lee-Anna said. "But let's think it through first. We go out together to retrieve Matheus and this entity decides to grab Elle while it's got her alone. Is anybody else reminded of King Kong?"

"A hole opened in the ground, and she fell in."

"Don't tell me the timing was random—I'm way past believing that. This being seems to control seismic activity at will, and it wanted Elle and only Elle for some reason."

"The reason seems obvious," Bheru said. "It can communicate with her. With the rest of us it only rampages through our minds. Perhaps it even considers her the only sentient one among us, and so, the only one who's interesting."

Alex looked up. "If that's true, do you think it will try to stop us? Close the crack on us, or rain down boulders."

"I don't think so. There's a good chance that it doesn't care what we do, but it simply wanted to bring Elle closer to itself."

"Presuming it exists somewhere deeper in the crust. But then, what's the connection with the creatures in the vent community?"

"I vote we go down and ask it." Lee-Anna's tone of voice made it clear that 'ask' was a gentle term for what she had in mind.

"It's not a democracy," Alex said. "I was put in charge, and I'm ordering you to save yourselves and go to the surface."

"Not going to happen," she said.

"God damn it!"

"If you think the entity is malevolent, that makes it all the more likely you'll need our help to rescue Elle. There's really nothing to argue about. We're only wasting time and she might be hurt."

Alex would have glared at them, but the suits didn't show faces.

"Is there any way for us to measure the depth of the crack first? Any sonar capability in these suits?"

Lee-Anna sighed. "No. An adaptation to the comm system was one of the things I was working on when Phillip invited us to join the mission. I guess we go in blind."

Without speaking, they moved Matheus' remains about ten yards away from the edge and let them sink gently onto the silt. Since each suit had a locator beacon that could be triggered remotely, they could find him again. If they came back.

"We should stick together—link arms and match our descent speed." Alex swam to Lee-Anna's side with Bheru on her other flank. "I suppose it makes us an easier target, but I have a feeling that if it's going to attack, it'll attack minds not bodies. Let's go."

As one, they kicked over the edge, heads downward at first, but then levelling out into skydiver position as they matched their buoyancy. The fall seemed intolerably slow, but Alex's suit display showed that they were dropping at about thirty-four feet per minute. Plunging into impenetrable darkness with sheer cliffs on either side demanded utmost caution. They'd be no help to Elle if they fell victim too.

The crevice was wide enough to swallow the hab, but no more. Their suit lights spilled across both walls. Alex tried to ignore the impression of falling into a volcano, clouds of silt billowing around them like dirty steam. The sea bottom probably comprised hundreds of yards of packed silt, but the walls looked much like any other soil, jaggedly ripped apart by the earth tremor. Occasional clods of dirt sped past, streaming dark grey comet tails until they vanished beyond the reach of the suit lights.

Their descent awakened a sense of the primal: regressing through time to ancient realms. No doubt the silt cliffs held decomposed remnants of ancient giants of the sea—whales and squid far larger than their modern descendants. Still deeper would lie scattered particles of former jungles, primeval swamps, and the denizens of Jurassic and Triassic land-and-seascapes. Alligators of nightmarish size. Gargantuan snakes. Thunder lizards.

None of that was a threat, though; so, why was his calm sometimes shattered by sudden fear and despair? Was his own mind becoming unstable?

The sound of Gary's voice jolted him out of his reverie.

"Can you hear me? Anyone. Please respond. If any of the crew of the American habitat can hear me, please respond. We'll hear you."

Alex had to work up some saliva and swallow before he could make any sound.

"Gary, it's Alex. We hear you, loud and clear. How are you getting through?"

"Alex, good. We weren't sure this would work. We sent a drone down to the edge of the new crevasse and it's relaying my signal. You went down into the chasm, didn't you? Are you all together?"

"It was my call, Gary. We're not leaving Elle behind. We're about half a mile down. Lee-Anna and Bheru are with me. Matheus ..."

"Yeah, the drone camera found Matheus. Listen, *Orion* has detected an acoustic signature we're almost certain is a Chinese submarine. Our assessment is that it's in firing position, probably ready to send a torpedo or mine into the crevasse within minutes."

"Nuclear?"

"No way to know. Small yield maybe. Fatal to you, either way. They'll be able to guide that fish down into the crack, above you; and when it detonates, the pressure wave will be channeled between those walls straight at you, amplified by compression as the crack gets smaller. I can't imagine Lee-Anna's suits are designed for that kind of sudden overpressure. Even if they don't crack ..."

"Our bodies will be turned to jelly from the shock waves," Lee-Anna finished for him. "I don't think Elle would survive in the hab either."

"No. I insisted that Captain Jensen send a warning message to the sub by acoustic transducer—my bosses are pissed off about that—but it's anybody's guess if they'll take it seriously."

"Well, our deaths will be for nothing if they don't, because this being isn't something that can be destroyed by a torpedo." Alex shook off the image in his head. "Do what you can, Gary, but don't endanger *Orion*. We're still going after Elle. We couldn't get somewhere safe in time anyway."

Resignation and frustration colored Gary's voice. "Good luck, people!" And then softly, "Go with God."

Bheru grunted at the echo of his own words to the departed Matheus. Then Alex asked them to switch to a suits-only sound channel.

"If anyone wants to spend their last minutes trying to tunnel into the muck for shelter, I won't stop you," he said. "But it won't do any good."

"Of course not," Bheru said. "And I agree with you that a torpedo won't kill the entity. I've been wondering how it could possibly control seismic activity, and I have a theory." His voice softened with something like reverence. "I believe this being can not only control the large sea life but also the very smallest: bacteria and archaea in their billions in every square foot of the seafloor around us. Such organisms use appendages to move around. Perhaps, acting together, such legions of bacteria might be powerful enough to move the soil they infest. Other forces of attraction and repulsion could be at work, too; so, the seafloor literally tears itself apart. Not truly a seaquake at all, but much more specific and controllable."

"Archaea are like tiny little sperm, for Pete's sake," Lee-Anna said.

"Yes, and what if their tails all pushed in the same direction at the same time? Anyway, it's a theory. The only other explanation I can think of is that the entity has learned to control gravity, and I find that harder to accept."

"What about magnetic repulsion—if it could change the polarity of molecules in the soil?"

"A magnetic field capable of pushing cliffs forty feet apart? Our suit gauges would be scrambled by something that powerful."

"But it wouldn't be on now. Only for the few seconds it took to open the crack."

Alex interrupted. "Whatever power it used, we need it to use it again to stop that torpedo. Try to project an image of the mouth of the crevasse closing again, or something like that. I don't know if it's paying attention to our minds, but Elle might pick up our thoughts and relay the message."

"Are you serious?" Bheru asked.

"Yes. If Elle is still alive, she should be able to read our thoughts."

"Good grief, that never occurred to me! Now I'm going to have to censor my own mind, am I?"

"Welcome to the club."

"I hope the creature remembers we're still in the crevasse," Lee-Anna muttered.

Their descent continued within a nebulous halo of blue-white light from their suits. Alex could feel a tremble from the arms of his companions. His own body was quivering too. It was a chill their heated suits could do nothing to prevent.

Though he couldn't risk closing his eyes, he tried to picture the mouth of the crack sealing itself to block a powerful explosion. On its own, his mind kept shifting to an image of Elle and he finally encouraged it to do so, as if indicating both the message and the intended recipient. Part of him was sure the exercise was sheer folly, but he tried to keep that voice muzzled. The back of his neck itched in anticipation of a deadly pressure wave.

Nearly fifteen minutes later, he gasped.

"She's here!" he said. "Elle's here. In the habitat, very near now." He pointed down and to the right.

"How could you know that?" There was a tremor in Lee-Anna's voice.

"I just do."

Exhilaration swept through Alex, but a sudden impulse made him rotate his camera view upward.

A searing line arced across the blackness like a bolt of lightning. The afterimage filled his mind.

"My God. They ...."

The impact knocked the breath from his lungs and smashed his face into the front of the suit. His whole body writhed, nerve ends dancing in agony. Breath sucked through his clenched teeth tasted like blood. A cacophony of piercing screeches and blatting horns assaulted his ears. Dimly, he sensed violent acceleration, the walls of the chasm rushing past.

Helpless. Defenseless.

Wrapped in torment.

Outer darkness oozing inward. Taking control ....

Flickering sparks dimming, one by one. Until ....

At last, it ended.

And he was still alive.

How?

"The entity must have closed the gap," Bheru wheezed painfully. "The explosion vaporized the blockage, but it was enough. Just. Even so, the warhead must have been a very small-yield weapon, or we would be dead."

"I'm running diagnostics on the suits." Lee-Anna panted. "Then I'll check our vital signs."

"You make good stuff, Dr. Cavallo," Alex said. "I'm grateful."

"All part of the service." Her light words didn't mask her distress. They needed to get to a place of safety to assess their injuries.

The shock had broken their grip on each other, but they hadn't drifted far apart. With a few kicks they were able to link hands again. The wave had pushed them downward an unknown distance; and within moments, their eyes registered a mere hint of a glow ahead. It congealed into the outline of an overhang, lit from behind.

Now the illumination grew quickly: they could make out a gleam of metal, and the glare of the habitat's lamps.

The egg-shaped hull was tucked under the overhang against the crevasse wall, but didn't seem to be resting on anything. Then Alex saw that the base was missing—gone for good this time. Only the hab's buoyancy was keeping it in place.

They just managed to get beneath the hull before a hail of debris obscured everything beyond its shelter.

They might still be out of luck. If Elle was badly hurt, or dead, who would open the airlock for them?

"Lee-Anna ..." He stopped as a bar of light appeared along the hull. It gradually widened, revealing the flooded airlock, and then closed after they had all squeezed through.

"Elle?" he called. "Can you hear us?" But there was no answer.

The draining of the lock seemed endless, and they shed their suits as quickly as the lowering water level permitted. There was a set of controls on the wall under a transparent pressure-proof cover and Lee-Anna waded toward them, but there was no need. The inner wall began to split apart the moment the water dropped below the door sill.

Elle stood there, clinging to the edge of the opening to keep upright.

Alex kicked out of his suit and rushed to her, wrapping his arms around her as gently as he could, then pulled back to look at her face.

Blood spilled down her cheek from an ugly gash on her forehead. Her eyes were aimed at him, but were blank, as if out of focus. She gave a violent shudder.

"Let's get her up to the couch," Lee-Anna said. "Very carefully."

Alex had to do the lifting. Bheru clutched his own abdomen, his face locked in a grimace. Lee-Anna could barely climb, hissing with pain at each step. With Elle over his shoulders in a fireman's carry, Alex pulled himself up the ladder as smoothly as he could to avoid jarring her. After easing her onto the couch, he got a wet cloth from the galley to clean her face. Its cool touch made her close her eyes in relief.

"Elle? Do you understand what I'm saying? Can you talk?"

"She may be in shock," Lee-Anna said, shivering badly, herself. "We should wrap her in thermal blankets."

"You and Bheru should get warm, too," Alex replied. "You both might have internal injuries. Where does it hurt?"

"My lower abdomen." Lee-Anna winced. "It's not good. There goes the sex life for awhile. What about you, Bheru?"

"My chest. A broken rib or two, perhaps." His breath was still a rasp, but at least there was no gurgle to indicate fluid in his lungs.

Alex quickly grabbed a pile of mylar foil blankets from the storage locker on the bottom deck and helped the others wrap up. Elle shifted listlessly when he covered her but made no other response. When she was fully cloaked in silver, he held her face in his hands and pressed his forehead against hers, so they were eye to eye. With all the concentration he could muster, he called to her with his mind.

Elle. Elle, it's Alex. Come back to us. Come back Elle.

There was no reaction. He kept trying, trusting that the others knew not to interrupt.

At last, her head shifted, and he felt her lips press against his. He returned the kiss with heat.

Pulling away, he said, "Can you hear me? Can you talk to me? Do you remember what happened?"

She took a few deliberate breaths and her eyes finally opened and seemed to focus on his.

"Alex. I'm all right. I'm safe." She swallowed, and her voice returned with more strength. "You're safe too.

You're safe." She pulled him into an embrace and began, softly, to cry.

50

April 3, 2042

"Did Phillip Watanabe put you up to this?"

"*What?* No sir. Why would he do that? He obviously went to a lot of trouble so no one would find out about it."

Gary felt like pacing, or rubbing his hands together, or doing *something* that would release the tension that coiled his muscles; but he needed to give the appearance of complete assurance.

"And no one else knows?"

"The captain must. He'll have to make sure *Orion* gets to safety. But no one else that I know of, sir."

The communications officer was sweating more than could be blamed on the heat. His name was Jervis something, Gary remembered. Jervis Lark. Seemed to be a straight arrow. Very efficient in the comm shack, from what he'd seen.

"Why are you telling me this, Lark? Aren't you afraid of betraying your captain?"

From the look on the man's face, that was exactly what he was afraid of. His Adam's apple bobbed.

"I'm certain the captain is unhappy about this and would do something if he could, sir. I thought you ... well, you seem to have exceptional contacts. And you're Navy, sir. Mr. Watanabe is ... I'm just not sure he's not ... well, exceeding his authority here, sir."

"Going rogue? Is that what you're afraid of?"

It wasn't an unreasonable fear. Phillip and his masters were devious bastards. In all likelihood the agent had the full approval of his superiors, but that didn't mean it was right. And Gary had a feeling the "superiors" were a small group that had grown cocky about circumventing the chain of command and were used to getting away with it. But this ...!

"When do you say this bomber is due?"

"Just before first light tomorrow morning, sir. I don't think they plan to tell *Orion*'s crew."

"I expect not—not before, and no explanation afterward, either. They'll let the crew assume that the Chinese sub fired a second torpedo—a nuke this time— and blew itself up—which will become the official version."

Lark just nodded. He made no move to leave. Clearly, he expected Gary to do something about the news that would involve the ship's communications station. But what? How could he, Gary, convince Navy brass that Phillip could somehow summon an Air Force bomber to drop a nuke on the entity? Even his future father-in-law would hesitate to believe him about something like that. Or, maybe the brass had signed off on it themselves! Hell, didn't a nuclear attack of any kind require the direct approval of the president? Who had the power to stop something like that?

The answer enclosed his stomach in a grip of ice.

The media.

If the bombing really did have top-level approval, the only thing that might have a chance of stopping it would be to go public with the whole story. An unknown intelligence at the bottom of the sea would be headline news on its own. But an American plan to nuke it out of existence and blame the Chinese, taking a whole Chinese sub crew with it—that would be an act of war. The planners of the scheme would have to back down, wouldn't they?

But going public was a preposterous idea. Although Gary knew someone pretty high up in the Thorson-Rodgers news corporation, she would never take his word on something this big—no one could. And that meant Gary would have to provide proof. Documents. Secret documents.

He would be court-martialed. The end of his career; almost certainly his freedom, too.

The end of his life with Naomi.

If he didn't, the entity would be murdered, along with the Chinese crew, and his friends in the habitat. Didn't that matter to Phillip? But then, Phillip Watanabe would do whatever he'd convinced himself had to be done, no matter who died. Obviously, he'd persuaded the highest authorities that the entity was a threat to many, maybe the whole human race.

Gary couldn't even be certain that Watanabe was wrong.

Lark stood, still waiting.

"I have no way to convince the brass about this without proof, Lark."

"But that's how I found out about it, sir. I was sent out of the room, but there was a record of the radio exchange that was somehow left in the system. I have a feeling the captain deliberately didn't erase it so there *would* be a record. To protect himself from blame."

"I don't just mean Watanabe calling in a bomb strike. I mean the fact that the bomb is intended to kill a non-human intelligence on the sea floor." Lark had to have been told that much while carrying out his duties. "For that, I'd need files that I don't have access to. Watanabe's own files."

He stopped and gave Lark a hard look. The man's face was turning red. He couldn't bring himself to look at Gary.

"Mr. Watanabe has his own laptop computer, but he was concerned about the threat to electronics from the thing down there." Lark cleared his throat. "So, he asked me to help him create backups on *Orion*'s battle-shielded server storage, as well as highly encrypted transmissions to an offsite storage facility, presumably on the mainland."

"But if they're so highly encrypted ..."

"Not the backups on our servers, sir. They're password protected; but protocol demands that the captain, myself, and my assistant must have access to all but the most top-secret passwords. Mr. Watanabe didn't ask for that level. An oversight, perhaps."

"Count on that." Shit. That changed things.

So, Lark was telling him that he could lay hands on Watanabe's complete records of the mission. With luck, and some time, Gary could find a few key reports, including the radio exchange about the nuclear bomber, and send them to his Thorson-Rodgers contact. He'd also have to convince the woman to publish it all immediately.

It was a hell of a long shot; and even if it worked, Gary's life would be ruined.

If it didn't, his friends' lives were over. A historical contact with another intelligence on Earth would be destroyed. And he would live knowing he'd let it happen.

He hung his head for a long time before finally raising it to look the comms officer in the eye.

"OK. Lark, you tell me what to do and I'll do it myself—I can't let you be implicated in this."

The other man looked puzzled, but nodded. He turned toward the ship's bridge and Gary followed.

Lark set up access to the files from Gary's quarters directly to give him some privacy, but the back of Gary's neck still itched as if Phillip might walk in at any moment. Lark had also revealed how to bypass ship's security for an outgoing message. Gary's knowledge of those procedures might be suspicious, but there would be no proof that Lark was involved.

Unfortunately, such a bypass would show up on telltales in the bridge computer. Captain Jensen would see it and have the ship searched.

Gary didn't have much time.

Not enough to spend it thinking about Naomi, and the loss of their life together.

In his mind, her face shone like the last glow of an ocean sunset on a welcoming island, her tight black curls like silhouetted vegetation. She could be a fashion model, instead of just a buyer; and, despite working in that shallowest of industries, she had exceptional depth. She devoted her time to charities, big and small. A rare gem of a woman he didn't deserve; but that didn't mean he didn't want her. Love her.

Admiral Sinclair couldn't have a son-in-law who'd been convicted of releasing Navy secrets to the media. Naomi would want to defy her father, but Gary wouldn't let her—it would mean cutting herself off from her family, her friends, her place in society. It might even destroy her career. The Admiral wasn't a vindictive man, but his disapproval would spread over their lives like a thundercloud.

And she might never be able to understand why Gary had done it.

He shook his head. He had to concentrate.

It was a relief to find that Watanabe's documents on the mission didn't include other military secrets that would put his fellow sailors at risk. But there was something else that made his heart sink.

Detailed personal information about Elle Travis, and her 'gift.'

So, Elle was a bona fide telepath who'd been tracked and monitored since childhood. Her full capabilities were unknown, but genuine—Watanabe assessed her as a potentially valuable intelligence asset. And it seemed her interaction with the entity may even have enhanced her natural abilities.

Damn. He'd been almost sure about her—she was too intuitive, and extraordinarily empathetic. But the official confirmation still rocked him. A lot of his thoughts around her had probably been insensitive. Were they outright hurtful?

His throat tightened. She would be devastated if her abilities became public knowledge—he'd come to know her well enough to be sure of that. She'd have no chance of ever living a normal life. Which meant he was going to have to spend precious time going through the reports to remove any mention of her.

He'd barely begun when there was loud knocking on the locked door of his room.

"Master Diver Cross? This is Captain Jensen. I need to speak to you. It's a matter of ship security." Was there reluctance in Jensen's voice? Probably, but he couldn't count on it, especially if Phillip Watanabe was out there too.

Should he respond? Make up some excuse to stall?

He said nothing, and deleted another file on the computer.

"Cross, if you're in there, open up. This is important. I have the security officer here."

Gary moaned. He had everything set up to transmit the whole collection of reports with one keystroke, but that would include far too much about Elle.

He'd accepted that his own life would be ruined, but not hers. Yet, if they stopped him, her life would end in atomic fire.

"Cross, we're coming in."

Naomi's face came to him once more, then Elle's. He asked them to forgive him, and swatted the keyboard as if it were a poisonous spider.

Then he held the power button to shut down the computer. Pulling half of his shirt free of his pants, he stepped toward the door just as he heard the scrape of a key in the lock.

"Dammit, Captain. It's the first chance I've had in days to catch a nap."

51

April 3, 2042

She was afraid it was a dream.

Alex was there, and Lee-Anna, and Bheru. Gathered around her, touching her, helping her. They were not dead, and neither was she, though she had feared the worst. Had been nearly certain of it.

She remembered watching them as they towed Matheus' body back toward the habitat. Then suddenly there had come a terrifying lurch; and the next moment, she'd floated from her chair while it slid out from under her.

The habitat was falling. Plummeting out of control. The base struck something and the whole hab rocked sideways, throwing her into the wall. Then the hab plunged onward, off balance, in a sickening spiral that held her pinned hard against the cupboards. A stabbing pain split her forehead; but when she reached a hand to touch it, she was catapulted into the ladder and slid down it to the bottom deck, cracking the top of her spine against each rung. The impact of her head against the floor made everything go black for a time.

Another bounce, and she was tossed upward, flung down, slung to the side. In desperation she crawled to the ladder and wrapped her arms and legs through the rungs. Her arms were nearly pulled from their sockets as the hab caught a ledge and tumbled end-over-end at least three times. With the violent crunch and clang and scrape of each collision, she expected to see water gush from a wall and bring her life to an end. But the tough walls kept the sea at bay, though loose items in the galley became projectiles rattling across the floor.

At some point, a long nightmare journey later, yet another impact produced a grinding crack; and suddenly Elle had weight again, as if the hab was wallowing in mud. But then, astonishingly, it began to rise, though it didn't go far. She heard a grating crunch from the roof three decks above that came with a jolt that broke her grip on the ladder. She grazed the ceiling of Deck One in an arc that left her in a heap on the floor, outflung arms barely saving her face from a shattering blow.

The habitat rang dully, rocked from side to side, and slowly came to rest.

Fear clutched her with cold fingers—fear for herself, fear for her friends. Tears spilled down her face mixed with something sticky and warm.

Her vision faded as if the hab had filled with blue smoke.

There were shapes in the smoke. Images.

Shapes in a sequence she felt she should understand.

There was a plain punctured by towering spikes. A castle filled with scurrying forms. A crack, a crevasse. Floating man-like shapes. A cylinder, gleaming darkly, a long tube trailing foam, and a cataclysmic explosion.

And then the habitat shook as if the end of the world had come.

Yet, somewhere in all of that, she had sensed Alex. The others, too, but mostly him. She had let her fear overflow into him; in part it was a call, in part a plea to keep himself safe. He would come to her in spite of the danger—she knew that without any doubt whatsoever.

That conviction was followed by puzzlement. Confusion filled her mind, but it came from *outside* her—a questioning that she had come to know only too well. She knew no way to frame answers, but simply opened her mind to allow answers to be found.

It was an examination that would have been a conversation, except for the lack of a common language.

There came a glimpse of Alex, but it slipped into the fog. Another glimpse, and she reached out a hand to him, or some part of herself. Dimly, she felt her body performing motions: standing, walking, touching, pressing. But her muscles were so weary, so very weary that she had a hard time pushing them to do ... whatever she was supposed to be doing.

Then Alex was lifting her. Embracing her. It couldn't be real, but she kissed him anyway, and he kissed back. Hard.

The fog began to lift, and she found that her mind could form words again. She said some, but wasn't sure they made sense. Alex seemed to like them. They made him cry, then laugh. They made him hold her again.

# # #

"Her body is covered in bruises, and she's taken another blow to the head, but I don't think it's life-threatening. A thick skull, that one, fortunately."

Lee-Anna had just finished examining Elle in the crew quarters and left her there to rest, but voices carried easily up the central shaft.

"What about you?" Alex asked. "That position can't be comfortable."

"Better than trying to sit. I suspect I've got some internal bleeding, but we don't have equipment onboard to check anything like that. I'm going to try kneeling over the couch with a cushion under my abdomen, unless anyone has a better suggestion." A sharp intake of breath showed that whatever movement she'd made, her body hadn't been impressed. "The stethoscope didn't pick up any sounds of fluid in Bheru's lungs, but I think he's right about broken ribs. We've got some compression bandage, so I'll try to wrap up his rib cage to keep it from shifting."

"I'll do it." Elle heard Alex go to the medical cabinet beside the galley.

"I think he's bleeding internally, too. Pale skin. Shivering. Signs of shock. Which is why it's important for you to stay still with your legs raised like that, Mr. Cyborg."

"You operate from a flawed assumption." Bheru painfully uttered a laugh that turned into a cough. "These legs don't have any arteries to rob my head of blood."

"Just do as you're told."

"We need to get all of you to the surface." There was no humor in Alex's voice. "I'll try calling Gary, but the relay drone will have been destroyed. Since the base was knocked off the hab, we just have to figure out how to push it out from under this overhang and it'll surface on its own. Maybe the water jets will move us far enough. The big question is whether the Chinese will think they succeeded or if they'll decide they need to take another shot."

Elle rolled off the bed, fought off her dizziness, and slowly climbed down the ladder.

"The bigger question is how to get out of the crevasse." They all looked at her. "The torpedo detonated a few hundred meters into the crack and vaporized the original blockage the entity had rushed into place, but the blast wave brought half the valley floor down afterward. Probably some big chunks of the ridge to the north, too. The crevasse is blocked again, much worse than before."

"How can you possibly know that?" Alex asked.

"The entity showed it to me."

"And you trust it?"

The question took Elle by surprise. The thought that the other mind could deceive her hadn't even occurred to her, and she said so.

"I don't suppose it told you how *it* can see all that, let alone split the ocean floor. In fact, if it could do that, why can't it just clear away the new blockage?"

"The little things in the dirt."

"The bacteria and archaea?" Bheru wheezed. "It does control them?"

"No." She looked into his face and then at Alex. "It *is* them. *They* are the entity."

"No!" Bheru slumped in the chair, his arms dropping by his side. "You can't know that!"

"I only know what it showed me. I'll admit it's not always easy to decipher its thoughts, but that one's pretty clear. The entity is ... perplexed by what it knows of me; and as it shows me images of how it perceives me, I am able to sense how it perceives itself." She shrugged her shoulders. "Maybe I should be saying *they*, except it doesn't feel like more than one mind. But those microorganisms are it. Them. Whatever."

"A collective consciousness," Bheru said, almost to himself. "A composite mind. Individual archaea like the neurons of a human brain, even if separated by great distance. Which means the mysterious energy we've been trying to identify must be the way its neurons communicate, like the chemical and electrical signals of our own brains."

"And that's why it can't just clear the blockage the way it moved things before." She looked at their faces, but they weren't getting it. "All the organisms close to the explosion were killed."

The group fell silent, as if trying to imagine the cost of such destruction.

She continued in a softer voice. "That was only the latest killing."

"What do you mean?" Alex asked.

"That sunken cargo ship full of toxins? The entity didn't just object to that on principle. Its organisms have slowly been absorbing those poisons from the ocean. Dying."

"Oh my God," Lee-Anna brought a hand to her eyes. "No wonder it hates the human race."

"But it doesn't ... it doesn't hate us. It simply has no interest in us at all."

When she had opened her mind, the entity had done the same; but it was impossible to summarize the flood of images, impressions, and sensations she'd experienced—far beyond what a human mind was meant to perceive and comprehend. Like a preschooler dropped into the Smithsonian without a guide, she had almost no understanding of what she was seeing, no sense of what she should look at or look for, and no way to know where any of the answers she sought could be found. And what little she did comprehend, she was at a loss to describe.

There was nothing friendly about the exchange—neither welcoming, nor unwelcoming. Nothing personal at all, merely a step taken out of practicality, or maybe just another example of that insatiable curiosity that had always been her strongest impression of the alien being. Though it gained some understanding of her and her race, it was not in any way gratified to have done so. In fact, she was sure it was repulsed by what it learned of humans. They were too changeable, mercurial even, with thoughts disorganized and trivial. Not mature. Not wise. Not worthy.

"It thinks of me as a ... fledgling, I suppose. An immature form of our species. I'd figured that out already. But it's been badly puzzled by the lack of any mature forms. I'm not sure what it means by that; but since I'm the only one who could communicate, and because I'm immature, it felt I should be protected."

"It made quite a sacrifice for you," Alex said.

"I think it sensed that the submarine was a threat—maybe it got that from me—but I don't think it had any concept of how much destruction there would be."

"Is it angry?"

"All along, my brain has been interpreting its states of mind as emotions, but they're not really comparable to ours. I sense no true equivalent to anger, or sorrow, or fear, in spite of all that damage. Just a sense that a threat had arisen and would have to be removed."

"What do you think it'll do?" Lee-Anna asked.

"Whatever it intended to do, I think it's already done it."

Bheru tried to find a more comfortable position but failed. "I still don't understand why it was trying to signal the Moon."

Elle shook her head. "That, I don't know. There was so much I couldn't understand."

Another long silence was interrupted by a gasp from Lee-Anna.

"An alert on the control board. There's a message coming through."

Elle raced up to the top deck with Alex close behind. She tried to fine-tune the incoming signal, but it was very weak. Finally, she was able to make out words against the background hiss.

Gary's voice.

"...timer in case we're taken out of action. If there's no response within 90 minutes, the package will automatically detonate. Repeating: We're trying to find a way to get you out. We've sent another drone to the crevasse mouth with a big package of high explosives, and it will try to burrow into the muck that's plugging the crack. The plug is thick, but the explosion might weaken it enough for it to break apart on its own. We're trusting that you've found someplace to shelter from falling debris, and we assume that if the entity could be hurt by our explosives, the damage has already been done. The problem is the unknowns. If that alien thing is still alive, we don't know how it will react after it's been attacked once already. And we don't know what the Chinese will do. The submarine hasn't moved since its torpedo went off—it appears dead in the water. But they might just be waiting for the alien to reveal itself, ready to fire again.

"There's more. Alex, our calculations show the Moon is coming into range again and, with the no-fly zone cancelled, our Pacific air traffic liaison warned us about a Chinese passenger jet on a heading to overfly the danger zone. Then we lost all radio and satellite communications—probably thanks to your entity—and so far, we haven't been able to warn it off. If you're able to hear this, let us know what you want us to do. We've set the drone's explosives on a timer in case we're taken out of action. If there's no response within ninety minutes, the package will automatically detonate."

The message continued to repeat. Though Elle sent an acknowledgement, it wasn't received.

"Oh my God!" she rasped, covering her face with her hands. *"It's happening again."* The haunting memory of her own flight and her first encounter with that incomprehensible mind merged with a nightmarish image of the hundreds of doomed passengers that Alex and Phillip's efforts had been too late to save four months ago. Now hundreds more might be racing unaware toward their deaths.

"Those assholes!" Alex hung his head over his knees. "It was way too early to drop the no-fly zone. The entity has probably scrambled the brains of everyone on that sub, and it'll do the same to *Orion*'s crew if the drone explodes. And the passengers on that jetliner just for getting in the way."

"Gary might be right, and the Chinese sub crew is just biding their time," Elle said.

"You don't believe that." He turned toward the manipulator arm control. "With the water jets pushing and the arm pulling us along, I think we can work the habitat out into the open. We've got to get Lee-Anna and Bheru to the surface; but if our timing is wrong, or the entity gets pissed or … Jesus, how am I supposed to know what to do?"

She felt his anguish more than she'd ever felt it before. This was the very thing he had dreaded most: the burden of a decision with lives in the balance.

He squatted to be on eye level with her and leaned in close.

"I think I know why the entity has treated you like a child and ignored the rest of us. And I think I know what has to be done to change that." He took her hands in his. "It doesn't respect any of us because we're not part of a collective mind. That's the only thing it would consider a mature form of our species. It can't accept that anything else could be fully intelligent. So … you have to make us into one. You've got to reach into each of our minds and pull our thoughts together. If you can do that, it might … it might actually talk to us. It might even care."

"*No!* No, I can't. I won't do that!"

His look said they couldn't afford for her to be unreasonable. But he didn't know what it was like. Most people had secrets and painful histories they would rather die than reveal. And such unconscionable exposure was exactly what he was asking her to do. He had no idea how much guilt she'd endured over things she'd seen and could never unsee.

He hadn't watched as all opportunities for love were destroyed by the unintentional violation of another's mind.

"Elle …"

"No! It's not possible."

Bheru's weakened voice came from below, though it no longer vibrated the floor. She could barely hear it.

"I think Alex is right. And wrong. Wrong to ask you to do something so abhorrent to you. So invasive. But I think he's correct about why the entity does not take us seriously and does not care what happens to us. Perhaps we are lesser beings and not worthy. We will find another way."

Alex went down the ladder and Elle followed him, though Bheru suddenly looked uncomfortable at her nearness. What was bothering him?

Oh. Her ESP. Of course. She sighed and took a few steps away.

Lee-Anna looked as if she had something to say, but chose not to expend even the energy needed to speak.

Alex kept calm with an obvious effort. "I'm going to free the hab and get us rising—we can't waste any more time." He turned to Elle. "Hundreds of innocent passengers will suffer what you suffered and worse. Or we can do something to try to save them."

"Even if she can contact the entity," Bheru said, "she won't be able to hold its attention if it comes under attack again."

Alex nodded. "I'll keep trying to reach Gary. Maybe we'll think of something."

He stepped to the computer console and tapped a rhythm on the controls. There was a surge as the directional jets began to thrust against the crevice wall. Alex raced up the ladder to the console for the robotic arm.

Elle did her best not to be sick.

52

April 3, 2042

"Their government's submarine probably just killed our habitat's crew, and you want to risk more lives to try to save these people?"

These people! Gary looked at Captain Jensen and fought to keep his anger in check.

His nerves were badly on edge. His ploy to stop the bombing of the entity valley had apparently worked, though not exactly as he'd expected. In an obscure text from an unidentified phone that had to be his Thorson-Rodgers contact, he'd learned that the government had been alerted to his information package and the news agency's intent to make it public once they could assess its content more carefully. That prospect had been enough to make Gary's superiors call off the bombing.

The delay in the story's release also meant that neither the news agency executives nor the Navy hierarchy knew about Gary's own involvement, but his bosses must suspect it. Right now, *Orion* had no external communications, but the hammer could fall on him at any moment, and there were things he had to accomplish before it did. Like saving the lives of hundreds of air passengers. And he didn't need the latent racism of *Orion*'s captain to get in the way.

"Is there still no response from the jetliner?" he asked.

Jensen shook his head. "Too much radio interference. My guess is that the Chinese got that ... *thing* down there pissed off, and it's still showing its displeasure."

"Listen, Captain, the people on that jetliner have done nothing wrong. They're not responsible for the decisions of their government. And if you don't want to be a part of this, your second-in-command has volunteered to take your place."

Jensen looked stung.

"I go where my ship goes. But I'm on the record as saying I don't think this will work."

"Noted. For now, I need you to get all non-essential personnel off this ship."

Jensen turned away and began giving orders to his crew. Gary didn't blame the man for his resentment. That Gary had been given full authority over this situation was probably just to provide naval command with a scapegoat if everything went sideways.

He looked at Phillip Watanabe.

"Aren't you going to transfer to the supply ship? There's nothing for you to do if you stay."

"Allow me to keep some appearance of authority," Watanabe said tightly. "I'll get Ranger to safety, but I'm staying."

"Does that mean you think the plan will work?"

"I have no idea, and I'm tired of guessing. I'm tired of this whole goddamned mess. But I think it's more likely the alien will concentrate on the submarine that attacked it than blindly flashing another message to the Moon."

"The sub crew is dead, or at least mental vegetables—I'd bet a month's pay on that. What I don't know is whether we'll be putting the jet passengers at more risk with our attempt to shield them. If that entity connects us with the sub that fired on it, *Orion* will become a target, and the jetliner could be collateral damage."

Phillip checked his watch, but Gary already knew what it said. He wished he could do something to speed up the evacuation of the ship, but he'd just be in the way.

Phillip gave a curt nod and left to look after his dog, Ranger. The whole crew had adopted the mutt; and if it was possible to keep him safe, they would. But what struck Gary was how a man like Watanabe could feel such compassion for his dog, yet be unable to consider that an unknown being might have compassion toward humans.

Gary looked out over the sea. *Orion* wasn't directly above the entity canyon, but forty-five minutes at flank speed would get it there. Only minutes ahead of the Chinese jetliner, if it had kept to its filed flight path. He'd only be able to confirm that, once the jet came within range of *Orion's* radar.

He wished now that he hadn't decided to leave so much time before the explosion of the drone down below. If the entity was going to attack *Orion*, it was better to know that as soon as possible. Maybe they could keep the bastard occupied and draw its attention away from the Moon. If only Jensen would get the damn ship cleared!

Gary glared at the communications panel in the radio shack, but it was stubbornly mute. Jensen was probably right that the habitat crew was dead, but he wasn't willing to accept that. Not yet.

Seven minutes later, the last tender to the supply ship cast off, and Jensen gave the order for *Orion* to get underway. Gary felt the surge of its powerful engines through his legs and gripped the back of a nearby chair; but couldn't bring himself to sit. You don't go into battle on your ass.

The course to the rendezvous above Ground Zero led almost directly into the prevailing west wind; and through the windscreen of the pilot house, he saw the bow turning blue water into creamy foam. Phillip had returned to the bridge.

"Why wait until the ninety minutes is up to detonate the drone?" he asked Gary. "There's no way the habitat can get to the surface unless the plug is cleared."

"We don't know where the hab is. They could be caught in the blast or buried by debris."

"A risk you may have to take."

"Or Alex and the rest might think of something. Even just a way to contact us."

"You put so much faith in Mr. Rhys?" Phillip asked.

"I thought he was your golden boy. Suddenly you're not so sure of him?"

"I didn't say that, but he's never been in such *personal* danger before. At least, not that we told him about." The man's cold smile made Gary uncomfortable.

"Well, he's on the scene and I'm not. That means he gets a little extra trust. Right now, we have enough on our plate. And though I care about the people in the habitat, there are more than three hundred passengers on that plane."

Long before they reached the target zone Gary's jaw ached from clenching his teeth. Although *Orion*'s radar was impaired by the entity's interference, it had received enough spotty returns to confirm the approach of the jetliner.

When *Orion* was five minutes away, he ordered the ship's EM field turned on. It was only meant for combat situations, usable for thirty minutes or less, so he'd taken the risk of waiting until the last moment to activate it.

A sailor stepped into the pilot house.

"I see a jet."

Gary followed him out into the wind and looked up, shielding his eyes automatically, though the sun was above and behind him. The first thing he saw was the Moon, distant through the dome of air but with nothing to show that it was a body hanging in space on its own and not a part of the sky. The sailor raised an arm to point, and Gary saw a short contrail to the southeast.

The jet was still a few minutes away.

But the Moon was overhead.

It suddenly seemed to jump closer, lighting up like an orange lantern against a cloth sky soaking up indigo ink. The heavens became shot through with deeper and deeper blue, and the Moon continued to swell until it filled all of Gary's consciousness.

He dimly heard gasps and cries from nearby. Strange gurgling sounds that may have come from his own throat. His legs collapsed and his back and head hit something. Had he fallen? He wasn't sure. He didn't even know if his eyes were still open.

Blue fog filled his head with a growing pressure, making it throb like a racer's heartbeat. The worst hangover ever. A killer, if it didn't end soon.

Dimly he wondered why the EM field wasn't working. Or maybe it was. Maybe he would already be irreparably damaged without it.

He thought about the jet, and hoped that *Orion* was absorbing most of the beam's energy. That would count for something at least.

He also thought of the habitat and its crew. If Gary didn't survive, there was still a chance the drone explosion would free them. That gave him some peace.

Then the fog grew very dark, and there was only the sound of pounding waves.

53

April 3, 2042

Elle's knees buckled and she clutched her head.

"What's wrong?" Alex leapt from the ladder to hold her up, but then put a hand to his own head. "Is it attacking us?"

"No," she gasped. "The Moon ...."

"I thought this thing's ... cells at the seafloor were killed."

"Only the ones near the blast."

"Oh, shit, no! The jetliner will fly right into the beam!" He squeezed her arms. "Elle, you've got to do this. You've got to do it now." He keyed a command to the hab's jets, and they shut down. He'd pulled the hull to within a few feet of the overhang's edge, but the rest of the maneuver would have to wait.

She could only nod her agreement and reach out with her hands. Hand in hand, they made their way to the others, and Elle clasped all of them in a tight circle.

She emptied her mind, making it a vacuum to draw in the energy that surrounded her: the thoughts, the feelings, the memories. With a deep breath, she submerged herself in a vortex of swirling currents.

The first image she can identify is a fly trapped between the glass pane and screen of a window. In some way, it's associated with Alex; but it is quickly replaced by a moving panorama of a city street under a highway overpass, seen from a car window. Clusters of people in tattered clothing huddle around makeshift fires, while others, like misshapen bundles, tuck into corners. A scrawny woman and a rag-covered child stumble onto a median strip, the woman's over-bright eyes showing fear and hopelessness. The view plunges into the woman's eyes as if down a deep well, and emerges into ...

A different streetscape that is broader and far more crowded, giving visual impressions of chaotic noise even before raucous sounds swell into being. Car horns, bicycle bells, shouts and curses in a guttural tongue, a roller noise that comes from a legless beggar on a slab of wood on casters. Then, up into the window of a hospital room—a view of legs on a bed, legs eaten away in great, gory patches until only stumps remain. The room is large and frightening, with a single wheelchair that might as well be the beggar's wooden cart. It begins to roll through a door ...

... into a hallway. No longer a hospital, but some other institution. A school. High heels click on linoleum, passing labs full of strange shapes and vivid computer displays hovering in the air. There is a sense of threat, though not physical. In the doorways are faces that smile and smile with reassurance and support, but turn to expressions of disgust and malice once passed by. One face (Kowaleska?) shines with triumph, but recedes, recedes until ...

... the view is a young boy's now (Alex?); and in it are other boys. One of them is young and frightened, forehead and cut lip bleeding. The others—five of them—are older and menacing in dirty jeans and big boots. As they approach, a hand reaches out to the young boy (brother? Aaron?) and pulls him into a run. It's a construction site! There are

trenches—thirty feet deep or more—but not wide. The brothers are nimble and gain distance on their pursuers, but another trench ahead cuts right across their path and is too long to detour. A narrow plank crosses it—a makeshift bridge that can be pulled away after they cross. Aaron is too afraid. Blood has run from his forehead into his left eye and wiping at it does no good. The hand reaches out again. They begin to cross. The plank is long and bounces even with their small weight. Aaron screams and falls.

As Elle tries to pull away, Alex squeezes her hand painfully hard.

Aaron lies at the bottom of the trench, looking up at the sky, struggling to rise but not able to make a sound.

His arms move. His legs do not.

Bheru:

A large cathedral-like space filled with people, the wall in view to the left is of dark wood, ornately carved. The facing wall is mostly windows, two stories high, three of them filled with panels of stained glass. In front of the windows is a raised gallery of spectators in formal clothes, behind carved marble pillars. A line of black-gowned figures makes its way to a stage. In the audience are many more black gowns with patches of scarlet or cream. As the line slowly moves, young men and women become visible on the stage, robed in black with flashes of purple.

There is a handshake, a red-banded tube of paper taken and gripped, but no feeling of satisfaction or pride. Only guilt, and the image of a plain red-granite headstone in a lonely cemetery.

Lee-Anna:

A handsome man in black boxers stands in front of a large mirror, holding a phone. A lavish hotel-suite. A mirror reflects an extravagantly trimmed four-poster bed painted salmon and pale gold. Glimpses of a female form kneeling on the bed as if posing.

A look downward shows shapely legs and breasts covered only in scraps of lace. A feeling of excitement, of daring. The man is taking pictures, and then moves closer, eyes filled with desire. But the room dissolves into nighttime on a city street. Strange faces, unexpected, unwelcome. Painful flashes of light burst across the scene from every direction. An urge to flee, to hide. To somehow erase shame, the sense of betrayal ...

Elle felt her face washed with tears, her body shaking. She had to stop this. She had to ...

There is another presence: familiar but still utterly alien. A spectral hand reaches through her forehead and deep, deep into a flashing pool within her that she has never seen before and did not know existed. It is a whirlpool of glittering colors that spark like gems and then, at the ghostly touch, open like flower petals to the sun.

The petals of color unravel and reveal darkness within: a gloomy hallway with a man slumped against a wall beneath a dim light fixture. A sharp smell of booze. A glass in Elle's hand, one-third full of amber liquid. Her first ever. The accomplice uncle grins and drinks from his own glass, then staggers closer—close enough for her to feel a waft of hot breath. This is not unwelcome.

But the touch of a hand on her breast is.

She pushes away, staggers to a door, closes it, blocks it with a chair. The concussive thump of a pounding hand echoes through the room but stops, eventually.

Footsteps. A slamming door. A car starting.

She pulls her phone from her pocket.

A vision of pale window curtains backlit by flashing blue and red lights.

Oh God. No more. Please.

What if the others ...? But of course, they've seen it. She was with them and they with her.

With the entity. The blue fog. The probing curiosity.

Yet she understood for the first time that its inquisitiveness was not a thing of urgency. It was a desire for knowledge, yes—for answers to many, many questions, but it was no burning thirst.

It is the novelty of a new encounter that changed things. A mind with multiple layers and startling complexity was a mind worthy of an exchange—a conversation.

The pain was gone, the pressure eased. The overpowering image of the Moon faded into the fog. *Orion* and the jetliner—they might be safe!

The entity sensed this feeling and asked the reason. The others were aware of the question, but only Elle could answer it. Uncertain where to start, she began to picture human technology, especially transportation. The fuselage of an airliner fading to invisibility, revealing the passengers—people—inside. *RV Orion* splitting to reveal others like her, connected to her by race and interest and need. Trains, buses, then towns and cities—all connected, spanning the surface of the planet.

Had she gone too far? Would it see the humans, not as equals, but as an infestation?

She withdrew a little, unable to control her shivering. Alex's arm slid around her and pulled her closer, his cheek warm against hers.

But her stomach recoiled as the entity once again showed her an image of a submarine suspended in the dark ocean, and a tremendous explosion that wrought a sickening collapse of the sea floor. There was a thick cloud of snow that was not snow but tiny organisms, their lives snuffed. After that, the view of a sunken ship, torn, twisted, bleeding inks of lurid colors into the surrounding sea.

Then there came images she had not seen: a waste-disposal barge being emptied. A tanker trailing a rainbow of poison stretching for mile upon mile. A river mouth gushing effluent. A floating continent of swirling plastic. An island and its atoll vaporized into mushroom clouds.

She sobbed and felt herself slip from Alex's arms.

We have done wrong. We have done harm, much harm. We are selfish, we are arrogant, we are ignorant.

Help us. Use your power to reach us, your ancient knowledge to teach us. Turn us from our ways by showing us the right path, the right way. You who have survived for eons without harming the life of our shared planet! Show us how it is done.

She was shocked to find herself on her knees, an appalling echo of childhood Sunday mornings. She tried to rise, but could not.

More shocking still was the entity's refusal of her request.

Did that mean that it truly was indifferent to other life forms?

No. It was ...

Dying?

The prospect made her breath catch.

Dying creatures lashed out in anger.

Yet she still sensed no animosity. There was regret, perhaps sorrow—its states of mind did not correlate precisely with human emotions. Most of all, there was a profound sense of loss. Disconnectedness. Dissolution.

It was losing cohesion! Too many of the individual members had been killed or were near death, and energy webs that connected the disparate parts were becoming too weak to keep the whole together. If not a complete loss of life, at least loss of mind.

No. She couldn't let that happen! Human hands had enough blood on them. She couldn't allow the only other sentient mind on the planet to fall victim, too.

She had bound the minds of four humans together—collectively many billions of neurons. Was she capable of holding more? Using her friends' mental energy to supplement her own?

She pictured her hands like claws digging deep into the core life force of the humans, drawing forth rippling currents that her hands sculpted into sparkling tendrils.

The blue fog was being shredded by a breath of extinction, and she cast forth the threads she had formed to stitch it back together.

It was too much. She wasn't strong enough. To reintegrate the whole would take everything she had. Nothing would remain of Elle Travis.

She choked out a silent scream.

54

April 4, 2042

It was a long time before Alex could be sure he was awake.

Awake, though not yet alone in his mind.

His first solid sensation was cold metal against his cheek. He had slumped against the ladder and was in danger of slipping into the shaft. He shifted to a safer spot and got up, then looked around, trying to slow his heart.

Nothing had changed within the habitat except for three forms slumped on the floor nearby.

He hurried to Elle and checked her pulse and breathing. She was alive and not in obvious distress. Gently raising an eyelid revealed a wholly dilated pupil that didn't react to the sudden light. His stomach sank. Either she had a serious concussion, or she was in the grip of a trance he didn't know how to break.

Reluctantly, he slapped her face. Again, harder; but there was no reaction.

The blue fog had not left him; and he felt puzzlement as he drew back his arm for another slap, so he didn't follow through. Instead, he gently laid Elle's head back on the floor and went to Bheru and Lee-Anna. They were both breathing but unconscious. Without knowing how, he seemed to understand that they were unconscious from their injuries, not some outside force.

But they all were slipping away from him. Without medical care very soon, they would be gone.

He was no longer immersed in Elle's interaction with the entity, though parts of the exchange seemed to have been intended for him to know.

There had been no second explosion at the mouth of the chasm—it was still blocked, and the entity had no means to open it. The habitat would never get through, would never leave the ocean depths. Could not take them to the surface.

But there was another way.

First, he had to consult the computer about the suits. He would need them to do something that would make their designers recoil in horror. The information wasn't easy to find, but he finally located what he needed and memorized the procedure.

Shaking with effort, one at a time, he hoisted each of his friends onto his back and carried them down to the airlock—though moving Bheru nearly defeated him. Then he set about programming their EV suits to respond to a very special command. For a terrible moment he was afraid that the suits' smart-processors would rebel; and then he feared that his crewmates' unconscious bodies would fail to trigger the suiting-up mode; but as he held his companions upright, the nanomaterial enveloped them, sealed itself, and activated the automatic life-support systems. His own suit did the same, but there was a difference. His was the only one that flashed a warning.

Its air-manufacturing unit had been damaged.

Internal storage might give him an hour or more of breathable air, and only if he didn't exert himself.

The suits were prototypes—there were no spares—and once they'd adjusted themselves to each individual, a restructuring was beyond his ability. At least he couldn't be tempted to swap suits.

The hab had fallen to nearly fourteen thousand feet—more than two miles down—which meant that even if he had a straight run to the surface and could achieve enough buoyancy to reach a rocketing 200-feet-per-minute ascent rate, it would take him seventy minutes to get there. Ten minutes too long, though that scarcely mattered because the only path he could follow was anything but straight.

The entity had shown him shafts that carried scalding water from the heated rocks of the deeper crust up to the smoker vents in the seafloor. One of the shafts had been exposed by the shock wave of the torpedo blast. A nearly horizontal branch of it opened into the chasm now, and rising hot water in its main channel produced suction that drew cold water in through the new opening. The result not only provided a detour around the blocked crevasse mouth, but offered a water temperature that was almost survivable.

Almost. It was still beyond the ability of the suits to cool their occupants without some additional means of shedding heat. Alex had thought of a way to provide that, but if the trick failed, he and his friends would cook like lobsters. Even if it did work, the suits might lose too much integrity and give way under the ocean's pressure.

No point wasting thought on that—there was no alternative.

But there was a choice to make.

If he abandoned his companions and went alone, there was a very slim chance that he could survive to reach the surface as long as the shaft didn't slow him too much. He might be able to make up for lost time once in the open ocean.

If he tried to tow any of his unconscious friends, he would not make it himself—the effort would cost too much of his already-insufficient air. But once above the ocean floor, he could at least release the others after making their suits buoyant—they would rise to the surface on their own where their locator beacons would give them a good chance of being picked up by *Orion*. Since the high-tech suits contained surface-pressure air, decompression wouldn't be an issue, no matter how quickly the suits rose.

If he tried to tow all of them, he might not even make it through the shaft to the open ocean, and they would all die.

Abandoning them for the sake of his own survival was out of the question, but should he risk all of their lives in what might be a foolhardy gamble? Did he have a duty to leave someone behind to give the others a better chance to live? Especially if any of the three was likely to succumb to their injuries anyway?

It was a moot point. He couldn't make such a choice.

He touched the logo on his chest. The reaching hands.

He climbed onto the lounge deck one last time and fired the water jets. The hab rocked and scraped against the overhead rock, then lurched free and shot upward.

He hurried down the ladder, sealed his suit, and flooded the airlock. With hard kicks of his fins, he pulled his crewmates through the opening, bound together with nano-reinforced rope. Once outside, he clung to the hab and waited. Its buoyancy would carry them up to the vent shaft quickly and without wasting his air. The drawback was that the hab was moving much too fast for the reach of its overhead lights. To make things worse, the last boost from the water jets had set the hull spinning, and the walls flew past in a blur.

If he missed seeing the vent, it would mean their death.

He needed help.

In desperation, he tried to tap into the blue fog that lurked at the back of his mind. It knew where the vent opening was.

Contact came, and with it an impression of Elle. His eyes looked down at her body, but the presence he sensed was in some kind of mental struggle within the fog. Swallowing hard, he pictured reaching out and clasping onto her with an unbreakable grip. He'd be damned if he'd let anything take her from him.

It was time to send his special command to the suits.

There was no change that could be seen. He could only trust that each suit had extruded a 'tail' of only a few hundred nanomodules in thickness, much too slim to be visible. If all went as planned, the tails would grow rapidly, unraveled by the current of the habitat's upward motion like a cat with a ball of yarn. Soon they would be hundreds of feet long, the actual nanomaterial of the suits themselves spooling away.

It was the only way he could think of to shed the deadly heat of the vent shaft's water. The temperature control system of the suits could quickly shift heat from place to place, nim by nim. When the crew entered the shaft, the tail ends would be left dangling behind, to carry the excess energy of the overheated suits back out to the cold water of the chasm.

That was the theory.

If the threads couldn't spool out as quickly as the shaft current carried the divers, or if the heat didn't transfer readily enough, he and his friends would cook. If the lines caught on a protrusion, they might yank a hole in a suit, or become suddenly taut and instantly deadly—sharper than any blade. If they drew too much material from any one part of the suit, its strength would fail and the occupant would die as Matheus had died, shredded by jets of water at unthinkable pressure.

He tried to push those pictures from his head.

Then his mind filled with a vision of the tunnel, and he launched them all away from the hab, feeling a pang of regret as his underwater home vanished forever into the blackness above. It had given them shelter in a hostile world, but they were on their own now.

He played his light over the wall and found the dark opening. Powerful kicks brought him within a few feet of the mouth, where the current pulled him like a fish on a line. Instantly, he was tumbling through darkness, careening into walls as the shaft curved and twisted. If there were protruding rocks ....

But there weren't—the passage of fast-moving water had worn the walls smooth. Eventually, he was able to keep from flinching at every flicker of the light.

His friends were tossed against each other and slammed into walls, a pounding certain to aggravate their other injuries, but his efforts to prevent it were futile.

The lurching and spinning nauseated him, and he worried about what would happen as the nano-'tails' became tangled. Part of him listened for the roar of an explosion, convinced that the drone would detonate at any moment. Would he feel it? Would the tunnel collapse? Or would the vent spit him out into a hellish fireball?

Discomfort turned to torment as the temperature rose in the suits. His breath became rapid and shallow in his body's vain attempt to dispel rising heat in its core. The contents of his stomach threatened to escape with every jolt, and each shock was repeated through the tethers of his three passengers.

Nothing could be seen but frenetic flashes of dusky surfaces. No way to judge distance or speed or depth. His suit's pressure gauge fluctuated wildly. Its external temperature reading had raced through the numbers and was now a blinking dash. The comm system delivered nothing but static. Warnings of all kinds showed as strobed icons blurred by salty sweat that poured from his forehead, though he'd muted the suit's harsh alarms.

He was a speck of dust in a tornado, rising, rising into unseen storm-clouds to be captured in a tumultuous hell forever.

His viewscreen flared red with a low air warning—twenty minutes, possibly less.

Air wheezed and bubbled through his sweat-covered lips. He had an impulse to hold his breath, but that was an unproductive primal instinct. Such deprivation would happen soon enough on its own.

Perhaps sensing the approach of death, his mind reached out for Elle. Her phantom presence was still there, clinging tenaciously to him; but blue fog overlaid everything—it pervaded and surrounded them. He tried to talk to the fog, but felt only indifference. It would converse through Elle or not at all; but he could detect no coherent thought from her. He hoped with every part of his soul that she was not lost forever.

An endless time later, he wondered if his brain had become starved of oxygen. Or poached. His blurry vision seemed to see ...

Ghosts.

Apparitions of white streamed around him in dense patches and thinner wisps. He felt tempted to speak to them, his only company in the confining darkness. Escaped souls. Specters of the deep sea. With a bitter taste in his mouth, he looked behind him at his trailing companions and hoped none of them had given up their spirits to this heartless night.

He was so focused on the apparitions that he didn't notice for nearly a minute that he had been spewed forth from a shattered crater into the cold calm of the open sea.

His numb brain tried to make sense of it.

He was free of the shaft, and there was something he must do.

What was it?

A raucous alarm sounded for thirty seconds.

Low air! his display flashed. Air was a thing you could only get up there, beyond the water, if there really was such a world and he hadn't just imagined it.

Cool, sweet air.

The temperature of his suit rapidly dropped, and renewed awareness made him jerk as if struck.

Jesus, he was above the ocean floor! It was time to send his friends on their way.

There was little point in trying to follow. He would simply stay behind and watch them go.

Programming their suits was nearly beyond his mental faculties by now, but at last he had them primed to inflate and go shooting toward the surface. He should offer some appropriate goodbye, but it was hard to think with his eyes full of fluid. Not sweat this time.

He snapped his head to the side to try to clear his vision.

And saw the drone.

His body began to shake. It took three attempts to activate his comm unit, and he had to lick his lips and swallow before he could speak.

He wasn't even sure what he said—something about stopping the detonation. Commanding the drone to drop its explosive. Hitching a ride. Getting emergency medical teams ready because his crew was badly injured. A warning about the razor threads of nanomaterial dangling from their suits. And the drone had better goddamn hurry to the surface because he was running out of air.

As he felt the drone lift off, towing its cargo of limp bodies, including his own, he turned his lights back to the vent just in time to see a monstrous phantasm rise from the silt and drift slowly with the current toward the open sea.

There was a time later when he made a tremendous effort to push his eyes open and was almost sure that the water had begun to get lighter. But then everything turned dark again.

So very dark.

55

April 5, 2042

Gary sat by Elle's bed in the sick bay and held her hand. There was no change. Her eyes were closed now, but the blankness he'd seen when the doctor had opened them briefly had chilled his heart.

Serious brain damage, the man had said. Nothing they could do about it aboard *Orion*. Medivac helicopters were on the way from Guam because Bheru and Lee-Anna were going to need them, too, though for physical injuries.

A selfish part of him feared Elle's recovery even as he hoped for it. He would have to confess what he had done. Tell her that, although Thorson-Rodgers had released only a very minimal, carefully screened and politically sanitized version of the information Gary had sent them, news outlets worldwide had jumped on the story of the entity and Elle's role in it as an authentic telepath who could communicate with alien intelligence, mind to mind. Reporters couldn't wait to talk to her. In modern tabloid-style media, her story got more attention than the discovery of a non-human sentient species on the Earth.

She would be devastated. She might even prefer it if she never woke up.

The Air Force had strenuously denied that it had ever planned to drop a bomb on the entity, and had found a scapegoat to blame for an "unauthorized and erroneous radio message"; but Gary didn't care about that. The more they denied everything, the less likely it was that his court martial would become a public spectacle, damaging to Naomi and her father.

Gary looked toward the bed to his left, still astonished at what Alex had endured, only to lose consciousness within minutes of rescue. Given oxygen immediately, his skin had returned to normal from the ghastly clammy blue when he was found; but he too might have suffered irreparable brain-damage. He hadn't awakened, and he might never do so.

Lee-Anna slept in the bed beyond Alex's, but it was only the sleep of exhaustion and her body's need to heal. Intravenous tubes replenished lost fluids. She would need an operation ashore, but the ship's doctor was confident that she would recover without lasting harm.

Bheru was under anesthetic in the ship's makeshift surgery while a team worked to stop the bleeding in his chest cavity and stabilize his broken ribs. In spite of his age, he'd been in good health and was mentally tough. He'd pull through.

Gary released Elle's hand, gently placing it on the bed beside her, and swiveled in his chair. He thought about calling the hospital corpsman down the hall to come to help him, but it hurt his pride to be lifted and carried like a little child. *Orion* stocked only three wheelchairs for emergencies, and they now had to be shared among fifteen of the eighteen crew members who had survived the last transmission from the entity. The other three could still walk with the help of walkers or crutches. Two men had died.

So, Gary shouldn't allow himself too much self-pity just because his legs would no longer respond to his commands. The doctor said that what they'd all suffered was similar to a stroke, so end results were equally unpredictable. Therapy often restored complete function; and if determination counted for anything, Gary was sure he'd be back to fighting trim within six months.

Just in time for workouts in the prison gym, once the court martial was through with him.

Phillip Watanabe hadn't been so lucky. He still couldn't speak, and it was unclear how much he understood of anything he was told. The most hopeful sign was his interaction with his most attentive caregiver, his dog, Ranger, who only left his master's side to answer the call of nature.

The Homeland agent's condition meant that all of the government brass was breathing down Gary's neck, demanding answers and status updates he still couldn't provide. He'd extrapolated what he could from the CPUs of the hab crew's EV suits, but it wasn't much. There was video, but any audio was inconsistent. He couldn't yet know why Alex had chosen to follow the vent tunnel or how he'd even found it. But then, Gary was equally uncertain how he, himself, had known that he needed to cancel the detonation of the drone's explosives. He only knew that he'd awakened from the entity's barrage with that strong imperative in his mind.

By the time he'd managed to crawl to the control center, dragging useless legs, there had been fewer than ten minutes remaining in the countdown.

He shuddered at the memory.

Then there was the mystery of how the killing emissions from the entity had been stopped. The jetliner passengers had suffered no worse than a few horrible daydreams. Gary was sure that it wasn't just a sudden act of compassion from the alien mind. His underwater team had done their job, and he fervently wished that someday he would know how.

The Chinese submarine appeared to be drifting with the current, and intelligence sources said that Chinese naval command had lost contact with it. Maybe that was why his own commanders had ordered *Orion* back to Guam for medical attention; but his paranoid side feared that US leaders were still preparing a devastating response to the threat the entity posed, and they wanted all witnesses out of the way.

He felt an overpowering sadness as he looked at the still forms of Elle and then Alex, both in the prime of life and, from what he'd seen and heard, probably in love. On impulse, he took their hands in his.

He nearly jumped out of his skin when they both awoke at the same instant.

56

April 6, 2042

The island of Guam was a hazy smudge on the horizon as Elle stepped to the ship's rail. She took a deep breath of sea air, glad to be free of the confining wardroom where naval brass had debriefed her. Having each of her friends questioned alone made her feel like a criminal, and it was counterproductive, too. It was only by hearing each other's slightly different versions of the same story afterward that her crew was able to fill in gaps to understand the whole narrative. So many things had happened, and so much of it no longer felt real.

This was her first chance to be alone since the habitat had descended beneath the waves. The feel of the breeze and warm sun was glorious. The blue sky and rippling water fed her soul. She hadn't realized how badly she'd missed all of that, and there had been a dark time when she'd thought that she would never experience it again.

The lengthy bombardment of questions had drained her. She needed some quiet.

Orion was never silent, but its crew was unnaturally subdued now, its decks hushed. What shocked her even more was the quiet within her own head. For the first time in as long as she could remember, there was no cacophony in the background of her mind. Though she had never been able to hear the thoughts of strangers clearly, they'd always formed a constant disturbance like the distant gabble of geese. Now that was gone.

It was gone!

It was like the time she had found a small cave on her uncle's rural property. Following it around three sharp bends, she had found herself in silence so profound, her ears had tried to fill the void with a low rustling hum like distant waves on a beach. Her brain had never experienced such a thing and did not know how to process it. Her mind was like that now. Thoughts bounced around a vast space like echoes in that long-ago cave; but they were her own thoughts, and only her own.

She had so fervently wished that the entity would cauterize that part of her brain—take away her 'gift'. Had it granted her wish? And, if so, what did that mean? How would her life change?

Could she really welcome it?

Yes.

Mostly.

Except she missed one of those other minds. One that she had touched often in recent days without meaning to, and then had desperately clung to for a time that had seemed endless. That mind had been her lifeline. Without it, she would have been lost—of that she was certain. Yet it was gone now, too. She would still be able to see him, touch him, use words to talk to him, but there would always be something missing.

Wait. If the entity had destroyed her ability, how did she know beyond a doubt that her mind and Alex's had clung to each other right until the moment they had awakened?

He was probably back in his quarters, resting after his debriefing—his had been the longest session of all, and he'd emerged looking very weak.

She reached out tentatively. Pictured his face. Imagined herself touching his cheek.

A warm glow began in her fingertips and spread until it suffused them both. He was thinking of his interrogation by the navy types and whether or not he had given a believable report, even though it wasn't the full truth.

In her mind his eyes opened, and he smiled.

Her own eyes filled with tears as she withdrew, heart pounding. She had her answer, and that was enough for now. There would be time for so much more.

Later, out of curiosity, she reached out for Lee-Anna and Bheru and found them both, though there was no sign that they were aware of her. It was the same with Gary. She could find nothing identifiable as Phillip Watanabe, which filled her with sadness despite everything. But what astonished her most was that she was able to sense her mother at home in Toronto, and then her boss in New York! Her boss had never been familiar enough for Elle to 'read.'

So, the thing she'd viewed as a curse all her life wasn't gone at all—instead, it seemed to be stronger than ever, forged into something of true power by desperate need. And she had been given control of it, or she had finally *taken* control.

That changed everything.

Maybe it could become a 'gift' after all.

57

April 6, 2042

As Elle was sharing the new extent of her abilities with Alex, Gary came toward them across the deck. Alex was sure that the strong-willed military man would remain vital and active; but for now, Gary's unfamiliarity with his wheelchair seemed to make him hesitant. Or was the hesitation for another reason?

Barely able to meet Elle's eyes, Gary told them what he had done and how much his desperate gamble had revealed about Elle's abilities. He showed her news reports on his tablet computer, though he had to hold it for her—she couldn't. He asked for her forgiveness, but it wasn't clear that she'd even heard him.

Alex watched her face freeze into a lifeless mask, its flame guttering. She looked like she'd just been told of the death of a loved one.

She had. The death of her own life; her hopes and plans for it. Freshly filled with new confidence and new faculties she couldn't yet comprehend, she'd allowed herself to imagine a future that was brighter than her past, only to watch that vision crumble into bitter ash at the first breath of reality.

Again, Gary asked for forgiveness. Again, she failed to respond. She didn't react at all.

"You'll be court-martialed," Alex interjected. Gary only gave a nod, then turned his face toward the sky, eyes wet.

He slowly rolled his wheelchair away, remorse making a shrunken shell of the vital man they'd known.

Alex gently took Elle's shoulders and turned her toward him. He had never seen such hopelessness.

"Maybe there's something that can be done," he said, meaning it, but with only a first hint of what that could entail.

Her mouth moved but couldn't form words. Instead, she collapsed into him and sobbed like a newborn.

After a very long time, he was able to help her to her quarters, where he left her weeping softly in the dark.

He made his way toward the pilot house and its radio room.

# # #

In the end, giving his agency minders access to his data cache on the dark web wasn't enough. Alex had known it wouldn't be.

So, he'd sold his soul. Again. Phillip Watanabe could be a cold bastard, but compared to his masters, he was only an apprentice.

The data cache had been Alex's protection. There was nothing to stop them from killing him now, and maybe even Elle; but he didn't think they would. As long as they didn't suspect him of planning to reveal their secrets, he was still valuable. Maybe even more so, with Phillip out of action. And in return for an indefinite commitment of service, Alex had been able to extract one extra concession to assist a truly decent man. That was worth something.

Numb, he went to his quarters and spent an hour attending to matters that included replying to a message from his father. Since Alex's name hadn't appeared in any of the news reports, it meant the congressman had learned the story some other way. Alex took great pleasure in being able to use the word 'classified' in his scant reply.

Elle was calmer when he returned to her room. He'd brought tea, and they sat on the bed together, drinking it.

"Gary had to do it," he said after a time. "We would have been killed otherwise. And I know he'd have kept you out of it if there'd been any way he could."

She nodded slowly. "Won't he be arrested for leaking secrets?"

"He'll have to leave the Navy, but that will be done quietly. And at least he won't go to jail."

"How can you know that?"

"I ... well, I just do."

She nodded again. "I'm glad. He made a terrible sacrifice for all of us." She held the tea in both hands, blowing on it to cool it. Alex knew by now that it was just a habit—the tea wasn't that hot.

"Did you read any of those articles on the tabloid websites?" she asked. "The interview with my mother?"

"She said your name is Elle Marcia Travis. I like it."

"She was saying they must have the wrong Elle Travis. They asked if she'd always known I was special. She laughed and said I wasn't. Just lucky and lazy."

"I'm sorry."

Her smile was melancholy. "I guess part of me knew this would happen if I came on the mission. It was history in the making—what were the odds I could stay anonymous? I knew all along, deep down, that my old life would be over."

"But you came anyway. I know you hoped the entity would take your gift away, but that wasn't likely."

"No." She looked into his eyes as if unsure that she could ever make him understand. "This thing could enter minds. Hijack minds. *Shred them.* To me, that's even more frightening than death."

"Yet you took that risk. You made that sacrifice. Why?"

"Who knows how many people—hundreds, thousands—might have become victims if something wasn't done? What was my life compared to that?"

Alex didn't trust himself to speak right away, so he stroked her shoulder and then kissed her. It was like a first kiss, and a many-years-together kiss, and a last kiss, all in one. She gave him a puzzled look.

"Your life won't be the same," he said, "but it may not have to be a disaster." He took her hands in his. "My contacts in government are willing to give you a new identity—get you started in a new life. You can hide from the media, and everyone else, if that's what you want."

"Like the Witness Protection Program?"

"Same methods. They claim they won't watch you, but I wouldn't count on that." Her response was a bitter laugh. Alex continued, "But it means you'd have to give up your family and friends; your job."

"Even my brother? He's the one I care about."

"It would be a big risk to cross the border into Canada to see him, though I know some people who might be able to help with that. No matter what, you'd have to be careful for the rest of your life. In my experience, successful investigative tabloid reporters are at least as persistent as cops, more cunning, and their most important qualification is lack of a soul."

She turned her gaze away as if imagining the possibilities, and the costs. When she turned back to him there was suspicion in her face.

"Those government assholes didn't just offer this out of the goodness of their hearts. What did you have to give them?" She gasped, her hand to her mouth. "Oh my

God, you agreed to keep working for them. You gave up your 'insurance policy'. Oh Alex!"

"Sometimes you really shouldn't read my mind." But he couldn't be angry.

"You can't! You can't give up your freedom for me." Then she stopped.

Her face sagged, robbed of its vitality.

"Oh God. You're giving me up too."

"How can we keep you hidden if you link your life to mine?" he said softly. "It wouldn't work. I'm known. A congressman's son. And I have to travel ... go to high profile meetings and to places where reporters are embedded with troops."

"But you *love* me. You can't hide that from me if you wanted to. And I love you. You can read it in my mind, too, can't you?"

He slowly nodded. The connection between them amazed him beyond words.

But he was still surprised by the look of determination that came over her.

"Phillip's agency could do it," she said. "Give me a cover. If they had a reason."

"What reason?"

"I'll work for them. I'll work with you."

He pulled away, stunned.

She moved closer. "What? You think they'd refuse me?"

"Of course, they wouldn't. But I can't let you do that."

"It isn't up to you. And you'd better believe that if Elle Travis, world-renowned mind reader offers her services to the shadow government, they're going to say yes and give me my pick of assignments. Which will happen to be the same as yours!"

He sat with his mouth open, completely outmaneuvered, and finally burst out laughing. Elle slid onto his lap and put her arms around his neck.

"Seriously, with my ability being so much stronger now, they won't be able to lie to us, or keep secrets from us. We'll always know what we're getting into. We'll do what they want, but do it our way."

"Jesus, Elle. Maybe your mother was right. Maybe they did have the wrong woman."

"That Elle Travis doesn't exist anymore," she said. And the rest of her argument was made by her lips pressed against his.

58

April 13, 2042

Lee-Anna and Bheru had plenty of company while they recovered from surgery, but the five friends didn't get a chance to be alone together until they finally managed to sneak away to a quiet beach one afternoon.

The beach was like something out of a tourist advertisement, framed by mangroves and ferns and towering coconut palms. The two patients weren't allowed in the water, and Gary was reluctant to leave his wheelchair; but Elle and Alex had reveled in the softness of the surf, and the penetrating heat of the sunbaked sand before rejoining the group on the shaded deck.

It was Bheru who raised the subject none of them could forget.

"So, what should we call this gathering? The Group Mind?"

"Not anymore." Elle smiled.

"Truly? My dear, I need to know if I have to keep censoring my thoughts. It's really rather difficult for a man like me, you know." He tried to smile but it didn't quite work. It hurt her to see him so deeply distressed and know that she was the cause.

She turned to Gary. He looked profoundly uncomfortable but answered her unspoken question with a shrug. "What happens in Guam stays in Guam."

Satisfied, she said to Bheru. "You don't have to worry. I have control of that now, and I promise not to read your mind without your permission. Unless your life is in danger. Or the fate of the world depends on it."

He looked nonplussed, then gave a loud laugh. There was relief in Lee-Anna's face, too. Elle felt herself relax.

"I'd like to explain what you saw … what you all saw … to get it off my chest," Bheru continued, shifting a little on the sand. "The view of the legless beggar, and my ordeal in the hospital requires no explanation. But the other was my convocation at the University of Glasgow. My very best friend at university had a brilliant idea for his master's thesis but dropped out because of mental health issues. So, I …" He paused and cleared his throat. "I took his idea and developed it, and it became the cornerstone of my career. But I never gave him credit. He took his own life not long after. I don't actually know that there was any connection, but I've always blamed myself." He looked up and his eyes were moist.

Lee-Anna put her hand on his shoulder and gave it a squeeze.

"In my early university research days," she said, "I had an enemy named Nicholas Kowaleska who accused me of stealing some of his ideas. I hadn't, but I lost grant money because of it and was under pressure to prove myself. So, I rushed an experiment and a big team-project failed. I never admitted I was to blame."

She gave an uncharacteristic blush. "The rest some of you already know. I let Chase Vizell talk me into posing for some boudoir pictures. There's nothing quite like seeing your goods splashed all over the internet."

Alex almost made a flippant remark, but Lee-Anna's obvious pain stopped him. Instead, his face turned serious.

"OK, if we're going to do confession .... My father used to drive me around the poorest parts of town—show me homeless people on the streets as some kind of incentive to work hard and make sure I'd follow in his footsteps, I guess. It didn't work, and he's never really forgiven me." He looked down at his hands and rubbed them slowly together. "But the thing I can't forgive myself for was when I was eleven. My brother Aaron was only eight and I found him getting a beating from some bullies. There were too many for me to take on, but I managed to help him escape. Except, as I was leading him away, he fell into a deep trench and ... he was never able to walk properly again."

"But he didn't blame you," Elle said softly.

"He didn't have to."

The group was quiet. A cloud passed over the sun.

Elle clapped her hands lightly. "The vision of my past that you saw was pretty self-explanatory. My good-looking uncle tried to get me drunk and have his way with me when I was fifteen. I managed to lock myself in my room, and when he drove off, I called the cops who arrested him for drunk driving. No one knew for sure what I'd done, and I never told. I just sent an anonymous note that broke up his marriage. Prick deserved it."

Gary laughed, covered his mouth, and then laughed again.

"Sounds like I missed a lot," he said, "but I don't understand why you're telling these stories."

"The entity is a collective consciousness," Bheru explained, and smiled at the bafflement on Gary's face. "It is made up of billions of living organisms spread throughout acres of seafloor. At least."

"The only way to convince it to talk to us was to form a sort of collective mind ourselves," Alex said. "Which meant letting Elle get inside our heads. All of our heads at the same time, so what one person saw, we all saw."

"Oooh, a little too much sharing for my taste." Gary pursed his mouth. "I can understand why none of you said anything about this at your debriefings."

"I would never have shared such painful memories deliberately," Lee-Anna said, "but now that they're 'out there' … I feel better somehow. Does that make sense?" There were nods of agreement, even from Bheru. Elle was surprised. She'd never thought anything positive could come from the exposure of private thoughts. Maybe human beings were too isolated in their individual minds for their own good.

Gary shrugged. "But I noticed Bheru said '*is* composed.' Present tense. You don't think the entity is dead?" He looked toward Elle.

"I had a strong sense that it was dying—poisoned by toxins from that sunken cargo ship and who knows what else? And certainly, billions of its organisms were killed by the torpedo blast. I tried to hold it together, and it survived long enough to show Alex the way to escape the crevasse, but after that …."

Gary looked at the ground, his brows knit together. "I shouldn't be telling you this. The brass isn't telling me secrets anymore, either—a friend got word to me." He took a deep breath and let it out slowly. "You already know there was a plan for the Air Force to drop a nuclear smart-bomb into the entity valley, but it was called off when I went public. Well, I've learned since, that the bombing went ahead a few hours ago, in greater secrecy. The government was determined to eradicate the entity. Now they feel confident that they have."

"That would be very regrettable indeed," Bheru said quietly. "Especially after your own sacrifice."

Lee-Anna hung her head. "It might have known how to reverse the acidification of the oceans. Maybe even something we could have used to stop climate change. What a horrible loss."

"I still don't understand where the Moon comes into this whole thing," Gary asked.

Bheru answered. "The entity is inconceivably old, but alone. It knew there was another globe in the sky and thought it might find a kindred being there. When it realized that it was slowly dying, I'd say it gave a cry for help."

"A deadly cry," Gary said. He stared at the ocean, probably reliving the past few days.

A voice called from behind them. A pair of sailors marched across the beach to Gary, and one said, "Court will convene with the admirals and their staff in thirty minutes, sir."

"That's not something I could forget, but I'll need a little help getting back to the van. I'm still amazed they gave me this free time without an armed guard at my shoulder."

Elle shared a look with Alex. He gave a reassuring nod.

Gary looked around the group. "I want you to know I feared the worse when I heard about this mission and who they'd put together to carry it out. But somebody smarter than me was right—you were a good team. It was a pleasure and an honor to serve with all of you."

After hugs and handshakes, Gary gave a nod to the burly sailors who hoisted him in his wheelchair across the sand toward the parking area. With the South-Pacific heat, their uniforms wouldn't look so fresh by the time they arrived.

Soon after, Elle looked up from their conversation to notice two other figures walking across the sand. Hospital orderlies come to fetch Bheru and Lee-Anna.

Alex saw them too, and spoke in a quiet voice. "There's something I haven't had a chance to tell all of you. Along the last part of the vent tunnel, I saw some pale shapes moving in the same direction as I was. Nebulous—they made me think of ghosts. Then, when the drone was just about to take us to the surface, I saw a huge cloud rise from the remnants of the smokers and drift off with the current. I could have been hallucinating at that point, but I think the cloud was real."

"That reminds me of the reproductive cycle of coral," Bheru said, eyes bright. "The entity's surviving organisms escaping to somewhere else? Maybe it's *not* finished. Maybe someday it will regain enough cohesion for a new consciousness to arise."

"It's probably best that Gary doesn't hear that." Lee-Anna smiled. "Keeping our personal secrets are one thing, but ...."

Lee-Anna and Bheru gave a wave as they left. They'd be spending another few weeks in Guam to recuperate, and Elle and Alex had no intention of leaving their new friends just yet.

When they were alone, she pulled Alex down to the sand and kissed him deeply. His warm skin felt so good beneath her, it was a damn shame that Guam's beaches were too popular to give them privacy.

Alex looked up at her with a sheepish smile. "You know, Lee-Anna and I are just ..."

She stopped him with a finger on his lips.

"No need to tell me that. I *know* there was nothing more than sex between you. I don't have to like it, but I think I can be persuaded to forgive." She gave a suggestive grin.

He gently touched her cheek. "You were the one I wanted to be with, all along."

"And now you are."

They kissed again and escaped into their own world of sand and sea and skin.

A long time later, as the sun touched the horizon, they walked along the beach.

"I still can't get my head around something I saw," Elle said. She took a deep breath. "It was toward the end, just before I woke up, as if the entity was giving me a parting gift of knowledge about itself. Bheru's right—it is ancient. But only Matheus saw what that really meant. All those millennia gave it a lot of time to grow and spread."

She looked into his eyes.

"I think it lives everywhere beneath the ocean. Maybe all over the planet."

He stopped walking, frozen in shock.

"One entity? Spanning the whole Earth?" Her reply was a nod. "But then what was it we encountered? Why did it try to contact the Moon from that one place?"

"Maybe a better description is one of many collective parts within a giant whole. Like the specialized lobes of the human brain. If I'm right, it's lived within the Earth's crust for millions of years, but is not always conscious. From time to time, it comes together and reawakens, perhaps with all of its memories intact, perhaps not. It must have been aware of the Moon for most of its existence, but maybe our own activity there made it think something new had come to life. I can't be sure of its motives. You know how alien it is."

He nodded. "Though not the kind of alien I was expecting. Hoping for. All along I thought it would be this super-advanced intelligence that would bring on a new golden age. The one thing I never expected was that it would have no interest in us at all." He made a face. "I sensed that it decided we were too ... changeable. Am I right?"

Elle nodded. "We're not even the same people we were when we started this mission, but I suppose something eons-old might get set in its ways."

"A bunch of uppity bipeds must seem like a flash in the pan."

"Maybe if we stick around for another million years it will take us seriously." She took his hand. "Are you terribly disappointed?"

"No, you know … I'm not." He gave a small shrug. "I've never been too impressed with the human race. I've seen too many of the horrible things we're capable of. Why I never paid attention to the good things, I don't know. Ingenuity. Optimism. Camaraderie. And self-sacrifice. It's all been there, even on my worst missions. And never more so than down in that habitat at the bottom of the ocean." He hesitated, then gave a laugh. "Damn, it sounds so corny, but … I was wrong. We have great potential as a species. We can find our own way."

After a moment, he said, "Do you think the entity will go back to ignoring us? Can we count on that?"

"I can't be sure. I wish I could."

She stepped a few paces into the surf and scooped up a handful of ocean. They were impossible to see, but she knew the water was filled with organisms—millions upon millions of them. Tiny manifestations of life.

She looked hard toward the sunset and saw blue fog.

Acknowledgments

The actual writing of a book is usually a solitary process, but the pursuit of writing as a passion and a career certainly isn't. Writers meet, read, listen, network, workshop, offer opinions and receive opinions about our work. We help, commiserate, praise and support each other. Above all, we learn from each other. In short, our journey as writers involves a lot of people along the way. Since *Oceanus* is my seventh published novel, by now that list is a long one, but I hope I've adequately thanked most of them in person and in earlier books.

For this novel specifically, I'd like to thank those who read an early version of the story and gave me invaluable feedback: my book-selling buddy and great thriller writer Dave Wickenden, the funny writer and longtime booster Matthew Del Papa, and husband and wife Rich and Sherry Schmidt, exceptionally diligent readers.

I'm also grateful to Arnie and Eini Sainio, my scuba diving instructors, for encouraging and enabling my love of the underwater world, while teaching me to travel there safely.

I've dedicated *Oceanus* to my editor of six novels and more, Robin Carson, whose contributions are so insightful, important, and enjoyable.

My cover artist, Juan Padrón continues to blow me away with his creations.

And I must always acknowledge the rock of my life, my wife Terry-Lynne, whose lifelong love and support are a debt that can never be repaid.

INDIGENT EARTH

The crimes of the past—the perils of the future.
500 years ago, the world's wealthiest abandoned a ravaged Earth and left billions to die of plagues and climate disasters. Now the space colonists plan to return.
Killian Morningcloud, a discontented Earth man from the stagnating communities known as Allocations, and Natira Celestia, a video celebrity of the off-world ruling class, are on a collision course. When they discover a secret that powerful people are desperate to hide, they face a brutal test of endurance and shattered dreams.
And their fire-and-water pairing will shape the course of the whole human race.

"... fun to read and thought-provoking. It is genuine, highly entertaining, adventure science fiction."
-- R. Graeme Cameron, *Amazing Stories* review

Buy yours: https://books2read.com/IndigentEarth

AUGMENT NATION

This is your brain on silicon.
Since the age of fourteen Damon Leiter has had a brain-computer interface implanted beneath his skull to correct a neurological disorder. As a teenager, it branded him as an outcast—as an adult it endows him with extraordinary abilities. He may represent the next step in human evolution. When computerized brain augments replace smartphones as the must-have status item, mega-corporations and governments conspire together and marketing becomes mind control. Damon is uniquely equipped to lead a worldwide resistance, but the fight may cost him everything.

"Scott Overton is a terrific writer and his vision of tomorrow is both realistic and frightening. Read this book!"
-- Robert J. Sawyer, Hugo Award-winning author

Buy yours: https://books2read.com/Augment-Nation

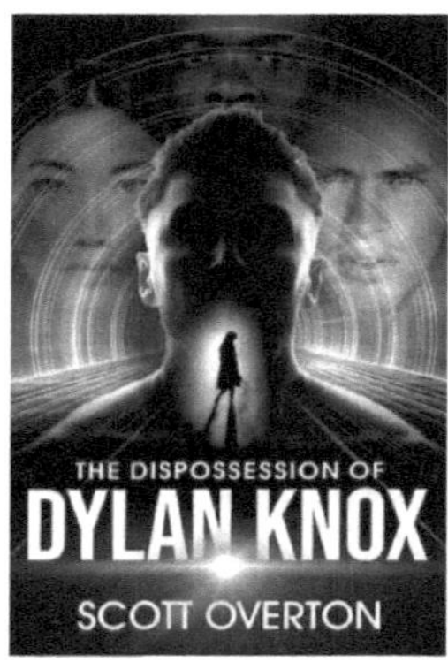

THE DISPOSSESSION OF DYLAN KNOX

Dylan Knox is not the man he was. He may be like no man who ever existed.

How do you *feel* if an old lover doesn't remember you? What do you *say* if they act like a different person each time you meet?

What should you *do* if they might be an impostor? Mentally unstable. A threat to the very security of your country.

Dylan's tale of a bold space mission, and a tragic accident is utter fantasy. Unless it's too crazy *not* to be true.

Brooke Chappelle has two choices: trust, or betrayal. And falling in love is the last thing she needs.

"The futuristic and technological elements combine seamlessly with political issues to create a plot that is timely and thought-provoking...will appeal to any reader who values the enduring human story of love and trust."

Renny deGroot—author of *Torn Asunder*

Buy yours: https://books2read.com/Dispossession

NAÏDA

The glowing structure at the bottom of a lonely northern lake is clearly not of this Earth, but scuba diver Michael Hart can't stay away. What it offers will change him forever, leaving him with astonishing abilities and a destiny he would never have imagined. Except it might be a destiny he no longer controls.

The actions Michael takes will make him a hero, or the greatest traitor the world has ever known.

Because he is no longer alone, not even in his own body.

There is another.

Naïda.

Readers say:

"A deep dive into the best parts of science fiction—thrilling and thought-provoking! *Naïda* is Overton's best book yet. I buy him on sight and never regret the choice."

"I COULD NOT PUT IT DOWN. ... Extraordinary. Enjoy."

Buy your copy: https://books2read.com/Naida

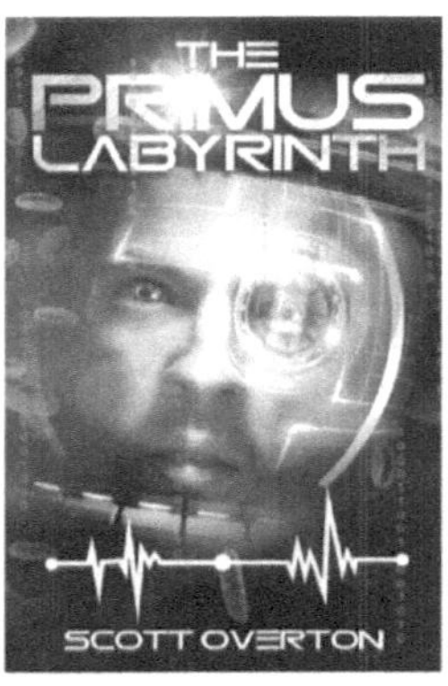

THE PRIMUS LABYRINTH

A woman's bloodstream has been seeded with destruction.

Curran Hunter almost died at the bottom of the ocean. Now an innocent victim will die unless Hunter can purge her body of deadly devices by piloting the *Primus*, a prototype submersible the size of a virus. Its control system uses *Virtual Reality*—its creators assure Hunter there can be no danger.

They are utterly wrong.

"Loved it! I give this book an enthusiastic four stars for its political intrigue, discussion of moral dilemmas, exciting action scenes, and fully fleshed characters..." Charlotte Graham—*Reedsy Discovery* reviewer

Buy yours: https://books2read.com/PrimusLabyrinth

BEYOND: Stories Beyond Time, Technology, and the Stars

Ride a bright flame of imagination across time and space with fifteen mind-stretching stories beyond time, beyond technology, and even beyond the stars.

A man who can walk through walls.

Agents who repair the mistakes of the past.

An invasion from beneath our feet.

A man who learns his replacement body was previously owned and died mysteriously.

A disastrous experiment to harness the awesome power of a hurricane.

Don't be afraid to go BEYOND.

"Scott Overton is a storyteller of boundless skill...a writer to watch." —Mark Leslie, author of *Haunted Hamilton* and *I, Death*

Buy yours: https://books2read.com/rl/scottovertonSFF

DEAD AIR

It's a hard thing to accept that someone wants you dead. It forces you to decide if you have anything worth living for.

When radio morning man Lee Garrett finds a death threat on his control console, he shrugs it off as a sick prank—until minor harassment turns into undeniable attempts on his life. When the deadliest assault yet claims an innocent victim, Garrett knows he has to force a confrontation.

"A gripping, insightful debut from a veteran radio personality and gifted wordsmith." —Sean Costello, author of *Here After*

Find out how to add these compelling reads to your own collection at <u>www.scottoverton.ca</u> .

Or <u>https://books2read.com/DeadAir</u>

ABOUT THE AUTHOR

A radio broadcaster for more than thirty years, Scott Overton described that world in his first novel, the mystery/thriller *Dead Air*, published by Scrivener Press. *Dead Air* was shortlisted for a Northern Lit Award in Ontario, Canada. But the rest of his writing is science fiction and fantasy, including his 2020 science fiction/thriller *The Primus Labyrinth*, the 2021 SF adventure *Naïda*, 2022's SF/psychological thriller *The Dispossession of Dylan Knox*, the chilling SF cautionary tale *Augment Nation*, and the thought-provoking SF adventure *Indigent Earth*. His short fiction has been published in numerous magazines and anthologies, many of those stories brought together in his *BEYOND* collections.

Now a freelance author and voice talent, Scott works from his home on a lake in Northern Ontario. His favorite diversions include scuba diving and a vintage sports car.

You can learn more and read free stories at Scott's website www.scottoverton.ca .

A Word to the Reader.

Authors cherish our readers and readers can become devoted to their favorite authors. We always hope so!

If you enjoyed this book please consider leaving an honest *review* wherever you bought it, or with any reading communities you participate in. After buying our books, reviews are the absolute best way you can help us continue doing what we do and bringing you the stories you want to read. Just a few lines will do, and I'd truly appreciate it.

Thanks, and I hope you'll look for my other books too.

www.ingramcontent.com/pod-product-compliance
Lightning Source LLC
Chambersburg PA
CBHW031642200726
48289CB00004BA/1190